MW00876517

In Plain Sight

By

Marlayne Giron

In Plain Sight

Book design copyright © 2011 Marlayne Jan Giron. All rights reserved.
Cover design by Karen Arnpriester
Interior design by Marlayne Jan Giron

Published in the United States of America by Marlayne Giron:

ISBN-13:978-1463789596
ISBN-10:1463789599
BISAC: Inspirational / Fiction

In Plain Sight

ଷ ഌ

Dedicated to:

My sister-in-law, Debbie – who really believes…

In Plain Sight

Table of Contents

In Plain Sight

Chapter One
"Crop Circles and Barn Raisings"

Jacob Lapp rolled out of bed at his usual time; 4:30 a.m., to milk the cows before sitting down to his usual breakfast of flapjacks, bacon, freshly baked bread, scrambled eggs and hot black coffee. The kerosene lamp he held aloft illuminated his breath in the frosty air as he strode in the dark to the barn. He could already hear his cows lowing...anxious for their udders to be relieved of milk. Nothing seemed amiss then in the dark just before the dawn so it was not until he had poured the raw milk into the pasteurizer and returned to his house in the growing light of day that he noticed his field of almost fully ripened corn had been completely flattened.

He stared in horror and disbelief, shook his head then rubbed his eyes, hoping that doing so would change what he saw but the damage was real. He walked to the edge of his cornfield with growing unease to survey the damage up close. A vast and intricate round design had flattened the stalks which stretched as far as his eye could see. Somewhere in the recesses of his memory the word crop circles sprung to mind. He had heard no machinery that previous night that could have caused such devastation. Despite the chill morning air a cold sweat broke out on his forehead. In his 30 years of farming Jacob had never seen anything like it. He would have to bring the matter up before the bishops immediately but before he did he would have to see what could be salvaged of his ruined crop.

Nineteen year old Rebecca Esh popped the trays of biscuits into the oven with a sigh. Every day it was the same routine: up at the crack of dawn, kneading and baking, cooking, canning, housework, washing, gardening and sewing. While the work was very satisfying, something inside of her longed to know what lay beyond the confines of her wonderful community. She had no desire to be out among the "Englisch" as the Amish called them. She had seen enough of her friends who left the community to experience the world "outside" only to come home unhappier than before; glad to return to the simple quiet life they had always known. No, what her heart longed for was found in the tomes that lined her bookshelf: adventure, fantasy, and wholesome historical romance and even some science fiction books. How she wished she could pop in and out of her books at will as a visitor; perhaps then that restless feeling in her heart would find fulfillment.

She straightened up from the oven to glance out the kitchen window just in time to see a silver flash above the hill behind their barn. Normally she wouldn't have given it a second thought; attributing the image to a passenger plane or blimp sailing over her area but when a bright blue beam of light shone down then disappeared it made her freeze in place. It was still yet early morning and she was only halfway through her baking. The rising sun was already turning the sky a pale pink so the intense blue light looked very out of place. She stared transfixed, oblivious to the flour floating down from her fingers and the sausages burning on the stove. She rubbed her eyes with the backs of her hands then shook her head. Surely she had imagined it…it couldn't possibly be what she thought it was. Time to stop reading science fiction novels and stick to Beverly Lewis she thought to herself. Her mother, Ruth, bustled into the kitchen with her arms full of dirty clothes destined for the washtub.

"Did you see that blue light?" Rebecca asked, a little crease appearing between her brown brows when she was particularly disturbed by something. Ruth looked at her daughter with an expectant smile as if anticipating a joke.

"Ach no. What blue light?"

Rebecca was at a loss to explain but tried anyway. "I saw a silver flash then a blue beam of light over there," she said, pointing out the kitchen window. Her mother set down the basket and looked out; seeing nothing unusual.

"You always did have a wonderful imagination!" she said, dismissing the subject. She nodded to the kneading board. "Tend to the dough," she gently reminded her.

Rebecca turned back around and finished working the dough, losing herself in the daily ritual of baking bread. Maybe I just imagined it; maybe my eyes are playing tricks. She set the loaves to rise and finished preparing the large breakfast for her father (Leroy) and sisters (Hannah, Mirriam and Mary) who would be coming in from the barn and chicken coop any moment with pails of fresh milk and eggs. After breakfast there was butter to churn and milk to be pasteurized for the ice-cream that sold at the Lapp Valley Farms ice-cream shop in Intercourse. They gathered around the large family table, bowed their heads in silent prayer then set to with gusto. After cleaning up, Rebecca became too preoccupied to think about the silver flash and blue light as she tended to her chores of helping her mother wash the clothes followed by more baking and then pegging the laundry to dry. By the time the morning chores were done, it was already time for lunch, clean up and a few precious hours spent talking and quilting with her mother and their immediate neighbors, the Zooks, Yoders and Millers on the wraparound porch.

"What are you bringing to the barn raising tomorrow, Ruth?" asked Ivy Miller, her closest neighbor and best friend.

"Probably a brisket," Ruth replied, pushing her glasses up on her nose to see her stitches better. "I plan to slow cook it overnight so it will be done by early tomorrow."

The following day there was to be a barn-raising for a newly married couple in the next district over. Rebecca would have to be up even earlier the next day to help with the baking and meal prep for all the families who were participating. They chatted on until late in the afternoon, working on the quilt that the Esh's planned to sell at the summer auction then they all left for their homes to prepare dinner for their families.

Rebecca had just enough time after dinner to squeeze in a little reading before heading to bed. She took her oil lamp with her out the front door and sat in her favorite place under the willow tree with an old quilt to keep the grass stains off her dress. The fireflies were already out and floating about her like fairy lights; the first stars already beginning to peep out. All was quiet save for the turn of the waterwheel at the nearby stream, the occasional clip clop of a buggy going by and the chirp of crickets. Sarah Miller had lent her a few of her books and she was anxious to start one of them. The first was titled: "Visitors From Another World" (which she quickly put to one side with a shudder) and the other was a medieval love story called "The Victor" which seemed safer considering her experience earlier that morning. She immersed herself for the next hour in knights, jousting and fair maidens then stood up to bid goodnight to the twinkling stars. As she turned back to the house, out of the corner of her eye she saw a falling star blaze across the heavens. It was so bright and so low it gave her a start of fear. Its trajectory also put it in the same place as the blue light which had appeared earlier. Gooseflesh crept up her arms, neck and into her hairline. She wrapped her shawl about her shoulders tighter and hurried into the house, feeling as though hidden eyes were lurking somewhere in the shadows, watching her every move. It was the first time on a balmy summer night that she was glad to be sharing a bed with her younger sister, Hannah. Despite her weariness, she fell into an uneasy sleep which ended all too soon with the crow of the rooster before dawn the next morning.

After all the necessary morning chores were done, her father and sisters got the buggy ready and helped to load it with all the food they would be contributing to the day's barn raising. The beef brisket and noodles had been prepared the night before and were now cool enough to pack. Rebecca was really looking forward to the barn raising. Despite the fact it was a lot of hard work, it was a break in the routine and a welcome chance to visit with a lot of other families, catch up on news, and sometimes even meet new people. Rebecca was approaching the age when Amish girls were courted as future brides but still had not met the one she felt her heart had been waiting for. Many of her closest friends were already in serious relationships and planning their simple weddings but she had mixed emotions about it all. She still felt too young and couldn't imagine being a wife and a mother in the next year or so despite all her experience in helping to bring up her younger siblings. Her heart longed to experience new things while at the same time feeling reluctant to leave her familiar life. Sometimes she felt like a little bird was beating its wings inside the cage of her breast, itching to take flight, while at other times it seemed content to nest.

They arrived at the barn site around 6:00 a.m. with a full day's work ahead of them. Ruth, Rebecca, Hannah, and her other sisters, Miriam and Mary unloaded and carried the baskets of freshly baked breads, pies and containers of beef brisket, potato salad, fruit salad and jars of corn, hot pepper, and spicy tomato relishes to the long tables already set up under large shade trees. They greeted their neighbors and set to slicing and squashing lemons for the gallons of lemonade they would need as the day wore on while others prepared sweet tea. Their brethren, wearing nail aprons and brandishing wooden boxes of hand tools, were streaming to the site, laughing and talking with one another as the sun began to spread its warm rays over the undulating farmland. At least 150 families had come to help build the new barn for the recently married Abram and Mary Zook and it has to be framed and roofed all in one day.

Although Rebecca was busy tending to the food and her siblings she had the strangest feeling of being watched. It grew so strong she had to stop what she was doing and look around several times to see who it was. Her sisters stared at her each time she did so; wondering what was bothering her so much. Finally it got to be too much. Rebecca stopped what she was doing and turned in a 360 degree circle looking for what or whom it might be. She noticed nothing. The women and girls were all busy with their chores and chattering away while the men and boys were busy pounding nails and fitting beams together but the nagging feeling just wouldn't go away. Then a low buzzing began in her ears; like a bothersome Bumblebee, then it grew louder and more alarming with each passing moment. She stared at her mother in mounting alarm, hoping she would notice the panic in her daughter's eyes but Rebecca could say nothing. She had been rendered mute. Then just as suddenly as it had begun the humming stopped and she found her eyes riveted upon the face of a young Amish man she had never seen before. He was brown haired and attired like everyone else but his eyes were shiny silver and fixed intently upon hers. Then the humming hit her body full force as they gazed at one another. The world about her began to rotate slowly as she continued to stare at him, unable to tear her gaze away from those incredible eyes; then she blacked out cold, falling where she stood as if struck by lightning.

From the blackness in her mind came the sound of faint voices calling her name. Rebecca slowly came to and found her mother and sisters bending over her with looks of concern on their faces.

"Ach! Are you all right, Rebecca?" whispered her mother, wiping her face with a cool wet cloth. "Are you feeling sick?"

Rebecca sat up with their help, not remembering that she had fainted at all. "I'm okay," she murmured, rubbing her eyes. They helped her stand to her feet and waited while she looked around. The work on the barn continued at a pace; unaffected by her little fainting spell.

"Do you feel good enough to continue?" her mother asked, caressing her pale cheek. Rebecca nodded; not wanting to make any more of a scene than she already had. She looked over at the barn to see if she could spot the young man with the silver eyes again but could not distinguish him from any of the other men working.

"Yes, I'll be fine," she assured them, embarrassed that she had caused a scene. She returned to the table and basket of lemons but kept stealing glances over at the barn. Once or twice she heard whispered snippets of conversation which ended abruptly as soon as she was in earshot but she managed to catch a few words here and there such as "cows" and "disappeared" which set her heart to thumping furiously. Soon she became too distracted with meal prep and serving to think any more about the young man with the strange eyes…until a break was called for lunch.

At noon the men put down their tools and gathered with the women at the tables under the cool shade of the maple trees and bowed their heads in communal prayer before sitting down to a feast. The women served the men first, filling their glasses with either sweet tea or lemonade and bringing platters of food that quickly disappeared. Rebecca was filling glasses as fast as she could; sweat trickling down her face and back when she suddenly found herself eye-to-eye with the mysterious stranger. She froze in shock, gaping at his silver eyes as he held up his glass to her. His eyes were absolutely mesmerizing.

"Rebecca!" she heard someone cry out when the glass pitcher dropped from her hands. Lemonade splattered all over the table, her dress and several men. They rose, wiping away the sticky liquid with their handkerchiefs and casting strange looks at her.

"May I?" said the stranger, taking a white handkerchief from his back pocket. He handed it to Rebecca with a bashful smile on his beautiful face. Rebecca accepted it but couldn't seem to move or drag her eyes away from his. Silence descended upon all as men and women alike turned to observe the shattered pitcher of lemonade and the young man with the other-worldly eyes. Despite their stares he seemed at ease and continued to smile at Rebecca as though he had eyes for no one but her.

It was her father who made the first move. "You are new," he announced, stepping closer. He looked him up and down as any good Amish father would. "What is your name?"

"Seth." The young man replied, turning and offering his hand in a warm shake.

"Seth....what?" repeated Leroy not accepting the proffered hand.

"Just Seth," smiled Seth, dropping his hand when it became apparent Rebecca's father wasn't going to accept it.

This brought an immediate frown to Leroy's face. He did not take to evasiveness. "Have you no family name?" he persisted.

"I do but it is impossible to pronounce," replied Seth apologetically.

Undeterred, her father continued his line of questioning. He stared hard at the Seth's bowed head. "Where is thy home?" By now a small crowd had gathered all around; the barn-raising seemingly all but forgotten for the moment.

Seth pointed over the rolling hills off into the distance towards the direction of Rebecca's farm. "There," he replied.

"I put little trust in the words of a man who will not meet my eyes," Leroy stated. In reply Seth lifted his chin and looked her father directly in the eyes. Leroy blanched...completely taken aback by his silver irises. His mouth opened and shut a few times; still at a loss for words, then he stood, took Rebecca by the shoulders and pulled her back, putting himself between them.

"You are not welcome here." Leroy stated, beginning to tremble. "You must leave."

Seth hung his head looking sincerely dejected. Rebecca felt sorry for him. He couldn't help being born with such strange eyes. Seth turned and walked away while everyone watched. Not until his form had disappeared behind a turn in the road did they begin to murmur amongst themselves or return to their lunch. An hour later the men and boys returned to the barn raising but the strange young man by the name of Seth had became the primary topic of conversation as they continued to work.

As she cleared the tables of dishes, cups and glasses, Rebecca kept stealing glances over her shoulder at the road he had taken; unable to take her mind off of him. Once or twice her father caught her in the act and shook his head at her; trying to discourage any further curiosity on her part but it only had the opposite effect.

By late afternoon the barn had been completely framed and the roof finished. The families would return the next day to finish the siding and painting before returning to their usual routines on their own farms and workshops. It was nearly twilight when their horse and buggy clip-clopped down the road back to their farm. The first stars began to peep out. Her father had been unusually silent on the ride home when normally he would hum a familiar hymn. This night he was deep in thought over the events of earlier that day. When they pulled into their drive-way Rebecca blinked and did a double-take. A pair of eyes seemed to gleam out at her from the other side of their hydrangea bushes but when she rubbed her eyes and looked harder they were gone. She clambered out of the buggy, helping her mother to bring in the empty food containers and baskets. Mary and Mirriam raced each other upstairs while Rebecca and Hannah helped their mom prepare a quick supper as well as food for the following day. They would have to be up early again the next morning to return and finish off the barn.

After supper it was time to get ready for bed. Despite her physical exhaustion sleep eluded her. Rebecca lay awake for hours, staring out her bedroom window at the silver crescent moon. In an odd way it reminded her of the strange boy's eyes.

Rebecca could have sworn that she had only closed her eyes for a few moments when the cock crowed at 4:00am the next morning. She threw the covers back, pushed Hannah out of bed, grabbed her shawl and together they went to the outhouse before changing their clothes and donning aprons to help with breakfast. Her mother was already up and working in the kitchen while her father was milking the cows. After a rushed breakfast, they all helped to prepare food for the day's lunch at the barn-raising then crowded into the buggy. When they crested the hill they beheld a site that made Leroy stand up and rein in Joe to a complete halt. With the backdrop of the rising sun, they saw over a hundred of their brethren with their buggies lined up alongside the road staring at the barn they had framed a mere 18 hours earlier. They were silent as gravestones, their arms hanging at their sides.

"Leroy, *was ist falsch*?" Ruth asked, craning her neck around to see past him but her question remained unanswered. Curious, Rebecca and her sisters tumbled out of the buggy and ran towards the line of Amish who continued to stare at the barn in silence. What greeted Rebecca's eyes had the same effect upon her as it had upon them: complete shock. The Zook's barn was still there but it was completely finished down to every last countersunk nail and the bright red paint and white trim. It defied explanation. It would have taken a hundred Amish working from dawn until dusk to complete what they now saw standing before them. Nothing was left to be done. The loft had even been stocked with fresh bales of hay.

Leroy stared at it; every bit as at a loss for words as the rest of his kinsmen. He had come prepared for a full day's work but there was nothing to do. Ruth went in search of her best friend, Ivy Miller while Leroy sought out Deacon Yoder who had been there the day earlier helping in the build. He too was staring at the completely finished barn as if it had appeared out of thin air; stroking his long salt & pepper beard and murmuring to himself.

All around him he could hear his Amish brothers muttering different variations of "*Was in der welt?*" but no one seemed to know who had finished the barn in absolute darkness the night before and without a sound. Rebecca looked around; her attention suddenly drawn to Abram and Mary Zook who were staring at the barn as though looking at a phantom. They seemed afraid to approach it as if it might come alive and bite them. They hurried past it to the line of Amish families and soon became surrounded, questions flying at them from all directions.

"Did you hear or see anything last night?"

"Do you know who could have done this?"

Their response to every question was a vigorous shake of their head followed by a frightened backward glance at the barn.

"I don't know if we want to put our livestock in there," Mary confessed, drawing her shawl about her tighter. "It gives me the willies just wondering who or what could have done all this without our hearing a peep all night. Not even our dog, Buddy, raised a whisker during the night and he'd bark at a dust bunny blowing across the floorboards!"

"We can't just tear it down and start over because we don't understand how all this happened," Rebecca's father interjected reasonably when a lull in the conversation occurred. "At the very least the bishop or Deacon should go inside and take a look around to make sure everything is…normal."

"If the bishops give their blessings then I suppose it will be alright," murmured Abram, exchanging worried looks with his new wife. She nodded in agreement but only half-heartedly. Deacon Yoder and Bishops Fisher and King were found and asked to inspect the barn. The sun rose higher and higher as they disappeared within to take a look around while the rest of the Amish waited from a distance for their verdict; as if afraid the barn doors would shut upon them and the entire structure take wing for far off places unknown. They exited half an hour later after a thorough inspection and pronounced the structure strong, safe and in every way ready for use. Abram and Mary Zook looked askance at their elders then bowed their heads in submission of their decision. Despite the unresolved mystery and their misgivings; there was nothing else to be done except to use the barn for its intended purposes. With that pronouncement, the Amish returned to their horses and buggies; shaking their heads and wondering what other bizarre events lay in store for them. First it was the crop circles and disappearing cattle; now barns were finishing themselves in the dead of night. The Esh's also returned to their farm in silence and performed their daily chores as usual but their thoughts were consumed with questions.

Chapter Two
"The Visitors"

Rebecca woke hours before the dawn despite her exhaustion to find her younger sister standing at the window as if in a trance.

"Hannah, what are you doing?"

Hannah stood rooted to the spot as if she had not heard her or was under a spell. Rebecca slipped out of bed, wrapping her shawl about her in the chilly air.

"Ach! Sleepwalking again," she muttered to herself, placing her hand gently upon Hannah's shoulder to guide her back into bed. Then she too froze; unable to tear her gaze away from the bizarre scene playing itself outside her window before her disbelieving eyes. A pattern of bright lights was swirling about their corn fields like some kind of strange light show. There was no sound save the violent rustling of the corn stalks as the green, blue and red lights danced above the field. In the barn she could hear the sound of Joe neighing, the mules braying and the cows lowing nervously as it rose higher and went from one end of the field to the other. She wanted to yell out for her parents or take cover under the safety of her quilts but she was too frozen with terror to budge. After several more moments the lights swirled higher and higher into the night sky until they disappeared into the clouds. Almost as if the spell had been lifted, they blinked and looked at one another in wild-eyed fear.

"Did you see what I saw, Rebecca?" Hannah whispered, trembling violently. "Should we wake *mamm* and *daed* and tell them?"

"Ach no! Are you *narrish*? They will just say it was a dream," Rebecca hissed back, pulling her back into bed and covering their heads with the quilt. Her heart was racing.

"Not if we tell them we both saw it!" Hannah insisted. "We can't just pretend it didn't happen!"

"Let's at least wait until the morning," Rebecca suggested, pulling her sister closer in her arms for comfort. "We can go out to the fields first thing and see if it left any marks, all right?"

"Wellllll okay," replied Hannah, "but I'm not going to get a wink of sleep now!"

"Me either," agreed Rebecca.

They lay still in each other's arms; the only sound their ragged breathing which seemed to take hours to calm down. At some point they must have fallen asleep because they were both startled when the cock crowed at 4:00 a.m. They were both up in a flash, wrapping their shawls about them while they ran downstairs and out the front door with the screen door slamming behind them. They raced across the grass lawn barefoot and to the edge of their corn field to gape at the sight. Their father and mother were only moments behind them having heard the ruckus they made; fearful that something bad had occurred. When they got to the field all they could do was to stare at the sight which greeted them. There were no words to describe how they felt. Almost the entire corn field had been flattened into an intricate pattern of circles and whorls that could only have been fully appreciated from several hundred feet in the air. Leroy stared at his corn field in grim silence, torn between anger at the senseless ruination of his crop and fear of the unknown cause.

"We saw lights last night." Hannah said, tugging on her mother's shawl.

Ruth looked down at her young daughter and clutched her close in her arms. "What lights?"

"Swirling lights…they made nee a sound," replied Rebecca. Both parents stared at her with almost accusatory glares.

"Why didn't you wake us?" her father asked; the rest of his unfinished sentence hanging in the air.

"We were afraid. We couldn't move or speak until after it was gone." Rebecca answered, hanging her head.

"Until what was gone?" Her mother coaxed, putting her arm about her shoulders.

Rebecca didn't know how to respond to the question. She had read enough newspapers and sci-fi books to hazard a guess but it sounded ridicules. "The lights," she mumbled at last. "They disappeared into a cloud."

Leroy and Ruth exchanged worried glances. Normally they would have passed it off to an overactive imagination but the visible evidence and Hannah's collaboration (who was not given to flights of fancy like her sister) made it impossible to dismiss.

"Saddle the mules then hurry in for some breakfast. We'll have to salvage whatever is left." Her father said grimly, going into the house. The strange lights and their source would have to take a back seat to saving what remained of his ruined crop. When that was dealt with he would meet with the bishops and discuss what, if anything could be done. The girls ran back to the barn and hurriedly saddled the mules to the harvester then tethered them to the hitching ring before going into the house to eat breakfast. They ate in silence; each one busy with their own thoughts as they tried to make sense out of all the strange things that had been going on lately. Breakfast done, they went out the front door only to be confronted by their second shock of the morning. The harvester stood just as they had left it to the hitching ring fifteen minutes earlier but now it was filled with ears of corn already cleaned, and piled up neatly; ready for market.

"Look, mamm!" Mary pointed, with a giggle; thinking it funny. Hannah might have been tempted to giggle had she not been so afraid. Leroy, Rebecca, and Ruth just stood staring at it.

"I'm heading over to get Bishop Fisher right now." Leroy said over his shoulder, climbing into the buggy. "Leave everything just as it is so he can be a witness."

His wife and daughters nodded obediently. If any of them had owned a camera they would have taken a zillion pictures by now of the lights, flattened field and harvester so they could have documented the evidence but that was impossible since the Amish did not own or use cameras. As their father sped off in the buggy for Bishop Fisher's farm, they trudged back into the house to forget the queer goings on to immerse themselves in their work. Rebecca was the last up the porch stairs when she heard a *Pssst!*

She looked to her right then her left, wondering if she was now hearing things as well. *Pssst!* This time there was no doubt; her ears were not playing tricks! The hydrangea bush next to the steps shook. Curiosity overcoming her fear, she stepped back down and peered closer. A pair of silvery eyes met hers. A scream rose in her throat but nothing would come out. The next thing she knew she was being pulled through the bush. She fell to her knees and found herself kneeling on the muddy ground before the strange looking young Amish man with the silver eyes who had been told to leave the barn-raising the previous day. He clapped his hand over her mouth just as she opened it to scream.

"Sssh! I mean you no harm!" he hissed. Rebecca stared at him, wild-eyed, trembling with fear. "Please do not be afraid," he whispered gently. His words instantly calmed her as if they were a command rather than a plea. She closed her mouth and he slowly removed his hand.

"Who and what are you?" she whispered fiercely. "Where did you come from? Are you responsible for all the ruined crops, the strange lights and...and...that?" She pointed at the neatly stacked piles of corn on the harvester.

"My name is Seth, I'm Plain just like you. As far as the rest of your questions: nee...a little bit...and jah," he replied, giving her a shy smile which made her heart beat a little quicker. Despite his strange eyes he was very handsome.

"What do you mean by 'nee, a little bit and jah'?" she frowned, not liking how evasive he was being.

"Nee: I am not personally responsible for the ruined crops...I am a little responsible for the weird lights...and jah I stacked the corn for you. I felt badly after what Silas had done and wanted to make up for it."

"Who is Silas?".

"My twin brother," replied Seth. "He looks just like me except his eyes are gold."

Rebecca stood up; she had heard enough. "Go away," she said, pointing up to the sky. "Go back from...from...wherever you came. You aren't wanted here! Haven't you caused enough damage? Bishop Fisher will be here soon and...well...I wouldn't be loitering about if I were you!" She pushed aside the bushes and stomped up the porch stairs and into the house, letting the screen door slam behind her; shaken to the core. Two of them! One with silver eyes and one with gold and both imbued with supernatural powers. For once she was glad it was wash day where she could immerse herself and her mind in massive amounts of dirty laundry. Perhaps by day's end she would be too exhausted to be woken up in the middle of the night by weird lights!

Seth watched her leave and stood up, smiling to himself as though he had just discovered something wonderful. He walked behind the house and disappeared into the corn field.

Her father returned with Bishop King following just behind in his own buggy within the hour. Rebecca watched them from her vantage point on the back porch where she was hand-scrubbing the laundry on the wash board. The two men walked out and inspected the flattened field then surveyed the perfectly stacked corn in the harvester. Every time she looked at him the Bishop was shaking his head while his hand continually stroked his beard. By the time her sisters joined her to help peg the first load on the line Bishop Fisher was already back in his buggy and turning his horse for home. Her father stood watching with a glower upon his face then went to work in the barn without a word to anyone.

Lunch and dinner were equally as silent. Even ten year old Mirriam and eight year old Mary who were normally chatterboxes ate in silence, continually casting worried glances at their daed and mamm who didn't speak at all; too lost in their own thoughts to discuss what the Bishop had said earlier that day. They all went to bed early with great apprehension; worrying about what the next morning would bring.

"Are you asleep yet?" Hannah whispered next to her.
"Nee!" Rebecca replied.
The two of them lay cuddled together in bed; exhausted but too fearful to go to sleep. Each of them stared out the bedroom window waiting for the light show to begin; too on edge to close their eyes.
"Do you think we'll see them again tonight?" Hannah whispered.
"I hope not!" Rebecca replied.
They got their wish but despite that it took them forever to finally fall into an exhausted but fitful sleep.

The rooster did not crow the next morning but everyone still woke up before the dawn mainly out of sheer habit. Rebecca's father and sisters went straight to the barn to take care of the cows (which were strangely quiet) and chicken coop to gather eggs while Rebecca and her mother began their baking and breakfast preparation. Her father and sisters appeared minutes later; their eyes round with fear.

"Leroy – *Was ist das*?" her mother asked. There was no way they could have gotten all the cows milked in such a brief space of time. "Are the cows all right?"

"The cows are fine." Leroy replied; tight-lipped. "We found them already milked and the milk in the pasteurizer."

"What?" cried Ruth in disbelief. Leroy sat down and put his face in his hands and began to pray silently. Rebecca became filled with righteous indignation when her father began to tremble. She left the dough she had been kneading on the board and marched out through the screen door; determined to give Seth and his brother a piece of her mind; heedless of the flour all over her hands.

"Seth! Come out! Where are you, Seth?" she hissed, hands balled into fists. "I know you're here somewhere! Come out… now!" She stood and waited for several minutes, getting no response then decided to try her luck in the barn. The cows all turned their heads to look at her but seemed peaceful enough. "Seth!" she repeated. There was a slight rustling in the hayloft above her and then his familiar face peeped out.

"Up here!" he whispered, beckoning to her.

She climbed the ladder and pointed at a floured finger at him; renewed anger flushing her face red. "Why are you still here? Do you have any idea what you are doing to my family?" she demanded.

"I just wanted to make up for all the damage," whispered Seth; his face the picture of genuine remorse.

Rebecca stared at him; pacified by his penitent (if misguided) attitude. "What are you talking about?"

"The field damage…the cows…the lights."

"Are you the ones who stacked the corn and finished the barn?" Rebecca asked, her voice softening a little.

Again Seth nodded then grabbed his stomach when it growled loudly.

"Are you hungry?" Rebecca asked.

Seth nodded and his stomach grumbled again in confirmation. "We both are…very," he replied softly, his silver eyes rising to meet hers. The moment they fastened upon her, Rebecca felt her heart quicken again; completely arrested by his handsome features. Despite his strange eyes and mysterious abilities; her heart could not help but go out to him.

"Kommen sie mit," she said gently, beckoning him down. Seth needed no further urging and practically slid down the ladder. "Where is your twin?" she asked. Right on cue Silas stepped into view from behind one of the cows. He looked exactly like his brother but there was a mischievous glint in his golden eyes which Seth did not posses. He too was clutching an empty stomach that was growling loudly. "I'll feed you both on one condition," Rebecca said, her face stern. "All the weird pranks and attempts to make amends have to come to an end; immediately and permanently. Do I have your word on this?"

The brothers exchanged glances then nodded in agreement; hunger was a good motivator. Rebecca nodded with satisfaction then led them out of the barn and to the front porch.

"Wait here," she commanded, holding up her hand. They froze on the lower step. Rebecca closed her eyes, breathed a silent prayer to *der Herr* to guide her then stepped into the house. All eyes turned upon her.

"I know who has been behind all the strange occurrences lately," she announced then faltered, wringing her floured hands together.

"Who?" asked her entire family in unison.

"It's the strange Amish boy with the silver eyes and his twin *bruder*."

"There's two of them?" he father replied with undisguised alarm in his voice.

Rebecca nodded. "One is Seth, father, who you saw at the barn raising and his twin is Silas. They seem to be quite remorseful over the trouble they have caused everyone."

"How would you know this?" her father responded.

Rebecca shifted nervously from one foot to the other, not knowing what the response was going to be when she told him. "...because they told me so. They are out on the front porch and they are very hungry."

Everyone rose to their feet at once; her siblings excited...her mother worried and her father angry.

"You brought them to our house?"

"No, *daed*, I found them hiding in the hayloft. They are waiting outside to give you their personal apologies." This last sentence she said as loudly as possible so that her voice would carry easily to the front porch. Leroy marched past Rebecca and threw the screen door open; ready to give the two boys an earful. When he saw them, heads bowed, hats in hand looking every bit as remorseful as his daughter had described, his anger dissipated somewhat.

"We are truly sorry for all the trouble we have caused," Seth said, elbowing his brother in the ribs.

"Please accept our apologies," added Silas. Then as if on cue, both of their stomachs rumbled loudly.

Leroy stared at them hard for a good long moment; his face softening. "When's the last time you had anything to eat?"

The brothers did some mental calculations using their fingers, exchanged looks between themselves then finally answered.

"Not since the barn-raising," Seth replied while Silas nodded in agreement.

"*Kommen sie mit,*" Leroy instructed, holding open the screen door. "Wash up at the sink then sit you down there." He pointed to the wooden bench at the family table. Like any good Christian, Leroy was not going to deny basic sustenance to a couple of penitent young men, regardless of their strange antics and eyes. The boys needed no further urging. They practically ran into the kitchen, pumped the water out of the sink and lathered their hands and arms all the way up to their elbows. Rebecca returned to kneading the dough and soon had the biscuits baking in the oven while her mother finished frying up the eggs, bacon and ham. Soon they were all seated around the long table, hands clasped and heads bowed as they gave silent thanks. Despite their ravenous hunger pangs, the boys politely waited their turn while the platters of food were passed around to them; however they were not shy when it came to the portions they took. They loaded up their plates with large mounds of food. Mirriam and Mary giggled constantly; finding the sight of young men shoveling food into their mouths as fast as they could a very funny sight. Ruth and Leroy ate in silence, casting glances at them every now and again as if to reassure themselves that they were no more than ordinary young men with healthy appetites.

When breakfast was done, Leroy stared at them over his mug of black coffee. "Where is your home?" he asked.

The brothers exchanged looks then pointed out the window towards the lightening sky. "In the tree?" Leroy smirked, trying to pin them down. Seth and Silas both shook their heads. "Where then, tell me!" Leroy persisted.

"If I tell you the truth, would you allow us to stay awhile and help you on the farm in return for room and board?" replied Silas, finding his voice.

"It does look like you could use some more men around here," added Seth; noticing that all of Leroy's children were female. "No offense," he added, looking specifically at Rebecca. She blushed and lowered her eyes.

"Ach! That depends upon your answer." Leroy replied noncommittally. All activity quieted as Rebecca's family awaited their response.

"You may find it impossible to believe us," replied Seth quietly.

"After what I've seen the past few days I doubt it," said Leroy patiently.

"We come from another world...out there," continued Seth; looking Mr. Esh right in the eyes. "I don't expect you to believe me but it's the truth. We never lie."

Leroy stared at him for a long moment, taking the young man's measure. Seth's face was open and sincere, nor was there any deceit in his eyes. "Thou art *narrish*," pronounced Leroy, shaking his head and setting down his coffee cup.

"I told you he wouldn't believe us!" hissed Silas, incensed at his brother.

"We're not insane, sir," insisted Seth, rising to his feet. "Do you want proof?"

At this, Leroy blanched. It was easier (and much more comfortable) to judge the two young men insane than to believe the clearly unbelievable. "You can offer proof?" He responded, incredulous.

"I would first have to obtain a solemn promise from you and your family that none of you will divulge what we are about to reveal to you." replied Seth; the *de facto* spokesman of the pair. "I know that an Amish man's word is his bond."

Leroy crossed his arms and smiled grimly at them; playing along. "All right, work in exchange for food and board on a trial basis," he agreed. "But if you violate my trust or bring any shame to my family or community neither of you will be welcome in Lancaster County anymore."

"...and your promise?" pressed Silas, his golden eyes large as millstones.

"I promise on behalf of my family and myself not to reveal your 'secret'." Leroy replied, thinking it little more than an elaborate practical joke and that once exposed, they would be well on their way out the door and hopefully out of the county.

"Follow me, then," responded Seth, turning around and heading out the back door. Leroy and Ruth exchanged worried glances. The brothers waited patiently for them to rise. After a long pause everyone got up from the table and followed the brothers outside. The dirty dishes, pots and pans were momentarily forgotten in the heat of curiosity Once in the yard, the entire family walked behind, trailing them like ducklings. The rising sun silhouetted the Esh family while they walked single file. They passed through their backyard, the house garden and barn until they finally stood at the end of their ruined cornfield. Leroy hesitated for just a moment then plunged into the open row after the brothers, wondering where on earth they were leading him.

They walked into the middle of the corn field where the flattened and now browning husks lay. Seth offered Leroy a bashful grin then reached up his hand and pressed his palm flat against the thin air. The scenery before them wavered, much like it would have done by heat thermals but the air was cool. Something slowly began to take shape before them…something enormous…and metallic.

The Esh family returned to their farmhouse in silence ten minutes later. None of them spoke to one another or knew what to say. Their entire foundation of reality had been shaken to its core. Rebecca had never seen her father so conflicted. Matters of behavior had always been clearly spelled out and taught throughout their community for generations but the Ordnung had no guidelines for something like this. They were sailing in completely uncharted waters. The brothers at least had the decency not to press the matter and followed behind her father in silence; wondering if Mr. Esh would go back on his word. Rebecca stole a peek at them as she made her way up the steps into the house. Their heads were bowed respectfully; allowing her father time to digest and process what he had just seen. The family retook their seats at the table, prayed in silence again and resumed eating their cold breakfast without conversation and without much appetite except for Silas and Seth who practically licked their plates clean.

After breakfast, Rebecca, her siblings and mother busied themselves with clearing away the dishes. Her father remained in his seat completely lost in his thoughts. The brothers waited on him in respectful silence, aware he was struggling with having to fulfill a promise he had never expected he would have to keep.

Rebecca was intimately familiar with how much and how long her father had longed for sons who could help him in the fields and with the livestock but she still wondered what his final decision would be. Finally Leroy cleared his throat and ran his fingers through his beard; something he did only when highly agitated.

This is it, she thought, casting a glance over her shoulder at Seth and Silas as she scrubbed the iron frying pan at the sink.

"As a Christian man I will honor my word," Leroy began, looking the brothers squarely in the eyes. "Food and lodging in return for good labor. There is to be no more damage either to my farm, nor any others. Is that clear? If you violate this agreement or do anything to dishonor my family I will turn you both out and have you shunned by the entire community. Are we clear?"

Despite their alien origin both of them seemed to be very familiar with the gravity of shunning. The brothers nodded solemnly; their strange eyes round with terror at the thought. There was no worse punishment than be treated as though you didn't exist.

"Rebecca will set you up with clean bedding in the barn but you may take your meals with us."

Seth stood up. "Thank you, sir. We won't disappoint you. Will we Silas?"

"No sir," replied the other brother solemnly.

"*Gut*," nodded Leroy, standing to his feet. "I will need some help plowing under the corn field you ruined."

The brothers hung their heads in shame and nodded. "Yes sir."

Dutifully they followed him out to the fields and Rebecca saw nothing of them until noon until when they took a break for lunch. They returned sweaty, dirty and exhausted followed by her father who was having a hard time trying to hide his smile of satisfaction.

"Go wash up first," he instructed, pointing to the kitchen sink. Rebecca had the noon table already set with a "dinner" of beef stew, mashed carrots and parsnips, fried noodles and a pitcher of ice-cold lemonade. After a brief silent prayer of thanks, they set to their meal with gusto.

"After lunch we go to Jacob Lapp's farm," Leroy informed them in a matter-of-fact voice. The brother's exchanged confused glances. Leroy explained. "He suffered the same damage as me so we are going to make restitution."

"Yes Mr. Esh," nodded Seth, throwing his brother a warning glance when he was about to protest their innocence. They finished their meal then joined Leroy in the buggy to ride over to Jacob Lapp's farm.

Rebecca did not seem them again until dinner time when they trudged into the house looking completely spent. She set plates heaped high with fried chicken, mashed potatoes with gravy and peas which they stared at listlessly. Her father had worked them over but gut!

They were almost too tired to eat but managed to soldier through.

"Not used to physical labor only using their muscles," Leroy said with a wink in his daughter's direction.

She nodded in silence; impressed with how he had so quickly adapted to the bizarre circumstances.

Afterwards they went to the barn to sponge bathe away the accumulated dirt and sweat of the day then collapsed upon their bed of hay in utter exhaustion.

Chapter Three
"You Can Never Travel Too Far for
Good Italian"

Although there was no email, internet, telephones or social media in the Amish community word still managed to spread like wildfire of the new additions to the Esh household. The gossip was already heading in a direction that Leroy had feared it might. He had already had been called to several meetings with Bishops King and Fisher the following week in which they had voiced their displeasure with him having taken in the young men but it always came back to the same thing: Leroy had given his word and now he had to abide by it.

Other than their strange abilities and unsettling eyes there was little else the bishops could find fault with and this especially seemed to vex them. They knew something wasn't right about them; they just couldn't identify exactly what it was. Leroy wasn't about to share with anyone outside of his immediate family his knowledge of the enormous metallic disc-shaped "ship" currently sitting in the center of his corn field; rendered invisible by technology that was obviously not of this earth. Either he would be branded a lunatic or much worse. The result would be shunning or expulsion from the community; he was caught between a rock and a hard place to be sure; bound by his word and trapped by their secret…

As luck would have it, Rebecca's home was to be the next location of the bi-monthly congregational meeting of their district. The family had gotten up at the crack of dawn and moved furniture around in all the downstairs rooms to make way for the benches and chairs that would hold the 100+ members of their congregation. Bishop King was the first to arrive with his family who (except for him) were all curious to meet the newcomers; especially his preteen daughters, Ruth and Sarah. They were followed by Deacon Yoder's family. The bishop and deacon spoke quietly with Leroy as the other families arrived but try as she might, Rebecca could not make out what they were saying while she helped prepare ham loaf, potato salad, lemonade, bread, biscuits, and pies for the noon meal; however it was patently obvious was how uncomfortable her father was by the set of his shoulders and tight jaw. She stole glances at him as often as she could while the elders spoke with him but when the two boys entered the house in their best white shirts, black trousers and jackets the atmosphere became tense and charged.

Bishop King and Deacon Yoder regarded the brothers with great suspicion and involuntarily shrunk away whenever they drew near as did many of the other Amish. It was obvious that Seth and Silas could sense their unease and did everything possible to be polite, unobtrusive and helpful but every glance at their strange eyes just made things worse. Most of their people appeared fearful of them.

It's a shame we Amish don't wear sunglasses… Rebecca thought to herself for the 100th time that morning. As the rest of their congregants arrived, took their seats and whispered amongst themselves, she began to feel more and more protective of the brothers and incensed at the unfriendly reactions to their presence.

Incensed, she marched up to Seth and took hold of his arm. "*Kommen sie mit!*" She steered them onto a small bench way in the back where he and Silas would be out of the way and took her seat next to them. She sat tall; silently daring anyone to bat an eye at them. The gossip was bad enough but to treat them like this in her own home really tested her limited patience.

By 9:00 am the house was filled with over 100 Amish men, women and children and by 9:10 am they were all singing and chanting hymns from the Ausbund. To Rebecca's surprise, Silas and Seth sang right along as if they had done so all their lives, without the benefit of a hymn book. This did not escape the notice of the other parishioners and it seemed to relax them a bit. Rebecca gave her kinfolk a triumphant smile of satisfaction whenever they reacted with shocked surprise.

Her father's best friend, Isaac Miller, was tapped that morning to give the sermon and with an understanding wink in Leroy's direction, he stood and began to recite from the 19th chapter of Leviticus: *"…and if a stranger sojourns with thee in your land, ye shall not vex him. But the stranger that dwelleth with you shall be unto you as one born among you, and thou shalt love him as thyself; for ye were strangers in the land of Egypt: I am the LORD your God."*

For the next hour he expounded upon the theme; elaborating on how showing charity to strangers, regardless of their peculiarities, was demanded by their Father in heaven. Silas and Seth listened intensely; completely transfixed; their twin faces alight with a joy that Rebecca could not help but marvel over. She took furtive glances around the room as Mr. Miller spoke and saw quite a few people squirming; especially Deacon Yoder and the two Bishops.

The sermon ended by noon and Rebecca could almost hear the audible sighs of relief which wafted about the room like a warm breeze. With another wink in her father's direction, Isaac sat down, a final hymn was sung and then everyone broke for lunch. In addition to the food the Esh's had prepared, all the other families had contributed as well. The men went outside or into the barn to discuss their livestock and crops; the women set up tables buffet style then assembled the many large platters of food by groups. They all paused for the quick blessing then everyone lined up in order from oldest to youngest. Silas and Seth went to the back of the line; the eyes of several of the Amish girls discreetly following them; obviously the object of great curiosity; especially Katie Zook. Rebecca did her best to swallow down her smile as she dished out the ham loaf.

"So where are Silas and Seth from?" whispered Sarah leaning forward.

Rebecca shrugged in response. She and her sisters had already been warned by their father not to reveal anything about the brother's strange abilities and especially not the invisible ship in their corn field.

"You aren't going to tell me anything, are you?" Sarah concluded. Rebecca answered with another shrug and an apologetic smile. Sarah sighed. "Very well, then, Becca! Where do you want to eat?"

"In our favorite spot of course!" Rebecca pointed. Together she and Sarah took places at the end of the line, filled their plates then went outside to find a place to sit in the shade under a large maple. They found Seth and Silas already there.

"Why aren't you with the other boys?" Rebecca asked them, sitting down.

Seth shrugged but gave no other response.

"We tried but it was clear we weren't welcome," Silas said.

This cut Rebecca to the heart. "I'm truly sorry," she said on behalf of her people.

The silence grew uncomfortable.

Sarah cleared her throat and addressed Rebecca. "Um, have you finished those books yet? Mary Lapp has been asking to borrow them when you're done."

"No, not yet," Rebecca replied between mouthfuls. "But I will soon." She cast a glance over at the brothers who were single-mindedly fixated on their plates and emptying their contents as quickly as possible. One thing sure didn't change; regardless of where they came from in the Universe; all boys consumed vast quantities of food as if they were continually starving. "Will you be staying to work on the quilt, Sarah?"

"*Jah*," replied Sarah. "I brought my sewing kit." They ate in companionable silence for ten more minutes then watched the brothers return their plates to the kitchen before heading to the barn for one more try to join in with the other young men to play or talk. They made several attempts to engage them but all shied away as soon as they approached; leaving them to stand awkwardly by themselves.

Rebecca watched angrily from a distance, her heart hurting for them. Almost as if he sensed it, Seth turned about and looked her right in the eyes. The forlorn look in his silver eyes was all it took to bring her up onto her feet. She ignored the humming in her head which usually accompanied his intense stares and marched to the barn in full sight of the entire congregation.

Sarah gaped after her; her spoon halfway between her plate and mouth; no doubt wondering what was Rebecca was going to do.

Rebecca walked up to Seth whose face lit up with joy at her approach. Silas, on the other hand, glowered at her. She ignored him.

"Kommen sie mit," she said, grasping his hand and hauling him unceremoniously out of the barn before the shocked and disapproving eyes of all around her. She marched him past the house and to the small pond at the back of their property which was surrounded by willow trees, one of which had a wooden swing hanging from it. Rebecca paced back and forth in frustration. She didn't like how they were being treated. They worked just as hard as everyone else! They hadn't harmed anyone or done anything inappropriate. They spoke

and behaved like any Old Order Amish in almost every respect except for their strange eyes but still her people were treating them like "*the Englisch*" or even worse.

She felt Seth's silvery eyes upon her as she tried to calm down but the more she thought about the morning's sermon and how everyone had still avoided them as though they had typhoid fever, the more agitated she became. She was muttering to herself and twisting her black apron into knots; wondering if it had all been an enormous mistake to invite them into her home and subject them to this treatment.

"Rebecca, calm down, please. What have I done wrong?"

Rebecca stopped pacing and stared at him; his handsome face and silver eyes imploring her.

"I just wish I could leave sometimes!" she blurted out; the words tumbling from her lips. They had been pent up inside of her for as long as she could remember. She had not yet chosen to experience her "Rumspringa" (running around) years but she still yearned to see and experience new things; she was just too fearful to take the chance. She knew of other Amish girls (like her friend, Hannah Yoder) who had left home and family who had still not returned and saw firsthand the heartache it had caused. Rumors swirled that Hannah had gotten mixed up in drugs and illicit sex; but no one knew of her whereabouts.

If only there was some way to experience what life was like elsewhere without running so many risks...

Seth's warm brown hand rested upon her arm, sending a jolt of electricity through her. Rebecca looked up at him; becoming lost in his incredible eyes; almost unaware that the world about her had begun to spin, first slowly then faster and faster. "Hold onto me and don't let go," Seth whispered, his eyes locked upon hers. Rebecca clutched his arms; unable to turn her face away from his. She felt his strong arms encircle her; holding her close as the wind rushed about them. Her stomach lurched but as long as she kept her eyes fixed upon his, she was able to keep the nausea from overwhelming her.

"What's happening?" she screamed but her voice was swallowed up in the maelstrom.

"Don't let go," came Seth's calm voice inside her head. Darkness swept over her and the last thing Rebecca remembered were his arms tightening about her before it finally descended.

She heard him call her name but it seemed to come from a great distance. Then she felt her face gently patted but it too seemed to belong to someone else and not herself. The black tunnel collapsed and light began to coalesce about her. Rebecca opened her eyes and found twin discs of silver concern staring back at her.

"We have to do something about your equilibrium problem," the three sets of lips floating above her face said.

"My what?" Rebecca sat up with Seth's help and tried to focus her eyes. She looked about her. "Where are we?"

The willow trees, swing, pond, farm house and grass were gone. Instead she found herself in a small cottage. The sound of waves crashing upon a shore through the nearby window brought her upright. She turned her head, staring with disbelief at sheer white curtains which floated and billowed with each warm sigh of the breeze.

"Where am I?" she repeated.

"We are in Southern California…Laguna Beach to be exact." Seth replied, helping her slowly back up onto her feet. Something felt wrong. Rebecca looked down at herself and gaped in horror. Instead of her "plain" clothes she was dressed in khaki shorts which shamelessly exposed her legs below the knees and a short-sleeve cotton print shirt with garishly bright flowers all over it.

"What did you do, kidnap me?" she shrieked, covering her mouth in horror. "How did you get me like this? My *daed* is going to throw you out of the house for certain!" Her voice grew louder and louder with each sentence.

Seth calmly stood with his arms crossed across his chest; an amused smirk on his face. Apparently he was accustomed to such reactions. Rebecca paced about the room in circles, oblivious to the charming décor as she made new discoveries about her changed appearance. The final explosion came when she discovered that her hair was no longer in its customary bun under her white linen kapp but flowing down her back in golden waves. She grasped the thick tendrils in each hand and shook them at him accusingly. "Are you determined to see me shunned?" she shrieked.

"Are you finished?" Seth replied calmly.

Rebecca stared at him, her entire body trembling with a terror she had never experienced before. She felt naked and exposed. If anyone caught her like this it would be terrible! Seeing her distress, Seth's eyes softened, changing from rye amusement to compassion.

Without thinking he held out his arms to comfort her. Rebecca collapsed into them; desperate for consolation though she knew the embrace was verboten. She began to sob uncontrollably.

"Ssshhhh, it's okay, Becca...don't worry. You won't be shunned," he whispered into her golden hair. "Be calm...be at peace."

His words sent the exact emotions through her entire body that came out of his mouth so that within moments she felt completely calm again despite her misgivings about her appearance and how she had gotten 3,000 miles away from her home. "I'm just doing what you asked; I took you away to experience life here from a different point of view."

"Jah...but- I didn't think you could actually do anything about it!"

"You didn't really mean it? I know better. I could feel the longings of your heart from low earth orbit!" Seth chuckled.

"Ach! What do you mean by that?" Rebecca demanded, grabbing a nearby throw blanket and wrapping it about her.

"What do you think I mean?" he replied.

They stared at one another for a moment while Rebecca pondered how wise it would be for her sense of security to respond. "Never mind...What if someone sees me like this I'll be shunned for good!"

"Who's going to see you?"

Rebecca just stared at him; the truth finally hitting her like a ton of bricks. "You're not playing games with me...we really are on the West Coast?"

Seth nodded.

"How...how did we get here?"

"I could try to explain it but you would need to at least have a basic understanding of quantum physics and trigonometry with a little H.G. Wells thrown in..."

"Are you saying we went through a Time Machine?" whispered Rebecca incredulous, growing pale again. She was well familiar with the works of H.G. Wells as he was one of her favorite authors; she just had never expected to be a character in one of his stories.

"No, we are still in the 'present' time; I've just teleported us somewhere else. No one is going to bat an eye at the way you look. On the other hand, you *would* draw a lot of attention were you "plainly" attired. Now, do you intend to spend the entire day cooped up in this charming little cottage or would you like to see the sights?" With this Seth opened up the front door to the cottage to reveal a steep flight of stairs which led down to a beach. "We could hunt for some seashells and sea glass before heading to the village for some sightseeing and window shopping," he grinned.

Despite her misgivings the temptation was too great. Rebecca had always wanted to visit Southern California…(something he seemed to have picked up on)…she might as well go exploring before facing the firing squad back at home. Maybe the time spent with Seth would help her think of a plausible explanation for why they were gone for so long and why.

"Lose the throw blanket; you won't need it," he advised.

She put it back on the couch and shyly accepted his offered hand. He led her outside and together they clambered down the endless rickety wooden steps to the beach below. It was low tide and the sand was filled with numerous seashells. Seth handed her a red plastic beach pail he had brought along and together they scanned the shoreline looking for treasures. The cool waves lapped at her toes; making her giggle every time they did so. Rebecca had to pause every few moments to admire the broad expanse of the endless sea stretching out before her across the horizon, glittering in the sun. Gulls and what she guessed to be Pelicans took turns dive bombing into the swells to catch fish. Despite the fact she had eaten a large Sunday dinner, she felt as hungry as though she hadn't.

"Hungry?" Seth smiled, carrying the pail back up the stairs for her. Rebecca nodded as she climbed, wondering if he planned to "transport" them to the village or if they would just go there the "old fashioned" way and walk. She entered the cottage and avoided her reflection in the hall mirror as he guided her out through the back door which led to a sidewalk just off Pacific Coast Highway. Outside cars sped by and tourists strolled, occasionally stopping to take pictures of the azure sea and picturesque landscape. On the inland side of the highway were shops and just behind them steep hills with cottages and mansions scattered all over. She had never seen such large homes perched so precariously on cliff faces before. They walked together downhill until they reached a boardwalk. They passed an old lifeguard tower which was surrounded on the beach side with basketball and volleyball courts. These were surrounded by grass and benches where people sat basking in the sun or holding up signs about war, global warming and politics. Rebecca looked down, suddenly realizing that Seth had been holding her hand the entire time. She should have pulled hers away but she found that she liked the way it felt. They made their way through the congested crosswalk over to where all the shops were located. His warm touch sent a tingle up her arm but she pretended to ignore it. Besides, she was too entranced with the storefronts. She didn't know where to look there were so many pretty and interesting things to see. They passed a Rocky Mountain Chocolate Factory shop with tempting trays of Carmel apples in the window and just past that was an Italian pottery shop. They continued walking until she found herself standing in front of Italian restaurant called Romeo Cucina.

"This is one of my favorite places to eat," Seth said, opening the door for her. "Their Tagliatelle Rustiche is the best!"

"What?" Rebecca questioned; her Italian nonexistent.

"Spaghetti with meatballs and tomato sauce," he explained with a grin, beckoning her in. A waiter showed them to a leather upholstered booth and handed them menus. Rebecca had never been to a restaurant other than the famous Shady Maple Smorgasbord in Lancaster County before and that had only been once. Since it was still early they were the only customers.

"Anything to drink?" asked the waiter, expecting an order for alcohol.

"Just two waters with lemon, please," replied Seth, taking charge. "We need a few more minutes please." Rebecca noticed that despite the darkened restaurant, Seth kept his sunglasses on in order to conceal his silver eyes; something he could not do in Lancaster County.

The waiter left and Rebecca examined the menu with dismay. "Don't they have anything else?"

"Such as?"

"Chicken? Noodles? Potato salad…Shoofly Pie…"

"I didn't transport you three thousand miles across the USA to my favorite Italian restaurant in Laguna Beach to eat Amish food!"

At that moment the waiter returned with an expectant look on his face. "We'll have two orders of your Tagliatelle Rustiche please." Seth handed the menus back with a smile.

"Excellent choice!" replied the waiter graciously, turning about to put their order in. Rebecca stared after him for a brief moment, wondering if there was any choice on the menu that would have elicited a *"bad choice…you should really choose something else"* from him.

She took a sip of her ice water, trying to appear nonchalant. "So how many times have you been here before?" She tried not to stare but he looked incredibly handsome in his sky blue, short sleeved shirt, khaki shorts and wind-tousled brown hair.

Seth grinned at her and offered her some bread from the basket. "A lot! There's also a great Irish Pub in Newport Beach I'll have to take you to called Muldoon's and a cupcake bakery nearby called Sprinkles!"

"I could never go to a pub!" Rebecca replied mortified.

"It's a restaurant just like this," Seth explained. They were interrupted a moment later when the waiter returned with two large white bowls filled with pasta that had a large meatball the size of a baseball in the center. The smell wafting up into Rebecca's nostrils was incredible.

"Grace first!" Seth reminded her, bowing his head. They gave silent thanks then Rebecca took a small forkful and tasted it. The first taste of the spicy tomato sauce made her close her eyes with pleasure.

"*Wunderbar!*" she declared, nodding enthusiastically, taking a larger bite. Seth grinned back; pleased she was enjoying it as much as he usually did. There wasn't much talking after that until their bowls were empty. Then the waiter brought over the dessert menu. Seth picked it up and waved it at her.

"Are you game for something besides Shoofly and Whoopie pies? How about trying Tiramisu and an espresso?"

"What's that?" Rebecca replied, unable to repress her enthusiasm to experience more new things.

"Dessert heaven and coffee on steroids," Seth replied. He held up two fingers to the waiter. "Two tiramisu's and espresso's if you please."

"Excellent choice!"

Rebecca covered her mouth to stifle the giggle. A few moments later he returned with two little cups of steaming black coffee and plates of what looked like a square of whipped cream dusted with cocoa powder. Seth waited and watched as Rebecca took the first bite. She closed her eyes as the mascarpone cream and lady fingers melted inside her mouth. It was absolutely wonderful; rich but not overly sweet. She was going to have to get the recipe and make it for her family! The only problem was figuring out how to tell them where she got it and why. When they were done Seth paid the bill and escorted her out to give her a brief tour of the village. They wandered from one charming shop to another where he let her admire the displays to her heart's content. Several times she caught him in the act of admiring her long golden tresses and felt a blush wash over her. It felt strange to have her hair hang loosely down her back and to be wearing clothes that exposed so much skin. It was nearing evening and the air was becoming chilly as the fog began to roll in. She began to shiver. Seth had thought of a lot but not about bringing a shawl to keep her warm! Seth walked her back to the boardwalk where they stood to watch the sun disappear into the gray clouds, his arm about her shoulders to keep her warm. They swiftly marched up the hill and returned to the little cottage.

He closed the door behind them. "Ready?"

Rebecca nodded a bit apprehensively; wondering how she was going to explain their absence. Seth took out what looked to be a regular pocket watch; something the Amish would never use. Again he put his arm protectively about her and pressed a button on the side of its case. A wave of dizziness hit her. Rebecca blacked out and the next thing she knew she was back home under the tree with the swing as if they had never left. This time the nausea and dizziness lasted only for a moment. She looked around; expecting it to be dark outside but from the angle of the sun it looked like only a few moments had passed at most. She found Seth standing very close; his arm still about her looking very pleased with himself. He was back in his plain clothes as was she. Reluctantly he released her and let her step back. The first thing Rebecca did was to check her head; her hair was tightly wound and in its kapp. It was as if she had never left except for her uncomfortably full belly and the rush of adrenaline which was coursing through her. She stepped back and stared at him in alarm wondering what he had done to her.

"Why do I feel like this?" she whispered, her entire frame trembling. "I've been working since the crack of dawn; I should be exhausted but I feel ready to jump out of my skin!" She clutched at her racing heart and pointed an accusing finger at him. "Did you drug me or something?" Her voice became shrill.

"Ssh!" laughed Seth, putting a finger to his lips.

"What is so funny?" Rebecca demanded. "Why do I feel like this?"

Seth returned her panicked stare calmly, the corners of his mouth twitching. "Two words: espresso and chocolate." "You'll be cleaning house all night until the caffeine wears off and then you'll crash. It won't be a pretty site…"

Rebecca just gaped at him. She should be furious with him but his smile was her undoing. She touched her tightly bound hair again, satisfied that no one would be any the wiser. "Let's get back to the house before we are missed!" She marched off, determined to make use of her energy surge by helping to clean up. Hopefully it would wear off by the time she was expected to join the other women quilting.

Seth followed after her still grinning but he didn't get far before he felt his twin pull him behind the barn and push him up against the wall; his golden eyes glowing with fury. "What do you think you're doing?" Silas demanded. "You know the rules!"

Seth scowled back at him. "So do you! It's all because of you that we're in this mess to begin with!"

"At least I kept out of sight! You're digging us in deeper. If this continues there's no way we're going to be able to return home without significantly impacting this world."

"I'll try to keep our footprint to a minimum, brother." Seth replied. "After all, how much of a "footprint" could we really leave in an Amish community? We'll be gone soon enough. You just focus on getting the ship back in working order!"

"Easier said than done…we sustained some pretty serious damage when we crashed into Mr. Esh's field. It's going to take months just for the energy cells to recharge. What about Rebecca Esh?" scowled Silas.

Seth stared back at him saying nothing. He hated it when his brother read his mind. "We're just friends…drop it," he replied.

Silas scowled. "I don't believe you. You know relationships on this world are forbidden. You better end it before it goes any further!"

"It won't go any further," Seth promised unconvincingly then fell silent. After all, what could he say? He was doomed from the moment he had laid eyes on Rebecca Esh at the barn raising. It had been like discovering a miracle; someone he had longed and searched the galaxy for all his life. That was probably why she had fainted when he stared at her. The emotions which had poured out of his heart upon recognizing his missing half were so powerful they had completely overwhelmed her. No matter which path he chose from this day forward; heartbreak was inevitable.

Chapter Four
"The Point of No Return"

By the time Rebecca had cleaned up the kitchen, the effects of the strange food had finally worn off; just in time to sit in the warm afternoon sunshine with her mother, sisters and friends to do some quilting and chatting. Every once in a while she stole glances at each face to see if any of them had noticed anything unusual, but they all seemed completely oblivious to her recent adventure. They chattered away happily about the latest engagements, weddings, newborns, and upcoming summer auction.

"This Shadow Star should fetch a good price at the auction, jah?" Rachel Fisher declared to no one in particular.

Ruth Esh nodded. "I have a couple more wall hangings to finish first and a good crop of berries so we will be bringing our jams as well. Those always sell *gut* to the *Englisch*. Much better than the Smuckers, *jah*?"

There was a general chuckle. They stitched a few more minutes in companionable silence.

"I think Seth is sweet on Rebecca!" Sarah blurted out with a giggle, sending her friend a teasing look.

All hands froze in mid-stitch and heads turned in Rebecca's direction. If murder had been permissible under the Ordnung Rebecca would have throttled her. Sarah instantly regretted her words but it was too late to take them back.

"Is this true?" Ruth asked her daughter.

"I honestly don't know, *mamm*, but even if he is; the feeling is not mutual!" Rebecca retorted, casting a withering look in Sarah's direction. This seemed to satisfy everyone. They breathed a collective sigh of relief and went back to their stitching. For some reason, this reaction irked her. Why should they feel relief when for all intents and purposes Seth was Amish? They worked in uncomfortable silence for the next ten minutes then gradually resumed their casual banter. Rebecca bent her head over her work and stitched with a vengeance, glad to have the spotlight off of her. Try as she might, however, she couldn't get Sarah's words out of her head. *Seth sweet on me?* The thought niggled at her mind for the rest of the afternoon until it was time to put away the quilting and prepare supper. She was the age when most girls were engaged, getting married or already starting families of their own but she hadn't had so much as had a single suitor yet. Not even Jacob Zimmer, who stared at her incessantly whenever he was near but was too painfully shy to utter a word. Nor had he ever come calling or offered to drive her home in his buggy after a singing even though they had known each other since childhood. He still stared at her like a forlorn puppy dog whenever they were in close proximity which earned him plenty of teasing from the other boys.

Rebecca was in the kitchen making noodles when Seth returned from the fields with his brother and her father to join the family for dinner, his silver eyes twinkling merrily at her. At that moment, Silas turned and gave him a warning look which plainly seemed to confirm what Sarah had declared earlier. The men cleaned up at the kitchen sink then sat down and all gave thanks to the good Lord who always provided and blessed.

"Mmmmm, what's this?" asked Silas.

"That is Mr. Esh's favorite: oven fried chicken, bread dressing and lima bean casserole," replied Mrs. Esh.

Her father cleared his throat. "Seth...Silas; you have done gut work these past week. Tonight you will move your things out of the barn and into the *dawdi haus* to sleep in proper beds. Rebecca will help get it ready for you."

Seth and Silas' heads popped up in delighted unison. "Danki, Mr. Esh!" The significance of his generosity spoke quiet plainly that he had 'accepted' them as part of his extended family.

Rebecca and Seth instantly locked eyes and he gave her a big smile which thoroughly warmed her soul. After that she ate with more appetite and a much lighter heart. Once dinner was over, she left clearing the dishes to her sisters and began collecting the things she would need. Silas went into the barn to retrieve their meager belongings while Rebecca used Seth as a pack mule, loading his arms up with a broom, dust cloth, mop and wash bucket while she collected fresh linen.

The *dawdi hause* had not been in use since her grandparents had died the previous winter. No doubt it was full of dust and cobwebs by now and would need a good scrubbing and airing out. She could hear her sisters chattering away at the kitchen sink, teasing and splashing one another as she led Seth to the smaller dwelling. Rebecca went inside, hung her lantern from the ceiling hook and began opening up all the windows.

"Put the mop and bucket down and take all the rag rugs out for a good beating," she instructed like a good *hausfrau*.

"Yes, mamm!" Seth grinned, tipping his hat. He went from room to room gathering up the rugs which required several trips.

"Hang them on the clothesline and use this." she said, handing him a rug baton.

Seth turned it over in his hand, staring at it with obvious confusion. "What do I do with this?"

With an exasperated sigh, Rebecca walked over, took the baton and whacked his behind with it; amazed at her own impudence. "You beat the dust out of it like so!"

"Ow!" Seth yelped, grinning at her as he left. He passed Silas on the way back from the barn.

"Why are you grinning like that?" Silas wanted to know. Seth shrugged then whacked his brother's behind. "That's why!" He laughed out loud.

"HEY!"

Silas entered the *dawdi haus* still rubbing his hind quarters.

Rebecca thrust a bucket of vinegar water and squeegee at him. "You will be washing the windows, inside and out. You'll need another lantern so you can see outside."

Silas nodded meekly. He was already exhausted from working in the fields but knew implicitly that the eldest Miss Esh would brook no argument. While he marched off to his assigned duty, Rebecca began dusting and washing down every surface. She smiled to herself as she listened to Seth smack the rugs with the baton, pretending he was doing battle with some unseen foe.

"Take that! And that!" *Whack. Whack.*

The surfaces done, she gathered up the sheets which had covered the furniture and wadded them up into a large pile. Then she went into a bedroom containing two twin beds and stripped them, adding their dirty linens to the growing pile. These she took outside and laid them on the grass before taking the broom and sweeping out the entire house. Although it was nighttime and the air cool, the work had her sweating. Next she wet mopped all the hardwood floors, pretending to ice-skate as she used her feet to dry them with a large towel. This too got flung outside onto the growing mound of dirty laundry. At that moment, Seth reappeared. He had sweat running down his face, neck and torso which plastered his blue shirt to his muscular body.

"The rugs have been beaten into submission, Miss Esh." He grinned at her. Rebecca stared at him and nodded; suddenly quite taken with how handsome he looked. Seth liked the way she looked at him. "What next?"

"*Ach*…ummm – here! Help me make up your beds and then I'll help you carry in the rugs." She pushed the laundry basket of clean linen into his arms and led him to the bedroom, feeling odd as she did so. She wondered for a fleeting moment if this was how it felt to be husband and frau.

As if he could hear her thoughts, Seth offered her a rakish grin. "Now what?" he asked, looking her up and down in a most flirtatious manner. Rebecca felt the heat rising to her cheeks; grateful it was too dark for him to see her blush. She selected a set of clean sheets and quilt and shoved them into his arms with a nervous laugh. "Make the bed, *dummkopf*! She turned away, taking her own set and showed him how to do it step-by-step on the other bed. Seth held up the sheet to his nose and took an appreciative whiff. It had come off the line earlier that day and smelled of clean air with a faint hint of lavender which they grew in the garden, dried and made into sachets for the linen closet. A few moments later, Rebecca turned to inspect his handiwork and found it to be typical of what a clueless male would do.

She shook her head and wagged a finger at him. "Tuck the sheets in, at the foot of the bed first, like so, then the sides." She bent down to show him then straightened up to find his nose bare inches from hers; his silver eyes fastened upon hers.

"Becca," he whispered, reaching for her hand. A loud squeal came from the window behind them; Silas making his presence known with the squeegee.

"Fresh pillow cases last." Rebecca swallowed. "Now we get the rugs." She turned and led the way to the clothesline where they hung, knowing he was right behind her. She knew his eyes were upon the back of her head and neck because she could feel his stare sending delicious shivers down her spine. Together they carried in the rugs and laid them back in all the appropriate rooms.

"You will want to sponge bathe before you lay down in those nice clean sheets. I'll start the water boiling if you'll fill the wash tub halfway using the kitchen pump." She dumped the dirty water out of the mop bucket into the yard and handed it to him.

"Yes, mamm," Seth nodded; carrying the pail to the kitchen pump as he was told.

Rebecca gathered up all the dirty linen into her arms and carried it to the front porch; an idea suddenly striking her fancy. She hurried into the main house and fetched a vase and pair of kitchen scissors. With a kerosene lamp lighting her way, she went into the flower garden, cutting a small bunch of purple coneflowers, black-eyed Susan's, lavender and Lamb's ears. She arranged them in a vase and set it on the small table in the *dawdi haus* before closing the door with a self-satisfied smile and returned to the main house. She found her mother sitting in her rocking chair, darning socks and mending. Her father was in his own chair reading The Budget. Her sisters had already gone up to bed.

Her mother looked up. "The *dawdi haus* is clean so fast already?"

"Jah, mamm; they are good helpers. I'm just going to set the kettle on so they can wash up first."

Ruth nodded and returned to her darning, humming an old hymn softly to herself.

Rebecca filled the large kettle, set it on the stove then sat down on the floor next to her mother, laying her head upon her knees, waiting for it to come to a boil.

Her mother paused, set down her work and stroked Rebecca's face. "They are good boys," she murmured.

Rebecca nodded; this statement warming her heart. Just as the kettle began to sing, Seth walked in.

"What now?" he asked, grinning at her. Rebecca pointed to the stove. "Use the hot mitts and pour it into the wash tub. Be careful, it is very heavy and the water very hot."

"Where do I get the mitts?" he asked, playing dumb since they were in plain sight. Rebecca sighed and wearily stood to her feet. She went over to where they hung and put one on each of his hands; playing along. She knew well he was using every trick at his disposal to be near to her. She smiled up at him and fished something out of her apron pocket, placing it in one of his mitts.

"Was ist das?"

Rebecca grinned up at him and pinched her nostrils. "Lavender soap to make you smell better!" She gave him a little push then wearily climbed the stairs to the room she shared with Hannah to read for awhile before going to sleep. She watched from her bedroom window as he struggled to carry the heavy kettle filled with steaming hot water into the *dawdi haus*, then turned her attention fully to her book after he kicked the door shut behind him.

Despite her exhaustion, Rebecca was reluctant to go to bed. She lingered in her rocking chair which looked out over the little dwelling, occasionally glancing up from the pages; not knowing what she was waiting for. About thirty minutes later she felt a distinct summons. She looked out her window again and saw a tall figure in the doorframe looking back up at her. Silver eyes gleamed up at her like twin stars; beckoning her like a hypnotist would his subject. She set down her book, stood to her feet and pressed her face against the glass. Too much glare from the lantern. She turned it off and looked outside again. Now she could see him better. Seth did not move or vocally call out to her but he was summoning her all the same. She couldn't tear her eyes away from his. Then powerful waves of emotion swept over her...deep longing...loneliness...and tentative hope. She knew these emotions were not hers but she felt herself succumbing to them all the same. Her body trembled in response. What was he doing to her? She shouldn't go; it wasn't proper but she found herself grabbing her shawl anyway then quietly tiptoeing downstairs. It was dark; her parents having already gone to bed. She walked barefoot out into the yard where he stood waiting for her.

"What are you doing?" she whispered; her voice tinged with fear.

"What am I doing, Becca?" Seth whispered in return. "Tell me."

"You've been calling to me for the past ten minutes!"

"I haven't said a word," he replied softly.

"I can still hear you! How are you doing this? I can sense your feelings!"

"You can?" he wondered, his voice lifting with surprise and joy.

"You aren't aware that you're doing this?"

"No...I didn't mean to disturb you, Becca-"

"You are disturbing me, greatly!"

His grin gleamed white in the pale moonlight. "You can feel what I feel!" The idea seemed immensely pleasing to him. He stepped closer. Rebecca took a step back, immediately wary.

"Don't be afraid, Miss Rebecca Esh," he whispered softly, reaching for her hand. "I won't do anything improper." He smelled clean and of lavender.

Try as she might Rebecca could not resist placing her small hand in his anymore than she could hold her breath for a week. Something about him drew her like a bee to flower. Warmth like liquid honey swept up her hand then arm at his touch, washing over the rest of her. Then images flickered across her mind like drawings in a picture book. Images from his viewpoint...of a vast, endless starscape flowing past, a world with a lavender sky and endless meadows of alien-looking flowers; people with silver and gold glowing eyes and then finally her farm but from a height that could only be described as dizzying. She stared up at him in wonder; understanding that he was sharing his world with her.

Such beautiful eyes he had; she was helpless against them. They drew her irresistibly deeper and deeper into his innermost soul. For a moment she resisted then she could fight it no longer. She swayed against him as his emotions hit her with an impact that took her breath away. Such loneliness...such longing...so unbearable. She was helpless against the onslaught. Tears filled her eyes and spilled down her cheeks as she continued to stare at him in the dim moonlight; communicating without speaking; intertwining without touching. It was like nothing she had ever experienced before and could never put into words. For a brief moment their souls were one.

"Nee!" she gasped. Rebecca swayed on her feet but Seth caught her in his arms before she went down and held her against himself; their faces mere inches apart. One arm supported her waist and the other cupped her cheek in his hand.

"Becca," he murmured. "I won't hurt you."

She stared deeply into his eyes and though their lips did not touch, they shared an emotional exchange so intense she could take no more. She crumpled into a dead faint. Seth lifted her into his arms and soundlessly carried her back into the darkened house. He studied her pale beautiful face as he trod upstairs, finally depositing her upon the bed next to her sister. Hannah didn't as so much as stir when he laid her down. For a brief moment he allowed himself a brief caress of her cheek then covered her with a quilt and returned to the *dawdi haus* deep in thought.

Tonight had irrevocably joined his soul with hers. Across the vast reaches of space his heart had finally found a home in Miss Rebecca Esh. Silas was right; there was no going back now but what was he to do about it? It wasn't allowed. He returned to the *dawdi haus* and lay down upon the bed she had made with her own hands. He flung an arm over his face. *Why oh why, Miss Rebecca Esh, did you have to be born into the one world where it is forbidden for us to be together?*

"You shouldn't have done that," said Silas' voice in the darkness. "You're only going to make it harder on both of you."

"I know."

"You need to end it tomorrow, Seth."

"Silas…I think she is my soul mate…"

"She is from a different world. You better have a deep heartfelt talk with the King before you imperil our world and destroy both your lives."

Seth uttered a deep shuddering sigh. Intellectually he knew his brother was right but his heart felt differently and right now it was in total charge of his will.

"Alright," he mumbled, focusing his thoughts so they would be in communication with their king. He lay silently for a long time; waiting for a response and for the first time that he could recall, it was purely a one-way conversation. There was no answer; none.

"Have you tried communicating with him since we crashed here?" Seth asked, sitting up.

"No, I've been too busy and too exhausted, why?"

"I can't hear him." Seth replied. "Do you think there is something wrong with this world that is interfering with his response?"

"I've heard rumors from others about that being the case; perhaps that is why it is forbidden to have direct dealings with earth dwellers."

Seth lay back down. Whatever the reason, he had received no guidance or response which left just his heart to battle it out with his mind while he struggled to fall sleep.

The next morning Rebecca awoke long before her usual time, thinking back on the night before. She lay quietly so as not to disturb Hannah, replaying over and over again the intense feelings she had shared with Seth. It has been incredibly intimate; to the point where she almost felt ashamed. But the more she thought about it and put it into perspective, the more she relaxed. They had really done nothing more than stare at each other in the moonlight for a few moments; nothing that could pointed to as a violation of the Ordnung. Her heart quickened at the memory of his silver eyes staring deeply into her own and how he had made her feel. After last night, she was positive he would begin courting her. With her father opening up the *dawdi haus* to them, she was hopeful that they might look on the match more willingly. After little more than a week the brothers had become quite indispensible to her family in helping to run the farm. Since their arrival numerous improvements and repairs had been made that had been put off due to lack of time and manpower. Her father seemed less weary and burdened since need no longer do the lion's share of the farming. He even behaved openly fond of them; slapping them on the back occasionally and joking. Perhaps a courtship would not be such an enormous hurdle after all...

The cock crowed, signaling the start of another day. Rebecca helped Mirriam and Mary to get dressed. They fixed each other's hair then together they all made a quick visit to the chilly family outhouse. From there they split up; Mary and Mirriam to the chicken coop to gather eggs and she and Hannah to the kitchen where their mother had already begun to prepare breakfast. Rebecca put her apron on; humming as she kneaded dough for biscuits eliciting strange looks from her mother and frowns from Hannah.

As the sun slowly rose upon the distant hills, she saw her father and the brothers emerge from the barn after having completed the milking and feeding. She rolled out the dough, cut it into discs, and laid them onto a baking sheet. When the oven reached temperature she slid the tray in; still humming happily.

Her father entered first, leaving his muddy work shoes outside as did Seth and Silas. Silas gave her a grim nod as he removed his straw hat and put it on a wall peg followed immediately by Seth. Rebecca's heart soared at the sight of him but he refused to meet her gaze. Stung, she watched in mute disappointment as he washed up then sat down at the table, avoiding her stricken gaze. All bowed their heads in silent prayer then helped themselves to the platters of freshly scrambled eggs and ham. Rebecca poured hot coffee into their mugs, sneaking glimpses at Seth to see if he would acknowledge her. He didn't.

Rebecca felt like she had been slapped in the face. What had she done wrong? Why wouldn't he look at her? Did he think her forward now? When the tears threatened to flood her eyes she got up and checked on the biscuits then sat back down.

Her sisters exchanged looks then shrugged, passing her moodiness off to her age but she could feel her mother's eyes upon her, then she looked over at the brothers. Seth sat with bowed head, pushing the food around on his plate with his fork the same way she was. Rebecca could see her mamm putting two and two together; it wouldn't be long before she figured out that something was clearly going on between the two of them. The smell of bread burning filled the kitchen.

"Becca! The biscuits!" cried her mamm.

"I'm sorry!" she exclaimed, jumping up to remove them from the oven. Two minutes more and then would have been burnt to charcoal. She set them to cool then plunked down again; still casting questioning looks in Seth's direction. Still he refused to look at her.

It was no use. She turned away and caught Silas staring at her and suddenly she understood. Seth's brother had said something to him! Rebecca glared accusingly at him; somehow knowing that this was all his doing. Silas averted his gaze and concentrated on wolfing down his breakfast like there was no tomorrow.

Her mamm had had enough. "Leroy, may I speak with you a moment?" she said, rising from the table.

Leroy looked up at her, his fork halfway to his mouth. A clear indication of how unusual and rare the request to interrupt his breakfast was. Rebecca pretended not to hear but her heart began hammering. She glanced again over at Seth who, although he was now eating with intense concentration, had gone quite pale. At that moment the timer went off, signaling that the biscuits were cool enough to serve. Rebecca got up, put them into a basket and brought them to the table; trying not to stare at her parents as they left the room to speak in private. The moment she heard the screen door slam behind them, Rebecca glared a warning at her sister's not to interfere.

"What's wrong with you?" she whispered to Seth, keeping her eye upon the front door.

"Nothing," he mumbled, his eyes fastened on his plate. "Everything is fine, Miss Esh."

He might as well have slapped her in the face as to address her so formally after last night's exchange. Rebecca's face transformed from one of crushed disbelief to anger. How dare he toy with her emotions as if they were some kind of plaything!

"Glad to hear it!" she responded, tight-lipped.

"Could you please pass the butter, Becca?" piped up Mary. Being eight years old she was completely oblivious to the tension between her sister and Seth. Rebecca passed the butter and shot an angry glare at Silas who was also keeping his head down with eyes glued to his plate.

There was no eating, now. Her stomach was in total knots waiting for her parents to return. Seth was behaving as cold as ice to her. "I have chores to do." She stood up with her plate, put it into the sink then turned about and left them all in the kitchen, stomping upstairs to gather up the rag rugs. She could vent her pent up emotions of betrayal by beating the dust out of the rugs and wringing out the wash with her bare hands. She was so angry she barely heard the screen door slam below, signaling the return of her parents to the kitchen.

"Rebecca!" summoned her father.

No longer feeling guilty, she stomped down the stairs, her arms loaded up with rag rugs and laundry. "Yes papa?"

"Is there something going on between the two of you that we need to know about?"

Rebecca dumped the rugs and laundry into a large basket, raised an eyebrow and smiled brightly at her father and mother. "Nee, daed, nothing at all." She trained her frozen smile upon Seth. "...ab-so-lute-lee nothing." She walked up to his place at the table and grabbed his half-finished plate. "All done? *Gut!*" She scraped the remains into the pail for slopping the pigs and it too went into the sink. Then she hefted the laundry basket onto her hip, turned on her heel and marched outside to commence the beating.

Leroy and Ruth stared after her then down at Seth who hadn't moved or budged an inch. His brother, Silas, on the other hand, seemed grimly amused. He got up, wiped his mouth and hauled his brother up with him.

"Time to fix the fence in the north pasture, *bruder*!" He grabbed two steaming biscuits out of the basket and towed his brother out the back door with him.

Ruth and Leroy turned to look at each other. "You see, I was right! He wants to court her," Ruth surmised.

"This shall not be," Leroy responded firmly. He sat back down at the kitchen table to finish his now cold breakfast.

Rebecca decided that beating an inanimate object was a good way to clear her head. She carried the basket out back, slung the rugs over the sturdy clothesline as Seth had done the night before and began swinging away. The harder she whacked, the better she felt. Once she had beaten all the dust out of the house rugs she started in on washing the quilts and bed sheets from the *dawdi haus* she had collected the night before. Over and over she replayed the previous night's encounter and this morning's rebuff in her mind; chiding herself for having shared her heart so willingly with a virtual stranger; *an...an alien for goodness sake!* Now he was treating her like it had all been a colossal mistake! She was so angry she could just spit. He really needed to be taught a lesson...but how?

Rebecca gradually became aware of his eyes upon her back but she refused to turn around or acknowledge him. Even from a distance of several hundred yards she could sense what he was feeling. Somehow after last night she had become emotionally linked to him and didn't like it one bit. He felt badly; he wanted to apologize. Too bad! Determined to ignore him, she gathered up the rugs and marched back into the house.

Her mother turned round and motioned her over to the kitchen stove. "Jacob Zimmer is stopping by today with his father to look at the new foal. I think it would be a nice gesture to offer them some lunch. Can you take care of it while I do the canning?"

"Jah, mamm." Rebecca immediately understood the unspoken purpose. They were going to put a stop to whatever they thought was happening between her and Seth by interjecting Jacob Zimmer inbetween them. His family had long been good friends with hers. Jacob was just a year older than her; with wavy red hair, sea green eyes and a tall, muscular build from working in the fields all his life. It was no secret that her parents had long hoped the two of them would eventually court but Jacob was too painfully shy to do anything.

"Let me just set the laundry to soak first." Rebecca put all the whites into the washing tub, added soap and bleach; agitated the water enough to disperse everything evenly then returned to the kitchen. If Seth was going to play these games with her heart then he would pay the consequences!

Her mother was too preoccupied cooking the berries down for jam to pay much attention to her elaborate preparations until it was time for the Zimmer's to arrive. Rebecca had just finished putting the final touches to the table on the front porch when her mother emerged and took in the site. Rebecca straightened, pleased with her work. There was a crisp, white tablecloth and a vase full of flowers from the garden. She had preset the table with matching china and glasses with crisp cloth napkins at each place. Just at that moment, the Zimmer buggy turned into the drive. Jacob's father, Eli, got out first; followed by his wife and younger brothers. All were very excited to see the new foal. In the distance she could see her father and the twins emerge from the fields to join them for the noonday meal.

"I see a place for everyone here except two," her mother remarked.

"*Jah*," acknowledged Rebecca. "The brothers will have to just eat in the *dawdi haus*." She said this last part loud enough for Seth and Silas to hear as they entered the yard to wash up. Instead of going into the main house, they made a left turn into their own. There was little reaction except for Seth's ears flaming red as he brushed past her; still avoiding her gaze.

Rebecca hurried down the porch steps to greet Jacob and his family.

"*Guder mariye*, Leroy...Ruth!" Eli and Leroy exchanged handshakes while their wives gave each other a warm embrace. They turned to regard Rebecca. "You have grown into a fine young woman!"

Rebecca bowed her head slightly, aware that Jacob was staring at her. "May I offer you some lemonade before you go to the barn?" She lifted a tray of glasses and lemonade pitcher up.

"*Jah*, that would be *wunderbar*!" Eli replied, elbowing his son in the ribs. Jacob blushed furious red and nodded obediently.

Rebecca handed out tumblers then filled each one with the cold beverage, beginning with Jacob's. The favoritism she displayed was not lost on either set of parents nor him. Rebecca was sure that the smile which broke out over his ruddy face was enough to capture the attention of Seth who she knew was watching them inside the *dawdi haus*. Rebecca didn't even need to turn around to see the jealousy he was feeling; she could feel it like searing hot waves washing over her. Jacob finished the lemonade in one long draught, wiped his mouth with the back of his hand and handed back the empty tumbler to Rebecca with an enormous smile. The rest of them set their empty glasses down then turned to go into the barn to look the newborn foal over. Rebecca went into the house to check on the meal. She heard the screen door creak open then heavy footsteps coming up from behind her. She turned round and found Seth staring at her. She turned back around without a word to continue the meal prep.

"You are ignoring me, Miss Esh."

"*Jah*!" she nodded.

"I don't like it."

Rebecca had enough. She whirled around, eyes blazing. "My heart is not some ball you can bounce back and forth as it pleases you. Now, I have to finish making lunch so please stay out of my way!"

She could feel the sting in his heart as her words struck home. Seth turned and left. Her parents and the Zimmer's returned from the barn fifteen minutes later, ready to discuss the purchase of the colt over a hearty lunch of beef and noodles over mashed potatoes. Rebecca carried the food out to the front porch with the help of her sisters. After a silent blessing, she began ladling out the stew; first to the Zimmer family (giving Jacob the biggest portion) and then her own. When they were all served she brought in the serving bowl and scraped what little meat, noodles and potatoes were left onto the twin's plates and sent Mary to deliver them to the *dawdi haus*. She returned to sit outside on the porch and eat; allowing the screen door slam behind her. Jacob's eyes were constantly upon her; inquisitive, wondering if he were misreading her overtures. She made sure to put all his worries to rest; refilling his glass with lemonade at every opportunity and offering him the first of the Whoopie pies for dessert. She ignored Seth who was boring holes into the back of her head throughout the entire meal. The Zimmer's lingered just long enough to settle on a fair price for the foal then made ready to depart for their own farm. Her parents and they talked quietly together as they made their way back to the buggy while Jacob kept glancing over his shoulder at her. With a brilliant smile and friendly wave goodbye, Rebecca turned her back and gathered up the lunch dishes to take them into the house. The moment she entered the kitchen Seth stepped forward and grabbed her arm; startling her. He must have entered from the back side of the house. She flung it off with a glare; almost dropping the dishes.

"Please Rebecca…I can't take this anymore," his silver eyes implored her.

"Sssh! My family will come back any moment! Go away!" she hissed.

"I don't like the way he looks at you."

"That is not your concern," Rebecca retorted, dumping the dishes into the sink and pumping out water furiously. "Don't you have the barn to muck out?"

She could feel his emotional turmoil quite plainly now that he was standing mere inches from her. As angry as she was with him; she found herself craving his nearness. The pull upon her emotions and heart was just too much. She turned the heat up high on the kettle so the whistling would mask their conversation.

"Please, go away," she pleaded. "Take your brother and leave our community before it's too late. Go back from whence ye came."

"We can't," he mumbled truthfully. "It will be months before we can get our ship repaired or fix our communication system so we can summon another to pick us up."

Months? For the first time that day they locked eyes. It was her undoing. The moment she gazed into his silver eyes she became lost in them. His irises were fathomless and mesmerizing; pulling her inexorably into their depths. His emotions swept over her. She felt dizzy.

Seth reached for her face. "Becca, please…" The room began to rotate about them and fade from view. She stepped towards him. At that moment her mother entered the house from the front porch followed by her younger sisters who had just returned from the house garden with their arms loaded with produce. The spell broken, Seth fled the kitchen with a heavy heart before they noticed him.

Rebecca turned about, struggling to calm her nerves and focus on the sink full of soapy water.

"Becca! The kettle is screaming. Take it off the heat!" Hannah groused, covering her ears.

Rebecca grabbed two mitts and lifted the kettle off, filling the sink with the hot water.

Hannah put her hands on her hips and cocked a head at her. "What's wrong? You look ready to cry or something."

"It's nothing," Rebecca sniffed. "It's just my allergies. I'll wash and you dry, okay?"

"Okay."

For the fifteen minutes Rebecca focused on just enjoying Hannah's company while they finished the dishes together. Then all of them helped their mother to wring out the laundry and peg it to the clothesline outside to dry in the warm afternoon breeze. It was busy work but left Rebecca's mind free to wonder how on earth she was going to get through the next few months. Perhaps she should go away for awhile...she had never gone on Rumspringa like so many others of her age. It might take her away from the farm long enough for the brothers to repair their ship and depart her world. When they were safely gone she could return to her normal life; allow Jacob Zimmer to court her and start a family of her own. She would have to wait, though, until after the summer auction to speak to her parents; they were entirely too busy preparing for it to be bothered with anything else at the moment.

Chapter Five
"What am I Bid?"

The Esh daughters could barely contain their excitement. The semi-annual Lancaster auction and flea market was swiftly approaching. It was a chance for them to socialize, hunt for bargains in the flea market, try new foods and meet up with families they hadn't seen much due to the distance separating them. Several days prior, Ruth and her daughters selected and packed up the goods they intended to sell. They had been canning like mad for months, harvesting berries, fruits and vegetables. It was not only to stock their cellar for the winter months, but to sell as well. The Shadow Star quilt had been completed the week before at a marathon quilting bee where upwards of twenty women had crowded into the Esh home for sewing, eating and socializing. The quilt would be up for auction along with several appliquéd wall hangings that Ruth, Rebecca, Mirriam and Mary had all worked on. Once all had been assembled, they were carefully packed in crates, then stacked and roped fast so they wouldn't shift about in the jostling wagon.

Everyone was up earlier than usual in the rush to get the morning chores done. The auction started early and they didn't want to arrive late. Mary and Mirriam had no need of the usual threats and prodding's to get out of their warm bed that morning to collect the eggs from the scolding chickens and help with breakfast. By the time 5:00 a.m. rolled around, the cattle were milked, the livestock fed and watered and a hot breakfast of fried cornmeal mush with tomato gravy, ham, bacon and fried eggs was waiting for them. The dishes were set to soak in the sink to be dealt with later that night upon their return and a brisket left to slow cook during the day for supper that night.

Seth and Silas rode with Rebecca's father on the wagon to keep an eye on their goods while she and her sisters crowded into the buggy with *mamm*. There was a great deal of giggling and squirming but soon everyone was settled.

Ruth gently slapped the reins on Joe's back. "*Geh* up Joe!" The buggy surged forward followed by the spring wagon which was pulled by their mules. It was little Mary's turn to sit up front with mamm so Rebecca was obliged to sit facing backward which seemed to please Seth to no end. He sat beside her daed on the buckboard while Silas rode in the back to steady the crates. Rebecca did her best to keep her face a complete blank for her daed's benefit but it was difficult when Seth alternated between grinning at her and staring longingly at her. She angled her body away from him; presenting a less inviting target while she concentrated upon her sisters. She had brought along a few Amish dolls for them to play with as well as some wooden toys to keep them occupied on the long ride. It was a fine morning with a beautiful blue sky, puffy white clouds and soft warm breeze. Numerous butterflies flitted amongst the mustard weeds that grew alongside the highway but other than the occasional impatient car which got stuck behind their buggy on the narrow road, there was no other sound except for the steady clip-clop of Joe's shoes upon the asphalt and her sister's chatter.

After half an hour their buggy came to an abrupt stop causing Rebecca to turn round to see what was happening. A long line of Amish buggies were lined up in a queue on the side of the road waiting to gain entrance to the open field where the auction and flea market had been set up. Automobiles were also lining up beside them along the road; idling their engines. The Amish covered their mouths with handkerchiefs to keep out the exhaust fumes but said nothing in complaint. It was just another thing to tolerate when living amongst the *Englisch*. After what seemed an eternity, the Esh's buggy and wagon entered the grounds where they soon found a place to hitch both the buggy and wagon. Seth jumped down out of the wagon and immediately helped Rebecca's sisters out of the buggy before extending his hand to her.

"Danki, Seth! Danki Seth!" Hannah, Mirriam and Mary chirped, hopping down like little birds.

"Miss Esh?" he held out his hand to her. Rebecca stared at it for a moment; her eyes wandering over to her father who was regarding them with an unreadable expression on his face. She accepted his hand and climbed down then immediately withdrew it.

"Danki," she murmured, hurrying to the wagon to help unload their goods.

"Mary, Mirriam, unhitch Joe and give him some oats and bucket of water." Her mamm instructed, her arms laden with a crate full of canned produce.

Her family had prearranged for their own booth and after a few minutes search found it with a sign overhead that read: **ESH JAMS, PRODUCE & QUILTS**. Unloading began in earnest.

Rebecca said nothing but noticed how much easier and quicker it went with two strong young men there to help out. An old wedding ring quilt in dark blue, green, black and burgundy was laid over the table that would bear the canned goods and Rebecca set about arranging a vase of raffia and sunflowers to help attract customers. On the clothes lines which acted as space borders, they pegged the wall hangings for display.

"Rebecca! Yoo hoo!" yelled a female voice. Rebecca turned around and felt her heart drop. It was Katie Zook; she had been hoping to avoid her. Rebecca plastered on a polite smile and watched the beautiful red head scamper up. Katie was the same age as she (they had attended the same school together until 8th grade) and also unattached. She always seemed to be on the prowl for her next conquest and had left a trail of broken hearts in her wake. She had always found something lacking in her suitors and seemed incapable of finding a man perfect enough to become her husband, though many had sought the privilege.

"*Guten morgen! Wie geht's?* It's been months since we last saw each other!" she gushed.

"*Gut,*" Rebecca replied standoffishly. Even though Katie was as "plain" as any other Amish girl, she still managed to stand out with her pansy-blue eyes, pale skin, and curly red hair that constantly found ways to escape her myriad of bobby pins and prayer kapp. Katie drew back from their brief embrace and stared over Rebecca's shoulder; her expansive blue eyes growing enormous with sudden interest.

"*Wer ist das?* (Who is that)?"

Rebecca turned round to find Seth standing just behind her. She jumped in fright; unaware that he had been there.

"Ach…this is just Seth," she replied, trying to sound nonchalant. "He's visiting with us this summer."

Rebecca watched with a combination of embarrassment, mortification and jealousy as Katie's gaze slowly traveled up and down the length of him; ultimately latching onto his strange silver eyes.

"Visiting from where?" she wanted to know; a grin spreading over her face that clearly indicated that she had found her next victim. Rebecca frowned; not liking what she saw. Most everyone else in her community had shied away from the brothers because of their strange eyes; which suited her and her family just fine, but Katie actually seemed captivated by them. At that moment Silas appeared to collect his brother. Katie's gaze bounced back and forth between the two of them like a ping-pong ball. One had metallic silver eyes and the other gold.

"We are from out of state," Seth replied truthfully with a polite hat tip. "Now if you'll excuse us…we have much work to do!" He took hold of Rebecca's arm and steered her away just as a small flock of girls joined up to join Katie in ogling the new Amish boys.

"Wer ist das, Katie?"A chubby brunette by the name of Annie Beiler wanted to know. "*He is sehr schee* (very handsome)!"

"Did you get a good look at his eyes?" stage-whispered a tall blond. "Have you ever seen such eyes before in your entire life?!"

"That one's name is Seth; he is staying with the Esh's." Katie replied in an all-knowing voice; the ring-leader of the group.

"Katie Zook – have you set thy kapp for a boy you've only just laid eyes on?" squealed Annie.

Katie stared back at her. "What if I have?" she challenged. "It sure doesn't look like Rebecca is interested in him! Seems to me that he is fair game!"

"There's two of them!" the blond hissed, pointing at Silas who had returned to the wagon for unloading. "They are both *schee!*"

Annie pulled on Katie's arm; already bored with the topic. "C'mon! Let's go to the food stands and see if the apple fritters or knee patches are ready yet!" The girls wandered off, arms linked.

Rebecca heaved a sigh of relief. If the brothers had planned to remain unnoticed; that had just all flown out the window. Katie Zook was a notorious gossip and she had an entire day in which to do damage with her wagging tongue. It wouldn't be long before everyone at the auction would be staring and gossiping about the brothers! Rebecca grimaced to herself as she listened to their fading chatter.

They sound like a bunch of yowling cats fighting over the same mouse! They didn't even attempt to hide their conversation from the brothers who were grinning to themselves as though they found the entire thing amusing. Rebecca cast a glance back at Seth and studied him for a moment; trying to see him the way Katie Zook did. Her eyes studied him intently for a moment starting at his feet then rising up his long legs to his broad shoulders, chiseled face and finally his dark wavy hair. At that moment Seth turned and stared back at her as if he had heard her thoughts; his silver eyes latching onto her own. She felt the pull of his emotions drawing her in just as he had the other night outside her window. A shiver ran up her spine almost as if he had caressed her.

"Rebecca the jams!" her mother gently reminded her. Rebecca swiftly turned her head away so she could concentrate on the work at hand; trying to erase the image of his hypnotic eyes and the effect they had upon her. Finally everything was unpacked and laid out in an attractive manner. The jams were all on one table; nicely labeled and the canned vegetables on another.

"Seth...Silas!" Leroy beckoned them. "I'm going to the auction barn to see the livestock and horses; you will come with me, jah?"

Rebecca did not react. Her father had not been blind to the growing attraction between his eldest *dochder* and Seth. She knew that this was another devise to keep as much distance between the two of them as possible.

"Jah sir," they replied. Seth tipped his hat to Rebecca, briefly touching her hand as he walked past. It was the lightest of touches but it sent a thrill through her entire body. Heat stained her cheeks red as she swiftly looked away; hoping her *daed* wouldn't notice. They strode off just as both *Englisch* and Plain customers began to walk up and down the aisles, looking for bargains.

Rebecca was kept quite occupied most of the morning ringing up purchases and by the time it was close to lunch they had sold out of all their jams plus two of the three wall hangings; collecting quite a bit of money in the process. Ruth counted out some cash and handed a little to each of her girls.

"We have done well today, my *kinner*; go and have some fun and bring back some coconut chocolate candy for me from the Zook's booth; they make the best!"

The girls jumped up and down with glee; tying the money into their brand new satchels. *"Danki, mamm!"* Then they all ran off except for Rebecca.

"You too, my *dochder*!" Ruth encouraged her.

"Are you sure, *mamm*? Wouldn't you like some company?"

"Ach, nee I'm fine. I'm going to sit awhile and chat with Iris Yoder here; we haven't seen each other since the last auction and we have much catching up to do!" Ruth waved her off and scooted her chair closer to the next booth over where Iris was sitting.

Rebecca left, searching for her sisters in the milling crowd which was not an easy thing to do since all Amish looked pretty similar at a distance in their identical plain clothes and prayer kapps.

"There you are!" murmured a familiar male voice in her ear. A hand caught her about the waist and spun her around. Rebecca looked up to found herself staring into Seth's face. He was standing so close that for a moment she thought her knees might go wobbly on her.

She mentally shook herself by the shoulders. *Get ahold of yourself, Rebecca Louise Esh!* Seth draped his arm casually across her shoulders and steered her towards the food stands where enticing smells set their mouths to watering.

"What do you want with me?" Rebecca whispered; the warmth and weight of his arm both irritating and thrilling.

Seth smiled down at her; turning her insides to mush. He bent his head down to whisper in her ear; his warm breath intoxicating. She closed her eyes; feeling a bit woozy.

"Fooooooood," he murmured softly then laughed; pleased at the effect he had upon her. "I'm hungry, woman, and have nothing with which to barter!" To demonstrate he pulled his trouser pockets inside out. "Ahhh, but I see that you do!" He lifted her arm which held the bulging satchel of jingling coins. His voice lowered to lecherous growl which was immediately followed by another laugh. "You have plenty!"

"Did someone say food?" Silas drew up on the other side of her. "I'm hungry!"

"Aren't you supposed to be with my *daed* in the auction barn?"

"They're castrating some livestock right now; we didn't want to watch." Silas explained with a shudder. Rebecca didn't know whether to laugh or be intimidated at being caught in-between two alien boys who were ravenously hungry. Silas put his arm around her shoulder also; making escape impossible. "Feed us and we'll leave you alone!" he growled playfully.

"*Ach*! You too! Here!" she opened her satchel and gave them each a small handful of coins. *Geh*! Fend for yourselves!"

Silas required no further urging. He made a bee-line for the outdoor kitchen where the aroma of barbecued chicken, apple fritters as well as pork and beans was coming from.

"Aren't you going to join your *bruder*?" Rebecca questioned when Seth made no attempt to leave her side.

"*Nee* – I may be hungry but I also want you to show me around," he replied. "Can we get lunch together first?"

Rebecca was about to say that she didn't think it was such a good idea when she spotted Katie Zook nearby, eyeing Seth as if he were a prize turkey. *She is just waiting for me to leave so she can sink her claws into him!* She turned her face upwards and favored Seth with an enticing smile. "Jah, Seth; I would be happy to break bread and show you around." She didn't have to look to know that Katie Zook was turning three shades of green.

This seemed to make Seth inordinately happy. For added affect, Rebecca laced her arm through his, casting a triumphant glance backward in Katie Zook's direction who was glaring daggers at her. *Der Herr, forgive me!* She thought to herself. She knew she was behaving badly but couldn't seem to help herself. Together they visited every food stand one-by-one so he could sample before deciding on what he wanted for lunch but the tastings only made it harder for him to decide; he wanted it all! They finally settled upon Barbecue sandwiches of beef and pulled pork in a robust tomato sauce, a side of coleslaw and apple fritters. Rebecca counted out the money and together they found a place to sit under a shade tree where they could eat together. After a brief prayer of thanksgiving, Seth sunk his teeth into the hot, succulent sandwich and groaned with pleasure. The juice ran down his chin.

"You act as if you have never eaten gut food before!" Rebecca noted, making no mention of the fact that Katie Zook and her friends had taken up an "observation post" not too far away.

"Not like this!" Seth replied in a muffled voice; cheeks bulging. "Where we come from food is a necessity…not a source of such…such…carnal pleasure!"

Rebecca stared at him; feeling her cheeks heat up. She had never thought of good Amish cooking as a carnal pleasure before. She watched him eat for a few more moments then took her own first bite with renewed appetite.

"Mmmmm!" she nodded in agreement. "*Ach*! It is very *gut*!"

Seth leaned in close his lips bare inches from her ear. "It is better than *gut*, Rebecca. It is sheer decadence!"

Rebecca wasn't sure what to do with this declaration so she just nodded and took another bite. In the distance she could see Katie continuing to stare at them with undisguised jealousy while her friends affected looks of shock.

"They're watching us very intently, jah?" Seth whispered between mouthfuls. "Shall we give them something to really gossip about?"

Rebecca nodded; unable to resist returning his grin; his suggestion too tempting to resist. For years Katie had flaunted her conquests about the community and now Rebecca had the opportunity to pay her back with some of her own medicine.

She broke off a hunk of apple fritter, leaned towards him as close as she dared and laid it against Seth's full lips. "Try this," she whispered, staring intently into his eyes.

His lips closed about the confection, just brushing her fingertips. "It is *wunderbar*," he nodded, pulling a strand of loose hair away from her face. Even from this distance they could both hear the jealous sighs, exclamations and gasps of shock coming from the group. It was working! They shared a conspiratorial grin for a moment then Seth leaned forward so his lips were near her ear.

"You are very beautiful when you're being devious!" he whispered. The sensation of his warm breath in her ear sent a thrill coursing through her entire body. Rebecca turned her head slightly and found herself staring at his lips which were bare inches from her own. They continued to form words but she had suddenly lost the ability to hear or think clearly. All she wanted to do was press her mouth against those lips of his...

"Rebecca!" The voice of her father immediately jolted her back to reality. She looked up to find him staring down at the two of them with a frown.

"Jah, daed? We were just eating lunch; Seth had no money." She held up the paper plate of food as evidence.

"The auction is about to begin," Leroy said with a jerk of his head. Seth got up immediately; popping the remainder of his sandwich into his mouth then brushed the grass off his pants.

"I'll see you later," he said, giving her a playful wink.

Rebecca nodded and remained where she was, staring after the two of them. *What was it about Seth that made her feel so...so-*

"Rebecca Esh! If you don't watch yourself you will be shunned for certain! Such brazen behavior!" Katie Zook plopped herself down beside her with a fake look of concern upon her face.

"I have not done anything against the Ordnung," Rebecca replied in her own defense, getting to her feet.

"It sure doesn't look that way!" Katie replied with a self-satisfied smirk. "You were behaving quite...uh.... intimately...for lack of a better word!"

Rebecca's face flamed red. She had heard enough! She was not going to subject herself to anymore of Katie Zook's malicious innuendos. "I need to get back to my *mamm*; perhaps I'll see you later."

Katie nodded; a devious smile upon her pink lips. "You can count on it!" It was definitely a threat.

Rebecca turned and marched off; not even having to look behind her to know that the rest of Katie's entourage had joined up with her to watch her flee. She ran through the aisles, ignoring the calls of friends from the other booths; finally reaching hers completely out of breath.

Her mother stood up. "Ach! There you are! Iris and I want to do some shopping and visit the flea market before our quilt goes up for auction; could you mind the booth for a while?"

Rebecca nodded, hoping her mother wouldn't notice her flushed face as she took her place behind the table. The two women left with their satchels and shopping baskets on their arms; still deep in conversation. Rebecca sat down with a heavy thud; her heart still pounding. *Why did she let Katie get under her skin like that? What did she care if Katie took a liking to Seth?* It shouldn't bother her...but it did. She closed her eyes, reliving the feeling of having his face so close to hers.

"How much for the wall hanging?"

Rebecca opened her eyes with a start and looked up to find an *Englisch* tourist admiring the appliquéd wall hanging she had made. It was deep red with a large heart in the middle and three tulips above. She was chubby, had brown hair and was wearing a straw hat, sunglasses and camera slung about her neck.

"I just love the quilts you Amish make!" she declared in a thick accent.

"Two hundred and fifty dollars," Rebecca replied politely.

"That's a heap of money for such a small wall hanging!"

"It is all hand pieced, sewn and quilted," Rebecca replied; already familiar with this line of protest. "It took a full month to make."

The woman nodded, obviously lusting after the quilt. "Well when you put it that way, it seems a bargain then," she grinned, taking out her pocketbook. She counted out the money from a large wad and handed it over to Rebecca. "I suppose $9.00 a day isn't too much to ask for such a thing of beauty!"

"Would you like a receipt?" Rebecca asked while carefully folding the quilt right sides together to keep it clean. She then covered it in plain tissue and put it into a brown paper bag with twine handles which she tied with raffia to keep it shut.

"Naaaaw…don't need the husband knowing how much I paid for it!!" The woman whispered loudly. "He'd have a coronary!"

Rebecca smiled; unable to help herself. She had been through this exact scenario many times before. She handed the bag over to the woman and waved goodbye. It was the last of the items they had for sale which meant that she was now free to wander around to her heart's content. She put all the cash into her satchel for safe-keeping and went in search of her sister's and mother at the flea market. She found Hannah, Mirriam and Mary first; all were munching on a large bag of home-made Cracker Jack. None of them had remembered to purchase the coconut chocolate candy their mother had requested earlier which meant that she would now be forced to go to the Zook's booth to get some. Another confrontation with Katie was sure to ensue. Rebecca sighed. Perhaps she would be in luck and Katie would be busy bothering Seth and Silas in the auction barn along with her cohorts. She approached the Zook's booth. She was in luck; it was just Katie's mother manning "the fort".

"May I get a bag of your coconut chocolate candy, Mrs. Zook?"

"Why of course, Rebecca! How is your *mamm*? I haven't seen her yet."

"She is *gut*; shopping with Iris at the flea market. She sent me over especially for your candy."

"Ach is that so?" Mrs. Zook filled the bag and gave Rebecca a second with a wink. The second bag is for you and your sisters to share!"

"*Danki*!" Rebecca smiled. Why couldn't Katie have taken more after her mother who was so sweet and generous? She wandered into the flea market until she found her mother and Iris looking over some used china.

"Here's your candy, mamm." Rebecca handed her the brown paper bag. "Mrs. Zook sends her greetings; hello again Mrs. Yoder!"

"Danki, Becca! I have been craving this all day! Did you sell the last wall hanging?"

"Jah, I have all the money in here." Rebecca indicated her satchel. Ummm…is daed still in the auction barn?"

"Ach no…he took the boys with him to save us some seats at the quilt auction. I was just on my way there myself."

They navigated through the crowds to the auction tent where all the big ticket items would be auctioned off to the highest bidder. Amish and *Englisch* came from miles around in the hopes of purchasing high-quality goods from quilts to furniture and even elaborate play houses for their children. Ruth spotted Leroy first where he had saved a row of seats. Seth looked up, his eyes going instantly to Rebecca; a broad grin spreading over his face. She felt her cheeks flame and lowered her eyes so her father wouldn't think she was encouraging him.

Silas cleared his throat. "Mr. Esh – there are some supplies I will need to get in order to fix our ship during the winter months so we can return home. I made up a list but we don't have much of your currency to barter with."

"Let me see this list," her father responded, extending his hand. Silas fished it out of his pocket and handed it over. Leroy looked it over in silence, his bushy eyebrows knitting together. "I am unfamiliar with these items. How can they fix something that came from…your home?"

"I have ways to adapt them to our use."

Leroy handed the list over to Ruth to look over. "This is a long list and will not be inexpensive. We will have to discuss this later; the bidding is about to begin on the quilts," he said, taking the arm of his wife. "If we fetch a good price we will be able to purchase some of those parts you need for your ship but not most."

"How much do you figure we will need to get all of it?" Silas replied with a worried crease in his forehead. The longer they lingered on Earth the harder it was going to be for his brother to part from Rebecca Esh. He had no wish to put up with his misery on the long journey home.

Leroy shook his head. "I really couldn't say, I would guess thousands," he finally replied.

Rebecca watched the brothers exchange looks then nod at one another as if they had reached a secretive agreement. They took their seats on benches amongst the other Amish and waited for the bidding to begin.

"Where is our quilt on the list, mamm?" Rebecca leaned over to look at the program.

"Ach! It is the very last item...not gut. There won't be as many people bidding which means less competition and less money. We will be lucky to make $500."

At that moment the auctioneer stepped up to the podium and announced the first item, a Dutch Tulip Lone Star quilt in deep reds, and navy blues on a white background. It was a large quilt that would normally go for $800. The bidding began in earnest with several Englisch bidding against each other to win the quilt. Rebecca sat patiently; barely able to understand the auctioneer because he was speaking so rapidly. Her sisters on the other hand found it immensely funny and giggled constantly. A slow hour passed in which 20 more quilts were auctioned off for an average of $700. With each passing transaction the crowd (which had been several hundred in number to begin with) thinned out more and more until there were perhaps only thirty left.

Ruth Esh shook her head. "Not gut...not gut at all!" she muttered.

Seth and Silas stood up and went onstage to display her quilt to the remaining bidders. The auctioneer began the bidding at $300. One or two hands went up and the price slowly climbed $20 at a time. Then the bidding began to peter out. If others didn't bid the auctioneer would have to call it sold at a horribly low price. As Rebecca scanned the seats, Katie Zook and her entourage entered the tent. They walked up the center aisle and took the empty seats in the first row. The better to ogle the brothers from, Rebecca guessed. She turned her attention back to the stage to find Seth staring at her; a ghost of a smile playing about his lips.

Watch this! came the words inside her head as the auctioneer yelled out: "GOING ONCE…!" his gavel poised to declare the bidding concluded.

Suddenly arms shot up all over the tent and the bidding began anew; this time in earnest. The price began zooming up by the hundreds and in moments was well over the $2,000 mark with no end of bidding in sight. Rebecca could feel the eyes of her mother, father and Katie Zook upon her but she dared not meet their gaze. She kept her eyes fastened firmly upon the auctioneer who was now mopping his florid face with a handkerchief; desperately trying to keep up with the bids. Once or twice she stole a glance at Seth who stood stone-faced by the quilt except for the mischievous twinkle in his silver eyes.

"Five thousand dollars for the Esh Shadow Star quilt…do I hear five thousand and a hundred?"

Word quickly spread through the fairgrounds that an incredible bidding war had broken out in the auction tent. The news that a quilt was breaking all records for price emptied the booths and had everyone who was left running for the tent to watch. Every vacant seat was quickly filled and soon there was standing room only but the bidding showed no sign of abating.

"Six thousand five hundred? Do I hear seven thousand?" The auctioneer was becoming hoarse and sweating profusely. Hands shot up again all over the tent. Now there were more than 100 people bidding on her mother's quilt. Rebecca caught Seth's eye. There was no doubt in her mind that the brothers were entirely responsible for the bidding war on the quilt; she just couldn't figure out how they were doing it.

"Eight thousand!" screamed the auctioneer. The crowd let out an enormous cheer. The bidding had become "the" show and everyone was curious to see how high it would go and who would end up with the quilt.

Rebecca looked over to see her *daed* and *mamm* exchange alarmed glances. They had obviously drawn the same conclusion as she and were not pleased. They didn't want to be responsible for taking advantage of people. Leroy stood up and stared down the brothers; making his meaning clear. Silas nodded and the bidding slowed down to two remaining bidders who seemed determined to win what was arguably the most famous quilt auction in all of Lancaster County.

"Make it stop!" Leroy mouthed to them when the price reached $9,000. The brothers shrugged and shook their heads in response indicating that the bidding was now outside of their influence and had taken on a life of its own.

The auctioneer paused for a moment to get a drink of water and mop his face again before continuing on at a much slower pace. When the price reached $10,000 one of the two bidders bowed out with a rueful grin and sat down; awarding the quilt to an *Englisch* man and his wife whom Rebecca recognized as the woman who had bought her wall hanging. The woman was jumping up and down with glee and raining kisses upon her husband who seemed giddy over his win. Seth and Silas unpegged the quilt from the display clothesline, folded it neatly and handed it over to the happy couple. Everyone in the tent stood to their feet cheering and clapping. This particular auction would surely be the talk of Lancaster County for many years to come!

The man counted out the money from a roll of bills and handed it over to Ruth Esh with a smile. She felt horrible for accepting so much money from him for a single quilt and tried to return $9,500 but he would not hear of it.

"You Amish certainly do beautiful work!" his wife declared, hugging the quilt to her bosom. "I've always wanted one of these!"

"We cannot accept such a large amount of money for the quilt," Leroy said, still trying to give the bulk of the money back. "Five hundred dollars is more than fair."

The woman pushed the money back and shook her head. "It's worth every penny!" she insisted with a smile then cupped her hand to her mouth to whisper loudly. "I'm spending my kid's inheritance!" Then she bellowed with laughter.

"Use it in *gut* health!" Ruth replied, still guilt-ridden. Rebecca, her sisters, Katie Zook and many other Amish were already gathering around to congratulate her.

"Too bad we can't bid on Amish bachelors!" Rebecca heard Katie whisper in a loud aside to her friends. "I'd bid all my savings to have a chance at either one of those two brothers!"

Rebecca turned round to say something but felt herself propelled away by Seth's arm about her waist. "Time to go, Miss Esh," he whispered, tipping his hat at Katie Zook. Rebecca bit back her smile and allowed him to lead her away. She still managed to get a good look at Katie Zook's face as they walked off together: it was turning pea-green with envy. The Esh family returned to their booth, broke it down, packed up the groceries and other items her mother had purchased and set out for the buggy ride home. The sun was setting but there was still supper to serve and the morning breakfast dishes to clean up. As Joe trotted along the street to their home, Rebecca struggled to make sense of her mixed emotions. She could tell her parents were none too happy about the exorbitant price paid for the quilt but they hadn't been able to do anything about it. Now there was enough money for Seth to purchase much of the needed items to fix his ship and leave by the next spring; a fact which filled her heart with dread.

Chapter Six
"A Stitch in Time"

As luck would have it, the next Meeting was held at the Zook's home so it was with a deep sense of dread that Rebecca helped her sisters pin up their hair into their prayer kapps and dress in their best Sunday clothes. Her mamm and daed, too, seemed quieter than usual and ate their breakfast of blueberry pancakes in virtual silence. It was the first Meeting since the auction and none of them knew what to expect from their community. To make matters worse, Seth and Silas had chosen again to eat breakfast by themselves in the *dawdi haus* which Hannah had brought over to them.

Once the breakfast dishes were cleared, Rebecca and her family exited the home to find the brothers waiting for them outside. Despite herself, Rebecca's breath caught in her throat at the sight of Seth in a new crisp white shirt, black trousers and jacket. Her mother had made them a new set of church clothes from the proceeds of the quilt sale figuring it was the least she could do (as well as to assuage some of the guilt she still harbored). Seth's eyes lit up with joy at Rebecca's response to his new attire.

The Zook farm was only a mile away and since the weather was mild, they decided to walk to the Meeting as a family rather than take the buggy. Hannah, Mirriam and little Mary held hands while Rebecca walked a few paces behind them beside Seth and Silas.

"It was very kind of your mamm to make these for us," Seth murmured.

"Jah it was!" agreed Silas.

Rebecca nodded then an awkward silence ensued, broken only by their footfalls on the asphalt road.

"Your daed offered to take us into town next weekend to purchase some of the parts we need," he continued.

"*Jah*?" whispered Rebecca even more softly. "It will be *gut* to return home?"

Seth cleared his throat and lowered his voice. "Becca – why is it that you never ask me questions about where we come from or what our world is like?"

"I think it is better that I don't know," she whispered. "Knowing you better will only make it harder when you leave."

This admission caused Seth to reach for her hand. "You are not the only one who will suffer when we do," he replied.

For the first time that morning Rebecca looked him fully in the eyes and as before, the torrent of his emotions swept over her. She stared back at him; barely aware that she was still walking on a road in Lancaster County. For a brief moment she allowed herself to succumb fully to his hungry eyes. The around world about them faded away and all that was left was the two of them, holding hands in the middle of rolling farmland on a quiet Sunday morning, staring deeply into one another's eyes. There was no use denying it: she wanted him to take her in his arms, hold her close and never let go. Sensing this, Seth drew closer, his hand reaching out to caress her cheek. At that moment her daed turned around and cleared his throat loudly. He might as well have dumped a pail of cold water on them both. Rebecca immediately extricated her hand from his, clutched her Bible and ran to catch up with her parents and sisters.

Seth let her go, his heart aching. Without a word his brother drew close and slung an arm about his shoulders to comfort him as they continued along; the morning quiet broken only by birdsong and the chattering of Rebecca's sisters. They arrived at the Zook farm-house 30 minutes later and were greeted at the door by Katie and her curious siblings. All had the same red hair and blue eyes and were obviously anxious to get a close up look of the brothers who had become the talk of the community.

"*Willkommen!*" Katie greeted enthusiastically, opening the door wide. Leroy, Seth and Silas all removed their hats and set them on pegs on the wall, giving her polite nods. About 30 other families were already crowding through the house for Meeting then going out back to gather in the spacious barn where benches and chairs had been set up. Ruth deposited her food contribution of Ham Loaf onto the kitchen counter before finding a seat with her daughters on one side of the barn while the men took their seats on the opposite side. After a brief silent prayer, they took out their Ausbund's to sing in worship. Rebecca did her best to keep her mind focused on singing and Bishop Fisher's message of Christian charity but it was difficult when Seth's face was directly across from hers. She refused to look directly at him but could still feel his eyes upon her every moment except for the few occasions when her father would look over at him. She could tell from the expression on her father's face that he had a good idea of what was going on between the two of them but since they weren't really doing anything other than looking at one another there wasn't a whole lot he could do or say about it, which seemed to frustrate him to no end. To make matters worse, Katie Zook had taken a seat directly behind Rebecca and had a great vantage point from which to observe what was going on. The Meeting ended at noon and everyone helped to rearrange the benches and chairs around the many tables that had been set up outside for lunch. While the men visited inside the barn and children played on the warm grass, the women set up a buffet line inside the house.

Ruth worked alongside her friends and neighbors as always but now she sensed an air of censure. Conversation seemed to die or end abruptly whenever she drew near; giving her the distinct impression that they were talking about her. True friendliness had been supplanted by mere courtesy. It was the closest thing to shunning she had ever experienced and it made her heart squeeze in pain. She wanted to leave but couldn't so she pasted a frozen smile on her face; fighting back her tears as she worked. Even her best friend, Ivy Miller, was behaving standoffish.

Leroy, followed by Seth and Silas, strode back into the barn where he found Isaac speaking with several of their mutual friends; obviously deep in conversation. The words "damaged", "total loss", "entire herd gone", and "crop circles" reached his ears. Leroy drew close then stopped in his tracks when they all turned around and just stared at him. There was no malice in their gaze but neither was there the usual warm greeting and shoulder clap. The brothers they eyed with deep suspicion.

"Isaac," Leroy said, tipping his hat. "Levi, Jacob, Abram...Mark."

"Leroy," they acknowledged.

"We've been discussing the recent incidents of crop damage and missing livestock." Isaac's eyes trailed over to the brothers who were standing behind Leroy.

"*Jah*," added Mark Zoosk, shaking his head. "I will have to plow under my entire field; it is a total loss."

Leroy nodded with deep empathy, his eyes downcast as he wheeled his hat about in his hands. "*Jah*, my cornfield, too."

Bishop King stepped forward. He and Leroy had not spoken together since the morning he had fetched him to explain the mystery of the miraculously stacked corn in his harvester. "Well praise be to *Der Herr*, Leroy, that it was not a significant loss like poor Mark here." He turned to the others. "Something or someone mysteriously salvaged most of Leroy's corn and stacked it in his harvester. *Der Herr sie gedanki, jah?*"

A murmur of half-hearted acclamations passed through their ranks but underneath it all Leroy sensed an undercurrent of unspoken accusation. Why had he been spared so much loss while they had suffered and how much did the mysterious brothers he had taken in have to do with all of it?

Almost as if the words had been spoken aloud, Silas grabbed his brother's arm, tipped his hat and hauled him out of there; leaving Leroy behind to deal with the mess they had made of his life.

"I told you we never should have come here!" Silas growled under his breath, marching as fast as his legs could carry him. "We've caused nothing but trouble!"

"We aren't responsible for the damage done to the other farms!" Seth replied, allowing himself to be hustled along. "We've got to get that transmitter fixed first so we can send word to the rest of our people so they stop inflicting so much damage!"

"Well until we do we better lay low; which means you need to stay away from Rebecca!"

"You might as well tell me to stop breathing, Silas!"

"Stop breathing then!"

The food was finally ready and all gathered together in a circle to bow their heads in silent blessing before lining up. The women and older girls took turns helping to pour the sweet tea and lemonade before getting in line last for the food. Rebecca carried her laden plate of ham loaf, German potato salad, and fruit over to a table where Sarah Miller, Katie Zook and her sisters were eating under a large shade tree. She took a quick look around but could see no sign of Seth or his brother amongst all the men who were seated together at another table. Where had they gotten to?

"Lose something?" Katie Zook inquired with a mischievous smile as Rebecca sat down. She saw Katie and Sarah exchange secretive smiles as if they had been discussing something privately before her arrival.

"She lost Seth and Silas!" Mary volunteered with a giggle, confirming their suspicions.

"Ssh!" Rebecca hushed her sister, laying her napkin over her lap.

"There's going to be a quilting bee after lunch, I hope you will stay!" Katie continued. "We're hoping some of that Esh magic rubs off on our quilt so it will fetch as outrageous a price as yours did at the auction!"

Anger boiled up within Rebecca but she tamped it down immediately; reciting Proverbs 12:16 to herself for perhaps the millionth time as a result of Katie Zook's needling: *"A fool shows his annoyance at once, but a prudent man overlooks an insult."*

Rebecca favored her with a forced grin. "I would love to come, Katie! I was hoping you would invite us! Mirriam will be happy to pick up the pins and needles from under the quilt too, won't you?"

Mirriam nodded enthusiastically, her cheeks bulging with food. "…and we'll all be sure to pray earnestly over your quilt as we work so it will fetch a great price at the next auction, won't we?"

Again everyone nodded, including Sarah, who couldn't help but grin at her and how she had turned Katie's dig back around on her while still behaving in a Christian manner.

Feeling much better, Rebecca put a large forkful of potato salad into her mouth and ate with relish while Katie sulked at having been one-upped. Once lunch was over the leftovers were wrapped up and the dishes cleaned and put away. Then the quilting frame was brought out as all the women and girls gathered around on chairs to begin work. Rebecca found a seat next to Sarah but her mother, arrived late with a face that appeared swollen from crying. She could find no free chair to sit in and no one was making an effort to accommodate her. Rebecca watched with silent frustration as her mamm stood forlornly with her sewing basket over her arm, staring around the circle of women who all refused to look at her. Before she could turn away in shame, Rebecca got up and gave up her chair to her mother, seating her between Ivy and Sarah Miller. "Here, mamm! I just remembered that I have to get something. Take my chair!"

Her mother nodded gratefully and sat down, still looking like she might burst into tears at any moment. All around the quilt frame the women quieted and bent their heads to their work while Rebecca left.

It wasn't right to treat her mamm this way! She fumed. She knew she needed to cool down before she opened her mouth and said something she would regret. It was a good excuse to go looking for the brothers. She found them on the front porch, eating their meal alone together on the steps.

She stared down at them with her hands on her hips. "You two have made a mess of things! You should see the price my mamm and daed are paying as a result of that obscene bid on her quilt! They are practically being shunned!"

Seth stood up, spreading his hands out towards her beseechingly. "Becca – the only reason we helped things along was so we could get the parts necessary to leave sooner. Isn't that what you all want?"

Rebecca's eyes filled with tears. "They're shunning her, maybe not "officially" but it's hurting her deeply. Can't you do anything about it?"

Silas looked up incredulous. "You're mad at us for getting involved but you want us to do it again? Is this kind of illogical behavior typical of all earth dwellers or just Plain folk in particular?"

"Silas!" groaned Seth, giving his brother a dirty look. "Shut up!"

Silas stood up. "I'm going back to the Esh farm now…alone!"

Rebecca covered her face with her hands to hide the tears which had begun to slide down her cheeks. Seth stepped forward and put his arms about her, drawing her close. "Don't cry, Becca…please."

Her shoulders began to heave as she thought about the injured look on her mamm's face.

Seth reached into his new trousers and pulled out a crisp white handkerchief. "Here, let's dry your tears. You can't let them see you upset like this." Gently he wiped her cheeks, then paused when she looked up at him; becoming lost in her dewy blue of her eyes. "Becca..." he whispered, bending his face down to hers. The next moment his lips were upon hers and his arms were sliding about her slim waist. The world around her ceased to exist; all she knew was the strength of his arms and the deepening passion of his kiss as she pressed herself against him. Somewhere in the back of her mind a small voice screamed that she shouldn't be doing this but she had lost the will to resist him. She returned his kiss fully; giving herself completely over to him as scriptures from the Song of Solomon flooded her soul. *Let him kiss me with the kisses of his mouth; for thy love is better than wine...*

Overwhelmed by her response, Seth lost all ability to hold his emotions in check. They poured into Rebecca's heart and soul like a river overflowing its banks. Under its relentless onslaught she felt her muscles turning to jelly; her legs going wobbly but Seth held her fast, tightening his embrace until a voice brought them both up short.

"Rebecca Esh!!"

Rebecca and Seth separated and turned to look upon the intruder with bewildered eyes. It was Katie Zook. Instantly their arms fell away from one another and Seth stepped back, not knowing what else to do. Rebecca just stared at her, not surprised to see a look of triumph as well as envy cross her perfect features.

"Your mamm sent me to look for you. She's not feeling well and wants to go home. I'm sorry if I interrupted some-thing...important."

Rebecca wiped her face, and pulled some wayward hair back into her kapp that had come loose. "Jah, will you go and tell her that I'll be right there, Katie?"

"I don't mind waiting!" Katie smirked, crossing her arms.

Rebecca nodded and without a second look at Seth, follow-ing her blindly.

Seth watched her leave, his emotions in tumult. Part of him was exultant; the other half filled with dread at what it might mean to her and her family. For the first time Rebecca had given herself completely over to him, and it left him wanting more. No matter what it cost, he would have Rebecca for his frau. He would either forsake his own world entirely or she would have to renounce hers. To separate would be akin to flaying himself alive. He shoved his hands in his pockets and slowly walked back to the Esh farm alone, wondering how he was going to explain it all to Silas.

Rebecca followed Katie Zook, barely paying attention to the looks she was being given by the other women in her community. She was too consumed with thoughts of being locked in Seth's arms and the way his lips had pressed against her own. He made her feel both completely lost and also fulfilled all at the same time.

When she came upon her family she found them all looking miserable. Mary ran forward with tears in her eyes and buried her face in Rebecca's chest. "They wouldn't play with me!" she wept pitifully.

Rebecca held her close and hugged her but she had no words with which to comfort her little sister.

"Where are the boys?" her father asked, putting his arm about her mother's shoulders whose eyes remained fastened sadly upon the ground.

"They already left for home, daed; I guess they didn't feel very welcome either."

"Jah," he nodded. Without so much as even exchanging goodbye waves the Esh family slowly trudged the mile back home to their farm in complete silence.

Chapter Seven
"Bothered, Bewitched and Bewildered"

By the time the Esh's arrived home they were all emotionally and physically drained. Her mamm took to her bed early where everyone could hear her crying into her pillow while Leroy tried in vain to comfort her. Hannah went straight to their shared room to bury her hurt feelings in a book while Mary and Mirriam commiserated in silence on the porch swing; their heads resting against each other.

Rebecca knocked on the door of the *dawdi haus* but neither Silas nor Seth responded. Frustrated, hurt and angry, she went to the kitchen to begin preparations for dinner alone. She cast frequent glances out the kitchen windows; waiting for the brothers to appear but they didn't until many hours later, both looking glum and downcast; Seth most of all. He went into the *dawdi haus*, not even pausing to glance at the kitchen window where Rebecca stood, waiting for him to notice her. Anger tried to flood her heart but she shoved it away; knowing she must not submit her soul to sin.

She went to the foot of the stairs. "Hannah! I need your help with supper; mamm is not feeling well!" Then she went to the front porch. "Girls! Time to set the table."

Mirriam and Mary got up; their eyes red and swollen from weeping. "Coming."

Hannah came down the steps, her eyes also swollen. Together she and Rebecca plucked, cleaned and cut up two chickens for frying. Then Hannah turned her attention to peeling potatoes while Rebecca baked more biscuits and prepared green beans.

"Can we make the sweet tea, Becca?" Mirriam wheedled. "We're done setting the table!"

"Jah, make plenty. It is warm today."

An hour later all was ready. Rebecca sent Mary to the *dawdi haus*. "Go fetch the boys and let them know supper is ready. I'll get *mamm* and *daed*."

Moments later her parents came to the table. Rebecca was shocked at the sight of her *mamm's* face, usually so joyful and serene. Now it was red and swollen from hours of relentless sobbing. Her daed looked grim and frustrated. Rebecca wrapped her arms about her mamm and laid her cheek against hers, whispering the words her mother would always say to comfort her whenever she was hurting.

"*Mamm*, remember the words of the Psalmist? *Weeping may endure for a night; but joy cometh in the morning.* Everything will be all right *mamm*; *der Herr* knows we have done nothing wrong."

Her mother nodded and patted her hand in an unconvinced manner. "*Jah*," was all she could muster.

Mary returned moments later. "They won't come." She announced. "They said they would be eating in the *dawdi haus* from now on."

The words struck Rebecca like a knife to her heart. Without a word she gathered up their dinner dishes, filled them with food and then handed them back to Mary; chewing on her cheek as she only did when sorely vexed. Mirriam followed her little sister, carrying out the utensils and an extra pitcher of sweet tea. They both returned moments later, took their seats at the table and together they all bowed their heads.

Rebecca closed her eyes. *Der Herr, please bring reconciliation between my family and our brethren. Please speak to all the hearts involved and where there is strife and fear; replace it with your love, understanding and peace.*

They ate in virtual silence; each lost in their own thoughts. When supper was over, they worked together in silence to clean up; the customary good cheer and fellowship gone. Her *mamm* returned to the bedroom, followed by her *daed*. Her sisters went also to their own bedrooms. It was eerily silent in the house where usually there was giggling and animated conversation. Rebecca climbed the stairs to her room with a hollow heart; images of her mother's stricken face, her sister's anguish, and Katie Zook's look of triumph still haunting her. She got ready for bed and peeked over at Hannah from her rocking chair. She lay with eyes squeezed shut but Rebecca could tell was not really asleep.

She sat and rocked in her chair for what seemed hours; staring out her window in the hopes of seeing Seth waiting for her outside. To make matters worse, she couldn't get the memory of his passionate kiss out of her mind. She replayed it over and over, wishing he would summon her outside again while everyone slept. She longed to have his arms about her; pulling her close; comforting her; feeling the pressure of his lips upon hers. She imagined her emotions like ghostly arms stretching out through her window to the *dawdi haus* where she knew he could feel them; every ounce of her being crying out for him. Still she waited and stared at the dark windows…holding her breath; hoping for any sign that he would respond. Nothing. She couldn't take much more of this! She stole a quick glance at Hannah to make sure she was finally asleep then slipped downstairs and out into the yard with her cloak wrapped about her; blatantly offering herself to him. She stood in silence; staring at his door as if she could make it open through sheer force of will. Except for the chirp of crickets, buzz of cicadas and pounding of her heart all remained still. After several long agonizing minutes she finally turned and walked back to her room feeling completely rejected. With hot tears flooding her eyes, Rebecca removed her prayer kapp, flung it across the room, and angrily brushed out her long tresses of wavy golden hair with vicious strokes.

Seth was in physical torment. It had taken every ounce of strength he possessed not to go outside and meet Rebecca in the dark of the garden. From his vantage point in the *dawdi haus*, he watched through her window while she took down her golden hair; his fingers itching to run themselves through its glorious mass. He could feel the pain in her heart as if it were his own. He shut his eyes, battling with himself to stay away when all he wanted to do was kiss her tears away and murmur against her lips that he loved her; that he wanted her as his mate…but it couldn't be; it was forbidden by their king. For the entire walk home and then again during their lonely supper Silas had laid into him about how much damage they were causing the family.

Silas had been ruthless. "How many times do we have to have this same conversation before you get it into your head that you can't be together?" Silas had railed at him. "It's going to take months to obtain and modify the parts to fix the ship! We need to keep as much to ourselves as possible and cause the Esh's no further trouble in their community! If you truly love Rebecca, then you need to do what is right by her and stay away so she can live a happy life without you! Sooner or later, we have to leave!"

Seth opened his eyes again, staring up at her lovely form in the window even after she drew down the shade. It mattered little; with his keen eyes he was still able to see her silhouette for a brief moment as she changed into her nightgown then the light was doused and he was standing alone in the dark with his aching heart. He balled his hands into shaking fists; his heart crying out with anguish.

All Wise King, please speak to me! Tell me what to do. How is this love I feel for her not of you when it overwhelms me so? I am willing to forsake my world and everything in it for her! Please tell me what to do!

There was still no response…just utter silence. Their king had never been silent like this on their world or any of the others they had visited in previous travels. The king had always responded with perfect wisdom but here he was silent. What was it about this particular planet that made communication with him so impossible? The distance Seth experienced was becoming equal to the heartache of losing Rebecca forever.

He had never known pain of such variations and intensity on other worlds. *How did Earth's inhabitants bear it?* He sighed and bowed his head. Now that Rebecca had given up and gone to bed, it made it easier for him to turn away.

Seth removed his clothing and slipped into the bed next to his brother's.

"I can't hear him anymore either," Silas announced in the darkness. "His messages are being blocked; something is terribly wrong with this world."

Seth made no reply, too mired in his own misery to respond.

When this elicited no response, Silas changed the subject. "I'm going to speak to Mr. Esh about taking us to the public library so we can use the internet to find a supplier of electro-mechanical parts."

Seth nodded glumly, little caring whether or not his brother could see him do it in the dark or not.

Silas continued. "With any luck we will have all we need by winter when we can work on the ship without dividing our time between the field work and the ship. Can you hold out for that long? Can you stay away from her?"

"I don't know," Seth mumbled.

"Look – it's only going to make leaving harder for both of you if you let this go on any further. I don't want to return home with a *bruder* who has left his heart thousands of light years away."

Seth did not respond; after all, what could he really say? His heart was already lost.

Rebecca awoke the following morning with a splitting headache; followed by a mental playback of the previous day's events. It was 4:30 am and time to get up but what she really wanted to do was to pull the quilts over her head and hide. With her mamm determined to stay abed it was going to be up to her to keep things running. She rolled out of bed with a groan, pulling the quilts off Hannah as she did so then went into Mirriam and Mary's room to rouse them. While the biscuits were baking, Rebecca tip-toed into her parent's dark bedroom.

"Mamm, how are you feeling today? Can I get you any-thing?"

"Nee," came the muffled voice from under the quilt. "I don't feel gut; I won't be getting up."

"Please, mamm. It hurts us to see you like this. We need you!"

Ruth's voice choked. "Not today, dearest...*ich kam sell neh geh!* This was followed by her mother's frame heaving with sobs under the quilt.

Rebecca turned away, her heart aching. "Perhaps later, then? I'll bring you in some breakfast on a tray?"

"I'm not hungry. Please just let me be for today."

Rebecca left, closing the door quietly behind her. She found all three sisters in the midst of the kitchen staring at her hopefully. She shook her head in response.

"Please set the table, Mirriam. Hannah – will you make a tray up for mamm in case she changes her mind? Perhaps you can coax her to eat."

"Jah," Hannah nodded, collecting a plate, utensils and tray that were normally only used when one of them was sick in bed. Rebecca checked on the biscuits; removing them from the oven to cool. Her father entered the house from the barn, looking as grim-faced as he had the night before. Neither Seth nor his brother was behind him; they were still sticking to their plan to eat separately. Leroy washed up at the kitchen sink and sat down, cradling his face in his hands. The sight of her strong father so down filled Rebecca's heart with both fear and anger. It wasn't right that they should be treated so over the auction of a silly quilt! But she knew it was more than just that. Their brethren still had not accepted the brothers into the community and now her family was paying the price for their mysterious ways.

"Becca the bacon is burning!" Mary alerted her.

Rebecca got a mitt and moved the cast iron pan off the stove to a folded towel on the counter. "Ach! I hope you like it extra, extra crispy! Mirriam – tell Seth and Silas that if they want to fill their bellies they will have to come fetch their breakfast themselves!" She had no intention of bringing the food out to the *dawdi haus* as if she were some kind of serving maid!

Mirriam ran out while Rebecca laid out the rest of the food on the table.

Silas answered the door.

"Becca says to come get your breakfast." Mary took hold of his hand and skipped back to the main house, dragging him along with her. Silas smiled despite himself; he sure liked having little sisters around.

When they got inside he took off his hat and waited; avoiding Rebecca's eyes while Hannah filled two plates of food and a thermos of hot coffee for him and his brother.

"Danki," he murmured, pushing open the screen door with his feet since both hands were full. Mirriam followed just behind with the thermos.

Rebecca allowed herself the brief luxury of peeking out the window while Seth opened the door for his brother but Silas and Mirriam obstructed her view. Mirriam then skipped back and seated herself at the table where all bowed their heads.

This time Rebecca prayed aloud. "Derr Herr, please be with mamm; help her to feel better. Please lead and guide us in thy perfect will."

"Amen. Amen. Amen!" responded her sisters, both surprised and pleased she had done so.

Her father patted her hand, smiling weakly at her. "Amen," he agreed softly.

Hannah brought in the breakfast tray to her mamm's room then returned to take her seat next to Mary. They ate in relative silence after that, each lost in their own thoughts. Rebecca glanced around the half-empty table; missing the animated chatter from her sisters, the strong masculine voice of her daed; and the comforting presence of her mamm. Most of all she missed Seth. He had completely withdrawn his feelings from her and she had not realized until that moment how lonely and empty she had always been on the inside until he had come along. It seemed more like a week since she had seen him last instead of a single day.

"Mary, would you please collect the dishes from the dawdi haus and mamm's room. If she hasn't eaten, see if you can coax her, jah?"

"Okay," Mary nodded eager to help. It took her only a few moments to collect the empty dishes from Seth and Silas which she stacked into the large sink. Evidently their appetites had not been affected in the least by recent events; the plates again looked as though they had been licked clean.

As the three oldest sisters worked to clear the table and wash the dishes, they could hear their youngest sister in their mamm's room, wheedling her incessantly to eat. She came out with a triumphant little smile five minutes later; having coaxed her to eat at least half.

Leroy wiped his mouth, stood to his feet and got his hat then bid her mamm goodbye. He was taking the boys into town so they could begin purchasing what they would need to fix their ship. He kissed each of his daughters' then hitched up Joe to the buggy.

Rebecca watched the door of the dawdi haus open from behind the screen door; not able to tell which brother was which since both kept their faces downward and hidden by their hats. Soon they were off; leaving Rebecca alone in the house to deal with the day's chores.

Seth rode in silence behind his brother, watching the Esh farm diminish in size as the distance between him and Rebecca increased. He had had to stop himself a hundred times from going to her, taking her in his arms and kissing the pain away; knowing it would just make things worse.

Silas' voice interrupted his thoughts. "Mr. Esh, in order to obtain what we need, I shall need you to set up a bank card account with your financial institution so we can purchase the items online."

"We Amish do not use credit cards," Leroy informed him. "We always pay in cash."

Silas nodded, understanding his objection. "Unfortunately we have to buy most of the equipment online and it is only possible using a credit card. The manufacturers are too far away and the volume too great to transport in your buggy or wagon."

"Most of it will have to be shipped to your farmhouse," added Seth.

"Will your bank allow you to set up such an account without having a picture I.D.?"

"Jah; they know me well there and Amish have set up merchant accounts in order to do business with the *Englisch*."

They arrived in town half an hour later. Joe was tied up to a buggy ring in front of the Bank of Lancaster and the three of them entered. After a short wait an account executive brought them over to his desk to set up the account.

"Please have a seat, Mr. Esh. What can I do for you today?" he said, motioning to three chairs. "How is your family?"

"They are all *gut*, Mr. Brown; *danki* for asking."

"There has been much talk about your quilt at the auction around here lately!"

Leroy tried to hide his grimace. He did not want to be reminded of the reason for their recent troubles. "Word travels fast," he observed.

"Well I have a buddy who was at the auction who owns a ham radio as do I. We were talking about it last night."

Leroy shifted uncomfortably. "I need to open a checking account with a line of credit, Mr. Brown."

"Of course! Back to the business at hand! Minimum deposit is one hundred dollars; five hundred if you wish to avoid monthly service fees."

Leroy reached into his back pocket and withdrew an envelope stuffed full of $100 dollar bills and laid it on the table.

Mr. Brown's eyes went as large as saucers while his eyebrows climbed high into his receding hairline. "I guess he wasn't exaggerating about the price you fetched on that quilt!"

"I will also need a $50,000 line of credit." Leroy added; the sum the boys had suggested to him earlier since some of the needed parts and equipment might run very high.

"Of course, it will take just a few minutes. I have special paperwork for you to fill out, being an Amish customer. I'll be right back with it."

While Leroy filled out the paperwork, the banker made small talk. "I guess you already heard the latest news?"

"Nee," Leroy shook his head.

"There's been more crop circles and funny lights in the sky. It has everyone around here a little freaked out! The UFO weirdoes are starting to flood the town."

Seth and Silas exchanged worried glances. *They needed to make contact with their people and soon, but how?* Suddenly a light bulb went on over Seth's head.

Seth leaned forward. "You have a ham radio?"

Mr. Brown nodded with evident pride. "Yes I do! It's been a life-long hobby of mine!" "Mr. Brown – we have cousins quite a long distance away to whom we need to get a message. If we provided you with the proper frequency and call number of their closest neighbor, might we borrow your equipment long enough to send them a message?"

Mr. Brown smiled, seemingly pleased at the thought of being of assistance to the usually self-sufficient Amish. "Of course! I'm off at 3:00 pm today and live only ten minutes from here by car. I'll be glad to drive you there." He was completely oblivious to Leroy's disapproving glower at the brothers.

Half an hour later they were out the door; ten thousand dollars lighter in exchange for a temporary plastic check card that would enable them to purchase what they needed through the internet.

Leroy waited until they were out of earshot. "Amish do not use 'ham radios' or credit cards."

"Mr. Esh, you heard what he said about the damage our people are still causing. If we can get a message broadcast out on his ham radio we can bring it to a stop. They don't understand the problems they are causing!" responded Seth.

Joe trotted along the road for another full block before Leroy answered them. "Very well, then; but only this once."

They pulled up in front of the Lancaster Public Library. He handed the check card over to Silas. "How much time do you need?"

"At least an hour to start; we may have to make several more trips here in order to get everything we need."

Leroy nodded reluctantly. He didn't like the idea of the boys using the library computer to get onto the "internet". Amish would never do such a thing and it would draw attention but it could not be helped. "I will be over at the Feed and Tack Store until then." He also planned to go into the Fabric & Quilt Shack to purchase some material and needles for Ruth, hoping the surprise might cheer her up.

Seth and Silas entered the air-conditioned library and went to the reference desk.

A teenage girl stepped up to help them with a pleasant smile. "May I help you?"

"Jah, we would like to purchase internet time, please."

"I will need your library card first," she replied.

"I guess we will need to get one of those first," Silas grinned sheepishly.

The girl blushed and pushed a registration form across the counter. "The bottom section is for Amish since you don't carry picture identification," she explained, pointing. Bring it back to me when you're done filling it out and I'll help you get set up."

"She likes you," Seth observed, jabbing Silas in the ribs with his elbow.

"Don't start, it's bad enough that you are already involved with one of them," Silas growled. Minutes later they were back at the reference desk with the completed form.

"Wow!" she said, staring at the page with open admiration. "I don't think I've ever seen printing that looked so computer-generated before! You must have won first place in penmanship in your school every year!" She typed the information into her computer behind the counter then handed them a library card. "Follow me," she said, leading them to a bank of computers. "I've entered your check card information so it is linked to your library card in our system," she explained. "All you have to do now is log-in with your library card number and reset the password to what you want; then you're all ready to go." She stepped closer to Silas, twirling a curl of her long brown hair between her fingers. "Is there anything else I can do for you?" Expecting them to ask what a log-in and password was.

Silas stared at her; momentarily distracted by her physical proximity. "Ach…no…danki! You have been wunderbar!" He said, laying on the Pennsylvania Dutch dialect extra thick.

She stepped back, the smile fading. "Okay, whatever…but if you change your mind I'll be right over there!" she smiled coyly and walked off, her hips swinging in her skin tight jeans.

Seth grabbed Silas by his suspenders and hauled him over to the computers. "Time to get to work, Romeo."

For the next two hours they poured over the websites of several electro-mechanical suppliers, racking up product orders that quickly burned through the $10,000 that had been deposited into the account earlier that day with only three-quarters of the needed items purchased. They worked with deep concentration, never noticing the strange looks they were eliciting from the other library patrons who thought it a very strange thing for two Amish boys to be on a computer at all, let alone for so long.

Seth was busy writing down the part and model numbers of the larger ticket items they still needed to purchase when he felt a hand come down heavily upon his shoulder.

"Since when do Amish go on computers? Whatcha doing? Looking at porn so your daed and mamm won't know about it?" accused a voice behind him. Seth twisted his head around to find a large male with pimples and a closely shaven head sneering at him. He had piercings in his face and ugly tattoos all over his upper arms. "Lemme see!" He pushed Seth to one side to look at the computer screen and seemed shocked to find not porn but an online catalog of electronic products.

"Ya gotta be kiddin' me!" His eyes narrowed suspiciously. "Just what are you Amish up to, anyway?"

Silas and Seth stared back at him. It was really none of his business what they were doing but it was obvious he and his small knot of friends weren't going to go away until he answered them. Silas stood up and cocked an eyebrow at him. "We're building a spaceship!" he said in his best Peter Laurie impersonation. He noticed a sci-fi book laying on the table nearby and held it up, slightly crossing his eyes at them. "Then we're going to the planet Uranus to meet blue-skinned women."

The teen with the shaved head just stared at him for a moment in utter shock then burst into laughter; clapping him on the back. "Hey you're funny!" he guffawed. A murmur of laughter erupted from his follower's right on cue. "I didn't think you Amish had any sense of humor!"

They walked off, still chuckling to themselves.

Seth exhaled loudly and wiped the sweat from his forehead with shaking hands. "That was unnerving; smart move *bruder!*"

"Hiding in plain sight, Seth; works every time." They returned to the computer screen; determined to get as much done before Mr. Esh returned to pick them up.

Leroy had never set foot into the Fabric & Quilt Shop before; this was his *dochder's* and *frau's* domain. The little bell above the door jingled as he entered; calling unwanted attention to himself. He stepped in and removed his hat; grateful that no one seemed to take much notice of him. He walked up to the counter where an Amish girl the same age as Rebecca smiled at him in greeting.

"Can I help you?"

"Jah; I wish to get needles for quilting and fabric."

"You will need to select the fabric first so I can cut it for you."

Leroy looked around; too nervous to move from his spot. He pointed to a bolt of cloth in solid hunter green.

The girl fetched the fabric, measured out three yards; cut and folded it in thirds then plucked a packet of quilting needles off the display rack on the counter. "Will that be all?"

"Jah."

She rang up the purchases. "That will be $26.45 *sei so gut.*"

Leroy counted out the cash and change in precise coinage, handed it over and took the package with a tip of his hat. "Danki," he murmured. He hoped Ruth would be pleased; he hoped it would help get her out of the bedroom and back to her cheerful self again. Next he went to the Tack and Feed Store to pick up some needed supplies. Several Amish buggies were parked out front; which, for some reason, made him nervous. He entered the store determined to get what he needed then get out as quickly as possible.

"Leroy!" said a voice as soon as he entered. He looked up and found his best friend, Isaac Miller standing there with his two sons, Samuel and John.

"Isaac," Leroy tipped his hat while noting the large bags of fertilizer piled high on a push cart. "For your soy field?"

"Jah – the crop will be gut this year; the profits should hold us over during the winter months; they just need some additional fertilizing."

Leroy relaxed a bit; the conversation with his good friend setting his heart at more ease. At that moment Deacon Yoder appeared with a push cart full of feed for his horses. He smiled and greeted Isaac but it faded away the moment he noticed Leroy standing there. For a moment the two men just stared at one another then Leroy backed away.

"I'll see you around, Isaac." He tipped his hat then escaped into the warehouse; completely shaken. Even his hands were trembling! He walked down one aisle after another, barely noticing anything until he calmed down enough to get what he needed. He shouldn't feel this way about one of his own people; especially the Deacon! He was a good man but their relationship had altered drastically ever since he had taken the brothers into his household.

He wandered for a good fifteen minutes and by the time he came to check out, Isaac and Deacon Yoder were already gone.

The short drive back to the library gave him ample time to mull over his tenuous circumstances within the community. He needed to get things back to normal as soon as possible or his family would pay an awful price. Seth and Silas were waiting for him on the front steps of the library when he pulled up in his buggy. They could tell from the expression on his face that something was very wrong but said nothing; not wanting to call attention to it. It was almost 3:00 pm; time to return to the bank and Mr. Brown. Leroy steered Joe back out onto the two-lane; driving in silence.

Mr. Brown was waiting for them in the parking lot, standing outside his car. "If you like you can keep your buggy here and I'll give you a lift to my home and back," he offered with a friendly smile, "I'm a good ten miles from the bank. Your buggy will be safe here and there's a water trough with fresh water for your horse."

Leroy nodded, tied Joe up and followed Seth and Silas to the banker's blue minivan. They soon arrived at a charming white clapboard Colonial style home with black shutters and the traditional tin star over the door.

"Please make yourselves at home; I'll just get the old girl warmed up."

Leroy's eyebrows climbed high. "Pardon?"

"I'm going to turn the ham radio on, she's a vintage model with vacuum tubes so it takes them a while to warm up," Mr. Brown explained with a sheepish grin. He might as well have spoken in Mandarin Chinese for all that Leroy understood him.

"Ach… jah…" Leroy nodded, pretending to comprehend.

"Could I offer you something to drink while you all wait? Soda? Water? Tea? And please call me Robert."

"Tea, *sei so gut.*"

Seth and Silas nodded, sitting down on the couch beside Mr. Esh, wheeling their black hats round and round in their hands nervously; worrying about how they were going to get him out of the room while they relayed their message in the native tongue of their world.

Mr. Brown poured them each a tall glass of iced tea; beaming with pleasure over the fact that he was being of assistance to the self-sufficient Amish. He ran upstairs to his office where they could hear him humming and flicking switches. "Should be ready in five!" he called down.

The three of them sipped their tea, nervous as can be.

"Okay, come on up!"

Silas got up first and led the way, followed by Seth and last of all Leroy. They entered the room where they found Mr. Brown beaming at them with pride. He stretched out his arms; indicating the myriad of electronic equipment, computers, printers and a large wall map with push pins stuck all over it. He beckoned Silas to sit in the chair of honor before his Lafayette HA-230 receiver and Knight T-60 transmitter set. Despite the fact that they were over 40 years old they looked as good as new. "Have a seat, young man! Now – what is the frequency you need?"

Silas paused for a long moment. He did not want this man knowing the unique frequency that would enable him to communicate with his people.

Think fast! He heard Seth screaming in his head.

"I know how to do it," Silas admitted, bowing his head with feigned guilt. "I used to be friends with an Englisch boy whose dad had one of these." He cast a worried glance over at Mr. Esh whose eyes had gone round at the whoppers he was telling. "Ach, but they have since moved away."

Seth's exhale of relief was explosive; drawing surprised looks from both Mr. Esh and Mr. Brown. Silas sat before the transmitter and donned the large earphones, spinning dials and adjusting settings so quickly that not even Mr. Brown could keep up with him. Seth watched him with baited breath; wondering how he was going to relay the warning to their people without their host becoming any the wiser.

Hiding in plain sight; trust me, his brother's voice said in Seth's head. Silas' back stiffened which telegraphed that he must have found the right frequency. With a grin and a nod of his head, Silas began jabbering away in the language of their home planet mixed in with a lot of "ach's...jah's and gut's" for good measure, all the while casting side glances in Mr. Brown's direction to see if he were catching on. Robert simply grinned at him and nodded; none the wiser, but Mr. Esh's mouth gaped open. When he was done, Silas stood up and laid the headphones down on the desk. He donned his black hat and tipped it in thanks to Mr. Brown.

"Danki, Mr. Brown! I was able to get a *gut* connection to our cousin's neighbor; he will relay the message for us."

Mr. Brown grinned at him and scratched at his head. "Please! Call me Robert! Well I'm glad to be of service! You'd think after all these years of living among the Amish I would have picked up on enough Pennsylvania Dutch to understand some of what you were saying but I couldn't make out a word of it!"

"Jah? Ach...well I do speak rather quickly!" smiled Silas, throwing a wink in his brother's direction. "Danki again, Mr. Brown."

"Robert! I'll take you back to your buggy; just give me a moment to power everything down."

The four of them went downstairs and waited by his car.

Leroy glanced back to make sure Mr. Brown couldn't hear him. "Were you successful in telling your...people what they need to know?"

"Jah; I explained quite clearly what they need to do and for the message to be relayed on to all new departures coming to this world."

"New departures?" repeated Leroy, turning pale. "Do you mean there is more of your kind coming here?"

Silas and Seth exchanged glances which led Leroy to believe that they had let slip information they shouldn't have.

"Mr. Esh; our people have been visiting this world for millennia." Silas admitted.

Leroy stared at Silas in shock; not quite sure how to process this disturbing new piece of information.

At that moment Mr. Brown joined them. "The van is unlocked, please be comfortable."

The three of them got in and rode in silence all the way back to the bank where their buggy was parked. Joe was still standing there patiently; occasionally helping himself to the water trough that was kept filled for the Amish and their horses.

"Danki!" Leroy said, exiting the van with another hat tip.

"Danki!" repeated Seth and Silas, waving goodbye with broad smiles.

The bizarre events in Lancaster County came to an almost immediate halt after their visit to Mr. Brown's home. There were no further reports of crop circles, missing livestock or what had become an almost nightly show of strange lights followed by ruined fields all over the county. Folks began to relax a bit and life for the Esh family slowly returned to normal. It was late summer and soon fall would arrive when they would harvest their crops and celebrate weddings in their community before settling in for the winter months.

Chapter Eight
"Something Borrowed and Someone Blue"

"Rebecca! The bread is burning! Where has your head been lately, my dochder?"

Rebecca came out of her stupor and rushed for the oven with her mitts. With a self-reproaching moan she pulled out two blackened loaves of bread that would have served for their lunches that day. Ruth began opening all the windows in the house to let the smoke out.

"Becca burnt the bread! Becca burnt the bread!" sang out Mary, thinking it quite humorous.

"It's not funny!" Rebecca scolded her while dumping the scorched loaves into the trash. "That was our sandwich bread! Hurry up and get ready! Where is Mirriam?"

"Ach, pinning her hair." said Mary; instantly downcast now that she realized she would be eating cheese and meat without the bread that day. Maybe her best friend, Sarah, would have extra…

Rebecca came out of the pantry. "Mamm, we're all out of flour and yeast."

"I'm out of other things as well; you'll have to go to Stauffer's and pick up some groceries. Perhaps you can drop the boys off at the library while you are out; they need to order more parts."

Rebecca quelled at this. She and Seth had been successfully avoiding one another for a few weeks and now she was about to be thrown back together with him in the buggy. "Can't daed or you drive them today?"

Her mother frowned. "Your daed is busy with farm work today and I have a to-do list as long as my arm. I would think you would enjoy a visit to town!" Her mother did not mention how nervous she still was to run into any of her friends.

Rebecca's shoulders slumped. "All right, give me your list."

Her mother smiled at her with great relief and opened her arms up for a hug. "Danki, Becca," she whispered; knowing her daughter understood. "I'll get the girls ready." She handed her a list along with some cash. "Treat yourself to a book while you're out; perhaps that new one by Jerry Eicher?"

"Jah," Rebecca nodded, forcing a smile for her mother as she undid her apron. The thought of being so close to Seth again was making her nervous inside but she couldn't tell if it was with excitement or dread.

"Hannah! Go hitch up Joe to the buggy for Rebecca!" Ruth yelled upstairs.

Hannah came down, bearing an armful of dirty laundry destined for the wash tub. "May I go with Becca, mamm? I haven't been anywhere in weeks!"

Ruth shook her head. "Nee, you'll be taking her place with me doing the laundry today."

Hannah groaned and let the screen door slam behind her as she stomped off to the barn to get the horse and buggy. Rebecca put the cash into a drawstring pouch along with the list.

Ruth embraced her again. "Perhaps you should get 10 lbs of flour instead of five the way you've been burning things lately," she smiled making at a poor attempt at humor. "Ach, Becca – you're shaking! Are you sick?"

"Nee, mamm – just a little excited to go into town." She hated fibbing but now was not the time to burden her mamm with her own heartaches. She turned with leaden feet and walked out of the house as if going to her own execution. She kept her eyes upon the ground; refusing to look up before climbing into the driver's seat. She waited as her passengers climbed in silently behind her then flicked the reigns. Joe took off at a brisk clip, throwing up gravel behind him. Rebecca focused her attention on the road; trying her best to ignore Seth's presence.

"Aren't you even going to look at me, Becca?"

His voice made her jump; but it also made her angry. "Why should I? You've been the one avoiding me for weeks!" She reproached him. "I'm just the driver today; pretend I don't exist; you must be good at it by now!"

His hand reached for her arm but she flung it off, angry tears stinging her eyes and making the road ahead blurry. "Silas – tell your *bruder* to leave me alone!"

"He's not here, Becca," came Seth's quiet voice from behind her. "I told him to stay and help your daed with the farm work while I went to the library today. I wanted the chance to be alone with you; to make amends."

Rebecca craned her neck around and for the first time in weeks looked him fully in the eyes; her face registering complete shock. She had not even noticed that Silas had not been there. The moment her eyes locked upon his she was lost. The reigns slipped from her nerveless fingers.

"Careful!" Seth cried, lunging forward to grab them. He climbed into the seat next to her and took over the driving until he could find a safe place to pull off the two-lane. He pulled Joe into a small parking lot under some shade trees. For a long moment they simply stared into each other's eyes; saying nothing then he couldn't stand it any longer. He took her face into his hands and pulled her mouth against his. He expected resistance; he expected her to push him back and slap him. What he hadn't expected was for her to slide her arms around his neck to pull him closer. The kiss deepened, becoming passionate. A moan escaped her lips and that was when Seth gently pushed her away. Rebecca stared at him; her heart pounding in her ears; her bosom rising and falling with emotions that had been pent up for weeks.

"You shouldn't have done that," she whispered. "We shouldn't have done that." She dropped her face into her hands. "I don't know what to think anymore, Seth."

"Becca…I love you. I can't deny it anymore."

"I love you too," she mumbled. "What are we going to do about it?"

Seth swallowed hard; knowing the next words he was about to utter would seal his doom forever; one way or another. "I'm going to ask your father for your hand." Rebecca stared at him, utterly shocked. Seth continued before she could think to protest. "I will remain here with you and be a good Amish husband." He wasn't going to tell her of the consequences to himself that would result; it wouldn't do any good anyway. His heart belonged to her now for better or worse.

"But-but…what about returning home?"

"Silas will have to go without me; my home shall be where you are if you will have me."

"My father would have to approve the match," Rebecca replied; not holding out much hope in that regard. "If he gives us his blessing, we will both have to be baptized first."

"Whatever it takes," Seth replied, bringing her fingers up to his lips and kissing them one by one.

Rebecca stared longingly at him. "Are you sure you want to do this?"

"My heart leaves me no other choice, Becca." Seth murmured, drawing her to him for another long kiss. After several moments, he pulled away and put the reigns into her hands. "You'd best take me to the library now."

Rebecca nodded but cuddled against him for the remainder of the ride, leaving him off at the library steps before driving Joe on to Stauffer's. She got everything on the list and then took a side trip to King's gift shop to find some books; her heart lighter than it had been in weeks. Perhaps life could really return to normal? If only her parents would give their blessing…!

She returned to the library two hours later to find Seth waiting for her. He climbed up into the buggy and with a grin, planted a kiss upon her nose. "That's the last of it; we shouldn't have to make any more trips to the library for a while. The rest of the equipment should arrive within the month. I'll help Silas fix the ship but he'll be returning home without me."

"First you must speak to my parents!" Rebecca reminded him; the knots twisting in her stomach. They held hands in silence on the way home, content just to be next to each other. Rebecca turned over in her mind every objection her father might come up with.

If he objected on the reason that Seth isn't truly Amish then she would demand to know in what respect! He ate, spoke, worked and even worshipped as one of them; why should his origin change anything? There was nothing in the Ordnung that forbid it; were not the *Englisch* sometimes baptized into their faith and then allowed to join with them in holy matrimony? Why should Seth be any different?

They arrived home just in time for lunch. Seth carried the groceries into the house for her then went in search of her father and his brother.

"Pray for me!" he said, brushing her cheek with his lips. Her mamm entered the room just at that moment; her greeting catching in her throat; her smile fading instantly.

"Mamm, Seth and I need to speak with you and daed about something very important," Rebecca said, going to her mother. Ruth looked from one to another; shock written all over her face.

"No," she whispered; already perceiving their intent. "He will not allow it!"

Rebecca gently took her mamm's hands in her own. "Why would he not permit it?"

"He…they are not one of us, my *dochder*!"

"In what way are they not one of 'us'?" Rebecca stood firm.

"Ach! You know how!"

"I want you to tell me! Have they not worshipped with us? Do they not dress and speak like us? Have they in anyway violated the Ordnung?"

"Nee," replied Ruth, shaking her head.

"Then why, mamm…why? We love each other! We wish to be married!"

"No!" shouted two male voices. They turned around to find Leroy and Silas standing just inside the door.

Leroy strode forward and grabbed Rebecca's arm. "Go to your room, now," he ordered her.

Seth rushed forward, his hands outstretched to implore him. "Mr. Esh-please!"

Silas grabbed him by the shoulders and spun him around. "No more of this, Seth! You've let it go too far!" He pushed him through the front door and into the dawdi haus while the tranquility of the Esh household erupted into sobs and words of rebuke. Silas slammed the door shut and stood in front of it to block it. "I thought we had this all settled."

Seth slumped into a chair and cradled his head in his hands. "So did I," he moaned. "I love her, Silas; I can't help it. The thought of living without her is killing me."

Silas squatted beside his brother and put his arm around him. "You know why we can't stay here; why you can't marry her! Think of what it will do to her even if you won't think about your-self!"

"Don't you think I have?" Seth growled, fighting back his tears. "It doesn't make it any easier; the heart wants what the heart wants and mine wants her."

Silas stood; his face somber. "Her father will never give his blessing."

"He might…if we persuaded him…"

Silas grew livid. "We are not going to influence his mind like we did the bidders at the auction, Seth! I won't allow it!"

Seth stood to his feet; his hands balling into defiant fists. "Then I shall have to speak to him man-to-man and make him see reason."

For a long moment the two brothers glared at one another; completely at cross-purposes.

"We'll see," Silas gritted out; tight-lipped. "Just let it rest for now; give him time to cool down."

Seth blinked; stunned that his brother had backed down so quickly. "All right, I'll let it be for now but my mind is made up. I'm going to take Rebecca as my frau and remain here."

Silas shook his head and walked out of the dawdi haus. *Not if I have anything to say about it!*

Silas entered the main house with hat in hand to find Leroy sitting at the kitchen beside his eldest daughter. Rebecca looked up; expecting to see his brother and in that moment…he knew; she had convinced her father to give his blessing to the match. Her eyes were ablaze with the fire of newfound hope. His heart sank; he had been hoping that Mr. Esh would do the dirty work for him but it was obvious Leroy had been no match for both his daughter and wife.

Ruth got up to embrace him as she would her own son.

"Silas, we have spoken on the matter and prayed to Der Herr!" She paused and turned to her husband; indicating that he should finish.

Leroy cleared his throat. "Except for thy strange origin there is no other reason I can find to refuse my daughter's wish to marry thy bruder if he agrees to live as one of us. You have both proven yourselves to me this past month and I would be speaking a falsehood if I did not tell thee that I have already regarded you as my sons for many weeks now."

Silas looked from Leroy to Ruth to Rebecca and back again; forcing a smile. "Danki," was all he could muster. Rebecca stood and gave him a brief hug; misinterpreting his reaction.

Silas put his hat back on and backed out of the room. Now it was solely up to him to save his brother from what would happen if they went forward with their plans to marry.

"I'll tell Seth the gut news," he murmured, turning to go. The screen door slammed shut behind him but he could still hear Rebecca and her mamm talking excitedly about plans to arrange for a wedding quilting bee and ceremony in late November. He needed to act fast before this madness went any further. He entered the dawdi haus but Seth was not there. He had gone into the barn to take out his frustration with the pitchfork and hay. Now was his chance. Silas went back to the main house to find Rebecca alone in the kitchen; elbow deep in flour, kneading bread dough; her face wreathed in smiles. He hadn't seen her this happy in months.

"I just wanted to tell you that I couldn't find him." He said to her, hat in hand. "I'm sorry this has been so hard on you both," he apologized, casting a nervous glance over his shoulder.

Rebecca grimaced good-naturedly at him. "Nee...I do not think you are; not at all."

"Why would you say that? Do you think I enjoy watching my bruder suffer? That I rejoice knowing that you and your family have been hurt on account of us?"

Rebecca shrugged; willing to forget and forgive all. She was too delirious with joy to let anything bother her now. "Everyone suffers," she replied as she kneaded. "Life is full of suffering; suffering is what conforms us into the image of our Savior."

"Savior?" Silas repeated, as if the term were unfamiliar to him.

Rebecca stared at him, perplexed. "You have sung from hymns with us in Meeting from the Ausbund. They all speak of our Savior, Jesus Christ. Why do you act like this is strange to you?"

Silas shrugged. "We had to be well prepared for our discovery sojourn here so we would fit in," he replied, putting phase one of his plan into action. "It involved much training which included learning your language, way of life, primitive belief system and 'hymns'."

Rebecca paused from her kneading to stare at him; not liking where the conversation was going. "Primitive? Is that what you call it? Primitive? Are you not also Christians just like us?"

"No! We have no need of a Savior where we come from; we have our King and that is enough." Silas replied with a smile, pounding the final nail into the proverbial coffin.

This was all just 'training' to you?" Her voice lowered to a whisper, her eyes widening with sudden comprehension. "You are not Christian? Not really Amish?"

"No more than you are subjects of our King," he replied, then added with a frown, "there is something desperately wrong with your world, Rebecca. We can't seem to hear him here; it has almost become unbearable; for both of us."

Rebecca gaped at him; her mouth hanging open in horror.

"What is wrong?" Silas asked innocently.

"It is bad enough that you are not Amish as you have pretended to be all this time; but to find out that you are not even…even Christian!" The betrayal of all she knew to be real was total and devastating.

"Look, it was never our intent to get involved like this; it just happened! I didn't want to come to Earth in the first place but Seth insisted."

"Get out!" Rebecca pointed to the door. "Get out…now."

Out of the corner of his eye Silas saw Leroy and Seth enter the family room. Rebecca rounded on Seth and pointed to the door. "Both of you…just get your 'ship' or whatever you call it fixed as soon as possible and leave us alone! I never want to see you again!" She ran from the kitchen; heedless of the flour and dough flying from her hands and fled upstairs to her bedroom, slamming the door behind her.

She flung herself on the bed, weeping with rage. She had never felt so angry or betrayed in all her life. To think that she had been willing to give her heart and hand to an…an alien in the most holy of covenants only to discover that he was not even a Christian! Her world was shattered. There was only one King and Savior who ruled over all and they did not even seem to have a passing acquaintance with Him! She pulled the quilts off her neatly made bed in a rage and flung them across the room. Next she picked up her hair brush and flung it against the wall. She spun in a circle; seeking what further damage she could do but found nothing left to throw. She needed to get away! She needed to get out now!

Rebecca ran down the back stairs so none could see her then out to the barn where she found Joe in his stall. With hands still caked in dough and flour, she put the blinders and traces on him then hooked him up to the buggy. She got in just as the screen door squealed open and shut with a bang; her father, mother and Seth all running towards her.

"Geh up, Joe!" she yelled, snapping the reigns hard on his rump. He took off at a gallop while she ignored their shouts and pleas to wait. Gravel sprayed behind the buggy; keeping them at a distance. She drove Joe mercilessly out onto the main highway; not bothering to even check first to see if it was clear of oncoming traffic. For the first time she applied the whip; driving Joe faster and faster; little caring what happened to her. Foam collected at his mouth as the horse strained to meet her demands for increased speed; his breathing became labored.

Seth stormed back into the house and grabbed Silas' arm. "What did you say to her?" he demanded.

"Where did Mr. Esh go?" Silas wanted to know; ignoring his question.

"To the nearest phone shanty to call the police; now answer my question!"

Silas threw his hand off. "Only the truth; Seth; something you should have done weeks ago instead of allowing yourself to become bewitched by an Earth dweller! I'm not going to stand by and allow you to ruin both of your lives and violate the primary decree of our king!"

"You don't know it would ruin our lives! No one has ever done it before!" Seth growled, dashing angry tears from his face. "We haven't even been able to make contact with the king to find out!"

Silas grabbed him by the shoulders and shook him. "You already know the law! No intimate relationships with anyone on this planet! His silence here should be enough to tell you that something is terribly wrong! Why else would they have need of a 'savior'?"

Seth's eyes grew large with sudden comprehension. "That's it, isn't it? You told her!"

"She figured it out on her own," Silas replied.

"If she hurts herself out there I will never forgive you!"

Silas regarded his brother with great sadness. "That's just the problem, Seth! We've come to a world where forgiveness is required in order just to function; where it had to be purchased in blood. That alone should make it clear to you how much we don't belong here." Silas turned and walked away; leaving his brother behind to wrestle with his thoughts.

Tears blinded Rebecca's vision as she drove the buggy aimlessly through Lancaster County. She should really stop and let poor

Joe rest for a bit but the ants crawling under her skin made it impossible to slow down. She was halfway between Strasburg and her farm when Joe came to a stop and refused to go any further. She looked down the road to make sure all was clear before getting out. She checked his legs one by one then finally bent to inspect his front left hoof. He whinnied softly as she lifted the foreleg. Fortunately there was no damage to his hoof but the shoe was hanging on by two nails. She would have to walk him carefully the five remaining miles home where she would have to face her parents…and Seth. A drop hit the back of her neck just below her kapp. She looked up to find the sky darkening with the threat of a summer storm.

Why now? She tried to think of the nearest Amish farm where she could take Joe to get re-shoed. The drops came down faster, followed by a rumble of distant thunder. She was going to get drenched. At that moment she heard the sound of another buggy approaching. It slowed to a stop just behind her. To her amazement, Jacob Zimmer stepped out.

"Rebecca!" he greeted in surprise, tipping his hat. "Is something wrong with Joe?"

"He is ready to throw his shoe," she pointed as he lifted the horse's leg to inspect it.

"Ach! You cannot walk him on this or he will go lame. I always keep a horseshoe kit in my buggy just in case; I can have this repaired in no time."

"Jacob Zimmer, you are a knight in shining armor!" Rebecca declared, swiftly wiping the tears from her face. At this Jacob's face flamed as red as an apple.

"Looks like rain, you best get inside your buggy," he suggested before ducking into the back of his to pull out a small leather pouch containing a hammer, pliers, file, extra horse shoes and a bag of tiny nails. Rebecca watched from the shelter of her buggy as Jacob pulled out the old nails from the Joe's shoe one-by-one, repositioned it correctly and pounded in the new ones; ignoring the rain which was now coming down in sheets.

"Danki, Jacob! Danki!" she said, truly relieved. "How can I show my appreciation? Would you and your mamm like to join us for supper later?" The question surprised both of them. *What was she doing inviting him to supper?* She had only just broken off all ties to Seth 20 minutes ago! She looked at him; half hoping he would refuse but Jacob was already nodding his head enthusiastically.

"Jah!" he said, climbing back inside the shelter of his buggy. "What time?"

Rebecca ignored the warning bells going off in her head. She would no longer allow her heart to rule over her. She was 19, a young woman ready for marriage and it was time to start living her life with a real Amish man.

"Five o'clock?"

Jacob's smile practically lit up the inside of the dark buggy. "Jah! Danki!"

"That will give me time to freshen up and get something nice prepared. Danki again, Jacob. Der Herr certainly must have sent you Himself! You were just in time to help me and Joe here." She didn't think it was possible for Jacob to blush any deeper red but this he did as he tipped his hat with a bashful smile before turning the buggy out onto the highway. Rebecca snapped the reigns gently and set off again, this time at a much more comfortable pace for her horse.

She arrived home an hour later, hoping to avoid both Seth and his brother Silas. There was no one. She unhooked Joe from the buggy spurs and led him into the barn where she first brushed the water and sweat down; then gave him fresh hay and clean water then covered him with a blanket. Hannah, Mirriam and Mary tumbled out of the house holding umbrellas and ran to the barn; their faces creased with worry.

Mary got to her first. "Daed called the police on you, Becca! Mamm is worried sick. Why did you leave like that?"

"Where did you go?" asked Mirriam looking up at her with concern.

"I needed time to think." Rebecca answered, walking with them back into the house; their arms wrapped about her.

"Are you really going to marry Seth?" Mary wanted to know.

"No!" Rebecca said loudly. That was the moment she saw him standing between the dawdi haus and the garden; his face desolate. She could feel his emotional agony the moment the words were out of her mouth. She tore her eyes from him; hardening her heart against him.

"Mamm's been in bed since you left," Hannah continued; shaking her head 'no' at Seth who looked ready to follow them in.

Rebecca patted Mary's back soothingly. "Everything will be fine," she whispered, wishing she believed it. "Jacob Zimmer helped me out of a pickle on the way home and I have invited him and his mamm to supper. Perhaps the company will make mamm feel better?"

Hannah nodded; still perplexed by her older sister's sudden change in attitude. "Jah…a visit from Rose Zimmer should cheer her. I'll go in and let her know so we'll have time to spruce things up a bit and prepare the meal."

"No, I'll tell her," Rebecca shook her head. "I owe her an explanation anyway." She left them at the door of her mother's darkened room and sat on the bed. "Mamm?"

Her mother sat up immediately and gathered her into her embrace. "Becca! Danki be to der Herr! Why did you leave like that? I thought you would be happy at receiving your daed's blessing!"

"I needed time to think, mamm." Rebecca said, unable to look her mother in the eyes.

Ruth searched her daughter's face, cupping her cheek lovingly in her hand. "Time to think and time to pray; it is a very important decision to become one flesh with another, my dochder. It is gut that you are not taking it lightly."

Rebecca nodded but said nothing. Her flesh and her mind had been at war with one another from the moment she had laid eyes on Seth at the barn raising months ago. Now he had been exposed by his own brother as a complete fraud in the most important sense of the word. She could not marry a man who did not truly share the same faith as she; no matter how good an actor he was; no matter how her flesh longed to be one with him. "Jacob helped me out of some trouble while I was gone; I invited him and his mamm to have supper with us tonight."

Ruth examined her daughter's face; understanding instantly what she was trying to do. "Are you sure this is what you want to do?"

Rebecca's face twisted with sudden emotion as the pain assaulted her again. She got off the bed and wrapped her arms about herself, refusing to meet her mamm's eyes. "I don't know what I want anymore," she whispered before fleeing to the kitchen.

For the next few hours the women busied themselves in the chopping, peeling, stirring and trussing; working in silence and giving Rebecca ample emotional room. Extra chairs were set around the dinner table which was laid with a clean table-cloth. By the time 4:00 pm came around all was ready. They stood under the shelter of the porch while the summer storm raged, waiting for the Zimmer's buggy to arrive; it came right on time.

"He's nothing if not punctual." Ruth remarked, squinting. "Is Rose with him? I can't tell." No one could mistake the tremor in her voice. If Rose Zimmer did not come with her son it would speak volumes that things were still very bad indeed for the Esh family in the community.

"I can't tell yet," Rebecca replied, straining to see.

"Me either," Hannah added.

Mirriam and Mary clutched hands, closed their eyes and prayed silently; afraid for their mother should Rose not be there. The buggy turned the corner into the driveway and everyone finally drew breath when they saw Rose's white kapp.

Ruth practically flew down the steps with an umbrella to greet her friend. "Rose, how happy I am to see you again!"

Rose stepped down and embraced Ruth briefly; they pressed cheeks. Jacob stepped out holding his umbrella aloft, his pale face already blushing furious red at the sight of Rebecca in her nicest blue dress; hat in hand. "Rebecca," he murmured in greeting. "It is gut to see you again!"

"Please come inside and be comfortable!" Rebecca beckoned them. "Can I offer you sweet tea or lemonade while my sisters tend to your horse?"

"I'll have sweet tea," Rose smiled watching the Esh girls squeal and shriek in the downpour as they ran the horse into the barn. "I'm sorry that Eli couldn't make it; he would have enjoyed seeing Leroy again."

Rebecca and her mother exchanged looks; happy to know that things seemed to have returned back to normal again. She filled Jacob's tumbler and handed it back to him with a plastered-on smile; hoping he would mistake it for shyness. Despite the fact that she had been the one to invite him and had set herself on an irrevocable course; her heart was not in it. "I hope you like roast duckling, Mrs. Zimmer…Jacob," she continued. "It's my mamm's special recipe."

"I haven't had duck in ages! It will be a treat." Rose replied, beckoning for Ruth to sit down and join her. "But what I really want is to catch up with your mamm. Can you spare her for a few minutes?"

"Of course!" Rebecca replied, turning back to the house to tend to the meal. She had three ducklings roasting in the oven and all three needed to be basted every 20 minutes. Jacob followed her in like a loyal puppy, sipping his sweet tea.

Rebecca opened the oven door and pulled out the rack with her mitt; feeling Jacob's eyes upon her as she bent over to baste the birds. "It was gut you came along just when you did, Jacob." She said; trying to keep her voice light. "I would probably be stuck out there still were it not for you!"

"I would always like to be there for you, Rebecca." Jacob murmured softly, closing the distance between them. Rebecca straitened, turned and stared at him; amazed at how his shyness had suddenly disappeared. Jacob's green eyes searched her face; his smile gentle. She stared back at him; feeling as though the entire situation was running full speed ahead without her. "I don't think it's any secret why you invited us here, is it?" he added.

Rebecca slowly shook her head, unable to back away from him; he had her trapped between his towering form and the open door of the hot oven. Sweat trickled down her back. "Excuse me," she said, turning round to slam the oven door shut.

"Say the word and I'll go to thy daed right now to obtain his blessing," Jacob continued. Rebecca blinked. This was progressing way too fast for her but she found herself nodding anyway. Jacob leaned forward and kissed her upon the cheek before turning to go.

"Wish me luck," he said and stopped short when he came up against Seth's looming form that was blocking the kitchen door-frame. Rebecca immediately felt guilt-ridden then angry at herself for being so. *What did she have to feel guilty about?*

"Excuse me," Jacob said, side-stepping around him. Seth stood rooted to the spot, ignoring him, his silver eyes filled with deep anguish as they bore into hers. A searing pain shot through Rebecca's heart; Seth was letting her have a taste of the agony she was causing him.

Stop him now, Becca...please!

She slowly shook her head at him. She had made her decision; she had set her course. She loved Seth...with every ounce of her being she loved and desired him...but she would not betray her Lord for him. Seth lowered his eyes then turned away, returning to the *dawdi haus* where he wouldn't have to witness what would happen next. Rebecca let him go despite her mind screaming at her to go to him. With leaden heart she turned back to the oven and numbly basted the meat, waiting for the footfalls of her father upon the floorboard which would signal her doom.

"Rebecca, I have just come from speaking with Jacob," said her father's deep voice behind her. "Is this true? Did you really wish for him to ask me for thy hand? What about Seth?"

Rebecca straightened, closing the oven door and nodded without turning around. She didn't want her father to see her face.

Her father's arms went about her. Gently he turned her about to face him and searched her eyes. *"Dummel dich net*, my dochder! Take your time; don't hurry! You don't have to do this now."

"Jacob is waiting for your answer, daed," she mumbled. "He will be a good and faithful husband; one which no one can object to…"

"I had already given my blessing to Seth," he reminded her gently.

Tears filled her eyes. "It can no longer be," she whispered; fighting to control her emotions. "I can't…he isn't…" The floodgates finally burst. Rebecca covered her mouth and fled upstairs to her room. She heard the creak of the floor boards below as her father returned to the dining room where no doubt he was now doing as she asked and giving Jacob his blessing. She poured water from the ceramic pitcher into the basin and splashed her face over and over; her emotions roiling. When she was sure she would be able to maintain her composure she returned downstairs to find her sisters gawking and Jacob Zimmer grinning at her. He held out his hand to take hers and placed a kiss on it; there was no delicious thrill coursing up her arm at his touch; she might as well have been stone.

Rebecca swallowed hard and did her best to return his smile while her siblings scowled at her from behind his back. "Hannah – would you help me to serve the ducks and dressing to our guests?"

"What is going on?" Hannah whispered to her when Jacob was out of earshot. "I thought you wanted to marry Seth! Now daed is discussing making the announcement about you and Jacob at next month's meeting after the harvest!"

"Ssh! Not now." Rebecca replied, pulling the roasting pans out of the oven. The grease in the pan sizzled as it hit the sides. The smell of duck, apples and sauerkraut filled their noses. She laid it on thick towels to let the ducks rest while Hannah scooped out the dressing and put it into a covered chafing dish to keep warm.

"You're breaking his heart; doesn't that mean anything to you?" her sister continued softly. "I see the way he looks at you; the way you look at him; it's not the same with Jacob!"

Rebecca turned to her sister, her eyes pleading. "I can't do this now…*sei so gut*…Hannah!" She dashed the tears from her eyes and shoved the chafing dish into her sister's arms. "*Geh!*" She pointed to the dining room, trembling violently.

Hannah left with a disapproving shake of her head while Rebecca plated the ducks onto a large serving platter. Thankfully her father and Jacob were deep in conversation and hadn't noticed the exchange. By the time she had poured out more beverages and brought the Brussels sprouts to the table she was calm enough to sit down beside Jacob and face "the music".

"Your daed will announce the engagement next month," Jacob confirmed, taking her cold hand into his from under the table. Rebecca nodded; feeling more like a prisoner condemned to die than a woman about to become a bride. This moment should have brought her joy; not dread. She stole glances at Jacob's face when he wasn't looking, a joy she had never seen before quite apparent upon it. Then it hit her; he had always desired to ask for her but had been too afraid of rejection. Since the moment she had given him the "go ahead" earlier that day he had become a changed man; a confident man. Jacob caught her staring at him and smiled. He had a kind face; he was a good man; she would have to learn to love him…*have to*.

They bowed their heads for the blessing then began passing the platters around. Rebecca served Jacob first as would be expected, then Rose; her parents and siblings then last of all herself. She pushed the food back and forth on her plate, listening to the conversations going on around her; her mind a million miles away. She wondered what Seth's world was like…who this King person was they always spoke about. She was barely conscious of Jacob squeezing her hand every now and then before returning to the conversation at hand as they finished their supper.

Then suddenly, unbidden by any conscious will of her own Seth's face materialized out of thin air in front of her; his silver eyes both longing for and accusing her. *Becca – don't do this!*

She stood up abruptly; terrified that everyone around the table had seen the same apparition as she. "Excuse me, I'll clear the dishes, mamm; you just sit and relax with Mrs. Zimmer. Would anyone like coffee with their Shoofly pie?" She was talking a mile a minute.

Becca – please come to me. Just this one last time!

It was so loud she was sure everyone must have heard it but no one seemed to. She gathered up the dirty dishes and took them into the kitchen.

"No!" she hissed out loud, dumping the dishes into the sink with a loud clatter and covering her ears so she wouldn't have to listen to him…as if that would do any good…

Arms slid about her waist and she jumped with a little scream; expecting it to be Seth. She found Jacob's face bare inches from hers. "It is all right now that I kiss you, jah?" he whispered, drawing her close. Rebecca resisted the urge to squirm away from him and allowed his lips to press against the corner of her mouth for a brief moment.

"Danki, Jacob," she smiled nervously, patting his arm as she would a friendly dog. "Would you like to help me get dessert on the table?"

"Jah," he smiled; pleased at being treated like a husband already. "What would you like me to do?"

Rebecca placed a pie in his right hand and a pie server in the other. "Take this to the table for me?"

"And then what?" he grinned, his double meaning unmistakable. She ignored him; feigning stupidity.

Becca!

"Then come back for the coffee cups, cream and sugar," Rebecca replied; ignoring Seth's summons.

Rebecca stop this!

"…and then?" Jacob whispered, enjoying their little game.

Seth's persistence was swiftly replacing her sorrow with anger. She'd show him! She smiled demurely up at Jacob. "…then it's dessert! Now geh!"

She pumped water into the sink and set both the kettle on to boil for hot dish water as well as the coffee percolator; humming loudly to drown out Seth's persistent voice in her head. Jacob returned moments later and favored her with another smile before carrying out the tray laden with cups, saucers, cream and sugar. Rebecca fidgeted; feeling like a long-tailed cat in a room filled with rocking chairs. She wasn't sure who was getting on her nerves more; Seth or

Jacob. The kettle sang and she poured hot water into the sink filled with dirty dishes to let them soak. She carried the hot coffee to the table and poured all around then plunked back down in her seat next to Jacob, putting her hands between her legs so he wouldn't have access to them anymore. By the time dessert was finished she was utterly exhausted. She lingered just long enough by the front door to bid Jacob and his mother goodbye; ready to flee to her room.

Mrs. Zimmer cupped her chin gently in her hand. "Gut nacht, Rebecca! We'll be seeing of lot of each other soon; your mamm and I have already set a date for the quilting bee at our home. We should all have it finished just in time for your wedding night."

Rebecca nodded in silent panic; dismissing the images of Jacob from her mind. Things were moving way too fast for her comfort. Jacob stepped up next.

"Gut nacht, Rebecca," he murmured, dipping his head to brush her cheek with his mouth.

"Gut nacht, Jacob." Rebecca whispered through lips that were turning white. The moment the door was shut she vaulted up the stairs to her room two at a time; leaving the clean-up to her mamm and sisters.

What had she done? Why had she set these wheels into motion? She wasn't ready to be Jacob Zimmer's wife! She wasn't ready to become one flesh with him under a wedding quilt!!! She barely knew him! She had not even been baptized yet...not been baptized...never had her Rumspringa...perhaps she still had an out...

She lay awake in her bed for hours, still awake even after Hannah had fallen asleep beside her. She studied her sister's sleeping face; so peaceful and serene. She couldn't remember the last time she had felt that way. Not since before Seth and Silas came into their lives. She wasn't ready to trade the familiarity of her sister with a man she barely knew; to whom she would have to belong to forever.

Rebecca! Come out to me. This time she had not imagined his voice. She turned her back to the window and put the pillow over her head. *Becca!* To drown him out she sung a hymn inside her head over and over. *Becca; I'm waiting for you.*

The pull was too great to resist; especially when she also desired to be with him. Of their own accord her legs swung out from under the covers and stood her before her window. Seth's form was hidden in the darkness below but she could see his silver eyes looking up at her from the yard like twin stars. *Please just talk to me; I promise not to touch you*, his voice said in her head.

She struggled internally but whether it was to ignore or succumb to him she wasn't sure. All she knew was that her legs and feet were tip-toeing downstairs and out the door; the dark grass wet beneath her bare feet.

Seth stood with his arms outstretched; a large blanket in his grasp to keep her warm. He watched her intensely as she walked towards him, her golden hair loose and hanging down to her waist; a sight only Amish husbands should be privy to. He wrapped the blanket closely about her and drew her body close to him to keep her warm. This felt like home; being held close in his arms. She felt different with him compared to Jacob Zimmer. His eyes burned into her own.

"I know you don't want to marry him," Seth whispered, gripping her shoulders. "It isn't too late; you have a month before it's announced. Come away with me!"

Rebecca shook her head; utterly forlorn. "How can I? We do not even share the most important thing in the world to me: my faith! I cannot be with someone who is not a Christian! I would bring shame and shunning upon myself and my family. I still have to live in this world, Seth; and you must return to yours…without me." Her head drooped as her own words brought the reality home. Her shoulders began to heave. The situation was entirely hopeless. She was trapped.

"Look at me!" Seth's hands cradled the back of her head and tilted her face up to his. His fingers twisted into her hair; his silver eyes growing large, pulling her into their depths. Rebecca swayed on her feet; her heart finally succumbing to him. His lips swept down upon hers; arms crushing her against him. She couldn't resist him anymore so she gave in; slipping her arms around his neck so she could pull him closer and parted her lips for him. Her heart felt as though it were straining through her chest to physically join with his. Unbridled joy exploded into her soul as she welcomed Seth into her heart; only dimly aware that they were sliding down together in the darkness onto the wet ground.

The cold blades brought Rebecca abruptly back to her senses. She pushed herself away; afraid of letting things getting too out of hand. It was no use. She wanted to be his but he was not really

Amish, not Christian…not even human. She gently pushed him away; shaking her head when his eyes questioned her.

"Nee," she whispered, struggling to her feet; her eyes pleading with him to forgive her. "Nee!" She wrapped the blanket about her, turned and fled back into the house; ignoring his silent pleas as she ran upstairs into her room. She could feel the raw pain in his heart; the emptiness she had left behind because she shared it too. Rebecca crawled into bed beside her sister and wept until she fell asleep.

Chapter Nine
"A Painful Decision"

The next morning at breakfast it was obvious to all in the Esh household that something was seriously wrong with her. Rebecca's face was puffy and eyes swollen; a sure sign that she had been crying all night. She assisted in preparing breakfast as usual but wouldn't eat; all she could do was push it around on her plate after the blessing. Hannah had brought the breakfast out for the boys to the dawdi haus but only Silas seemed to have an appetite. She returned moments later with Seth's full plate; shrugging her shoulders at her parents.

Ruth set down her coffee cup. "Rebecca, what is the matter? Have ye ought of which you wish to speak to us?"

Rebecca nodded; avoiding his eyes. "Jah, mamm; I want to go on Rumspringa before you announce the engagement."

Ruth stared at her; thoroughly shocked. They had both thought the engagement to Jacob much too rushed; her subsequent misery only confirmed it.

"I think that is a good idea, my *dochder*," her daed agreed to her amazement. "We have put some money aside for just such a day."

She had expected an argument or at least a lecture on how she should not play around with Jacob's feelings and behave in such an erratic manner. A ghost of a smile came to her lips. "I think it best if I leave home as soon as the arrangements can be made. I would like to stay away until the spring." She had no intention of remaining home while Seth and his brother worked on the ship; he held too much temptation for her. Last night she had come dangerously close to defying every ordinance of the Ordung. She could no longer resist him; she had to get as far away as soon as possible; before she brought shame down upon all of them. "Perhaps I could visit our relatives in Indiana?"

"The Millers?"

"Jah, Ruth Miller and I have often corresponded and we are close in age. I could share a room with her."

Her mother stood, collecting the dirty dishes. "I will write them tonight then, after we clean up from supper." She bent over and kissed her daughter tenderly on the top of her kapp. "But I will surely miss thee, while you are gone, my Rebecca."

"Thank you, mamm." Rebecca sighed a bit relieved; however she had yet to confront Jacob with the news. She helped to clear the table from breakfast then immersed herself in chores; making a concerted effort to avoid coming into contact with Seth. In this at least, she had her father and Silas' help. Silas did not allow his brother to approach the main house and her father kept him so busy all day he had no time to think let alone give him an opportunity to summon her again.

Jacob showed up unannounced that afternoon and offered to drive her to the post office as an excuse to be with her alone; unaware that she was planning on 'running away from home' and him. Rebecca bounced along in the seat next to him; allowing him to hold her hand but inwardly struggling with how to tell him that she would be leaving soon. In the end she was a coward and said nothing; allowing him to kiss her cheek before returning for his own home. From the moment she dropped the letter into the Out of State mail slot at the post office it felt like a countdown to doom.

For the next three weeks she worked hard at avoiding both the brothers as well as Jacob who was now coming by at least three times a week to leave her small gifts or notes in the mailbox. Even out of sight she could feel Seth's pain. On a moment-to-moment basis she was forced to steal herself against the growing ache to be held in his arms and kissed until nothing else mattered. It almost drove her mad knowing that all she had to do was whisper the word 'yes" inside her heart, go out to him and he would be there…waiting for her. She shook her head, trying to concentrate on her work. She was leaving soon for Indiana and he would be leaving for…well only *Der Herr* knew where.

Once the brothers were gone, she would return, get baptized and ask Jacob for a longer courtship before announcing the engagement. Her mamm had already been spoken to his in private about holding off on the quilting bee until after she had returned. It seemed an eternity before the Miller's letter arrived welcoming her.

It was now late August and the fields were swiftly ripening to the harvest. Her father and the brothers were busy from dawn to dusk tending to the livestock, cultivating fields, and making as many improvements upon the farm that they could fit in. They were so exhausted by the end of each day that they did nothing but eat and sleep in their spare time.

Rebecca had yet to break the news to Jacob that she would be leaving for Indiana. She dreaded the inevitable confrontation knowing how it would hurt him but her mamm was insistent that she be honest with him and let him know herself. It wasn't right to keep him in the dark like this.

She would wait until the letter from the Miller's arrived to tell Jacob. She would have to do it just before the Meeting service the Sunday following when there would be too many people around to even think about making a scene.

After the second week the letter from their cousins arrived in the afternoon mail. Rebecca held it in her hands, staring down at the envelope as though it held her execution orders. With a sigh she tucked it into her apron and walked back to the house to help her mamm to make jam from the last of the summer berries.

The screen door slammed behind her. "Mamm, the letter from the Miller's arrived."

Her mom wiped her hands on her apron before accepting it. "Ach, that is gut; let us see what they say!" She opened it up and read aloud.

Dear Ruth, Leroy and Rebecca: Wie geht's? We are all well and were very pleased to receive your letter. We would be happy to host Rebecca. Ruth is very excited to have someone her own age join her in shopping at the mall, see movies and run around in blue jeans…

The letter went on for a half page more, discussing family matters, the latest weddings, births, and auctions before finally concluding with: *"…please be sure to let us know the day and arrival time of Rebecca's train so we can be there to greet her. All our love and affection to you in our good Lord's name…Rachel Miller."*

Ruth turned to her daughter with a compassionate smile on her face. She knew well the heartache she had been trying to hide. "When would you like to leave?"

Rebecca's heart melted within her. Her mamm never failed to understand her deepest, unspoken emotions. She put her arms around her mother and laid her head against her bosom. "As soon as possible," she said in a muffled voice.

"All right then. I will have thy daed take you into Strasburg this weekend to buy the ticket. You will leave the week after that; it will give my letter enough time to reach the Millers." She kissed the top of her head affectionately. "The berries have cooled enough to handle, let's get them into the jars before we start pickling the cucumbers."

For the first time in several weeks Seth (joined by his reluctant brother) came into the main house for supper with his brother that same night; almost as if he knew about the letter and that his time was running out. He said nothing but his eyes continually pled with her throughout the meal; driving her to distraction. Her parents pretended not to notice and welcomed them; content to let her adventure in Indiana work everything out.

"Thy *schwester* is traveling to our cousins, the Miller's, next month," Leroy announced to all at the table after they had offered the blessing. Seth kept his eyes fastened on his plate, but Rebecca could instantly sense his panic.

Hannah, Mirriam and Mary were immediately excited. "May we go too, mamm?"

"It will be a while before you are of age for Rumspringa," Ruth responded, passing around the tureen of Onion Rivel Soup. "Rebecca – can you ladle some out for your schwesters?"

"Jah mamm," Rebecca stood and picked up their bowls one by one to serve them.

"Silas and I came here on a form of Rumspringa," Seth announced; startling Rebecca. She spilled some of the steaming broth onto the table. She grabbed a dishtowel and mopped it up as she cast a warning glare in his direction.

Leroy and Ruth stared at him, their mouths slightly agape; not expecting to hear this kind of information.

Silas put in his own two cents. "We have something similar from where we come from only we call it discovery."

"Jah?" Ruth and Leroy exchanged looks. It has been months since the boys had appeared and they had almost completely forgotten about their mysterious origins. The brothers had assimilated into the plain lifestyle so well that Leroy had come to think of them as Amish.

"Gut," her mother nodded, just to be polite. It was obvious she did not want to delve into the subject matter much further; it was just too unnerving. Ruth lifted a platter of oven fried chicken. "Dark or light meat?"

The brothers visibly deflated; the Esh's having made it quite obvious the topic was 'verboten'. "Dark please," Silas mumbled. Ruth speared a whole leg of chicken and plopped it onto his plate. She turned her questioning gaze to Seth. "The same please," he mumbled.

There were a few more minutes of quiet chewing.

"Becca, when are you going to tell Jacob that you're leaving?" piped up Mary.

"Soon," Rebecca mumbled, refusing to look in Seth's direction. She could feel his silver eyes burning the proverbial holes into her.

"I think you've gone *narrish*!" Hannah said with a shake of her kapp; never one to hold her tongue. "First you agree to marry Seth then change your mind! Then you want Jacob to court you, change your mind again and now you're going on Rumspringa!"

"Hannah!" both parents scolded at once.

Rebecca could feel her face heating up; she could fee herself turning three shades of red.

"Well I just don't think it's fair!" she finished; realizing she had gone too far.

Rebecca stood up; her appetite gone. "May I be excused, mamm?"

"Jah," Ruth said, giving Hannah another withering look. Rebecca fled the table and ran upstairs where she wouldn't have to endure Seth's wounded emotions.

She changed into her sleeping gown, undid her hair and brushed it out then settled into her rocking chair to block the world out with a good book. An hour or so later, Hannah entered the room looking thoroughly remorseful. Rebecca studiously ignored her.

"I'm sorry, Rebecca. Please forgive me…I shouldn't have said what I did; please don't be angry with me anymore."

Rebecca put her book down. "Hannah, I know I have acted narrish for the past few months; I just don't know what to do anymore!" She covered her face with her hands. "I shouldn't love him but I do. We can't be together but it's all that I think about. Why couldn't I feel this way about Jacob? That would solve everything!"

The sight of her older sister so distressed filled Hannah's heart with compassion. She closed the distance immediately and the sisters embraced.

"Forgive me; sometimes I get envious of you, being the eldest and the first to do everything," she admitted.

"Well this time I'm not the one to envy," Rebecca whispered, resting her chin on the top of her sister's head. "This is just killing me; I don't know what to do anymore."

Hannah looked up at her. "You mean choosing between Seth and Jacob?"

"No; between doing what I know to be right and doing what my flesh wants."

"I don't understand," Hannah confessed.

"...and I don't think I could explain it to you right now," whispered Rebecca, returning to her chair. "Just pray for me, Hannah. Pray that *derr Herr* will strengthen me to choose the right and narrow path instead of the one that will lead to destruction."

"Rebecca; you're scaring me...what do you mean destruction? It surely can't be as bad as all that!"

Rebecca closed her eyes; fighting against the summons that had been beating upon her brow for the past fifteen minutes. "It is; just pray for me."

Rebecca watched as Hannah stepped back to regard her; her brown eyes large and serious. Something in Rebecca's face must have finally registered with her because she nodded and went immediately to her knees before her bed to silently intercede for her sister. Rebecca knelt beside her, turning her soul over to *der Herr*. She ached to go outside to Seth, fall into his arms and become lost in his mesmerizing eyes...to feel his lips ravaging hers...

"Becca you look funny; are you alright?" Hannah was kneeling next to her; having finished her prayers.

"Nee," she shook her head. How about if I brush your hair before we go to sleep?" she desperately needed to distract herself.

"Would you, Becca? We haven't brushed each other's hair in such a long time! I would love it!" Hannah hurriedly took off her kapp and removed the bobby pins, letting her light brown hair cascade down her back. Together they sat upon the bed and took turns brushing out each other's hair; eyes closed with pleasure. Rebecca realized how much she missed sharing such an emotionally intimate time with her sister; the closeness did much to take her mind off Seth. Twenty minutes later she became aware that he was no longer outside 'calling to her'; having given up.

Rebecca gave Hannah a grateful hug. "Thank you, Hannah."

Hannah hugged her back, pulling the covers over both of them. "For what?"

"For being such a *wunderbar schwester*."

"I want to go to Strasburg and see the train museum!" Mirriam bemoaned the next morning at breakfast; crossing her arms over her chest. "Why did daed have to choose wash day to take you to Strasburg?"

"Me too!" added Mary.

"Hush now and finish your oatmeal pancakes!" Their mother scolded them. "You're going to need all your energy to help me get the wash done today."

Rebecca said nothing; not sure whether she felt more disappointed or relieved that Seth and his brother had chosen to eat in the dawdi haus that morning. The family finished breakfast and the remainder of their morning chores while her father rigged up Joe to the buggy. Soon just she and her daed were off on the half hour ride to Strasburg. They hadn't gone on an outing alone together since before Hannah was born. She cuddled up next to him and he put his arm about her to keep her warm. It was a little chilly outside with ground fog that still hovered over the road and fields. Joe's steady clip-clop-clip-clop upon the asphalt was a familiar and reassuring sound. They passed farm after farm in the rolling countryside, making steady progress through West Lampeter and finally arriving at the Strasburg train station by mid-morning; not talking but just enjoying one another's company. Leroy helped Rebecca down then tied up Joe to the hitching ring. Together they walked hand-in-hand inside the large train station and went to the nearest ticket booth.

"I wish to purchase a round trip ticket from Strasburg to Shipshewana, Indiana - departing next week."

The clerk checked her computer screen and punched a few keys. "That will be $125.00 total." Leroy pulled out his billfold and counted out six twenties and a five dollar bill, pushing it through the window.

"*Danki daed*," Rebecca murmured.

"*Gern gschehne my dochder*." He tucked the tickets and receipt back into his billfold and together they left the station. Then he paused as an idea popped into his head. He smiled invitingly at her. "Would you like to go the train museum while we are here as you used to?"

Rebecca's eyes lit up at the suggestion. Strasburg was home to a toy train museum that had five elaborate layouts where as a little child she used to love spending hours just gazing at the clever dioramas. When she was little her parents would make monthly pilgrimages there then follow it up with ice-cream at the Lapp Valley Farm which used milk from their cows in return for a small discount. They were wonderful memories. They spent the next hour admiring not only the trains but the reactions of other children who were seeing it all for the first time. Then it was a short buggy ride to Lapp's for ice-cream where they picked up a gallon each of chocolate and vanilla. They returned home in early afternoon. The clothesline was half hung with dresses, nightgowns, aprons, shirts, trousers and sheets. Mirriam, Mary and Hannah paused from their work to run out and greet them.

"We brought some Lapp's ice-cream!" Rebecca grinned, holding it up. Her sister's squealed with delight. "Let's get it into the freezer before it melts. Can we have it after supper tonight?"

"Just in time to help peg the wash, Becca!" Hannah informed her, hauling her out to the backyard. "We left the fitted sheets for you."

Rebecca grimaced. "Ach, Danki! You left the worst for last just for me!" They put the ice-cream into the propane powered freezer then returned to the backyard to finish pegging the laundry on the line. The warm breeze billowed out all the clothing like sails upon a many-masted ship. Leroy greeted his wife on the front porch and handed her the tickets.

I'll take the letter to the post office as soon as you have it written; I want to make sure it arrives at its intended destination. Where are the boys?"

"They finished the fence as you asked and are now in the barley field. I will be sorry to see them go, Leroy. I will miss having two such hard working boys on our farm, jah?"

"Jah – they have done much to help me but also much to trouble me," Leroy grunted; staring at his eldest daughter whom he must soon send away. As much as he had come to depend upon the brother's help the thought of how it was affecting Rebecca was causing him no end of stomach trouble. Her eyes had taken on dark circles; she was hardly eating and her once ready smile had disappeared. He feared for her welfare if things did not change soon. It was a great relief when Rebecca herself had suggested traveling to Indiana. He had every intention of making sure she stayed there until they could repair their ship and return from wherever it was they had come from.

Ruth turned to go into the house. "I'll write it now. There's some lemonade and lunch on the porch if you want."

"Danki" Leroy hitched Joe to the rail and gave him some oats as well as a pail of water before helping himself to the lemonade. There was also some leftover ham loaf and potato salad. He and his horse had just enough time to finish their respective meals when Ruth returned with the letter for the Miller's, advising them of the train number, date and time of Rebecca's arrival.

She handed it to him with a womanly giggle. "I feel like a covert spy in one of my suspense novels! Can you also bring me some items from town? I made a short list."

"Jah - when Seth and Silas come in from the fields have them muck out the cow stalls and pitch in some fresh hay. That ought to keep them preoccupied until I return." He untied Joe and looked across to his daughters who were laughing and chattering as they hung up the laundry; his heart filling with love for them. They were the apple of his eye. He would not have any of them hurt, not if he could help it! He left for the post office, dropped off the letter then went to grocers to pick up the flour, corn meal, dried beans, peas and sundries on the list, returning just in time to observe Seth and Silas heading for the barn. From their bowed heads and posture he could see they were exhausted. Gut! Better to keep him too busy with hard labor than to let him moon after his eldest. An idle mind is the devil's playground! He brought Joe and the buggy into the barn, unhitched him and curried him before covering him with a blanket and replenishing his hay. From the back of the barn he could hear the sound of the brothers speaking quietly in a foreign language as they shoveled the manure and carted it out in a wheelbarrow to dry in the sun. Once or twice he heard Rebecca's name mentioned. It would be a heavy load off his mind and heart once she was well on her way to Indiana and out of Seth's reach.

Leroy carried the groceries into the kitchen and handed them over to his wife. "Give the lads extra helpings for the gut work they have done today; enough to make them very drowsy after supper!"

"Jah," nodded Ruth, understanding his intent. "Ice-cream should do the trick!"

"Make sure it is only vanilla!"

Dinner that night was a heavy meat and potato combination with braised Brussels sprouts. There were also large glasses of milk instead of sweet tea or lemonade. Rebecca had just finished setting the table when the brothers trudged in to clean up at the kitchen sink. Her heart dropped; she had hoped they would stick to eating in the dawdi haus but apparently Seth had other ideas.

They had been out in the warm sun for the first half of the day working in the fields and the second half in the barn. They plunked down at the table out of sheer habit; closed their eyes and waited with droopy heads for the rest of the family to appear; already half asleep. Her father and sisters arrived moments later; covering their laughter with their hands before taking their seats; then all bowed their heads. That is when she heard it…Rebecca peeked at Seth and Silas from under her lashes. They were snoring; and in unison! Despite her emotional anguish a tickle of mirth pricked at her heart. Mary began to giggle first; following by Mirriam and then Hannah. Rebecca didn't want to laugh but couldn't force down the giggles which erupted from her throat. She ladled out helpings to the brothers after the blessing was given.

"Ach! Dat is not enough for two just hard working men!" her mother chided. "Give them a bit more, Rebecca!"

Rebecca dutifully scooped out two more large heaping portions and slapped them onto Seth and Silas' plates. They were so weighted down with food they almost dropped them. Although they were famished, it took them forever to eat. They were so tired they seemed to chew in slow motion. Mary and Mirriam had to take turns prodding them every few minutes during the entire meal so they would finish what had been put on their plate. Her mother had seasoned the meat extra well, which engendered much drinking of milk. Hannah and Rebecca exchanged looks; figuring out what their parents were up to and finding the entire thing hilariously funny. They erupted into intermittent giggles throughout dinner but the brothers were too tired to notice.

After the dishes were cleared Ruth carried in both gallons of ice-cream and set them on the table while the girls ran to get fresh spoons and small bowls. She scooped out hefty portions onto fresh berries for each of the boys who stared at it with weary curiosity.

Hannah spooned some chocolate into her mouth and sighed with pleasure. "Why aren't you eating? Haven't you ever had ice-cream before?"

"What is it?" asked Silas, sniffing at it.

"Frozen cream and sugar, *dummkopf* ! Try it! It's *wunderbar*!" she exclaimed.

Seth took the first taste and the moment it melted upon his tongue he was "hooked". "Mmmmmmmmmmmmmmm!" he exclaimed, waking up a bit. He shoveled an enormous spoonful into his mouth; with gusto.

"Careful!" warned Rebecca as Silas followed suit but it was too late. Both boys soon dropped their spoons and clutched their foreheads, gritting their teeth in agony.

"Ahhh! My brain is going to explode!" moaned Silas.

"What have you done to us?" Seth demanded, squeezing his eyes against the throbbing pain in his temples. They writhed in agony.

"Ach! You did it to yourselves!" Ruth laughed, covering her mouth with her hand. Even Leroy could not hide a smile.

"Did what?" Seth and Silas laid their pounding skulls into their arms upon the table, still moaning and squirming.

"You gave yourselves brain freeze!" Mirriam exclaimed. "It happens when you eat too much cold stuff at once, *dummkopfs*!"

The pain soon passed. From then on the brothers took much smaller bites and suffered no further insult.

Dessert finished, the girls rose to clear the dishes. Rebecca's mom relieved her of her armful. "Rebecca – would you draw water for hot baths? I think Seth and Silas should be rewarded for all their hard work today."

Rebecca stared at her. "Soaking bathes?" she asked incredulously. A soaking bath was a rare and incredibly extravagant treat. Something they had rarely experienced; having taken sponge baths most of their lives.

"Jah," Ruth confirmed, looking her right in the eye.

"Jah, mamm," she agreed, wondering if this was to be a nightly ritual until she left. It was so transparent: work them hard, wear them out, fill their bellies, warm their weary muscles and ensure an exhausted night's sleep with no interruptions. Rebecca picked up several large pails, filled them with water from the pump sink and lugged them into the dawdi haus while her mother put a large kettle on to boil. Silas and Seth were completely oblivious. They may have been well educated on the ways of the 'plain folk' where they had come from, but subterfuge was obviously not one of them. It took several trips but soon there was a steaming hot bath for both of them. Leroy had moved one of his larger water-tight containers into the dawdi haus which was just big enough to accommodate a young man. Ruth handed them bars of soap and some towels and shut the door on them while her daughters finished cleaning up the kitchen in the main house. After an hour Ruth began to grow concerned that that one or both of them had fallen asleep and drowned in the process. At her urging Leroy poked his head in to check on them and found them both half-submerged, their heads lolling back, snoring softly. Satisfied, he helped his wife to get them toweled off and dressed them. Then they half carried/half walked them to their beds as Hannah, Mirriam and Mary watched through the windows; giggling uncontrollably. Their father had never, ever done such a thing in all their lives so it was truly a sight to behold.

If Rebecca had not been pining for Seth she too might have found the entire scene funny. At least there would be no late evening summons tonight; her parents had made sure of that. She wondered how they had found out about them.

This routine was repeated daily for the rest of the week leading up to Rebecca's departure. Each night she sat in her rocker with her book open; unable to concentrate or think of anything besides Seth; a hollow feeling growing in her heart where his feelings had once found safe harbor. She should have been relieved and grateful but instead she missed and longed for his voice and gorgeous silver eyes. Instead of reading her book her eyes would just stare unseeingly at the page while she relived in her mind how it felt to be wrapped possessively in his arms and kissed over and over again. Seth filled a void in her soul she had not known existed until the moment he had appeared at the barn raising. The thought of being with him terrified her and the thought of leaving him devastated her. She shouldn't tempt fate but couldn't seem to help herself. She closed her eyes for just a moment, allowing her thoughts to reach out to him. Nothing. She tried harder but still got no response. She sighed, opening her eyes just in time to see a shooting star blaze across the night sky.

Rebecca closed her book and laid it next to her packed suitcase. Tomorrow she would leave for her cousin's and would never see Seth again. If only she could have bid him a final goodbye. She crawled in next to Hannah and lay there; staring up at the ceiling, waiting for sleep to come.

Chapter Ten
"Rumspringa Abroad"

Rebecca rose before the dawn and looked out her window hoping to catch a glimpse of the brothers before they disappeared into the barn. She could see the faint light of a kerosene lamp bobbing up and down as her father entered to harness Joe to the buggy but the brothers were nowhere to be seen. Evidently her father wanted them to sleep in this morning until she was safely on her way. Rebecca clutched her shawl about her as she visited the outhouse then returned to the warm kitchen where her mother was already busy frying eggs and baking the morning biscuits.

"Guder mariye, my dochder!" greeted Ruth, kissing her forehead. "Do you have everything ready? I will be missing you sorely these next few months!"

Rebecca wrapped her arms about her mother's waist, hiding her face in her shoulder. "I will miss you too, mamm," came her muffled voice.

"Hurry now and get dressed; thy train leaves very early, jah? There is a basket on the counter so you and your daed can eat on the way to Strasburg. I have packed all your favorites: cinnamon rolls, spiced compote and hot coffee."

Hot tears leaked from under Rebecca's eyelashes. She was really going to miss her mother terribly. "I love you, mamm."

Ruth stopped what she was doing to embrace her. "Rebecca! *Es wird nichts so heiß gegessen, wie es gekocht wird* (things are never as bad as they seem)," she murmured.

Rebecca clung to her. She loved the smell and feel of her mother; loved the sound of her gentle voice. She felt ashamed of herself: here she had been obsessing only about Seth and forgetting how very much she would miss her home and family. She had not realized until this very moment how much she would miss the most important person in her life: her mother. Before separating, Rebecca kissed her mother on both cheeks then gave her a fierce embrace.

At that moment her father appeared in the doorframe. "We must be off if we are to make your train in time." He picked up Rebecca's suitcase. "When the boys get up send them out to work the north field today," he informed his wife. "They have a lot to do so you might want to have one of the girls bring lunch out to them later."

Her sisters came into the kitchen and each one gave her a hug and kiss goodbye. Rebecca took the basket from the counter and clutched her shawl tightly about her; trudging through the front door as if going to her own execution. She cast a glance at the dawdi haus hoping to catch one last glimpse of Seth; her heart sinking when she did not. She would never see him again; never feel his embrace or taste his kisses again. The sudden dose of reality just made her feel more despondent than ever. She climbed into the carriage. She needed to use this time away to forget him and learn to think of Jacob as her future husband. The thought was anything but comforting.

Her father climbed up beside her and flicked the reigns. With a short jerk, Joe turned the buggy about, trotting down the driveway for the main road which led towards Strasburg.

"Pour me some coffee from the thermos, *sei so gut*," her father requested; unable to use his hands. Rebecca untwisted the cap, carefully pouring the hot liquid for him and handed it over before pouring some for herself. She did her best to eat the fragrant cinnamon buns but they only seemed to stick in her throat regardless of how much coffee she drank. Her father pretended not to notice; eating as he guided Joe through the undulating countryside. It was so early there were hardly any other buggies or cars on the road. They arrived at the Strasburg Train Station a half hour later where a few commuters were already standing about, checking on their train's schedule. Leroy tied Joe up then helped Rebecca down; carrying her small suitcase for her. All it contained was a few changes of clothes, her Bible, brush, extra kapp and toothbrush. They walked hand-in-hand until they found platform #9. The train was already there, its loud engines idling. Rebecca climbed onboard and took the basket and suitcase from her father.

"Der Herr be with thee, my dochder. Write us as soon as you arrive."

"Jah, papa."

Leroy kissed her forehead and stepped down as she made her way inside to find a seat near a window. She settled down and waved at him through the glass, putting on her bravest smile. To her amazement, her father's eyes were moist with tears. Suddenly she wished she had hugged him longer and told him how important he was to her.

It must be a difficult thing to let your eldest take wing, she thought to herself. The train gave off a warning blast on its horn and began to slowly move forward. Leroy kept pace down the platform, waving goodbye until he could go no further, then he was lost from Rebecca's view. She settled back in her seat with a shuddering sigh; allowing the tears to flow freely. She no longer cared about putting on a brave face. Had she done the right thing in leaving?

A hand stretched out with a handkerchief. "Don't cry, Becca,"

Rebecca jumped and clapped her hand over her mouth; her eyes growing larger and larger as she stared at the person only two feet away from her across the aisle. It was Seth and he was grinning from ear to ear. All she could do was gape at him; not sure if she was imagining him or not.

"Come here," he beckoned to the empty seat beside him. Without thinking of how improper it looked, she flew across the aisle and into his waiting arms. The *Englisch* passengers didn't give it a second thought but those who were Amish eyed the two of them with stern disapproval. Rebecca was instantly aware of her *feaux pas*. For his part, Seth was so overjoyed at her response that he thought nothing of hugging her back until he caught a glare from an older Amish woman.

"Cousin Rebecca!!" he exclaimed louder than he had to. This seemed to mollify the small group of Amish travelers. They turned back to their books, knitting, and private conversations.

Rebecca suddenly came to her senses. "What are you doing here?" she demanded in a fierce whisper. "When daed finds you missing he will put two and two together and then I will surely be shunned!"

"I'm going on Rumspringa with you," Seth informed her. "I teleported to Strasburg and got on the train before you did. Your daed will never 'miss me' because I am in the time in-between time." He held up the mysterious pocket watch which defied the natural laws of nature. It was the same device he had used months ago to take her to Southern California.

He held her hands, staring at her with a sad smile. "I tried to stay away, Becca. I really did," he whispered. "I understand what you're doing and why but I-I just couldn't let you go and then return to my world without at least a memory to take with me; something that would make spending the rest of my life separated from you by millions of light years more tolerable."

Rebecca stared at him; her heart swelling with pain. "I understand," she nodded.

Seth stared deeply into her eyes. "I know you do." His sad smile almost broke her heart. How could she possibly deny him when her own heart ached to do the very same thing?

"I promise to behave properly if only you will agree."

Rebecca paused a long time; weighing the potential consequences such an adventure could bring then concluded she couldn't get much more heartbroken than she already was. "Very well, Seth...a lifetime of memories to take home with you," she agreed, laying her small hands in his. He clasped them gently but firmly, intertwining his fingers through her own so that she could not tell which were whose.

Seth leaned close; ready to give her a kiss but then remembered where they were and sat back, still holding her hands.

He changed the conversation by shaking his head. "Rebecca Esh, you suffer from an appalling lack of curiosity."

She blinked at him. "I what?"

"Still not one question about myself! Where I come from or what my world is like? Aren't you the least bit curious?"

Rebecca glanced about them fearfully. "Sssh! You are speaking too loudly! Some of these people are from my district! Do you want word to get back?"

"I wouldn't be too concerned: look closer." Seth replied. Rebecca leaned past him and carefully looked around. Then she did a double take. The scenery outside the train windows was blurred and frozen in place and all the passengers as well. It looked like she was sitting inside a life-sized diorama. "Now look outside again," he whispered, putting his arm about her shoulders to cushion the coming shock.

Rebecca twisted her head around and looked outside. Instead of the familiar Pennsylvania countryside with its Amish farm houses and barns, she found herself looking at a tall range of mountains with craggy peaks tipped with snow. In the foothills below the peaks she saw castles and below them what looked like quaint German villages. Sudden nausea swept over her as she lost her equilibrium. The world about her rotated crazily and she blacked out.

Seth has been expecting this reaction. Rebecca fell heavily against him. He held her close in his arms; waiting for the effects of the space/time travel to wear off. For the first time in over a week he could openly admire her golden eyebrows, pale lashes and porcelain skin. He felt both protective and possessive of her. He knew that she was trying to leave in the hopes of beginning a new life…a life that did not include him. A life that would see her joined to another man…Jacob Zimmer. A wave of heat washed over him. The thought of her being embraced and kissed by anyone other than him made him physically ill. He knew with every fiber of his being that they belonged together. If only he could communicate with the king, he felt that they could find a way to be together!

Rebecca slowly began to wake up. Seth waited patiently for her eyes to open, placing a gentle kiss between her brows.

Her eyes flew open and she instantly sat up. "Where are we?" She looked out the train windows again to see the bucolic German scenery. She turned around to stare at him; her face a mixture of disbelief and slowly dawning delight. "Are we really in Germany?"

The expression on her face was his undoing. Seth leaned in and placed a brief kiss upon her lips.

"Oops, I promised I wouldn't do that," he chided himself with a grin. Rebecca's head swam with the effect it had upon her; unable to believe she had done such a forward thing in public. She glanced warily about the cabin at the other passengers only to discover that they had all changed identities. Instead of *Plain* and *Englisch* passengers she saw tourists with cameras, businessmen in suits working on laptops and young adults with backpacks. They were no longer 'frozen' but talking amongst themselves in German, Dutch, French and other languages she could not identify. All were completely oblivious to the kiss she had shared with Seth. Seth continued smirking at her then did a slow, appreciate once-over appraisal which made her extremely nervous. It was a good thing she was dressed plainly or she would have thought…she looked down at herself and immediately gasped in horror. She was no longer in her blue dress, black apron, bonnet and shawl. She was attired in blue jeans, a long-sleeved white cotton top and her hair was hanging loosely down past her shoulders! She went beet red.

"Don't panic!" Seth calmed her, patting her hand. "You look like any other plain girl who has gone on Rumspringa. I thought you might like to see the origins of your family before going to Indiana?"

This brought her up short immediately. She covered her mouth with her hand; her eyes going wide. "Ach, no! The Millers! They are going to be frantic with worry if I don't show up tonight."

Seth cupped her face in his hands. "Rebecca, do you honestly think I would do anything to jeopardize your standing in your community? You will arrive on schedule in Indiana tonight at 7:00 pm and no one will ever know that you spent Rumspringa in Bavaria, Germany.

She stared at him aghast. "Then what about you? My daed will be greatly alarmed when he discovers you missing; he may even suspect…"

"-nothing." Seth interrupted. "He will suspect nothing. I have slowed down time in order to be with you," He held up his strange pocket watch. "For every hour that passes in Lancaster County a full day and night will have passed in ours. You will arrive in Indiana with no one the wiser and Silas will cover for me until supper time. Your mamm sent us to work in the fields all day after he left for the train station. We have at least 6 days here…or 6 hours local Lancaster time to spend together; making some wonderful memories."

Rebecca dropped her head in her hands, struggling to understand. It was all so confusing.

Seth continued. "I promise to treat you with the utmost respect and courtesy; I won't even kiss you anymore if you don't wish me to…"

Rebecca looked back up at him at this; her heart pounding. The emotional pain she had bottled up inside her for the past few weeks suddenly drained away. For the next six days she could forget about the rest of the world and just be with him. Her other friends had done a lot worse during their running around years (drinking, experimenting with drugs, body piercings, illicit sex)…she leaned forward and kissed his cheek of her own accord then rested her forehead against his, re-entwining their fingers.

"I may let you kiss me," she finally confessed with a deep sigh. "My heart has been yours since you dragged me through the hydrangea bush."

Seth nodded and slowly sat back; taking in the full impact of her admission. Her heart was his and that was enough. "There is so much in this world of yours I would like us to see together, Becca! I wish we had more time together but six days will have to be enough."

Rebecca suddenly frowned. "Six days also means six nights; what are we going to do about those?"

Seth gave her a wicked smile and leaned close as he whispered. "I'm afraid we shall be sleeping in separate rooms; as far apart as can be arranged."

Rebecca turned a furious red. "Ach how you tease! What else besides my 'origins' in Germany would you like to show me?"

"I would love for us to stroll along The Champs-Elysées in Paris, France or share a picnic lunch in Tuscany, Italy among the sunflower fields."

Rebecca's eyes sparkled with anticipation. "Can we really do all those things? Won't it cost a lot of money!"

"I put some aside from the proceeds of the quilt auction," Seth replied, showing her a small wad of cash.

Rebecca's eyes grew wide. "I've always wanted to travel and see the world, Seth…how did you know?"

"I felt it in your heart," he replied quietly. "I feel what you feel, remember? It was your heart that drew me to you…to Earth…to Lancaster County; I could feel you calling out to me from light years away; I just didn't know what it was until I saw you at the barn-raising."

Rebecca took this in and after a long pause nodded. "I never told anyone this but in the past year or so when I couldn't sleep, I would look out my window up at the stars and…"

"…and what?" Seth whispered, his silver eyes beginning to glow with a light that reminded her of the very stars she was telling him of.

"Pray. I would pray to Derr Herr to bring me the one he had chosen for me,"

Seth merely stared at her as if in shock.

"*Was ist los?*" she asked him.

"That was about the same time I had the calling to go on discovery."

"Seth, do you think…could it be at all possible…?"

"Becca – until I can make contact with my king and find out for sure I dare not assume anything."

A tiny flicker of hope kindled inside Rebecca. "Seth…suppose you were able to make contact with him and, and he confirmed that we…that you and I…I mean…what then?"

"Becca I'm almost too afraid to hope," he replied, "but if I could finally speak with him and learn his mind…and he gave us his blessing then nothing in the universe could keep me from you! I would stay here and become your husband."

"You would have to become a Christian first and be baptized."

Seth took her by the shoulders, his face deadly serious. "I will become whatever I have to be, my dearest Rebecca; just so we will not be parted from one another ever again."

Rebecca swallowed hard and nodded. "Then you must make every effort to contact him and find out. At the same time I will pray and seek Derr Herr."

The matter thus settled, at least for the time being, Seth turned the conversation back to a lighter topic. He sat back in the seat with her hands in his.

"I would like to show it all to you but since we only have six days I thought we would start here first. Have you ever been to Disneyland or seen picture of it?"

She shook her head, excitement beginning to build. "Nee, why?" She had heard of the "Magic Kingdom" from her other friends who had run around and visited Southern California. It had sounded like a wonderful place. "Never." She glanced out the window again and saw what looked like to be a fairytale type castle far off perched on a lone hill. She pointed. "Is that where you are taking me?"

Seth nodded. "It is called the Neuschwanstein castle or "Cinderella" castle."

Rebecca continued to stare at it in awe. "It's beautiful."

Seth kissed her hand and clutched it to his chest in unmistakable glee. "Just wait until you see it up close! The inside is magnificent!"

"Jah?"

In Plain Sight

Seth pulled a brochure from a backpack he had stowed under the seat and read aloud. "Listen to this: *King Ludwig II started construction of Neuschwanstein in 1869. It took over 24 years to build at a cost of $89 million dollars at the time. The double-storey throne room reaches fifteen metres in height and is encircled by galleries on both floors. Its extravagant decorations dazzle in gold and blue and the walls depict canonised kings performing noble deeds..."*

Leroy arrived home to find several buggies parked in his driveway. One of them he recognized as that belonging to Bishop Fisher. A sense of foreboding settled upon him as he tied Joe up and walked up the porch steps into his home. As he guessed, Bishop Fisher was there as was Bishop King, Deacon Yoder and Isaac Miller. All had their backs turned to him when he came through the screen door but the stricken look on Ruth's face made his heart drop. They turned when they heard him enter the family room.

Isaac looked him directly in the eye, his mouth set in a grim line. "Leroy, something has happened."

A lump formed in Leroy's throat. He gestured to some chairs. "Won't you please be seated?" They remained standing...an ominous sign.

"There has been more crop destruction, Mr. Esh." Bishop King informed him with a frown.

"...and more livestock missing," added Deacon Yoder.

The news hit Leroy like a ton of bricks. The community had gone back to normal for a few weeks; ever since Silas had used the banker's ham radio but it had been short-lived. Normally he would have commiserated with the news and wondered along with them as to who was behind it all but the looks on their faces spoke plainly whom they already suspected.

"You have been harboring those...those...strange boys here for months, jah?"

Leroy nodded. His eyes strayed back to Ruth who looked terrified and was twisting her apron in both hands. "They were hungry and asked if they could work in exchange for food and shelter. I did what any good Christian man would do. They have been good workers."

"My entire field of soybeans is ruined." Isaac said; his usually friendly faced strained. "I was days away from the harvest and now it is a total loss. My cows are gone too; every last one of them."

Leroy stared at him in shock. "I am so sorry, Isaac. I will do everything in my power to help, you know that! The boys could not be responsible for this travesty." He blurted out.

"How do you know this?" interjected Deacon Yoder suspiciously. "Do they always do their chores under your direct supervision?"

"No, it has not been necessary," Leroy said, feeling as though he had just plunged a spade into the ground to dig his own grave. It was an odd and shameful sensation to feel guilty for something you weren't sure you were responsible for.

"Do you never send them into the fields while your attention is elsewhere?"

Another shovelful. "Yes, but they have proven to me that they can be trusted."

"They have been of great help to Leroy," Ruth interjected, stepping forward. "They have become like sons to us. They have not given us any cause for worry."

Bishop King turned from her to Leroy. "Is this true? No cause at all?"

Leroy hesitated for but an instant; his thoughts immediately seizing upon Rebecca which they instantly misinterpreted.

"Mr. Esh, if you are willing to make restitution on their behalf to Mr. Miller we will consider the matter closed for the time being..."

"Of course I will." Leroy began but was interrupted by Bishop King's upraised palm.

"However, if there are any more of these strange incidents a district meeting will be called. You best speak to those boys and explain clearly to them what the consequences of their actions can be." They turned to go, tilting their hats to Ruth. "Gut morgan, Mrs. Esh."

Leroy stood mutely, watching his best friend, Deacon Yoder and Bishop King leave without so much as a handshake; another ominous sign. Isaac's rebuff hurt more than their veiled threats. The screen door closed softly behind them. Leroy waited until their buggies turned into the lane then faced his wife. "Where are the boys?"

"They are working in the fields." Ruth replied softly, her face creased with anxiety. "Leroy, I'm sure there must be a good explanation for all this."

Leroy reached into a kitchen cabinet and pulled out a tin box that held a good portion of their savings. He would have to go to the bank to get the rest. He hoped it was enough. He paused at the front door. "I should have given him this while Isaac was here but I was in too much shock. I am going to the bank and then on to Isaac's farm to recompense him. When I return I want to have a serious talk with both of them. They were supposed to have put a stop to all this weeks ago."

Hannah, Mirriam and Mary appeared just in time to hear these last few words. "What is wrong, daed?" They looked from their father to their mother and back again; having never seen them look so worried.

Ruth drew her daughters close to her side. "Leroy, I know those boys; they made us a solemn promise; they could not be responsible for this mischief!"

Leroy closed his eyes. "I know this too but it won't matter. Obviously their message did not reach all their people. It won't matter to the bishop, Deacon or Isaac who did these things. The boys will be held responsible regardless, as will we for harboring them because of the nature of the destruction. If this continues our entire family could be expelled from the community. We could lose everything." He turned to go, his heart leaden. Though he felt certain it had not been Seth or Silas who had destroyed Isaac's crop, the accusing look in his best friend's eyes was more than he could bear. Though it broke his heart to do so, he would have to turn the boys out of his farm; he could not allow his family to suffer such dire consequences.

Rebecca and Seth alighted from the train and stepped out on the platform at the Füssen train station. Seth held her hand as he guided her through the crowds, out onto the street and to a nearby bus station. Rebecca could not help but marvel at his efficiency and courtesy. He opened doors for her and insisted on carrying her suitcase as well as his own heavy backpack. The air was warm and scented with the smell of wildflowers. He purchased two tickets and soon they were boarding the bus towards Schwangau which would take them to the village of Hohenschwangau. Rebecca could not tear her eyes away from the scenery as it rolled by. It reminded her of Lancaster but behind the rolling foothills were tall majestic mountain peaks. Lush fields of alfalfa and hay passed them by as well as fields of sheep and goats grazing interspersed with picturesque villages. Before long the bus arrived in Hohenschwangau. Rebecca's anticipation at seeing a real castle was making her giddy with excitement. Seth took her hand again and guided her to the Hotel Müller where horse drawn carriages were lined up.

Seth pointed. "Choose! Hiking on foot, tour bus or horse drawn carriage, milady?"

Rebecca covered her excited smile with both hands, hardly daring to breath. She pointed to an open carriage pulled by two snow white Andalusia horses. "Buggy of course!"

Seth slapped his forehead. *"I'm a dummkopf...Amish!"* He walked up to the driver and handed him some money, extending his hand to help Rebecca up. "Milady?"

Rebecca giggled and accepted his assistance, sitting down on the luxurious leather. Seth climbed in beside her. "I feel like Cinderella!" she whispered, admiring the beautiful carriage. Unlike the other buggies lined up in the queue to transport visitors up to the castle, theirs was a high gloss white with red upholstery and bedecked with real flowers and a two-seater. The driver wore special livery that harkened back to the 1800s. He flicked his whip and the horses took off at a brisk clip, their harnesses jingling merrily with tiny silver bells. They wound their way slowly up the steep road which led towards the castle.

"Are you sure we are on the right road?" Rebecca asked, observing that they were the only ones. She saw no pedestrians, cars or other carriages.

"Absolutely," Seth murmured, brushing the top of her hand with his lips. Rebecca did a double-take. Except for his silver eyes, his entire appearance had changed. He was wearing clothing that reminded her of the fairytale picture books she loved to read as a child. He even had a dark green cloak clasped at the throat with a golden chain and jeweled broaches.

She ogled him. *"Was in der welt?"*

Seth grinned. "You don't look too bad yourself, Becca!"

Rebecca glanced down and gasped. Instead of blue jeans and the plain cotton top she now found herself in the most exquisite, full length gown of midnight blue velvet, bedecked with pearls and gold stitching all down the sleeves with a caplet to match on top of her flowing hair. "*Was in der welt?*" she repeated. It was definitely not plain! "Change me back at once!" she hissed, laying her hands over her exposed collar bone.

Seth was struggling not to laugh. "Change you back to what? Jeans and t-shirt or plain and simple? Make up your mind!"

"I can't be seen like this!"

"Why not?"

"...because!" Rebecca sputtered, turning murderous eyes on him. "It isn't plain!"

Seth waggled a disapproving finger in her face. "Rumspringa!" he grinned by way of explanation. "If you don't like this I can always model your outfit after say....hmmmm...the infamous Hannah Yoder!"

Rebecca drew away from him with horror at the thought. Hannah Yoder had been one of her good friends until she had left to run around the year before. She had never returned to her family and there had been talk that she had become like "the English". Rebecca and her family had been present in the Yoder's home when Hannah's parents had received a certified letter postmarked from Philadelphia. It contained a brief letter stating that she was not returning and had a photograph of a young woman they no longer recognized as their plain daughter. Hannah's hair had been cut short, spiked straight out in all directions and sported every color of the rainbow. Her nose, eyebrows and ears had multiple piercings and her bare arms were covered with tattoos. Her parents had mourned her as one dead and prayed for their daughter to come to her senses but so far nothing had been heard from her in months.

"How do you know about Hannah Yoder?"

"Ah...now you finally ask a question!" Seth replied. "Are you sure you want to know the answer? It will be difficult to hear it."

Rebecca withdrew her hand and thoughtfully chewed her lip. Was this really a road she was ready to travel down? Of course she had been always been curious about him and where he had come from; she had just been too scared to ask about it. "Not yet, I think," she replied softly to the steady clip clop of the horses along the steep road. "Can't you just answer my question about Hannah Yoder? Do you know how she is? Do you know if she will ever come back?"

Seth laid his hand on top of hers. "You really miss your friend, don't you?"

Rebecca nodded. "We are all very worried about her; there has been no word for months now."

"If you knew the truth it would be much worse." Seth replied and immediately regretted it.

Rebecca's head snapped up. "What do you mean? Is she in some kind of trouble?"

Seth fingered his pocket watch and closed his eyes, concentrating intently. In the blink of an eye he faded from view and reappeared again. "She has gotten herself mixed up with some very bad people," he replied. "They lured her into a snare months ago by making false promises and have been holding her captive since. They make a habit of preying off innocent girls who venture into the big city alone. They made her write the letter and change her appearance so her parents would think it was all her idea."

Rebecca clapped a hand over her mouth, horrified. "I don't know how you know all this but we must do something! Now! Immediately!"

As much as he wanted to argue with her, Seth knew she was right. He could not in good conscience insist continuing on to tour to the castle as though nothing were wrong when her friend was in mortal danger. "This will not be easy on you," he warned. "I may have to do and say things to get her out of there that are not in accord with the Ordnung. Do you understand?"

Rebecca nodded, terrified but determined to rescue her friend.

Seth adjusted the tiny knobs on the watch. *"Daumen drücken* (cross your fingers)!" The next instant the world about her contorted and the usual nausea swept over her. The carriage, horses and German countryside vanished and were replaced by a dark hallway with filthy doors on either side. The cries and screams of young children could be heard coming from within various apartments.

Seth placed a hand over her mouth. "Don't scream," he whispered, pointing down. A rat the size of a small cat scurried past them and disappeared around a corner. It was only his hand over her mouth that muffled the scream that rose in her throat. He waited until she calmed down and raised a finger to his lips. "Stay right here and no matter what happens, don't move. I'll need you to draw Hannah out of that room so we can teleport together back to her home." Rebecca glanced down at herself and saw that she was back in her plain clothes again. She looked back up at him then went pale as Seth withdrew a gun from the back pocket of his blue jeans. Where had that come from? What was he going to do with that?

From the other side of the door came a whimper. It was Hannah! Seth threw himself bodily against the door, tearing it from its hinges. Inside Hannah screamed. He stumbled inside the dank room and caught his balance just before crashing into two large men. Rebecca watched from the hallway struggling not to scream. Two large, scary looking brutes were on either side of her friend. One had her short spiky hair in his grip and the other's arm was poised in mid-swing. Her face was black and blue and her eyes almost swollen shut. They froze; caught completely off-guard.

Before they could react, Seth was pointing the gun at them. "Let her go...now." He ordered in a no-nonsense voice. The two men complied, lifting their arms high and staring in shock at his silver eyes which were glowing white-hot with rage. Rebecca hurried forward and grasped hold of her friend.

"Please don't hurt me!" Hannah whimpered, unable to recognize Rebecca through her swollen eyes.

"It's me, Rebecca Esh! Come with me now, Hannah!" She put her arm about her and propelled her through the door while Seth covered their escape. "Don't be afraid! Come with me!" Together they stumbled into the hallway. Seth slowly backed away, his gun still aimed at the two thugs. "Rebecca, I need you to hold this!"

Rebecca stared at him. Surely he was not asking her to hold a gun?

"I can't teleport us back! I need my hands free!"

Rebecca shook her head vigorously. "Do not ask this of me! *Ich kam sell neh geh!*" Then she watched in horror as the two thugs slowly lowered their arms and began advancing on him with dangerous sneers.

"Rebecca!" Seth growled, one hand pointing the gun, the other fishing for his pocket watch.

The thugs drew closer, sensing they had an opportunity to exploit. "Wassa matter, sonny boy?" one of them sneered, edging closer. "Pretty little Amish girl won't obey your commands?"

"Looks like we got three for the price of one," said the other, looking Rebecca slowly up and down. It filled her with disgust but she still could not bring herself to take the gun from Seth.

"Rebeccaaaaaaaaaaaa!" he pleaded. The thugs were almost within arm's reach of him.

Someone stepped in front of Rebecca, took the gun from Seth and pointed it at eye level at the two men. It was Hannah. Months of beatings and abuse had hardened her. Her arms trembled as she pointed it at them. Not out of fear but out of rage.

"No!" she told them. "NO MORE! I am going home to my family!" They froze; the look in her eyes telling them she was in deadly earnest.

"Got it!" cried Seth pulling Hannah by the waist into the hallway where Rebecca stood still rooted to the floor. The movement caused her fingers to squeeze the trigger. Instead of a loud BANG a stream of water squirted directly into the nearest thug's face.

"Why you!" he bellowed, running forward to tackle her. His arms encircled empty air and his body fell with a heavy thud onto the floor. It was too late…all three of them had vanished into thin air right before his eyes.

The next thing Rebecca knew they were standing in the Yoder's front yard. She experienced just a brief moment of passing nausea but poor Hannah had fallen to her knees and was retching onto the grass. Rebecca knelt by her friend's side.

"Rebecca we can't linger here," Seth warned. At that moment Hannah's mother came around the corner of the house with an armful of clean laundry.

"Hannah? HANNAH!" The laundry fell in a cascade onto the ground as she rushed across the yard towards her daughter.

Seth grabbed Rebecca's hand and yanked her behind a shrub, feverishly working the tiny dials on his watch.

"Hurry!" squeaked Rebecca, panic rising. "She mustn't see us!"

Mrs. Yoder knelt beside her daughter, tears of joy streaming down her face then her attention was drawn to the bush. "Rebecca Esh, is that you?" She left her daughter for a moment to peer around it then rubbed her eyes. For a split second she thought she had seen Rebecca and an Amish boy huddled upon the ground but now there was nothing. She stood and turned about in a full 360 degree circle, scanning the horizon then rubbed her eyes again.

"Mamm?" moaned Hannah.

She hurried to her daughter's side and clutched her to her breast, rocking her with fresh tears. "*De Herr sie gedankt! De Herr sie gedankt!* (thank the Lord)"

"Mamm I'm so sorry," Hannah sobbed. "I was held against my will; they altered my appearance..."

Seth collapsed back against the carriage cushions, shutting his eyes and breathing heavily. "That was too close."

Rebecca looked about her. They were back in the white carriage, and no further up the hill than when they had "left". The driver hadn't so much as even turned around to see what was going on. It seemed like they had been gone no longer than a "blink of the eye". She turned back to Seth and took his hand in hers; he was trembling. "*Danki, danki* for rescuing my friend."

"I may have just jeopardized everything by doing so," Seth sighed. "No doubt she will tell her mother who it was that rescued her and what happened. If we're lucky they might attribute it to drug abuse but I'm pretty sure Mrs. Yoder got a glimpse of us before we teleported back here."

The full weight of his words pressed in upon Rebecca's heart. What would await them when they returned home? It was all so confusing jumping in-between time and traveling vast distances without moving. She drew his hand up to her cheek. "You rescued my friend from a horrible fate and for that I will always be grateful."

Seth turned his head to look at her, his silver eyes blazing with an intense light. A rush of warmth swept over Rebecca that issued straight from his heart. The world around her faded from view; all she could see were his beautiful eyes. They stared intensely at one another for a few moments.

"Rebecca," he whispered, leaning towards her. Their lips met briefly then he drew back, a sheepish grin on his face. "I keep forgetting myself."

Rebecca nodded; she ached to kiss him also. The carriage pulled to a stop and the driver helped both of them down. That was when she finally took real notice of the castle rising high above her. She tilted her head way, way back; her mouth hanging open in awe.

"It's just like a fairytale!" She looked around. "Why are we the only tourists?"

Seth shrugged but his smile made it evident that he had done something to arrange it so. Together they walked through a short tunnel and stepped out onto an iron bridge that crossed a deep chasm with a waterfall far below. The height was dizzying.

"This is the Marienbrücke over the Pöllat Gorge." Seth read from the brochure.

Rebecca shook her head. She was terrified of heights. "Ach! You're narrish if you think I'm walking across that!" Her stomach was churning.

Seth held out his hand; his smile irresistible. "Yes you are," he coaxed. Rebecca continued to shake her head, imploring him but he ignored it, walking backwards with her hand in his. "Just keep looking in my eyes and don't look down."

She walked a few more paces and felt the wind upon her face; it billowed out her velvet dress like a wind sock. Down below she could hear the rush of the waterfall. "Don't look down!" Seth reminded her. After a few moments she was across the bridge. He kissed her forehead. "That's my brave girl." The ordeal over, she continued on a bit more bravely then found herself standing before the castle gatehouse. Hand in hand they entered the first level to explore the throne room, grotto, singer's hall, salon and kitchen.

Jessica Lynch turned to her office neighbor, a seasoned reporter who had been with their station, WGAL, for over 20 years.

"Hey Hal; just got off the phone with my buddy over at the Pine Grove Police Department."

"Yeah?"

"Remember the story we did about that Amish girl who ran away from home about a year ago?"

"Barely,"

"The story about Rumspringa gone haywire? The girl who went all Goth? You know, tattoos, body piercings…the whole nine yards?"

"Oh yeah….poor parents. What a shame," Hal nodded.

"Well seems like she just appeared out of thin air on her parent's front lawn today, tattoos and all. Seems she was abducted into white slavery and miraculously got away. They're filing a report over the parent's protests. Think we should do a follow up piece? *Amish girl learns lesson the hard way!"*

"You'll have to run it by Gil first, Jess." Hal replied, meaning their producer.

"Already on it!" Jessica grinned.

Leroy slowed the buggy down as he approached Isaac Miller's farm; having just come from withdrawing most of his savings from the bank. Isaac's soybean field ran along the highway and as far as the eye could see it was scorched black; a smoking ruin. Leroy's heart sunk to the depths of his soul. Isaac had not exaggerated; it was a total loss and just before the harvest! If Leroy lived two lifetimes he could not save enough money to recompense him for all the damage done. He fought down the anger which rose in his heart. What kind of people did the boys belong to who could do such a malicious, senseless thing? He turned his buggy onto the road which led to the Miller's house and soon drew up before the barn. Isaac, Bishops King and Fisher were there, as well as Deacon Yoder and a few other families. All ceased speaking and turned to see who had come. Silence fell.

With leaden feet, Leroy stepped down and approached his dearest friend.

"Isaac," he said, unable to meet his friend's eyes. "I do not know who or what is responsible for the damage to your fields but I have come to offer my help." He held forth the wad of cash.

Isaac stared at him; struggling with his emotions. He knew his friend was offering him all he had. "Danki, Leroy, but I cannot accept the money. The good Lord gives; and the good Lord takes away; shall I not receive the bad as well as the good from His hand?"

"At least allow us to help you plow under the field and replant it for the next harvest. I will pay for all the new seed."

"Us?" repeated Deacon Yoder, his brow furrowing with disapproval. "Do you mean to include those two...boys you are harboring on your farm?"

"Yes, they are good workers." Leroy replied, turning to him. "I know they have strange eyes and come from...another community...but as long as they have been with us they have abided by the Ordnung. They could not have done this thing; I have worked them to the bone this past week."

"If this is so then why do you offer me your life savings?" Isaac asked softly.

Leroy squared his shoulders and looked his friend straight in the eye. "Because you are my closest friend, Isaac, and I would not see our friendship damaged for anything. The boys and I will be back here first thing in the morning with our team and we will not rest until your field is replanted." He extended his hand, not sure Isaac would take it.

All fell silent, wondering what Isaac would do. He heaved a heavy sigh, closed his eyes, and grasped Leroy's hand in both of his. "You are my good friend," he whispered. "I welcome your help."

With a nod to the bishops, deacon and others standing about, Leroy returned to his buggy and drove home much lighter of heart than he had been since earlier that morning. As soon as he got home he would find the brothers and tell them what happened and what they were going to do about it.

Silas just happened to glance up in time to see Mr. Esh's buggy approach in the distance when he paused from his work. It was still quite far away but it would only be five minutes or so before he came into clear view. He stared at Mr. Esh's face intensely while beads of nervous sweat broke out on his forehead. Silas could not read his thoughts *per se* but he was able to glean some meaning from them. It became immediately clear that Mr. Esh wanted to speak to both of them but Seth was gone; gallivanting off somewhere in Europe with the oldest Esh daughter. In sudden panic Silas dropped the hoe and fumbled in his trouser pocket, withdrawing his own version of Seth's 'pocket watch'. He set the dials and pressed a button which started it buzzing violently.

"Hurry up, Seth!" Silas muttered under his breath, eyeing the approaching buggy.

Rebecca paused from admiring the elaborate murals in the throne room then looked all about her, wondering where the buzzing sound was coming from. She turned to Seth who was engrossed in his brochure. "Do you hear a bee?"

He stared at her with a blank look then went pale.

Mr. Esh's buggy drew up to where Silas was working. Silas had turned his back to the road still pressing the panic button on his device while pretending to hoe.

Mr. Esh climbed out of the buggy. "Silas! I wish to have a word with thee, where is thy bruder?"

Seth fumbled about, checking hidden pockets on his costume as though a mouse were running wild under his clothing. Rebecca stared at him, half amused and half worried. *"Was in der welt?"*

Suddenly he stopped squirming and with a panicked look on his face, disappeared into thin air without a word of explanation. Rebecca gaped at the empty space where he had once stood, flabbergasted.

Silas stalled for time. He turned and cupped his hand to his mouth and yelled out. "Seth! Seth! Mr. Esh wants to speak with us!" He turned back to Mr. Esh. "I think he's further down the row."

Silas slowly made his way to the buggy where Mr. Esh waited standing directly in front of him so he could block his view of the field. "Yes sir?"

Leroy leaned to one side to look past him. "Where is thy bruder?" he repeated.

Good question, Silas thought to himself. He shuffled his feet; glad that he had been sweating from his labor so it would mask the nervous flop sweat that was now running down his front and back. *Where on earth was his brother?* "Out there," he muttered.

Leroy shaded his eyes to peer past Silas into the distance, oblivious of Silas' golden eyes that had grown as large as saucers. Leroy jumped in fright when he felt a hand upon his shoulder from behind.

"Guten morgen, Mr. Esh," greeted Seth, walking around him to stand by Silas' side.

Leroy paused a moment, waiting for his pounding heart to settle down. "I've just come from Isaac Miller's farm," he informed them, carefully gauging their reactions to see if they had any prior knowledge of the damage done to his friend's crop. They continued to stare at him in polite silence, no guile upon their faces. "His field of soybeans has been destroyed, burnt to the ground." This time there was a reaction but it was not one of guilt; just sorrow. "Do you know anything of this?"

The boys exchanged glances and seemed to be conversing without speaking. They turned back to him.

"No, Mr. Esh. We had hoped to put a stop to it when we used the banker's ham radio. Evidently our warning was not properly conveyed," replied Seth. This was not something that Leroy had expected to hear. It had become too easy to forget that they were not of earth.

Leroy shook his head. "You two may not have been directly responsible but it is you...and me who are being held to blame. I can't very well tell my brethren about your kind and what you are. They would think me narrish."

"We are sincerely sorry for the trouble our people have caused you, Mr. Esh; I can assure you it has been completely unintentional."

Leroy took a moment to chew on this fact and when he looked back up he was still visibly troubled. "I'm not sure I even understand what you are."

"We will have to get another message out," Seth replied. "Do you think you can somehow help us to use that gentleman's ham radio again?"

"I will do my best," Leroy replied, feeling deeply unsettled. He had seldom if ever given much thought to what lay beyond the borders of Lancaster County let alone the vast expanse of the universe and now he was being asked by the brothers to again help them communicate with other foreign beings. It was just too incredible to even give credence to; perhaps he was narrish after all. He couldn't return with this excuse to Isaac, deacons, and bishop. They would all think him insane or worse. In either scenario they were still certain to blame the boys and shun his entire family for having taken them in.

He looked at them imploringly. "Is there anything you can do to guarantee that this won't happen anymore? The welfare of my community and family are at stake."

Silas and Seth exchanged sorrowful glances. "We will do our very best, Mr. Esh. We love your family; we don't want anything to happen to you either."

Leroy nodded. "I will do my best to get you back in front of that radio equipment. In the meantime, you will both have to make restitution for the damage your people have caused. Tomorrow morning the three of us are going to the Miller's farm to plow under his ruined crop and replant it."

"Yes, Mr. Esh," the brothers replied, looking truly remorseful at the thoughtless exploits of their own people.

Leroy turned to go, his shoulders stooped with the burden he carried. "You will need to get as much of this field harvested as possible today. I will send Hannah out with a good lunch for both of you." He climbed back into his buggy, flicked the reigns and headed back for the barn.

The brothers watched him go; feeling truly bad for their host. They had grown to respect and care for him and the entire family a great deal; it pained them to know they was causing him so much trouble.

Once he was out of earshot Silas angrily turned on Seth. "That was too close! I thought you were going to stay away from Rebecca Esh! You could have at least told me face to face what you were up to! I don't appreciate getting a note after the fact!"

Seth hung his head. "I can't," he mumbled. "I can't explain it, Silas, but it's like…it's like I've been living a half existence until I met her. No matter how hard I try to stay away, her soul calls out to me…oh, no! Rebecca! I have to go!"

"No, wait!" Silas protested, but it was too late. Seth vanished in the blink of an eye. He threw his hoe down upon the ground in disgust and paced back and forth. How was he supposed to harvest the enormous field all by himself?

Rebecca glared at him. "You left me for hours!"

Seth shook his head then nodded, remembering the time differential he had set up between the two locations. "I had no choice, Silas pressed the panic button."

Her eyes narrowed. "What does that mean?"

"Your father wanted to speak to us; I had to be there or he would have suspected something."

"I don't like this at all," Rebecca fumed. "This feels like I'm intentionally deceiving my entire family and this I will not do!"

"You are away on Rumspringa," Seth pointed out truthfully. "You will arrive in Indiana right on schedule; how is it deceitful?"

"I can't tell you how but it sure feels that way. What did my father need to see you about that made Silas panic?"

Seth was hoping that she would forget to ask this question. He shrugged nonchalantly. "He wants Silas and me to help on Isaac Miller's farm tomorrow." It was the truth; it just was the minimal truth.

Rebecca stared at him. "What happened?"

Seth swallowed hard. "His entire field of soybeans was destroyed."

Rebecca clapped a hand over her mouth; realizing what a hardship this would mean to the Miller family. Then she grew suspicious. "Did Silas have anything to do with this?"

This accusation really rubbed Seth the wrong way. "Why are you so quick to blame my brother?"

She crossed her arms. "Well wasn't it your ship that destroyed my father's corn field in the first place?"

"That was an accident! We crash landed; and as I recall, it was I who salvaged most of the crop by stacking it up in the loader without being asked!"

A small knot of tourists rounded the corner of the great hall at that moment and stared curiously at them; thinking them part of some historical reenactment since they were in period costume. Many looked away in discomfort while others took out cameras to take photographs. Rebecca turned her back and hauled Seth out of the room; it was against the Ordnung for her to be photographed.

"How did Mr. Miller's entire field get destroyed?" she demanded. "I thought you sent word out to your people?"

"We did but evidently some didn't get it. They aren't doing this damage on purpose."

This did nothing to mollify Rebecca. "Then it is complete disregard for the work and property of others! Isn't there anything else you can do to stop it?"

"Rebecca, we can't communicate with any of our own kind unless we use the banker's ham radio or until we get our ship fixed enough to send a message. We will have to send another transmission from Mr. Brown's ham radio again. As it is, we have precious little time left together before I have to return to Lancaster to help Mr. Miller tomorrow."

"Then why don't you 'teleport' to one of your other ships and explain how what they are doing is wrong?"

Seth shook his head. "If I could I would have done so before now! They all have force fields to protect the hulls from damage – there's no teleporting through them!"

Rebecca closed her eyes and held her throbbing head in her hands. It was just too much to take! She was arguing with an alien boy about the how's and why's of teleportation onto interstellar spacecraft. She looked up and found him waiting patiently.

"Becca, I promise to make everything right before we have to…leave."

She nodded and allowed him to slip his arm around her waist and lead her out to a high balcony of the castle which overlooked the snow capped mountains. The sight was breathtaking.

"So beautiful," she sighed, unable to help gazing with wonder, the breeze lifting her hair like a golden cloud.

Seth's hand cupped her cheek and turned her face back to his. "Yes you are," he murmured, his silver eyes pulling her to him. The next thing she knew his arms were fully encircling her and his lips were upon hers. She melted into him, not even aware that her own arms had gone around him to pull him closer. They kissed for a long moment and it was very sweet.

"Oops, shouldn't have done that," Seth grinned at her.

"So you've said," Rebecca returned his smile. She laid her head upon his chest and closed her eyes. "What are we going to do now?"

Seth drew back and gently stroked aside the hair that was blowing across her face. "We are going to make a lifetime of memories together in the time we have left and then face harsh reality."

Rebecca's eyes nodded sadly. "I don't know if I will be able to bear a life without you in it. Somehow you must find a way to hear from your king and find out what can be done."

Seth forced a cheerful smile and took her hand. "Let's complete the tour then head down to the restaurant for some authentic German Schnitzel, jah?

"Jah," Rebecca nodded. They caught up with their guide and finished out the tour of the magnificent castle in the enormous kitchen then together they walked hand in hand to the Alpine restaurant located just outside the castle walls and shared Schnitzel with noodles and authentic German sauerkraut.

Chapter Eleven
"Caught in the Act"

Leroy arrived home and unhitched Joe from the buggy, leading him into the barn for some well earned water and feed. He climbed the porch steps and entered his home; sitting down heavily in his favorite chair. It had not been a good day. He lifted his hat and combed his thinning hair back with calloused fingers; his thoughts consumed with Isaac Miller's ruined crop of soy beans. Hannah came up from the cellar; her arms laden with jars of pickled vegetables. When she saw her father looking so troubled she set the jars down on the coffee table and went over to him. Leroy did his best to smile reassuringly but it didn't fool her. Hannah bent down and kissed him on his cheek then straightened back up to gauge his reaction. Leroy smiled up at her; his daughters' affections had always been a constant source of joy to him.

"Where is thy *mamm*?"

"Stocking the cellar with the jars of sauerkraut we just pickled. Would you like some sweet tea, *daed*?"

"I would," he replied. "The boys will not be coming in from the fields for lunch so you will need to take it out to them. They will be plenty hungry."

Hannah poured him a tall glass of ice-cold tea then returned to the kitchen to make sandwiches for the brothers. Along with these she packed potato salad, fresh fruit and two large thermoses containing lemonade and sweet tea then put them into a large, insulated plastic cooler with bagged ice.

"They are working the north field. Take Matilda instead of Joe," he instructed, meaning their mule.

Fifteen minutes later Hannah was riding Matilda to the north field in search of the brothers. It was a warm day with a bright blue sky and puffy clouds floating overhead. Bees and butterflies flew among the crops and flowering weeds that bordered the service road. Though she had become accustomed to having the brothers around, knowing that they were not of this world still intimidated her a little bit. It was a difficult thing to understand; there was nothing in either the Bible or the Ordnung that was of any guidance in the matter except perhaps the verse which spoke about dealing with angels unaware; however, she seriously doubted that Seth and Silas were angels. An angel would not be making cow eyes at her oldest sister all the time the way Seth's did. This elicited a giggle as she searched the field rows for them. She drew near hoping to catch a glimpse of their straw hats and blue shirts among the rows of deep green. She made a slow circuit around the field, shading her eyes from the sun's bright rays. Suddenly, she spotted movement. She cupped her hand to her mouth to call out their names then froze; watching in amazement as one of the brothers fiddled with something in his hands then raised both arms heavenward. A soft rumbling began underneath the earth, building to a muffled roar; the warm air about her vibrating. Amazement transfixed her as she watched thousands of objects rise up slowly from all over the two acre field, collect together in mid-air then pile themselves neatly into crates which, when filled, then stacked themselves neatly on the loader. She was sitting only mere feet away so was able to get a good look at what it was: bell peppers. At that moment, Silas turned around with a self-satisfied grin on his face to find her staring at him. His smile froze then disappeared entirely as he eyes traveled to someone behind her. Then he went white as a sheet. Hannah turned around on the mule to see what he was looking at and found an Amish buggy behind her with Deacon Yoder in it; on his way home from the Miller's farm. He was staring past her at Silas in abject horror.

"This work is of the devil!" she heard him mutter under his breath. Before she could even think to react, he snapped the reigns and took off. Cold terror gripped her heart as she turned back to Silas who stood gaping after the buggy.

Fear choked Hannah's throat. "Silas! That was Deacon Yoder! *Ach*! Do you know what you have done?!"

Silas stared at her, his golden eyes round with fear. He nodded; regret etched all over his face. "I have put your family in danger of shunning."

"Not just shunning," Hannah choked, barely able to get the word out. "Expulsion! I must go tell papa at once!" She slid off the mule, thrust the basket into his reluctant arms then climbed back on, not even thinking to ask where Seth was. Silas avoided looking in her eyes but Hannah could tell the effect her words had upon him because he looked racked with guilt. She turned Matilda about and kicked her in the sides, urging her back home. Of course the mule would pick that particular moment to act like one. Matilda turned round to look at her then brayed in protest. Hannah kicked harder; to no effect. The animal then did what any stubborn mule would do; she sat down on her back haunches and refused to budge, with Hannah hanging on for dear life. If the situation hadn't been so dire, Silas might actually have laughed but as it was he had no patience for the stubborn animal either. He left the field, clambered through the split rail fence, reached into his pocket and thrust something under its' hind quarters. There was a loud buzz and a tiny flash of light. The mule reared up quick as a shot with Hannah still hanging on; trotting off as fast as its legs could carry it.

"What did you do to Matilda?" came Hannah's voice as the mule sped away.

"Alien version of a cattle prod!" she heard Silas yell in response. Hannah did not see him fumble with his strange device to set off the panic button again; she was too involved with trying to stay upon the mule's back. She made it back home in record time but not before Deacon Yoder beat her to it. She could see him speaking to her father and mother from a distance and both of their heads were bowed low.

"Faster, Matilda, faster!" she urged, still a ways off. By the time she rode up to the house the Deacon was already leaving in his buggy. Her father and mother were still on the porch steps with stricken looks on their faces.

Hannah jumped off Matilda's back; allowing the animal to run back into the barn by itself. "Mamm, daed – what is it?"

They looked at her but could only shake their heads sorrowfully. Hannah's heart plummeted when she saw that her mother's eyes were filled with tears. They went slowly into the house and let the screen door shut behind them; leaving her to stand outside to wonder what Deacon Yoder had said to them.

"Not again!" Seth moaned, feeling the panic button go off again. Rebecca was biting into schnitzel with noodles as he took the device out of his pocket, pressed a button to silence it then put it away again.

"Why does it keep going off like that? I thought you had settled everything."

"I did."

"Well perhaps something else came up. Aren't you going to see what the matter is?"

He shook his head stubbornly, taking a large bite out of his own meal. "No." he said through a large mouthful.

"But it might be important!" Rebecca urged, growing concerned. Two panic alarms one right after the other; something had to be very wrong.

"Rebecca – I only have this one last 'day' with you; I'm not going to allow anything else to disrupt it. Whatever it is will just have to wait; Silas will have to learn how to deal with things on his own for a change!"

"But..."

Seth took her free hand in his and kissed it, his silver eyes imploring. "Trust me, Becca." An irresistible sense of calm flowed into her which she instantly recognized as emanating from him. She fought it for a moment then relented and let the peace wash over her. She was no match for his powers of persuasion. It should have frightened her how easily he could manipulate her feelings but she supposed it was easier to do so when she was a more than willing 'victim'. She didn't want her time alone with him to be spoiled with another interruption either.

"Very well," Rebecca sighed giving in.

They ate their lunch in relative peace after that and finished it off with loud belches that drew looks from those sitting nearby.

"Now this is what I call a *gut* meal!" Rebecca nodded. "I will have to cook this one at home."

Seth grinned at her in amusement and belched loudly again as he wiped his mouth. "Good appetite!"

Rebecca stood up and grabbed him by the hands. "Where to next?" Her eyes were dancing with excitement now that she had given herself up to the adventure.

Seth grinned at her. "When did you get so daring?"

Rebecca tucked her arm through his. "Just now when I realized how very little time we may have left with each other. I once saw a travel book about the canals in Venice...would it be possible...could we...?"

Seth pressed his cheek against hers. "Say it, Becca, tell me what you wish for."

"Take me to Venice," Rebecca sighed, clinging tightly to him. Seth removed the device from his pocket and still embracing her, set the dials. The next instant the earth revolved about them like a whirlwind then all went black.

Hannah slowly climbed up the porch steps to her home and entered; afraid of what she might find. Her mother's face was buried in her hands and she was trembling. Her father stood before her, his eyes shut; obviously struggling to maintain his composure.

"What did Deacon Yoder say, *daed*?"

"We have been given the warning," her father replied. "Deacon Yoder is convinced the boys are from the evil one." He raised his head and looked her in the eyes. "What is it that he saw that would make him say such a thing, Hannah?"

"He harvested the peppers using magic." Hannah replied.

Her father stared at her, incredulous. After having experienced so many mysterious and unexplained phenomena at the hands of the two brothers; it shouldn't have seemed absurd anymore, but it did. "Deacon Yoder witnessed this?"

Hannah nodded then grew animated at the memory of it. "You should have seen it, daed-mamm! Silas lifted his arms and all the peppers just twisted themselves off the stalks then the bins stacked themselves up when they were full!"

Ruth stared at her daughter, her knuckles covering her mouth; her face streaked with tears. If the situation hadn't been so dire she might have been tempted to chuckle. *"Ach! O mein Gott!"*

Hannah nodded then blurted out, "I sure wish I could make our crops do that!"

Her father suddenly erupted into laughter, unable to help himself. Ruth looked at him as if he had gone mad. Leroy held out his arms to his daughter and gathered her into his embrace. "The good Lord knows the truth," he declared. "We will all pray together and commit our way into His care, *jah*?"

"Jah," whispered Ruth, nodding, not knowing what else to do. Together they all got down on their knees, joined hands and bowed their heads to pray in silence. Mary and Mirriam entered the house at that moment, dragging Silas with them who truly looked miserable. They joined their parents in kneeling upon the floor and all bowed their heads. After a long silent entreaty to the Almighty, Leroy lifted his head and looked around and then he looked back at Silas. "Where is thy *bruder*?"

After a night's rest at a local youth hostel, Seth teleported them into a Venetian apartment located near the Santa Lucia train station. Hand-in-hand they walked until they came to a large canal filled with a long queue of bobbing Gondolas and water taxis. Seth helped her into Gondola first before climbing in after her. Rebecca leaned back against the cushion and stared about her in wonder as the Gondolier pushed away from the dock. In minutes they were out in the Grand Canal, surrounded by other Gondolas, water taxis and boats. Seth cuddled next to her, drawing a blanket over their laps. To her delight and amazement, the gondolier began to sing out loud in Italian in a beautiful tenor voice.

"If only you could bring him home with us for the next meeting!" Rebecca whispered. "It would be *wunderbar* for him to join in with us on the singing!"

"You're going to give yourself a good case of whiplash if you keep doing that!" Seth grinned; watching her trying to take in the sights on both sides of the Canal.

"It is so beautiful!" She exclaimed, her face lit up with joy. "This is so much better than a book; except for the fishy smell!" She pinched her nostrils for emphasis.

"If we time it right, we might be able to make the Bridge of Sighs by sunset."

"The Bridge of Sighs? What is that? It sounds very romantic."

"It is and it isn't," Seth replied, picking up the brochure to read aloud. "The view from the Bridge of Sighs was the last view of Venice that convicts saw before imprisonment. The legend suggests that prisoners would sigh at their final view of beautiful Venice out the window before being taken down to their cells…"

"How sad!" Rebecca interrupted.

Seth continued. "...local legend says that lovers will be granted everlasting love and bliss if they kiss on a gondola at sunset under the bridge and be in love and happily married for the rest of their life."

Rebecca leaned back with a troubled look on her face. "If only it could be true!"

Seth nodded. "If nothing else, I would still like to share a kiss with you at sunset under the bridge; it will be a wonderful memory to take home, jah?"

Rebecca blushed a deep red then looked about; pretending to admire the beautiful palazzo's which lined the Grand Canal for a brief moment. "What happens after sunset?" she finally asked, turning back to him with haunted eyes.

Seth shrugged. "Paris? The Eiffel Tower? Wherever your heart desires."

Rebecca shook her head. "Ach...no! After all this?"

His face fell. "A train to Indiana...Isaac Miller's farm...reality." The device in his pants pocket buzzed again. Seth took it out, silenced it again then shoved it back in with a glower.

Rebecca frowned at him. "Why do you keep doing that? Seth, something must be wrong otherwise why would it keep buzzing like that?"

Seth shrugged, not wanting to appear alarmed. The sun was already heading for the horizon. He tugged on the Gondolier's pant leg to get his attention. He didn't want to miss floating under the bridge at *sunset "Ponte dei Sospiri, per favore signore, anche urgenza!"* He waved around some lira as extra incentive.

It took every ounce of self-discipline Silas possessed not to fling his device against the wall in frustration. Seth was ignoring his summons and Mr. Esh was beginning to doubt his excuses that his brother would be arriving at any moment. After praying with the family he was able to buy some time by offering to go out in the field and bring him back personally. He left the house then as soon as he was out of sight, made a right turn and ran into the field where their cloaked spacecraft was hidden, muttering alien epitaphs under his breath in frustration. If Seth wouldn't respond to the panic button then Silas would have to take more forcible measures! By experience his fingers found the hidden panel which would gain him entry inside the ship. There was a soft hum as it recognized his fingerprints followed by a soft click when the hatch cracked opened. He looked about carefully to make sure no one was watching then entered the ship.

It was a mess inside; a result of crash landing in the field. Everywhere he looked he saw some kind of damage that would have to be fixed but what drew his attention now was a particular control panel that would help him to locate and retrieve Seth. He had to clamber carefully over exposed wires and other things in order to get to it. He just hoped it was still in working order. It seemed to have sustained the least amount of damage compared to the rest of the ship.

Seth sensed that the sun was setting but it was difficult to tell because of all the buildings lining the canal on either side which blocked his view. Rebecca was working herself towards a whiplash; her head swiveling constantly this way and that to admire the picturesque homes, shops and bridges as well as the other gondolas which passed them by. Quite a few of them seemed to be making a beeline to the same destination as they and he worried that they might be crowded out at the Bridge of Sighs by all the traffic. The race was on to see who would make it there at the exact perfect time.

Their gondolier stomped to get their attention. "Signore!"Signore!"

Seth and Rebecca looked up then followed his pointing finger with their eyes. "Ponte dei Sospiri! (The Bridge of Sighs!)"

They were only about 20 yards away and the church bells had begun to peal; signaling that sunset was approaching.

Sweat streamed down Silas' face and body as he struggled with the controls. It was a typically muggy Pennsylvania summer evening but the inside of the ship was an absolute misery. The cloaking device may have protected the hull from external damage and spying eyes but it didn't allow for the free exchange of air. The in-ship teleporter was really Seth's area of expertise but Silas had used it enough to know how to accomplish his current goal. Finally he got it turned on; the control panel lights lit up and began blinking; waiting for him to input the origin and destination coordinates.

Seth pulled Rebecca close to his side and held her hands in his. "We're almost there."

She turned to him and smiled; a deep blush crimsoning her cheeks then turned her gaze back to the bridge which was only a few feet away. They counted down the moments as the bridge slowly seemed to float towards them. A half dozen other gondolas were also attempting to float underneath it at just the right moment. Seth had promised their gondolier a handsome tip if he got them under the bridge before the last bell tolled. The Gondolier poled with all his might; determine to earn the extra money. Now they were only a couple of feet away.

Seth turned Rebecca's face to his and brushed aside her glorious golden hair so he could fully appreciate her face. "It's time, Becca."

Rebecca nodded then closed her eyes for his kiss as they passed under the Bridge of Sighs which would eternally unite their hearts as the legend promised.

"WHAT DO YOU THINK YOU'RE DOING?" Seth approached Silas, his hands balled into fists. "Do you have any idea what lousy timing you have?!!"

Silas stood his ground. He crossed his arms, glowering at his brother. "You wouldn't respond to the panic button!"

"I had a good reason!!"

"I don't care what the reason is, Seth! You have to make an appearance for Mr. Esh, right now! He is beginning to suspect something is wrong."

Seth closed his eyes and groaned as he thought of Rebecca, floating alone under the Bridge of Sighs without him, before they even had a chance to-

"All I asked was for one day; one! You couldn't even handle that!"

Silas shook his head at his brother. "You are so far gone you can't even think clearly anymore!

Seth sat down with a thud and put his head into his hands. "You've no idea," he whispered.

Silas laid a hand on Seth's shoulder; pitying him. "Look – just make a brief appearance and I'll send you right back."

"All right," Seth mumbled, defeated. "She's going to be hopping mad when I return…"

Silas hauled him to his feet and shoved him towards the door. "Serves you right for falling in love with a forbidden one!"

They jumped out into the cornfield, sealed the door behind them then turned towards the farmhouse; instantly freezing in their tracks. Deacon Yoder was sitting in his buggy staring at them from the dirt road which ran alongside the field. *What was he still doing there?* They saw fear in his eyes and also something else; it looked like determination. He gave them both a disapproving scowl then turned the buggy about and headed off, leaving them both to wonder what further damage they had just caused and how he might have interpreted what he had just seen. From his viewpoint it would only have looked like they magically appeared out of thin air into the field…

"Let's get to the house now." Seth said through gritted teeth. They walked together in silence; a growing sense of ominous foreboding descending upon them. They entered the Esh dwelling and found Leroy and Ruth in the kitchen talking quietly.

Upon hearing the screen creak open and slam shut, Leroy looked up and motioned the brothers over. "It seems the *der Herr* has seen fit to try our faith most earnestly. Deacon Yoder was here; apparently he saw you harvesting the peppers in a most…unconventional manner and believes you to be a servant of the evil one."

Seth stared at his brother and mouthed the words: *What did you do?*

Silas removed his hat and knelt before Leroy, dragging his brother down to the floor with him. "It is worse than that, Mr. Esh," he said, unable to meet their benefactor's eyes. "He just now saw us exiting the spacecraft in your corn field. The look on his face was…uh…very disturbing."

Leroy and Ruth exchanged horrified glances then fell mute; the enormity of the news not lost on either of them. The brothers stared sorrowfully at him; hats in hands; feeling awful for all the trouble they had caused.

"What will you do now?" Seth whispered.

Leroy sighed deeply and closed his eyes. "I will entrust my family to *der Herr's* care; who made heaven and earth."

"*Jah!*" agreed Ruth vehemently though she looked badly shaken. "We have done nothing more than take in two Amish boys who needed food and shelter in return for good labor; how can they expel us for this? We will trust *der Herr!*"

Seth and Silas nodded in agreement. "We also; we will entrust this situation to our All Wise King." Leroy and Ruth said nothing, out of respect for the brother's beliefs; but wondered who their "All Wise King" was that they so often mentioned.

Having settled the matter in her heart, Ruth regarded the brothers. "Have you had anything to eat today?"

Seth remained silent; he didn't dare confess that he had dined on a Schnitzel with noodles in Bavaria the day before or the hearty breakfast at the youth hostel earlier.

"No, not yet," Silas responded. "Hannah left our lunch out in the field where we are working so we'll just eat that." He elbowed Seth in the ribs; giving him the signal to start backing up.

"Jah, gut," murmured Leroy absently, waving them off to finish their work in his fields. "Get as much work done as you can today; we are leaving early tomorrow for Isaac's field."

"Yes sir," Silas replied, pushing his brother through the door ahead of him. Once outside, Silas grabbed Seth's arm.

"Look, return to Rebecca but only long enough to say your farewells and get her back on the train to Indiana."

"But-"

Silas turned on his brother, his face grim. "We've done enough damage to this wonderful family; it needs to stop."

Seth hung his head and nodded reluctantly. For once it was his brother behaving like the responsible one and he the fool. He felt ashamed. He just wasn't sure what kind of reception he was going to receive from Rebecca when he returned.

"Get back here as soon as possible." Silas said, gripping his shoulder.

"Alright," Seth nodded, withdrawing the device from his pocket. The world spun briefly and the next moment he was back in the gondola. Rebecca was gone. He clapped a hand against his forehead; what had taken ten minutes back in Lancaster had translated into an hour or more in Italy because of the time differential. He looked around frantically but found no one except the gondolier who was staring at him as though looking at a ghost. The man's mouth fell open in a silent scream and the pole dropped from his hands. Seth dived for and caught it just before it disappeared under the water.

"Where is the young lady?" he gasped, peering about him frantically.

The gondolier couldn't answer; he was too gripped with terror at witnessing the same person disappear then reappear in thin air before his very eyes. Seth tried asking him again, this time in Italian: *"Dove è la mia lady amico?"*

This tact seemed to calm the man down enough to answer. *"Ha lasciato* (she left).*"*

Cold dread filled Seth's heart. "How long ago? *Quanto tempo fa?"*

At this point the gondolier shut his mouth and extended a trembling hand, palm up. He may have been frightened but that didn't seem to affect his penchant for greed any; he wanted payment first. Seth dropped in a few Lira.

The Gondolier pocketed the money and snatched back his pole from Seth. *"Due ore, forse più* (two hours perhaps more).*"*

"Two hours! Where? *Dove hai lasciato lei?"*

The gondolier stuck his hand out again; Seth deposited another Lira. *"Ponte de Rialto,"* he replied.

Rebecca had gotten out just after the Bridge of Sighs. Seth dug into his pocket, fished out his wad of Lira and waved it at the gondolier as incentive again. "Take me there, pronto!"

The gondolier nodded enthusiastically and turned the boat about, poling back for where Rebecca had gotten off. Evidently no translation was needed when there was plenty of money to be made, Seth thought ruefully. He only hoped he would be able to find her wandering among the shops near where she had gotten off. It would take about fifteen minutes to reach the place which would give him some time to think of how he was going to explain all of this to her.

Chapter Twelve
"Venice Interrupted"

Rebecca had never felt so conflicted in all her life. She was simultaneously simmering with rage while also fighting down her fear and overwhelming disappointment. Seth disappearing at the very moment they had been about to kiss under the Bridge of Sighs was obviously a sign from *der Herr* that it was not meant to be. Filled with sheer panic which was quickly followed by anger, she had pleaded through her tears to the Gondolier to let her out at the very next stop. She then had fled, covering her ears from the string of curses he flung at her for not paying the fare and had run blindly until she found herself staring at her reflection in a shop window somewhere in Venice. She was halfway across the world in a foreign land with no money, ignorant of the language and completely alone. Her anger at being left to fend for herself quickly crowded out any disappointment or sadness she harbored about the Bridge of Sighs. She was trembling violently which elicited sympathetic stares from those who passed by her.

What was she supposed to do now? She was completely lost. Rebecca covered her face with her hands and let the angry tears spill down her cheeks.

"Signorina? Che io sia d'aiuto?" said a masculine voice, startling her.

She jumped a little and looked up to find a handsome young Italian man smiling gently down at her. "Ach! You frightened me!"

He smiled; his teeth very white in contrast to his deeply tanned skin and riveting blue eyes. Rebecca could not help staring at him. "You are Americano, no? Do you speak Italiano?"

"Nee? I mean I'm not? I mean…*jah*…I am…American; actually Amish," she went crimson; she was babbling away like a *dummkopf*!

The Italian took her hand in his and patted it, his icy blue eyes twinkling. He was obviously flirting with her. "What is Amish?"

Rebecca opened her mouth; ready to explain then realized it would be too tedious to make him understand. "I am plain."

He stepped back for a moment, still gripping her hand and slowly ran his eyes up and down, a rakish smile spreading over his face. Rebecca was clothed modestly but her hair hung down her back in thick waves; golden in the warm Italian sun.

He shook his head. "No! Not plain...*bello!*"

There was no point arguing with him. She studied his handsome face for a moment. Perhaps she could take advantage of his interest and get him to help her? She pointed to herself. "Rebecca."

His smile broadened exponentially. "Rebecca? *Bellisimo!*" he bent over her hand, kissed it then pointed to himself. "Alessandro."

"Alessandro," Rebecca repeated, gently extricating her hand. It did nothing to dissuade his enthusiasm.

"Rebecca, would you do me the honor of joining me for some espresso and biscotti?" He gestured towards a café that had tables and chairs set up in front of it. The large and magnificent cathedral of St. Mark's stood across the square. Rebecca couldn't help gawking at it. Alessandro took her silence as acquiescence and gently (but irresistibly) began pulling her towards the café. Alarm bells began going off in her head but her good sense was no match for her empty stomach and a determined Italian. She had not eaten in hours and was feeling dizzy from hunger. Perhaps just a quick bite with her handsome new benefactor would not be so bad? It would give Seth time to return and find her; if he ever did...

"Danki," she smiled and allowed him to tuck her arm through his as he led her to the café. The sign read: Florian. He held out her chair for her then seated himself. A waiter appeared a moment later with menus. Rebecca took one glance and realized with dismay it was all in Italian including the prices but she was absolutely famished; she would just have to take her chances. She pointed to an item with the longest name, figuring it would have the greatest amount of food then handed the menu back to the waiter.

Alessandro also ordered two espressos and biscotti; (whatever that was) then leaned forward and recaptured her hand. "What brings such a plain beautiful girl to Venice, Italy?"

Rebecca was rendered mute by this question. She knew he was just trying to make small talk and be nice but there was no way she was going to be able to tell him the truth. The waiter reappeared a moment later with two tiny ceramic cups of dark liquid that smelled like coffee and little cookies. She stalled for time by taking a sip of the thick liquid and immediately began choking. It was like drinking hot mud! Alessandro stood and gently patted her on the back until the coughing spasm passed. Tears ran down her cheeks as she fought to control her choking. She pointed at her cup. "What is that?!"

"Espresso…coffee…you do not have before?"

"Nee…it is very strong!"

He sipped his, grinning as he nodded at her.. "Si…si…a bit of an acquired taste, no?"

Rebecca nodded, still finding it difficult to speak without choking. She took a sip of water, hoping it would help.

"Where in America, plain girl?" Alessandro persisted in his broken English.

"Bird-in-Hand," Rebecca finally managed after several more sips of water. Alessandro stared at her as if she had spoken gibberish. "Pennsylvania," she clarified.

He nodded, smiled and dipped his biscotti into his tiny cup before popping it into his mouth. "You would like to see more of beautiful Veniza, no?"

"No? Uh – I mean…yes! Uh-No?" His way of speaking was thoroughly confusing her. The waiter reappeared with his round tray and set before her a steaming plate of noodles and what looked to be a variety of seafood she couldn't identify. She had taken a great risk in picking blindly off the menu and now she would just have to eat it. Why couldn't Seth have disappeared while they were still in Germany? At least there she knew she liked the food. Alessandro stared at her plate with widening eyes; mentally calculating how much this snack was going to cost him at the most famous caffé in all of Venice. He waited politely as Rebecca bowed her head then began to partake of her meal. Despite her initial misgivings, she discovered it was actually pretty tasty…as long as she didn't know what she was eating…

Alessandro took that moment to light up a cigarette; oblivious to her frown of revulsion. "Rebecca…tell me…are you alone? Where are you staying?"

"Rebecca!" yelled a voice in the distance. Relief flooded her soul; it was Seth. Both she and Alessandro turned at the same moment to watch him run across St. Mark's Square towards them, waving his arms. Pigeons scattered and flew in all directions. He arrived at their table, breathless from his exertions. Rebecca watched in smug amusement as the scene before him began to register. Her fork was poised in midair with a scallop impaled upon it and a handsome Italian with a cigarette hanging from his mouth was sitting across from her, holding her free hand and scowling at him.

"I've been running all over Venice looking for you!" Seth announced in a voice that should have engendered at least a small degree of sympathy. It had the exact opposite effect. All the anger, pain and frustration came boiling to the surface.

How dare he vanish like that and leave her all alone in a foreign country then to just reappear and assume that everything was as before?! She popped the scallop into her mouth and chewed leisurely, pretending to care less. "Ach! Really?" She stole a glance at Alessandro who was now grinning. She gestured to him. "Alessandro…this is Seth…Seth, this is Alessandro." The two nodded at each other, obviously wondering who was going to win the prize of Rebecca's company. "Alessandro bought me this meal," she volunteered, hoping her meaning was clear.

Seth cleared his throat; taking the reprimand. He reached into his pocket and withdrew some Lira and set it on the table. "Thank you for taking such good care of my fiancé while we were separated from each other."

Alessandro pushed the money back towards Seth and took another drag on his cigarette, rudely blowing the smoke into his face. "Any man who allow such a lovely woman to wander alone in the streets of Veniza is not worthy of her!"

Rebecca watched Seth wave the smoke away. He coughed then stood up, pulling her up with him; he had had enough. "Time to go, Rebecca. The day is growing old."

As tempted as she was to teach Seth a lesson, she knew she had no other choice but to go with him; Seth alone held the means by which to get her back on the train and der Herr only knew what Alessandro might expect in return for buying her such an expensive meal. She looked upon his disappointed face and smiled sadly. "Danki, Alessandro, for taking such good care of me, I'll never forget you." She meant every word.

Alessandro nodded; knowing he had been defeated. Then like a true Italian gentleman he stood and kissed her hand in farewell. "Arrivederci, Rebecca bella!" He pointed his cigarette at Seth. "You! Take better care from now on or you may not be so lucky next time!"

Seth grinned at him, and put his arm around Rebecca, steering her away. "I will!" As he walked her away back towards the Grand Canal, Seth exploded with relief. "I know you're on Rumspringa, Rebecca...but did you have to throw me over for the first charming Italian you meet?" He was only half kidding.

She knew he meant it in jest but there was definitely an undercurrent of jealousy. *Good! It served him right!* "I was *hungrig*," she replied in her own defense. She stopped in her tracks and faced him; her anger returning in full force. "I didn't know where you went, or why or how long you would be gone! He offered to help me! What else was I supposed to do?"

Seth took her hands in his. "Look, it wasn't my doing, Becca! Silas pulled me back because I wouldn't respond to his summons."

"Why did you not respond?"

Seth swallowed. "I didn't think the situation was as grave as it was."

This had a sobering effect upon her. Fear replaced the anger. "What happened?"

"Deacon Yoder witnessed Silas harvesting your father's crop..."

"Why is that bad?"

"He did it using what looked like to be supernatural methods."

Rebecca covered her face. *"O mein Gott!"*

"He also saw us exiting our spacecraft."

"Ach no!" Rebecca's legs buckled out from under her; she collapsed onto her knees on the pavement. This was all becoming a bad nightmare. "This will result in shunning and expulsion for sure, Seth! My family is going to suffer the consequences of your carelessness!" She collapsed against him, shaking uncontrollably. "Take me back now...this instant. I need to be with my family!"

"Rebecca – think about what you're saying! I can't take you directly back to your farm...at least not yet; we will have to wait until your train reaches Indiana then get you on the return train for home immediately."

"I have no more wish to carry on this deception to my family!" She growled under her breath. "I will confess in penitence to them and hope they will forgive me. Were I already baptized they would not be able to do so. We must go back now and try to undo all the damage you have caused. Perhaps if you explained the truth to Deacon Yoder he might understand. He is a very good man..."

Seth shook his head sorrowfully. "You would not say that if you had seen the look on his face."

"Just take me back to my family, please!"

Seth slowly withdrew the device from his pocket. "Very well," he sighed, holding out his arm to her. "Stay close."

"Hal – we just got another one!" Jessica Lynch knocked on the shared partition wall. Hal stood up and peered over it at her computer screen and let out a long whistle.

"I feel like we're Mulder and Scully from the X-Files!" he exclaimed, watching the aerial footage of another elaborate crop circle spotted in Lancaster County.

"Who from what?" replied Jessica Lynch who was still only in her twenties. She did not recognize the reference to character names from the once popular 1990s television show.

"Old television series about aliens...I believe you can rent them on DVD now," he explained, then he shook his head. "I can't believe I'm referring to the 1990s as old...where has the time gone, eh?"

"Old is a relative term," grinned Jessica. "Einstein's theory of relativity states that time differs in relation to mass and gravity."

"Oh is that so?" Hal replied. Their newsroom at WGAL had been abuzz for weeks over the numerous videos that had come pouring in from people's cell phones as well as YouTube and other sources with footage of elaborate crop circles and strange lights appearing all over normally bucolic Lancaster County. To add to the mystery, many local "English" farmers had been reporting missing livestock in numbers too alarming to ignore. Investigations had turned up nothing so reporters were now being sent out into the field to question both English and Amish farmers but the latter remained tight-lipped and refused to talk to the press which was not unexpected. Though they said nothing it was clearly evident they were greatly disturbed by the strange events.

"What do you think is going on, Hal?" Jessica asked.

He scratched his day-old beard. "I really don't know what to make of it," he replied. "I've never seen anything like this in Lancaster. If it weren't Amish farms I would say it was some elaborate hoax but the Amish would never do such a thing to their own fields and the last thing they would want is all this attention."

"Look! I just got an email back from Gil. He gave me the go-ahead to interview that family whose daughter just mysteriously returned. He's letting me take a news crew out so while I'm there, might as well gather more information about those crop circles and take footage." Jessica plopped back down in front of her computer and began banging away on the keyboard.

"You can try all you want but the Amish are not going to cooperate and tell you anything, Jess; no matter how much damage they have incurred." Hal snorted with a shake of his head. "They aren't going to let a bunch of '*Englischers*' run rough-shod all over their fields to get a 'story'."

Jessica shrugged. "Well the airspace above their farms is public domain; there isn't a whole lot they can do to stop news choppers from taking aerial footage, now can they?"

Hal sat down heavily and bit into a doughnut with a shake of his head. "The Amish are not going to like this one bit! The last thing they want is for their lives to turn into a three ring circus!"

"The news recognizes no man's privacy!" Jessica sighed with a grin.

The dizziness wore off quickly and Rebecca found herself again sitting on the train to Indiana. She glared at Seth; ready to do vocal battle.

"I'm sorry, Rebecca," he interrupted her, fiddling with the device before fading from view again. "But I'm not going to risk ruining your reputation with your family over me. You can get off at the next station and perhaps get back to Strasburg by evening without anyone being the wiser."

The next moment he was gone and Rebecca was left alone in her seat on the train, fuming.

Deacon Yoder pulled his buggy onto his property, unhitched his mare and led her into the barn, his shoulders stooped with what felt like the weight of the world upon them. Outside the sun was shining, the birds were singing and all appeared to be at peace but inside, for the first time that he could recall; his heart was filled with doubt and terrible fear. His chest hurt the entire ride home and a horrible pain had been growing in his right arm. The crop circles and missing livestock had been bad enough but in the past few days he had witnessed things that had no human or Biblical explanation for them. He had been wary of the two brothers with the strange eyes from the beginning and had been willing to overlook their oddities as long as they drew no attention and conducted themselves according to the Ordnung but no plain folk….no human could do the things he had seen those two doing. They were of supernatural origin and judging from the damage they were causing, they surely could not be benign! He could not dismiss the images of bell peppers culling themselves by means of magic or the two young men materializing before him out of thin air in the midst of Leroy's cornfield. There was no guidance in the holy scriptures for these things so now he was at a total loss and feeling as frightened as he had ever been in his life. He sunk to his knees in the straw and laid his arms upon his milking stool, bowing his head in prayer.

He desperately needed guidance from on high. He believed by faith that supernatural beings existed but it was quite another to discover them living amongst his fellow brethren in broad daylight! Something had to be done…everyone was looking to him as though he had all the answers…but he didn't. He didn't know what to do.

"Jacob?" His wife, Ruth, entered the barn and saw him bowed down in seeming grief. She knelt beside him and put her arms about his shoulders. *"Was ist los?"*

"Pray with me, Ruth. Pray for *der Herr* to guide me," he whispered brokenly. Searing pain suddenly gripped his chest. He fell onto his back, gasping at the crushing pain in his chest. "Ruth, hurry! My glycerin tablets!" But he knew it was already too late.

Ruth struggled to her feet in a panic. "Where are they?"

"Night…stand," he whispered then grasped her hands. "Ruth, don't leave me."

"Jacob! Jacob!" she screamed, falling to her knees beside him as his eyes rolled back into his head. It was no use running to the phone shanty to dial 911; he would be gone by the time they arrived. She cradled his head in her lap and wept bitterly; consigning his soul into der Herr's hands.

The next main station stop was Columbus, Ohio. As soon as the train came to a halt, Rebecca was out the door with her suitcase in hand; eyes scanning the platform for anyone who could be of assistance. She spotted a man in uniform and went up to him.

"*Sei so gut*...I need your assistance. Can you tell me how to find the platform for the train to Philadelphia, Pennsylvania?"

"Ticketing agent is over there," the man pointed, not even pausing. He continued on his way while Rebecca looked where he had pointed. She hurried forward and found a line of people in front of her, waiting to purchase tickets. She looked around, searching for signs that might direct her to the right place then decided to wait. After a good thirty minute wait in line she learned which platform the train would depart from with five minutes to spare before it left.

When she was resettled in her seat and able to breathe a sigh a relief the anger came flooding back in. This whole charade seemed like an enormous waste of time when Seth could have more easily teleported her back to the farm with him. Now she had at least another four hours of wearing herself out with worry before arriving in Philadelphia. From there she would have to figure out a way to get from the train station back to her farm. She checked her satchel and counted out the cash her daed had given her; hoping it would be enough for a taxi ride home.

Seth returned in time to help his brother finish harvesting the field before returning to the main house to clean up and make an appearance at the family dinner table. The Esh's were all unusually silent that night; the sense of gloom palatable.

Leroy was too consumed with his thoughts of Deacon Yoder to be of much conversation and Ruth was too worried about him and their circumstances to make any small talk. Hannah, Mirriam and Mary were all moping at having to take on all of Rebecca's chores while at the same time missing her.

Seth finally cleared his throat. "How bad was Isaac Miller's field, Mr. Esh?"

Leroy barely looked up. "Very bad," he mumbled. "It will take us a full week to plow it under and prepare the soil for replanting."

"We could help to speed things up, if you wish..." Seth began to offer.

Leroy's response made everyone jump in their seats. He slammed his hand upon the table. "NEE! No more shenanigans!" He pointed his finger at both boys. "You will make this restitution by the sweat of thy brows!"

Seth and Silas stared at him then nodded; their eyes large with fear. He had never exhibited anger before. Their appetite disappeared.

Seth stood to his feet. "May we be excused?"

Ruth glanced at Leroy who went back to pushing his own food around his plate then nodded on his behalf. "Jah...go to thy rest; you will need it for tomorrow and the days that follow."

Silas followed his brother out the door to the *dawdi haus* where they sat down heavily upon their respective beds.

"He's really angry," whispered Seth.

"Yeah and he doesn't even know about you and Rebecca enjoying Rumspringa together in Europe yet!"

Seth fell back onto the bed and crossed his arms over his eyes. His heart ached with missing her already. There would be no good memories of her to take home with him and he still could not make contact with their king. Perhaps it would be good to toil in the muggy fields under the hot sun; the work would alleviate his feelings of guilt and keep his mind off of her.

Outside their window they heard the sound of a buggy coming into the driveway. They peered out and watched an Amish man knock on the door of the main house.

Leroy opened the door and stepped out; his face creased with concern.

The man removed his hat. It was Bishop King.

"Leroy, Deacon Yoder has gone on to be with the angels; he died of a heart attack earlier today. I've just come from his home."

Ruth joined Leroy at the door. "Ach no!" she cried, clasping her heart. "How is Ruth? Is she alright?"

"Her children are with her but she is understandably distraught."

Leroy shook his head, feeling horrible. "This is my entire fault," he muttered.

"Ach, no Leroy! Jacob had a bad heart; he's been seeing a doctor for years now. Do not take this burden upon yourself. Der Herr knows the number of our days and it is in His hands when we go."

"Would you like to come in?" Ruth beckoned him, opening up the screen door.

"Nee, danki – I must get on home. You were my last stop. Perhaps you could pay a visit to Ruth Yoder tomorrow?"

"Of course I will!" Ruth replied, her heart breaking for her friend's loss. "Where have they put him?"

"I've had blocks of ice brought over to keep him cool until tomorrow when his body can be prepared," Bishop King replied tipping his hat. "Now if you'll excuse me I should be going. Isaac's field will have to wait until after the memorial service and burial." He returned to his buggy and drove away.

Seth and Silas left the window and returned to their cots.

"What do you suppose they mean by 'gone on to be with the angels'?" Silas wondered.

"Not sure but it doesn't sound good," Seth replied, a shadow of sadness falling across his heart. "Did you see the look on Mrs. Esh's face? It was as though it was the worst thing she had ever heard."

"Why would they need ice?" Silas wondered aloud; deeply disturbed by what they had heard.

Their conversation was interrupted by the sound of the dawdi haus door creaking open. They both stood, waiting to see who would appear and wondering if Mr. Esh had changed his mind and was going to throw them out after all.

Hannah appeared around the corner bearing a covered tray in her hands. She placed it on the small table in the eating area. "I brought your dinner," she explained with a shy smile, removing the dishcloth.

"Danki, Hannah…you really didn't have to do this."

Hannah shrugged. "I don't mind; just bring the dishes back when you're done. You can leave them on the front porch if you like then just knock on the door and I'll get them." She closed the door behind herself.

The brothers took their seats at the table and stared at the food.

"I can't eat," Silas admitted.

"Neither can I."

"We need to hear from the king," Seth said; talking more to himself than to his brother. "Perhaps if we do it together we can get through?"

Silas nodded."It's worth a try." They had been making too many decisions on their own without the benefit of their sovereign's guidance.

"We still need to figure out a way and time to get back onto Mr. Brown's ham radio again and send out another warning!"

They returned their untouched plates as Hannah instructed then re-entered the *dawdi haus*. They sat face-to-face and clasped hands. Silas looked at his brother. *Ready?* Seth nodded then they both closed their eyes and directed their thoughts towards their king.

Hannah was at the kitchen sink, washing up their dinner dishes when she saw it. The window over the sink looked out upon the *dawdi haus*. "Mamm! Mamm! Look!" she pointed excitedly out the window; suds dripping from her soapy hands. Ruth hurried over and stared out the window. All was dark upon their farm except for twin beams of silver & gold light which ascended to heaven from inside the *dawdi haus*.

She went pale. "Leroy! *Schnell*!" At the urgency in her voice, Mary and Mirriam scampered up; jumping up and down to see out the window. Hannah lifted Mary up to the counter to get a better look. Leroy joined them a moment later and all stood in silent wonder to stare at the two beams of light.

"Do you think its angels come to visit?" Mary asked; her blue eyes round with wonder. No one answered her. For the next few minutes the beams continued to ascend but stopped just shy of the cloud line where it dissipated. Mary hopped down while her parents turned away from the window.

Ruth clutched her husband's arm. "Leroy?" She wasn't even sure what to ask him. He turned to her and shook his head; as mystified as she was. "Do you think it was from a…ach…you know…another spaceship?"

"It wasn't coming down from heaven it was trying to go up to heaven!" Mary piped up before her father could venture a guess. They all turned to her. "I always see that light coming out of their heads whenever they pray!"

Leroy and Ruth exchanged glances; not knowing what to make of her declaration. Leroy sat down on a nearby bench and beckoned Mary to his lap. She sat upon his knee, looking up at him with round solemn eyes.

"You have seen this light before?" he asked gently. Mary nodded. "Why have you never told us?"

Mary shrugged then giggled a little. "I didn't want you to know that I peek during prayers!" she admitted. "Sometimes I hear music too."

This statement really got their attention. There was no music in Amish homes or even in church except for when they were singing the Ausbund. "Music?" repeated Leroy; incredulous.

Mary nodded, her faces dimpling with a joyous smile. "It sounds like angels singing!"

Ruth turned to Hannah and Mirriam. "Have you heard this music too?"

Hannah shook her head but Mirriam nodded. "I have heard this music, *daed*; it is very beautiful."

Hannah stared at her younger sisters. "How come I don't hear it?" The disappointment in her voice was unmistakable.

Leroy abruptly stood up; setting Mary back onto her feet; he needed time to think; first Deacon Yoder and now this. "Time to go to bed now, *kinner*!" This was met with disappointed groans all around but they trudged dutifully upstairs anyway with Hannah leading the way with an oil lamp. Once they were out of earshot Leroy and Ruth stared at each other, then Ruth wrapped her arms about him and laid her head upon his chest. He could feel her trembling.

"What do you think it all means?" She asked him.

Leroy patted her back to comfort her but he didn't know what to say. "I do not know," he finally admitted; his emotions warring within him. *Were the boys truly from another world as they claimed or were they angelic visitors?* He wasn't sure which one frightened him more. "Let's get ready for bed then pray about it," he suggested. Ruth nodded, entering their darkened bedroom by touch. They prayed earnestly that night and even peeked at each other but saw no lights ascending as they did so.

Once they saw all the lights go out in the main house, Seth teleported back to the northbound train. As he feared, Rebecca was not in her seat and her suitcase was gone. He went from car to car searching every seat for her twice before giving up. He still felt terribly bad about Deacon Yoder and decided to pay a visit to his home before returning to the Esh farm.

He entered the darkened house and bumped against the kitchen table. On top was a large mound covered with cloth. Seth pulled back the fabric and caught his breath for he had never looked upon death before. Deacon Yoder's face was still as stone; almost as if he was sleeping, but his skin was cold to the touch. Underneath him were blocks of ice to keep his body cool.

"What a curious practice," Seth thought to himself. From the back of the house he could hear weeping and see the faint glow of lantern light. He tip-toed down the hall and peeked into the room. Ruth Yoder sat at her foot powered sewing machine stitching together pieces of white fabric; tears were running down her face as she grieved.

The look of pain on her face was enough to break his heart. Compassion for her sorrow washed over him. Seth returned to the kitchen and laid his hand upon the still body in farewell for just a moment before leaving. "I'm sorry." He whispered.

The funeral for Deacon Yoder was held the following day. Ruth Esh had left early to help her friend prepare the body. Leroy and the boys arrived later in the spring wagon. The service was conducted in his home first and then the pine box containing his remains was moved into the barn for a larger service before being buried in a plot of land set aside for this use on his farm.

Chapter Thirteen
"Restitution"

Dawn on the day following the memorial came all too soon for the boys. It was still very dark outside when the rooster began to crow; signaling that it was time to wake up and begin another long day. Seth rolled out of bed first, followed by Silas. They hurriedly dressed and were met by Leroy as usual to start their early morning chores in the barn. As they trudged behind him, Seth's thoughts strayed to Rebecca; wondering where she was at that moment and how angry she probably was with him. She had looked furious when he had left her so he was not looking forward to the inevitable confrontation when she returned.

The cows seemed unusually agitated that morning. They were mooing incessantly and constantly shifting around in their pen; making it extremely difficult to milk them. The other livestock were behaving oddly as well. Leroy said nothing to the brothers who were becoming frustrated in their attempts to complete their chores; every bit as bewildered by the animal's behavior as they were. He went from animal to animal to calm them down; his patient efforts eventually enabling them to complete their tasks. All three of them were carrying the last pails of fresh milk across the lawn when a low thumping noise began to sound in the distance. Leroy turned slowly in a 360°circle, scanning the horizon. The noise grew louder. Suddenly a helicopter appeared over the nearest hill, flying low over his farm. The noise was deafening. All three dropped their pails in sudden fright then they watched it fly away.

"That was a news helicopter!" Leroy exclaimed; recognizing it from the station that had covered the Amish school massacre a few years earlier. He stared at the brothers then down at the growing pool of spilt milk. "Don't say it," he warned.

Seth and Silas blinked at him. "Say what?"

"It's no use crying over spilt milk!" Leroy retorted a bit surprised. When he looked back and found them studying him as if he had gone *narrish*, he couldn't help but smile. "Never mind," he added.

Obviously, they were not well versed in Earth's colloquialisms to understand and for some reason he found this amusing. They finished up, pouring the remaining raw milk into the pasteurizer to process before heading to the house for their waiting breakfast.

They cleaned up and took their places at the table. After a long moment of silence, Seth and Silas became slowly aware that several sets of eyes were peeking at them; even Leroy and Ruth were doing so. They straightened up; wondering what was going on.

"Aren't you going to turn your head lights on?" Mary piped up.

"Our head lights?" Seth and Silas stared at her, confused.

"Jah! Yours is gold and his is silver - just like your eyes!" She pointed first to Silas then Seth.

Enlightenment dawned. "Ach! That is just our communication light," they nodded. "It doesn't seem to be working properly here."

"It stops before it hits the clouds!" Mirriam volunteered.

Ruth decided enough was enough. "*Kinner*! Time to say the blessing!" This time they all bowed their heads and no one peeked. They were just passing around the plates of food when they heard the sound of automobile wheels crunching on the driveway.

"Mary! Mirriam! Sit back down!" Ruth demanded but they were already out the door.

"It's Becca!" they squealed in unison running outside.

Seth rose instantly to his feet, wondering if he could get out the back door and hide inside the dawdi haus before she spotted him. Silas gripped his arm and pulled him back down while the rest of the family went to the door to greet Rebecca.

"Rebecca - *was ist los?*" Ruth Esh's voice rose above the din of her younger daughters who were squealing with joy.

The door opened wider and Rebecca stepped through, her eyes scanning the room for Seth. "I-I got off in Columbus and rode all night back to Philadelphia…" Her eyes locked upon him; her expression inscrutable. "From there I took a bus then a taxi."

"Rebecca the Miller's will be worried sick! They were waiting for you to arrive! How could you do this to them?" Her mother chided, twisting her apron round and round in her hands.

Rebecca hung her head. "I'm so sorry, *mamm*. I can use some of the money left to send them a telegram so they won't worry."

"You will also write them a letter of apology!" her father scolded. "They have probably gone to a lot of trouble for you; not to mention how disappointed Ruthie must be."

Rebecca listened quietly and nodded; knowing she had caused great worry and inconvenience to her cousins. "You are right; I will write them a letter right now; but I'm so tired; could I go into town a little later and send the telegram?"

This seemed to mollify her parents but she could tell that her mother was still very upset by the whole scenario.

"Ach! Oh mein Gott, was waren sie denken?" She said with a shake of her kapp. Then the matronly instinct kicked back in. "Jah; of course you should rest first. You must be exhausted from riding all day and night!"

"Yes but I'm hungry too. May I have breakfast first?" Rebecca set down her suitcase and took a seat next to Seth as if nothing were wrong. He retook his seat; his sigh of relief almost audible.

"Becca! Seth and Silas have head lights!" Mary informed her.

"They what?"

"Mary – not now; your schwester is weary from travel!" Ruth warned, setting out a plate, glass and utensils for her eldest.

Rebecca bowed her head briefly; aware that Seth's eyes were studying her then she dug in. For the next few moments there was just the sound of clinking silverware and eating until Leroy cleared his throat.

"Deacon Yoder passed away; we buried him yesterday."

Rebecca looked at her father in shock. "What happened?"

Leroy shook his head sorrowfully. "Heart attack." He looked her in the eye. "So why have you returned so suddenly?"

"I was homesick," she replied between mouthfuls. It was the truth; she had spent several days away from home; long enough to experience real homesickness but she knew that only a day and a half had passed for them. Trying to figure out how the time differential worked was giving her a headache; that and riding a train nonstop for 12 hours.

They finished their breakfast and while the younger girls cleaned up, Rebecca trudged upstairs to her room for a few hours rest without another word or glance at Seth.

"We have a very long day today and tomorrow. I expect good work out of both of you." Leroy said as they took their plates to the sink where Hannah and Mirriam were already splashing each other with soapy water. They went to the barn to get Joe.

"What just happened?" Silas wanted to know once they were safely inside. "She acts like she just came back from running an errand instead of…well, where exactly did you take her?"

"Bavaria first, then Venice."

Silas frowned. "So this was your swan song, jah? No more cow eyes and late night trysts in the front yard? You've made some memories and now we can concentrate on fixing the ship and getting out of here?"

"Not exactly,"

Silas began to turn red. "What do you mean by that? You promised me!"

"I know what I promised but I also can't deny how I feel about her, Silas; I want to find a way for us to be together."

"Out of the question!"

"Not if I can make contact with the king!"

"Look just the fact that we can't should tell you why he has laws against joining with anyone from this world. He's not going to change them just for you!"

"I have to at least still continue to try," Seth mumbled angrily. They heard the screen door slam, signaling that Leroy had left the house.

Silas let out a long exasperated sigh. "Look, first things first. We make restitution to Mr. Miller then we get back on that ham radio set. If our people don't stop making their presence known the press is going to descend upon this farm like a hornet's nest. That helicopter was looking for something!"

They exited, leading Joe out to where the buggy and Leroy was waiting for them. They climbed into the back and rode in contemplative silence. Every few minutes they could hear the sound of other helicopters circling over farms that had crop circles in them. After fifteen minutes they pulled up to Isaac Miller's farm where a news crew had set up their cameras to record the latest, mysterious damage.

"Oh-oh."

"Keep your eyes downward and put your hand in the way if they try to photograph you." Leroy instructed over his shoulder. Several other Amish buggies were already lined up; men from their district had come from all over to help restore the Miller's crop.

"Help me unload the seed, boys." Leroy said, tying Joe up next to the other buggies.

As soon as they clambered out the news crew trained the cameras on them. Seth and Silas averted their eyes, lowered their heads and raised their hands.

"Sir! What can you tell us about the mysterious damage to all the Amish farms?"

Leroy refused to respond, turning away to lift and drop the heavy sacks of soybean seed onto the shoulders of Seth and Silas.

"Have you sustained any damage to your field? Have you heard of all the strange lights that have been seen over Lancaster County lately?" The reporter was relentless but Leroy and the others just kept on behaving like she wasn't really there. Frustrated, they trained their cameras onto the brothers again whose faces were hidden by their black brim hats and sacks of feed.

"Have you seen any suspicious people in Bird-in-Hand lately?"

"Nee," Seth grunted, turning away to follow Leroy into Isaac Miller's barn.

The camera crew watched in frustration as the Amish moved away from them, leaving all their questions unanswered.

"Pack it up, they ain't gonna talk." Jessica grimaced, turning off her microphone. "We'll just have to keep our ears open, eyes peeled and hope this happens to an 'English' farmer who still hasn't gotten his 15 minutes of fame..."

"Let's just stay for another hour or so, maybe something interesting will pop up," suggested the cameraman.

Jessica cocked an eyebrow at him. "You're kidding me, right?" She tapped the microphone against his skull. "Helloooooooooo? Interesting? Amish?! The two words don't mix."

Rebecca descended the stairs after a brief nap with a letter for the Millers and satchel in hand. "I'll be back in an hour or so mamm. Do you want anything from town while I'm out?"

"Jah – pick me up some batting at the Fabric & Quilt shop – enough for a king-size quilt. We have to start on the next one right away if we're going to have it done in time for the fall auction."

She went outside and carried the scooter down from the porch. Mary ran up followed closely by Mirriam and Hannah.

"Where are you going, Becca?"

"Into town on an errand for mamm."

"Would you give me a ride before you go?"

"What about me? I want a ride!" Mirriam whined.

"The scooter isn't big enough for you and me," Rebecca explained, lifting Mary before her.

Mary and Mirriam stuck out their tongues at each other.

"It's not nice to rub it in!" Rebecca scolded her, pushing away. "You're going to have to take turns pushing too; I'm not going to do all the work!"

Mary leaned her head back against her sister's chest, closing her eyes for just a moment so she could enjoy the wind whistling through her kapp. "Just like flying!"

They went around the perimeter of the house then Rebecca let her off at the front porch. She took it out onto the road, riding it into town. First she went to the Post Office to drop the letter apologizing in full to the Miller's then to Western Union to send them a telegram. Rebecca felt awful for the trouble and worry she had put them through. Words on a piece of paper didn't feel like it was enough but there was no other choice. It was getting close to two o'clock when she finally arrived at the fabric shop. She was tired, hot and sweaty.

The bell above the door tinkled as she entered. Cool, air-conditioned air washed over her.

"Rebecca Esh!" crowed a familiar voice.

Rebecca turned and found Katie Zook and her mamm carrying several packets of cloth remnants.

"Looks like we had the same idea! Mamm – we should pay special attention to what fabric Rebecca buys and do the same; maybe then our quilt will fetch thousands of dollars too!" Her sarcasm was unmistakable.

"Hush, Katie!" Mrs. Zook scolded, thoroughly embarrassed. "Becca – I thought you were going to Indiana to visit cousins? Was I misinformed?"

Rebecca stared at her; momentarily panicked at how to answer. "My plans changed at the last moment," she replied truthfully.

Katie stared at her hard. "Just couldn't stay away from those boys your family adopted, jah?"

"That's enough. Be still!" Mrs. Zook snapped; having had quite enough of her daughter's tongue.

"Yes mamm," Katie replied, unfazed. "Where's your buggy, Rebecca? I don't see it outside."

"I rode the scooter. Daed had to go to the Miller's farm today."

"Ach jah! He suffered horrible damage!" Mrs. Zook shook her head in dismay. "There has been far too much of that lately!"

"Jah," agreed Katie with a nod; getting in her final dig. "It all seemed to start about the same time those boys showed up at the Zook's Barn Raising."

"Ach! We're leaving, NOW, Katie!" Mrs. Zook cried, lifting the fabric out of her daughter's arms and dropping it onto a nearby counter. She pushed Katie ahead of her and through the door without buying anything.

Rebecca was not sorry to see Katie go. She had the batting cut to size, paid for it in cash then returned outside to begin the long ride home. Just as she exited the shop she spotted the unmistakable red hair of Jacob Zimmer in his buggy. She turned her back swiftly, pretending to look in the shop window as it flew past; hoping he hadn't recognized her. The sound of the horseshoes kept up their steady gait but she didn't breathe a sigh of relief until his buggy was out of sight.

That was too close. If Jacob had seen her in town when she was supposed to be in Indiana he would first have a lot of questions she couldn't answer and then he would pick up courting her where he had left off. That she just could not deal with right now. She only hoped that Katie Zook would not think to tell him about seeing her. For the first time in her life she was thankful that the men of her community did not engage in gossip the way the women did.

Leroy, Seth and Silas entered the Isaac Miller's barn, stacking their large sacks of seed next to the others.

Isaac stepped forward to greet Leroy, giving him a brief back slap. "Danki," he said. He jerked his head in the direction of the news crew. "They have gone to every farm in the county trying to get an interview or footage of the damage."

"And?" Silas questioned, trying to appear calm.

"They've run into the typical roadblock of Amish noncompliance," Isaac smiled. "I think the best they have been able to get is aerial footage.

Leroy nodded; looking as relieved as he felt. "The life of a reporter in Lancaster County must be a pretty frustrating one!"

With that said, the men poured the seed into large tub for the horse-drawn planter while others lined up several team of horse-drawn cultivators across Isaac's field to plow under the ruined crop. The day was already promising to be a sweltering one. It was only 8:00 am and already 82 degrees. Women and girls were already at work making up large quantities of sweet tea and lemonade to keep the men hydrated under the hot sun.

For the better part of three hours, Seth and Silas toiled beside Leroy to rectify the damage their people had visited upon the undeserving Amish. Their shirts and trousers were plastered to their sweaty bodies while the rich earth caked their shoes and pant legs. They called a break at noon for a good rest under the shade trees and hearty lunch of tuna and cream cheese and Pennsylvania Dutch sandwiches. By noon the temperature had reached a sweltering 99 degrees.

Seth and Silas were almost too exhausted to eat but did so knowing they would need the nourishment for the worst part of the day. They each gulped down two glasses apiece of lemonade before turning their attention to the sandwiches.

"I sure wouldn't mind some cloud cover and a cool breeze right about now," they heard Isaac Miller mention to one of the older Amish men. Seth and Silas exchanged looks…*did they even dare?*

"Me too, Isaac! Couldn't you have arranged for your crop to get ruined in the spring when the temperatures aren't in the 90's?" joked another. A general murmur of grim humor circled about the tables. It was only noon and they still had at least another five good hours worth of work ahead of them during the hottest part of the day.

"What could it hurt?" Seth whispered to his brother. "They'll attribute the miracle to der Herr anyway!"

"It sure would make the work easier and go quicker," Silas added. They stared at each other for a long moment then reached a silent agreement. Silas reached into his pocket and fumbled with a small gadget.

"Be careful, just have it change gradually and make sure it doesn't affect the weather patterns over a widespread area!"

"I know what I'm doing!" Silas hissed in return. Seth looked about to make sure no one was looking, biting into his sandwich so as to appear normal.

"Okay it's done," he said, shoving the device back into his pocket. He took another large bite of his sandwich. "Say, this is really good!"

"Der Herr be praised!" cried a voice from another table a few moments later. Seth and Silas looked over then up to where he was pointing. Instead of a golden haze, puffy clouds began to congeal overhead; the temperature began to drop. Everyone paused from their meal to watch in wonder as more clouds formed. A gentle breeze began to blow, drying their sweat-soaked clothing.

"Derr Herr be praised!" exulted another.

Most seemed happy about the change while others scratched their heads. Leroy Esh was staring daggers at them; already having figured out what was going on then he slowly and imperceptibly shook his head at them. Seth returned his stare and also shook his head. It was too late now; if they reversed what they had done it would look even more suspicious. The men swiftly finished eating; wanting to take advantage of the cooler temperatures before the mercury rose again.

"Just wrap it back up in the wax paper and put it in your trouser pocket!" Silas suggested, getting up from the table to return to the field. "We'll just have to eat them as we work."

"Please tell me you got that," Jessica said; turning to her cameraman with saucer-sized eyes.

He nodded, patting his camera as though it were a favorite feline pet. "Oh I got it, alright. This is better than getting a full-face interview with a stubborn Amish man."

"I want to review every millisecond of tape you got in *slow-mo* before we send it to Gil," Jessica emphasized. "I'm so glad I listened to you for a change and we waited around."

"This footage is going to put you on the network's radar for sure, Jess – especially the sky footage showing clouds forming only over that farmer's field."

Jess nodded gleefully as she helped to pack up the van. "Yeah, it's not every day you catch a glimpse of an almost perfect rectangular formation of cumulus clouds!

"Get on your cell as soon as we're on the road and call Matt in meteorology to see if he can pull up a Doppler map of this area. Have him run a time-elapsed graphic for us starting around noon-time to show as complementary footage."

"Fox 29 - here comes Jessica Lynch!" announced her cameraman.

By 5:30 p.m. Isaac's field had not only been completely cultivated but over half the acreage had been re-sown with new seed. As if to lend a supernatural blessing, a gentle rain came drifting down just as everyone got back into their buggies for the return ride home.

"Danki, Leroy for all your hard work today," Isaac said, leaning his head into the buggy before they departed. "I can finish up the planting myself tomorrow."

"We will return tomorrow as well, Isaac." Leroy insisted. "I would not have it any other way." He slapped the reins and Joe pulled away. When they were out of earshot Leroy turned about and gave the brothers what his daughters often referred to as "the evil eye".

"I don't know how you did it but don't ever do it again," he warned them.

Silas and Seth stared back at him; all innocence. "Do what?"

"If you were younger I would take the strap to you both!" he said with a shake of his head.

"Strap…a form of corporal discipline," Silas recited as if reading from a dictionary.

Seth punched him in the arm. "Shut up!"

"What?

"Quit while you're ahead!"

Chapter Fourteen
"The Game is Afoot"

Jessica and her cameraman, Ted Booker, arrived back at the newsroom two hours later after fighting the horrific Philadelphia traffic for the last half of the trip. On her desk was a DVD from the Meteorology department in response to her request.

She tossed her purse and keys onto the pile of file folders strewn all over her desk. "As soon as you have that video from the farm cued up, let me know."

Ted saluted. "Aye, aye mon cap-e-tain!" Then he left for the Camera Department. "Give me 30 minutes."

Jessica stuck the DVD into her CPU and waited for it to load. It was just raw Doppler footage of Lancaster, magnified to display a wide swath of farmland in the area in which they had been earlier that day. The time signature was for 1100 hours to 1400 hours. For the most part the Doppler showed no cloud cover and then at 1215 hours cloud formations began to appear over a tiny section of farmland. She rolled her mouse over the image, right-clicked and zoomed in. Her pulse began to race as she watched the impossible happen. The Doppler showed clouds forming but only over a few specific acres of farmland and the outside borders of it formed an almost perfect rectangle; straight lines were not a natural phenomenon in nature.

"Holy moly!" she swore under her breath. She time stamped the part she wanted to air then she turned to another monitor and began pounding away on the keys while she waited for Ted to notify her that the video he had recorded earlier was ready for viewing. Her phone jangled; causing her to almost jump out of her chair in fright.

"Meet me in Engineering," said Ted's voice, then the line went dead. Jessica stuffed her purse into her locking file drawer and bolted for engineering; almost knocking down a few interns on her way. When she arrived she was breathless.

"Ted, if we can find anything on the video you shot I think we have a big story here!"

"We'll see!" He pointed to a chair before the massive control panel and flipped off the lights. The video of the weather change was everything she could have wanted and then some.

"Roll all the way back to the beginning and see if we can find anything unusual." She instructed.

They watched the monitor first at normal speed then slowed it down, muting the audio as they watched numerous Amish arrive at the farm and unload bags of seed. They watched it over three times before Jessica slumped in her chair.

"Damn," she muttered. "I was really hoping we'd find something or someone that would explain that weird weather phenomena!"

"Let's try it one more time only let's go frame by frame and see if we find anything," Ted suggested.

"Do you have any idea how long that will take?"

"I'll pay for take-out if you order it," he grinned. "Philly Cheese-steak, Thai, Chinese or Sushi?"

"Sushi, *always*."

Jessica pressed a speed-dial on her phone, waited a moment then gave the order. Then she handed the phone off to Ted who provided his credit card.

"Fifteen minutes for delivery," he said, handing it back to her. "Ready?"

Jessica nodded, her face resting on her hand; preparing herself for a long boring night. Halfway through and two hours after they had eaten they were both yawning and ready to call it quits.

She checked her watch. "I have to get up early tomorrow," she yawned, stretching her arms over her head.

Ted stared at her; his eyes going large. "Wait a minute!" He dialed back the video ten minutes then pointed with excitement. "There! Look!"

"What?" Jessica stared at the screen. "Just an Amish boy checking his pocket watch, what about it?"

"Just humor me here for a sec." Ted said, flipping open his new iPad2. He went onto Google and typed in a question: Do the Amish use watches? Wiki Answers was the first hit followed by some Amish sites. He scanned the information as she let out another yawn then slammed his palm down on the table, making her jump again. "Amish don't use watches! I thought something was weird but it didn't hit me until you checked yours!"

"That's not enough to go on; the most that would do is get the poor boy shunned; providing his family even saw the newscast!" she grumbled.

"Let's just concentrate on the footage that this kid is in and see what else we find." Ted cajoled her, definitely feeling like he was on to something.

"Ted, darling, you know I hate to say this and sound like such a prig but those Amish all look alike!"

"Look, if I'm wrong I'll give you my box tickets to the next Phillies game! They're right behind first base."

Jessica's jaw dropped. "Deal!" She sat back down and struggled to concentrate.

"Okay here he is and what looks like his twin brother when they first arrive," he narrated, slowing down the video. "Now they're holding up their hands to block the camera like good Amish boys…whoa! What was that? Did you see that?"

"See what?" Jessica leaned in.

"Look at his eyes; it's just for a split second…wait…I'll pause the image. Okay – now look!"

Jessica sucked in her breath. "I never noticed that before." She turned to Ted. "His irises are shiny silver!" She deflated a bit. "It could just be a trick of the light, you know."

"Let's keep watching. Okay now look – they've got those seed sacks over their shoulders and their heads are down but I managed to get a close-up right about here…*OH WOW*."

"There's two of them!" Jessica screeched. "They're twins but one's got golden eyes and the other's is silver!"

Ted shook his head. "That is just too freaky looking!"

At that moment Jessica threw her arms around him, hugged him and planted a big kiss on his cheek. "I got my story! I owe you big time!"

"I want a Starbuck's card with a year's worth of weekly hot mochas and croissants added on it!"

"You got it. I'm heading back to my desk to start writing an investigative piece. This is bigger than just one segment; I'm going to Gil and have him approve some additional vouchers and transportation so I can go back to Lancaster and do some snooping around."

"I want to come with you!"

"No, it will just be harder to get information if a camera is sticking into everyone's face. Just do your best to edit out all the footage that isn't pertinent to the story and then match it up with the Doppler footage we have because it's a *Dusey*!"

She got up to leave, hauling her large purse over her arm.

"Jess-"

"Yes, Ted?"

"What exactly is the story?"

Jessica shrugged at him with a conspiratorial smile. "That's the $64 thousand dollar question now then, isn't it?"

When their buggy pulled into the Esh driveway, Seth wasn't surprised to see Rebecca waiting for him. He clambered out reeking of sweat; his lower half caked in dirt from the Miller's field.

"There's dinner waiting for you in the house after you wash up," she said; her face still unreadable.

He wanted to take her hands into his and search out her feelings but Mr. Esh was watching and she had erected an emotional barrier that he couldn't seem to penetrate.

"Danki," he murmured, removing his hat as he entered. His thick brown hair was plastered to his skull. He left his muddy shoes outside along with Leroy and Silas and headed right for the kitchen sink. After thoroughly washing their hands, arms and dirt-streaked faces and back of the neck they took a seat at the table. It was filled with fresh bread, Beef Brisket, Pea Salad, and Apple Dumplings.

"How did it go today?" Ruth asked, ladling out generous portions to the men.

"Gut, we got much done. We should be finished with replanting by tomorrow evening."

"Some packages arrived today from the Oops man!" Mary chimed in.

"You mean U-P-S," Hannah corrected, rolling her eyes.

"That's what I said! It spells Oops!"

"Where are they from?" Leroy wanted to know, slathering a large pat of butter of his slice of pumpernickel.

"They are probably some of the parts I ordered through the library computer," Silas said. "You should start getting quite a lot of them over the next few weeks as the orders are filled. Hopefully they will all arrive before winter so we can finish work on our ship and be off."

"Is there a safe place we can store them to work on later?" asked Seth.

"I have a workshop behind the barn that hasn't been in much use lately, you can store your parts there." Leroy sighed.

"Mr. Esh?" Silas continued.

"Jah?"

"If you don't want there to be any more unfortunate 'incidents' we need to get back on that gentleman's ham radio again and broadcast another warning. I would also like to get word to my people to drop a handheld communication device for our use so we won't have to bother that banker again after this. It's similar to a cell phone the *Englisch* use."

"Just keep it out of sight somewhere safe," Leroy replied wearily.

The family continued eating in relative silence but every once in a while Seth would steal a glance at Rebecca who was refusing to look at him. At times like this he wished he could read minds; her silence was killing him. After supper they all took sponge baths and went right to bed.

Seth lay on his cot with his arms behind his head, looking out at her bedroom window. A lantern flickered softly for a while then went out but still he stared; longing to feel her in his arms again, smell the fresh scent of her hair...

"Give her up, Seth." Silas advised him in the darkness. "You had your chance now it's over. Let her go."

"Not until I can speak with the king. Not until I hear from his own mouth that I cannot become her husband and remain here."

"Perhaps you should find out from her first if she even wants to be your frau anymore after that fiasco? It sure doesn't look like she does."

"Be quiet! You weren't even there," Seth seethed. "You didn't see the joy on her face! You don't see the way she looks at me when our hearts intertwine...you don't know the way she responds when we kiss."

"Yeah? Well I saw the way she was tonight and to me it looks like it's over."

Seth threw a spare pillow at his brother. "Go to sleep already and let me be!"

"I can't believe you're refusing me after everything I have shown you!" Jessica Lynch exploded, tempted to throttle her producer with her bare hands.

"Look, there's a lot more important stuff for the station to spend money on than a wild-goose chase for aliens in Lancaster County! It sounds crazy even when I say it! I gave you the crew and equipment just for today; that will just have to be the end of it! We've got the entire Middle East melting down, political scandals, tornadoes and flooding to report on while corporate is simultaneously trimming our budget…"

"But what about the Amish men with the strange eyes and that bizarre weather incident?"

"Drop it Jessica. If you want to do some digging on your own time and come up with something reportable I'll consider reimbursing you, but unless you have more to show me I just can't do it."

"Arrrrrggh!!!" Jessica screamed, flinging her purse out of his office in frustration. She pointed a carefully French-manicured finger at him. "All right then! Have it your way! I'll take my own recorder and do it on my own time; I believe I have at least four weeks of paid vacation time coming to me!"

"Now just a minute!" Gil protested. "You just can't walk out of here and disappear for four weeks!"

"Do I really need to get the State Board of Equalization involved and have them investigate all the unpaid overtime, weekends worked and lunch breaks I've skipped?" she countered. "If not, just say the word, Gil!"

Her producer drooped; he knew when he had been beaten. "Fine – four weeks' vacation and not an hour longer or you'll be packing up your cubicle. Bring me back something great and we'll talk promotion."

Jessica crossed her arms; flexing her power. "I want to move up to the network. I want a shot at filling in for the anchor."

Gil just stared at her; shocked at the audacity. "You must think you're on to something really big."

"I don't just think; *I know*. See you in four!" With that she snatched her purse off the floor, slung it over her shoulder in a wide arc and marched out of the station offices to her car.

The next morning at breakfast, Rebecca still refused to look at Seth. She was polite to him but that was about it. The silent treatment was eating him alive on the inside. She had completely shut herself off from him emotionally and physically; making him increasingly desperate to get in communication with their king so he could finally make a sanctioned offer of marriage. Until he could give her real assurances that he wasn't going away, she would do whatever it took to protect herself.

They ate swiftly, finished up the planting at Isaac Miller's farm early then were driven into town by Mr. Esh to see if they could talk the banker into letting them borrow his ham radio one last time.

"Well hello there, Mr. Esh!" he greeted as they entered the air-conditioned establishment; obviously pleased at seeing them again.

Seth removed his hat but kept his eyes downcast. "Mr. Brown, I hate to impose again but we were wondering if there was any possible way we could borrow your ham radio again to send another brief message to our cousin?"

"Of course! Of course! I would be most happy to be of service!" he grinned. He checked his watch. "I work until 5pm today so it will be a two hour wait."

"That's fine," Silas replied. "We need to go home and wash up first anyway; we'd hate to get dirt and sweat all over your nice automobile."

"Sounds good to me! See you at 5:00 pm!" he nodded, turning aside with a wave to welcome another customer.

The three of them returned to the buggy just as a young woman with long blond hair stepped up to the outdoor ATM to get some cash. She paid little heed to them as they turned away and drove away in the buggy; then she finally did a double take.

Jessica Lynch didn't know much about the Amish but her recent research on them as a result of the crop circles story had brought up the fact that they didn't have checking accounts or credit cards...*so what were three of them doing in a bank?*

"Hurry up, hurry up, hurry up!" she groaned at the sluggish ATM machine. If she didn't get in her car soon to follow their buggy she'd lose them. It was late afternoon and there were already half-a-dozen Amish buggies out on the road already; all of which looked exactly alike. Finally the machine spit out her money and card which she jammed into her purse while racing to her car. She put the car in reverse and then had to slam on the brakes as an old woman directly behind her in a gold Ford Taurus began to back out at a snail's pace; her car beeping a warning as if it were some kind of delivery truck.

"Oh nooooooooooooo not NOW!" Jessica banged her head against the steering column as the old woman backed up one inch at a time. After several minutes wait the way was finally clear until a split second later when another car got in her way to pull into the stall the old woman had just vacated. "Arrrrggghhhh!!!" she screamed under her breath. She finally gave up all hope of pursuit when a mother pushing a stroller and three kids appeared in her rear-view mirror. "I'm cursed; that's what it is…" she muttered in defeat; then an idea hit her. She turned the car off and went into the bank.

"How can I help you?" a middle-aged woman greeted her with a broad smile.

"Umm, this is going to sound rather funny, but…I just saw three Amish people exit the bank and I was wondering…is it normal for them to have bank accounts?"

"Not for personal banking but many of them have business-es or work at businesses that require them to have merchant accounts in order to conduct transactions, why?" The woman replied.

"Oh, I'm a reporter doing a story and I was just curious…" Jessica replied mysteriously.

The woman's eyes grew large with sudden interest; she leaned in close. "Are you here to do a story on all the crop circles and weird lights?" she asked *sotto voce.*

Jessica smelled a potential ally. "Maybe," she replied with an engaging smile. "Why? Do you know anything?"

"Well nothing first hand but it's been the main topic of con-versation around here for quite a while!" the woman replied conspi-ratorially.

Jessica dug in her purse and handed the woman her press card. "Well if there's anything you'd like to share feel free to call my cell. I'll be in town for the next 4 weeks on a working vacation."

The woman giggled and pocketed the card as Jessica turned to leave. Just before she exited the door the woman closed the gap between them and leaned forward to whisper again. "I don't know if this would be of any interest to you; but those Amish you just saw leaving the bank?"

"Yes?"

The woman looked around surreptitiously as if she were a clandestine spy in a suspense novel. "I only got a glimpse so I'm not positive…but two of them had the strangest eyes…"

Jessica's heart began to pound with suppressed excitement. "Really?"

The woman nodded.

"Can you tell me who they were?"

Suddenly the woman straightened becoming all business again. "Certainly not! I'd be violating privacy laws!"

Jessica instantly deflated; she forced a friendly smile. "Well thank you anyway. Please feel free to call me should anything else interesting come up!"

She went back to her car and speed-dialed Hal's office number.

"Speak fast," said his voice before the second ring.

"Hal – I got a lead on the Amish boys with the weird eyes."

"Already? That was fast!"

"It was sheer dumb luck but I missed a golden opportunity to follow them home. They were in a bank conducting some kind of business…"

"Amish don't have personal bank accounts," Hal stated.

"I know – that's why I went inside!"

"Did you find out anything?"

"Just that the two young men in question were in here not more than five minutes ago so I know they must live within a 20 mile radius."

"Well that's something; not much, but something," he allowed. "Why aren't you following them? I thought your nickname was the bloodhound!"

"The fates intervened…don't ask for the details."

"So where are you staying; the Day's Inn in Intercourse?"

"No! If I'm going to be here 4 weeks I'm going to be comfortable. I booked a B&B in Bird-in-Hand; if I can come back with a good enough story it will all be reimbursed."

"…and if you don't?"

"Then I've had a nice vacation for the first time in five years. Look, I gotta run; any recommendations for a good place to eat around here?"

"Yeah – the Shady Maple," said Hal.

"What's that? Fine Dining? Not on my budget."

"It's a famous Smorgasbord; reasonable and all the food you can eat. Ask anyone there; they'll tell you!"

"I'll Google it and get directions; Smorgasbord sounds great right now; I'm starving."

At that moment a car honked at her; the driver growing impatient at waiting for her spot.

"Gotta go Hal; I don't have my Bluetooth on."

"Later."

Leroy and the brothers arrived home twenty minutes later to find Ruth, Rebecca, Hannah, Mirriam and Mary all busy pegging the mountains of freshly laundered bedding and clothing in the warm summer breeze. Leroy went into the main house followed by the brothers.

"I think we should bring Mr. Brown some kind of thank you gift," Seth said when thee had finished washing their hands and face. "I'm going to ask Mrs. Esh if she wouldn't mind baking something for him."

"Sure you don't mean Miss Esh?" Silas countered with a lift of his eyebrow.

Seth walked out the door; ignoring him. He found Rebecca on the service porch, wringing out another load of laundry. He stared at the back of her head nervously; wondering how to break the ice when she suddenly turned and froze upon seeing him. For an instant he thought he saw the glimmer of a smile then she set her face into stone.

"Jah?" There was no warmth or welcome in her voice.

"Becca, please don't be like this; it's killing me," Seth murmured, spreading his hands out plaintively. "I'd rather have you yelling at me or throwing things but this emotionless apathy…I just can't take it. I still love you; I still want you as my frau; don't you feel anything for me anymore?"

Rebecca merely stared at him; unmoving then her lip trembled. "No," she whispered, turning away from him. Seth closed the distance instantly; seizing upon the chink in her emotional armor. He spun her around, seized her face in his hands and slanted his lips upon hers. For a moment she stood unresponsive but then her arms snaked about him to pull him closer; pressing herself full length against him. It was all the encouragement he needed to kiss her with the unbridled passion that had been pent up inside of him for days. He could taste the hot tears sliding down her cheeks upon his tongue. After several long moments he reluctantly pulled away.

He stared at her with renewed determination. Her eyes were no longer cold but feverish with desire. "Rebecca Esh; as long as I live you will have no other husband but me," he swore. "If I have to forsake my own world and all I hold dear to have you; I will."

Rebecca nodded but still said nothing. Then she lifted her arms for him again and smiled.

Seth pulled her close, nuzzling her cheek and neck. "I have a small favor to ask, Becca," he murmured, breathing in her fresh scent. Her arms tightened about him.

"Anything," she whispered in his ear; sending a thrill coursing down his spine. "What do you desire?"

Seth gently separated from her and gave her a rakish grin; causing her to blush crimson. "I want you to make me some Whoopie pies for the banker."

Rebecca stared at him; caught completely off-guard then she shoved him playfully. "Ach! You're impossible! First you beg for forgiveness then you try to seduce me when all you really wanted in the first place was WHOOPIE PIES!"

Seth caught her by the waist again and drew her close. "That's not all I want," he retorted with a happy smile, "but until we are wed it's what I am willing to settle for."

Rebecca sighed and gazed her fill of him; happy to have the millstone gone from her heart. She took his hand in hers and laid it over her heart to show him that all was forgiven. "How many do you need?"

"Half a dozen in an hour?"

"We've only just made up and you're already making demands!"

Seth drew close until their lips were only a kiss apart. "I plan to make plenty more once we've exchanged our sacred vows. I'll finish up your share of the laundry if you'll bake those pies."

"You'll never hear the end of it from my sisters!" she grinned at him, ducking into the kitchen.

"Or my *bruder*," he yelled over his shoulder as he hefted the basket full of wet linen up into his arms.

Two hours later they were back at the bank, waiting in the buggy for Mr. Brown to exit. On Seth's lap was a small baker's box filled with the freshly-made Whoopie pies.

"Howdy Mr. Esh!" Mr. Brown waved, oblivious of his fellow employees exiting the bank behind him.

"This has to be the last time," Leroy warned them softly before climbing out. "It's drawing too much attention."

"Jah, it will be," agreed Silas, climbing out and keeping his eyes lowered. They left a bucket of oats and pumped fresh water into the trough for Joe then climbed into the familiar mini-van.

"We brought you a little thank you gift!" Seth said, offering the banker the box.

"Well that's awfully nice of you!" Robert smiled accepting it. He lifted the lid and grinned with pleasure. "I've always wanted to try one of these! May I?"

All three heads bobbed in affirmation.

He picked one up and paused before taking an enormous bite. "Don't tell my wife; I'm supposed to be dieting!" Whipped cream leaked out of the corners of his mouth as he shook his head in unadulterated pleasure. "Oh man…that's good!" He licked his fingers before buckling up. "Put your seatbelts on!" he reminded them cheerfully.

For the next fifteen minutes he chattered away, completely unaware that the conversation was entirely one-sided with only a grunt here and there to encourage him. He parked the van and carried the box into the kitchen.

"Lil! We've got some visitors!"

A pretty brunette came out to greet them. Leroy, Seth and Silas instantly removed their hats and cast their eyes downward.

"Well, welcome!" she said, taking the box of pies from her husband. "Can I offer you anything to drink?"

"Nee," Leroy shook his head. "But danki – we will only be but a moment."

Robert vaulted upstairs; taking them two at a time. "Come on up fellas!"

With polite nods, all three followed him up to his hobby room where the radio was already warming up. He beckoned Silas to the seat. "It's all yours, son!"

"Danki, Mr. Brown."

While Robert indulged in another Whoopie pie, Silas swiftly dialed in the correct frequency and began jabbering away; not neglecting to throw in some of the more commonly-known Amish phrases as before. After only three minutes he was done and changing the frequency so their benefactor would not know what it was.

Silas stood to his feet and put his hat back on. "We shouldn't need to bother you again, Mr. Brown; we surely appreciate your help."

"Mi radio esta su radio!" he grinned. "You can come back as often as you like as long as long as you bring me more of these!" He waved a third Whoopie pie in the air before stuffing it whole into his mouth. They waited for him to dispose of the "evidence" before following him downstairs.

"Leaving so soon?" his wife said, looking a bit befuddled.

Robert pecked his wife on the cheek on his way out the door. "I'll be back in 30 minutes Hun; dinner can wait for an hour or so; I'm not hungry." He shoved the box of pies into her arms and beat a hasty retreat when she lifted the lid to peek.

"Robert Allen Brown –how many of these did you just eat?" came her voice through the door as it sailed shut.

They arrived at the bank which was now closed and got back into the buggy to return home, waving goodbye to the genial banker as he backed up and drove off.

"Were you successful in your endeavor?" Leroy asked, snapping the reins.

"Yes – there should be no more incidents and a hand-held communication device will be deposited for our use sometime within the next few days." Silas replied. They rode in silence the remainder of the trip while Silas ignored the questioning looks Seth was giving him. They couldn't very well discuss the matter he had posed to his people of his bruder being granted permission to marry a woman of earth in front of Mr. Esh; they might slip up and mention Rebecca's name.

Rebecca was waiting for them at the front door; a welcoming smile on her face.

Chapter Fifteen
"Eavesdropping at the Shady Maple"

After several wrong turns and numerous stops to ask directions, Jessica finally found the Shady Maple and was now standing in the parking lot; ogling at what had to be the world's largest Smorgasbord.

"Holy mackerel; it's the size of two Costco's!" She made her way to the upper level where the line of locals and tourists was already out the door. She checked her email on her Android then punched in the address for the B&B where she was staying so the navigation app could steer her to her lodgings after it grew dark. After a ten minute wait she was paying her $25.00 to the cashier and wandering among the numerous food stations to see what she wanted to eat. The sight of so much food in one place was simply overwhelming. She decided to be good and start at the salad bar, piling her plate high; determined to eat her money's worth.

On her second trip back her plate was stacked with fried chicken, brisket and creamed corn. As she walked back to her table she found herself stuck behind a small group of long-haul UPS drivers who were off for the night. She smiled to herself, admiring the manly legs under the brown uniforms; remembering a story she had covered on all the women in offices who were besotted with their particular delivery man. Dimly she became aware of their conversation; her journalistic ears pricking up when she heard the words "crop circles", "weird lights" and "hate driving at night in middle of nowhere with all the weird stuff going on". Since she had her purse with her, she decided to follow them and see if she could commandeer a nearby table so she could continue eavesdropping. As luck would have it, a table was available just on the other side of the aisle from them.

She set her tray down, fished out her Android and found the app for recording audio then set it on the table; hoping it would pick up their conversation clearly despite all the background noise.

"I'm telling ya, Craig – you don't want to be driving the 222 after midnight," she heard one of the drivers say to the other. "Ask any of the locals around here! The teenagers don't even go out after midnight anymore; they're too scared stiff!"

"I had a green beam follow my rig for the better part of five miles," another said in-between mouthfuls, "…before I pulled off into one of those truck stops. I had to change my underwear I was so scared."

"What do you think this all is?" another asked.

"I don't know but it's getting worse. There's talk of aliens hiding in plain sight but I won't believe it until I see one up close."

Jessica suddenly became aware that the conversation had stopped and that all four UPS men were staring across the aisle at her.

Her hand had been poised halfway to her mouth with the same piece of fried chicken for the past ten minutes.

"You gonna eat that, lady or just memorize it?" one of them grinned at her.

She went red. "Sorry, I just couldn't help overhearing your conversation is all. Aliens huh?"

The smiles disappeared suddenly. "You aren't with management, right?"

Jessica blinked, not comprehending. "Management?"

They nodded.

"Oh! You mean UPS? No – I'm just here on vacation!" She almost added that she was a reporter then thought better of it. "So lots of weird stuff going on, eh? I guess I won't be driving after midnight."

"You heard that?"

"Yup."

"Stay on the well-lit roads too after dark."

Jessica nodded and reluctantly returned to her food; her stomach all in excited knots. She pretended not to pay them anymore attention while her cell continued to record their conversation which then switched back to talk of regular work. She ate as slowly as she could, not wanting to miss anything but the dessert table was calling her name and it was getting late. She opted for soft serve ice-cream, nuts and syrup then scooted out of her booth with a goodbye smile to the UPS men who were also getting ready to leave.

"Happy delivering," she waved, instantly realizing how totally lame she sounded.

"Oh yeah, thanks!" grinned the one named Craig. "After this last stop I'll be done for the day; 24 packages all to one Amish farm, then I can go to sleep."

At this Jessica's internal radar went up. "Wow that's a lot of packages for one place!"

"Especially for an Amish home," Craig nodded. "We've all been placing bets on what's inside them."

"What do you mean?"

"Well they're all mostly from hi-tech companies which is why it caught our attention; Amish never order that kind of stuff; in fact they rarely if ever get UPS deliveries at their homes; only to the businesses they work at."

Jessica tried to remain calm but too many alarm bells were going off in her head that she had stumbled upon something huge. "I don't suppose you could reveal where they're going to?" she responded, turning on her most winning smile.

"Sorry, no." Craig smiled apologetically. "I already told you too much. Now if you'll excuse me?" He hurried off to catch up with the other drivers who were already heading to their separate trucks. Jessica was tempted to follow him but she was wearing high heels and would have to run the equivalent of an entire block just to get to her vehicle; she wouldn't make it in time.

"Damn." She trudged down the parking lot and made a quick visit to the Shady Maple market for her free loaf of bread and some snack foods and bottled water before getting into her car and punching in the address for the Rocky Springs Bed & Breakfast Inn. It was 7:00 pm but still light outside. She followed the robotic voice as it directed her where to drive, passing Amish buggies every once in a while along the way. Every time she saw one she tried to get a good look at the people riding inside but it was nearly impossible and she almost ran one off the road into the ditch.

"I'm so sorry!" she yelled out through her open passenger window at the frightened family. After a fifteen minute drive she found the Inn; a lovely two-story structure made entirely of brick. She checked in and lugged her laptop and suitcase up to her second story mansion bedroom which included free high-speed internet access. She flopped on the bed, turned on the laptop and signed in while waiting for Hal to pick up his cell phone.

"Talk," came his voice on the other end of the line.

Jessica grinned even though he couldn't see her. "Got another lead! I'm feeling pretty lucky!"

"Let's hear it."

"I overheard and recorded the conversation of several UPS drivers at the table next to me; they were all talking about UFOs."

"Interesting; anything of use?"

"Well I still have to go over the audio again but one of them was mentioning how he had over 25 packages of hi-tech parts being delivered to a local Amish farm and how weird they all thought it was."

"That is strange," Hal agreed. "Don't suppose he was willing to be nice and share the address?"

"I asked and no; he refused; however, he and his compatriots all warned me about not driving around in the dark here because of all the weird stuff going on."

"He might have just been pulling your leg, Jess."

"I don't think so because I overheard them all talking about it before they ever noticed me..." she interrupted herself with a big yawn. "I'm going to go now, Hal. I'll email you if anything more turns up."

"Try to actually take some vacation time while you're on vacation, kiddo," he advised.

"I will – tomorrow I'm going to go into Bird-In-Hand and do a little sight-seeing while I snoop around. Night, Hal."

"Night, Jess."

She hung up the phone, hooked up her Android to her laptop using the USB port and transferred the audio she had recorded earlier while she unpacked. Twilight was approaching. She took a bottle of water and notebook out to the Inn's deck and watched with child-like delight as the fireflies came out. Living in a city apartment, she didn't get to see them much anymore and she had forgotten how enchanting they were. They were like tiny fairies that rose and descended in the foliage under trees and bushes and above the grass; their little bodies blinking on and off like Christmas lights. She found it difficult to tear her eyes away but managed to scribble down a few leads to follow up on the next day.

That evening after supper Rebecca was waiting for Seth in the front yard. "I am going to have to tell Jacob the news soon," she said as they ducked behind the corner of the house; holding hands. "Sooner or later he's going to find out I never went to Indiana and he's going to come calling."

Seth nodded, unable to help but feel sorry for his competition. "What are you going to tell him?"

"Ach! I don't know! There is still the matter of what to say to my parents as well! I've made such an awful mess of everything!"

"Becca – perhaps you should wait until I've heard back from our king?"

"Who is this king you constantly speak of?" she blurted out; feeling a bit of animosity for him. "Why do you need to hear from him first?"

"Finally a question! And here I had assumed you were the one female left on earth who had lost her capacity for curiosity!" Seth grinned, trying to make light of the situation.

"If we are to be joined together as one then I need to know more about you," she admitted, fingering the collar of his blue shirt. Her light touch sent delicious shivers coursing down his spine. "I need to know that you will be baptized into our faith and truly become a believer; that you are not just going through the motions so you can please my people and be with me."

Seth lifted her fingers to his lips and kissed them one by one. "It's that important to you?"

Rebecca nodded and lifted her blue eyes to his. Instantly his own began to glow white hot; she felt heat entering her and spreading throughout her torso and limbs. For a long moment they stood; lost in one another's eyes; their souls silently intertwining. "It means everything to me, Seth. I have to know that you truly believe and have embraced der Herr as your own before I can give myself to you."

Seth drew her close and cupped her face in one hand. "Whatever it takes, Rebecca, I will do it," he swore, his voice shaking with the intensity of his emotions. "I will embrace your faith and make it my own once the king has given me his blessing to do so."

"What is your king's name, Seth?" Rebecca whispered, tracing the fine angles of his face and the dark stubble upon his upper lip with her finger.

"We are not permitted to speak his name or refer to him as anything other than our 'king' but I am permitted to write it down for you," he replied.

"He sounds very stern," Rebecca replied.

"Stern but fair; we serve him out of love."

"Then he is a benevolent king?" She stood on tip-toe; her lips bare inches from his.

Seth was finding it hard to concentrate. "Completely," he murmured.

"Seth…"

"What?"

"Kiss me already!"

He needed no further encouragement. He pulled her close and found her lips waiting for him. It was a sweet kiss; brimming with all the promises he wanted to fulfill in order to make her a proper Amish bride.

"Perhaps you should write his name down for me now," Rebecca smiled shyly, stepping back; her face flushed.

They went to the dawdi haus together where she found some pencils and blank writing paper. At that moment they heard the sound of a large vehicle pulling into their driveway.

"It's the Oops man! It's the Oops man!" Mary sang out from the front porch, hopping down the steps to greet him.

"Probably delivering some of those things we ordered." Silas said, hurrying past them outside.

"Go ahead; keep writing!" Rebecca reminded Seth. Seth grasped the pencil and going from right to left, scribbled down alien-looking symbols onto the paper which she did not recognize. He handed her the paper and she turned it this way and that but couldn't make heads or tails out of it.

"Seth!" called his bruder's voice from outside. "Can you give us a hand out here? Grab a lantern and let's show him where the workshop is."

"Coming!" Seth hollered back. He gave Rebecca a little push out the door. "Time for you to clean up from dinner, my little Becca; and time for me to stack all those boxes in the workshop."

"Ach! All right!" she grimaced, folding the paper up and tucking it into her apron. Outside was the UPS man in his traditional brown uniform holding onto a hand dolly that was stacked high with boxes from several high-tech companies.

"This way," Seth pointed, leading him to the workshop. After three more trips all the boxes were neatly put away.

The UPS driver held up his large electronic clipboard. "Sign here Mr. Esh, please," he smiled, indicating a small LED screen.

"I'm not Mr. Esh – I'll have to get him. Can you wait a moment?"

"Sure," smiled Craig. He looked down to find little Mary staring up at him. "Hi!" He squatted down so he was eye-to-eye with her. "What's your name?"

"Mary," she giggled. "You're the Oops man!"

"I'm the what?" Craig grinned.

"The Oops man!"

He decided to play along. "Do you know why they call us that?"

Mary shook her head.

"Because when a package is marked 'fragile' we throw it harder!" Then he laughed at his own joke.

At that moment Leroy Esh appeared. "Jah?"

"Since your name is on the invoices I have to have your signature," Craig said, holding up the electronic clipboard.

Leroy stared at it for a moment; not quite sure what to do; he had never seen one before.

Craig handed him the plastic stylus. "Just sign your name here like you would on paper."

Leroy signed and then turned to go back into the house. "Danki,"

Craig spun the hand dolly around and pushed it over to his large brown van while Seth and Silas followed behind. "So whatcha up to?" he grinned, just trying to make light conversation. "Science project?"

"I guess you could say that," Silas nodded, wishing he would leave already.

Craig slammed the door shut, gave them a friendly wave then drove off; little Mary waving until the delivery van was out of sight.

Seth's exhale was explosive. "I thought the guy would never leave!"

"As soon as we get Mr. Esh's harvest in we'll start adapting those parts," Silas said, shutting and locking the workshop's double doors.

"Silas, we have to talk."

"If it's about your staying here you'll just have to wait until you hear from the king because until then; it's a moot point."

"I may stay regardless," Seth replied quietly.

Silas looked at him in horror. "Don't…even…go…there," he warned, struggling to find the right words to say. In the end all he could do was shake his head: "NO!"

But Seth couldn't leave it alone. "Silas, please try to understand…"

In response Silas grabbed him by the front of the shirt and pushed him backwards until his back hit the wall of the workshop with a bang. "You will not be the first among our people to commit sedition!" he gritted out through clenched teeth. "Especially not over an earth-dweller; the result of which would be cataclysmic for all of us."

For the first time in his life Seth experienced fear at his brother's words. He knew that Silas had spoken the truth; that his act of following the desires of his heart could doom his planet. Their king was benevolent but he was also just and would brook no disobedience. In thousands of millennia no one had ever done so. Just entertaining the idea of doing so for the love of Rebecca could potentially lead to catastrophic consequences, not just to him but his home world as well.

He slumped. "It hasn't come to that yet; perhaps he will grant me my request…"

Silas let go of his shirt and shook his head in reproach. "Do you actually think you're the first to fall in love with one of them? He is not going to change his law just for you! He has good reasons for forbidding it and you know well what it is!"

Seth did not reply. What his head knew and his heart, body and soul wanted were two entirely different things; he had never felt so torn in two.

"Just let it be for now, Seth," Silas pleaded, his hands gripping his shoulders. "Please; I beg of you!"

Seth nodded but still said nothing which just worried Silas all the more. His hands fell off and hung at his sides; he felt absolutely powerless to make his brother see reason. "It's getting dark; I'm going to bed." He turned away and walked to the dawdi haus; leaving his brother behind. Seth looked up hopefully at Rebecca's window but it had already gone dark; finally he too went inside and lay awake for hours; rehearsing how he would present his petition to the king as soon as he had the communication device.

Rebecca was not asleep. She had listened to the entire exchange between the brothers and it had made her blood run cold. Until that moment she had only been worried about her family, their standing in the community and Jacob. The notion that their love for each other might cause cataclysmic trouble for Seth, Silas and their world was frightening. Though she knew next to nothing about where they came or their world, a nameless terror had arisen in her heart. She loved Seth with every fiber of her being and more than anything desired to be his frau but could she really allow him to make such a tremendous sacrifice just for her? For some reason the entire scenario reminded her of something important and familiar but when she tried to put her finger on what it was; the thought evaded her; it just kept dancing around the periphery of her memory like an elusive phantom.

Chapter Sixteen
"The Whoopie Pie Hits the Fan"

The sound of birds singing outside her window brought her to irritable consciousness. Jessica opened one eye then the other, trying to locate the alarm so she could fling it across the room when she realized that it was nature calling and therefore had no snooze button. She was well accustomed to the sounds of the city outside her fifth level apartment; the almost nonstop honking horns, people yelling and what seemed like the never-ending road demolition and reconstruction. Those she could sleep through with no problem but not a flock of birds cawing, whistling, and singing simultaneously out her window.

She flung the covers back, shrugged into the thick complimentary terry cloth robe and shoved down the double-hung window with a bang. The birds outside flew away instantly.

She stumbled across the creaking hardwood floor to the bathroom to answer the second call of nature then upon checking the time, hurriedly dressed for breakfast, clipping up her long blonde hair to look more presentable. She had 20 minutes left before the Innkeepers put the food away. She hurried downstairs to find the dining room half-empty. She settled herself at a table for two, admiring the red toile wallpaper contrasted against the black colonial style furniture and Persian rug upon the hardwood floor.

"May I offer you some coffee?" The Innkeeper greeted her, appearing with a coffee pot in one hand and juice pitcher in the other.

"Absolutely," Jessica said, pushing her cup forward.

The Innkeeper poured, continuing with polite conversation. "Where are you visiting from?"

"I guess you could say I'm a local; I'm from Philly," Jessica replied, taking a sip of the steaming brew. "Mmmmm this is really good."

"Today's breakfast offerings include homemade blueberry and bran muffins. There's also fresh fruit, homemade granola, pastries, bacon, sausage, cottage potatoes and broccoli quiche. It's all buffet style on the board there so just help yourself. We also have fresh squeezed orange *(here she lifted her pitcher as evidence)* and cranberry juice. Please let me know if you need anything; refill on your coffee, water; or if you would like information on sites to see, tickets or reservations." Jessica was impressed; it was a well-rehearsed speech without a hint of boredom at having to repeat it endlessly to every patron who entered the dining room.

"How about a good lead on all the UFO stuff that's been going on around here?" She grinned up at the Innkeeper; attempting humor.

The Innkeeper's smile instantly vanished and a look of terror filled her eyes. "That's not funny," she whispered and hurried back to the kitchen.

Jessica craned her neck around 180°degrees to watch her disappear behind the swinging door; not knowing whether to laugh or apologize. Apparently it was no laughing matter around here; the woman looked completely shook up. She got to her feet, found a stack of lovely china plates at the sideboard and filled her plate before returning to her seat. On the way she caught a glance at the local newspaper. **STRANGE OCCURRENCES COME TO ABRUPT HALT** teased the headline. She set her plate down then snatched up the paper bringing it back to her table. For the next hour she scanned various articles which described the nightly routine of strange lights, damaged crops, missing livestock and resulting paranoia that had gripped the populace of Lancaster County. She read further and slumped. Great...just great; it had all come to complete stop the day before she arrived.

"Damn; what lousy timing!" Perhaps it was just a lull and would restart before she had to return to Philadelphia. If it didn't and she couldn't provide Gil with a major scoop, she would have to empty her savings account to pay for all the expenses on this trip which had been intended for Hawaii! By the time she remembered to eat, everything that was supposed to be warm had gone cold and vice versa. She tucked the newspaper under her arm, went to her room to shower then was back in her car and driving to town to see if she could wheedle any additional information out of the woman at the bank. She parked her car and surreptitiously scanned the street; hoping to find a horse and buggy nearby. No such luck. She gathered up a local map and Tour Guide book and entered the bank; waiting for her eyes to adjust.

"Welcome! How can I be of assistance? Would you like one?" greeted a male voice. Jessica turned round to find a middle-aged man holding up a baker's box.

"What are they?" she asked, just to be polite; her eyes searching the interior for the woman.

"The Amish call them Whoopie pies," he smiled.

Jessica's ears instantly perked up. She gave him her best thousand watt smile. "Did you make these yourself? she asked, selecting one and peering down at his name tag. "...Robert?"

"Me? Oh no! I can't bake to save my life. No – these were a 'thank you' gift from some of my Amish customers," he said proudly.

A low volt of electricity began to ascend up her spine. "Thank you gift?"

"Yes...I let his boys borrow the use of my ham radio a couple of times to get in contact with a neighbor of their cousins or something like that. My wife didn't want me eating all of them so I brought them in to share..."

"I didn't know Amish used ham radios," Jessica purred, opening her green eyes as wide as possible. It had the desired effect; her knock-out looks and undivided attention loosened his lips like a good bottle of wine might have done.

"Oh they don't! It's not allowed...they don't usually have bank accounts either unless it is a merchant account for their business."

She took a nibble just to stall for time. "So did the boys bake these for you?" she asked, batting her lashes at him in blondified wonder.

"Oh no!" Robert giggled; actually blushing furious red. "I'm sure Mrs. Esh or one of her daughters did that; Amish men don't bake or cook."

Esh. She had actually managed to weasel a last name out of him! She wondered how far her luck would hold..."I hear tell that Amish have very large families; like Catholics and Mormons do," she smiled, taking another bite of the Whoopie Pie even though she was already stuffed to the gills.

"Oh yes, they do! They need them to work their farms; just like how America used to be; the more kids the better!"

"So do you know the Esh's well? How many kids do they have?"

"Well I only met the two boys and the father," he babbled on. "Fine looking young men but with the strangest eyes..."

Jessica tried not to gasp aloud but the low voltage shock of electricity instantly cranked up full blast into Giga watts.

"Strange eyes?" She tried to maintain a calm voice but her lips had actually gone numb.

"Gold and silver...never saw anything like it before."

She was close to going apoplectic with joy but she managed to contain herself enough to take out her guide book to further the illusion that she was just a tourist. Her hands were shaking as she handed it to him. "I actually came in to see if I could get a local's recommendation on some of the sites around here. Would you mind?"

She only half-listened as Robert prattled on about the many attractions she could find in Intercourse as well as Bird-in-Hand; her mind racing a mile a minute.

"...then there's the Central Market at Penn Square..." she dimly heard him say.

She had stayed long enough. "Robert! I can't thank you enough for taking the time to help me," she interrupted; so happy she could have kissed him. "And thank you for Mrs. Esh's wonderful Whoopie pie! It was heavenly."

"Well you're quite welcome!" he grinned, watching her edge backwards to the exit doors.

Jessica gave him a friendly goodbye wave then practically flew out of the bank and bodily crashed into her own car; gasping for breath. Her asthma always did kick in when she got excited. She clawed through her purse for her inhaler and took three deep drags first before dialing Hal's phone and getting inside.

"What?" he answered in his typically brusque manner.

She was still struggling for breath. "Esh!" she managed to get out. "Esh!"

"Jess – what are you talking about? Is this some new curse word you've learned that you want to try out on me?"

She wanted to bang the cell phone on the dash in frustration but it wouldn't have accomplished anything. She struggled for breath and calm.

Hal waited patiently...accustomed to her breathing struggles. "Just let the inhaler do its' job, honey. I'll wait."

Jessica laid her head back against the rest and closed her eyes, struggling to calm down and just breathe. Finally her airway began to open up. "I found them, Hal! The boys with the strange eyes; the last name is Esh – can you Google it?"

"There wouldn't be any point," he said, in a sorry-you're-out-of-luck voice. "Amish live in a totally closed, nontechnical society; they wouldn't leave any kind of digital footprint."

"What about the online yellow pages?"

"They don't have phones."

"Look – the banker told me they have businesses, people can't do business without phones...just try it will ya, Hal? We've got nothing to lose!"

"Okay, okay give me a sec."

A car honked at her in the parking lot; another driver exasperated at waiting for her stall. What was it with these impatient people??!! She hooked up her Bluetooth, started the car, backed out, and began driving aimlessly.

"Well I'll be – the Amish do have an internet presence!" He admitted.

Jessica bobbed up and down with excitement. "Send all the hits you get to my email; I'll be able to view them from my Android."

"Are you sure?"

"Yeah – I'm sure. How many could there be? *The Amish don't leave any kind of digital footprint!*" she mocked him good naturedly then hung up. She drove through the rolling countryside for a good fifteen minutes before happening upon Kitchen Kettle Village. A line of cars and tour buses were waiting to turn into the large parking lot.

"Looks like as good a place as any to kill time," she muttered to herself, getting in line behind a large SUV crammed full of people. In ten minutes she was parked and walking towards the row of shops. She wandered in and out of the Vera Bradley shop, picking up a new purse that caught her eye then to the Canning Kitchen where shelf after shelf was stacked high with jar upon jar of jams, jellies, preserves, butters, relishes, pickles, salsas, dressings, syrups as well as baked goods which were all on display and available for sampling. Ten minutes into her shopping she got Hal's email.

HOLD ON TO YOUR PANTYHOSE warned the subject line. She scrolled down and groaned aloud. "ESH FOODS; ESH QUALITY HOME IMPROVEMENTS; ESH DAIRY; ESH EYECARE; ESH PUPPY MILL ALERT; ESH QUILT FETCHES EXORBITANT PRICE AT RECENT AUCTION…" It was the equivalent of looking up the surname of Chin in the Beijing White Pages. She'd have to wait and go through them on her laptop back at the Inn.

Seth finished harvesting the final row just as the sun set across the Esh farm. It had been two days since Silas had broadcast the "cease and desist" warning to their people along with their special request. The communication device was due to arrive almost any time. Seth was both anxious for and dreading its arrival; one way or another it would herald the end of one way of life for him. Silas turned the mule team towards the barn with their last load of hay. Tomorrow they would plough under the field so it could lie fallow for the winter months. Leroy saw them coming and opened the barn door wide and together all three labored to store the bales into the loft. It was hot, sweaty and dirty work and by the time they were done, all three of them had hay sticking in their hair (and Leroy's beard) despite their hats.

"Mmmmm is that my favorite dinner I'm smelling?" Seth asked, breathing in a deep whiff of the wonderful aromas wafting from the Esh kitchen windows.

"Jah, the women are making oven fried chicken tonight." Leroy nodded. "But first we clean up gut; Ruth will not abide hay being tracked into the house; either by foot or head."

Silas punched his brother in the arm; trying to reignite their friendship. "You look like a scarecrow! You'll need to take a curry comb to that head of yours first."

"Hey! What was that?" Seth pointed to the field where their ship was hidden.

"Falling star," Leroy grunted, wiping off his clothes and running his fingers through his head and beard.

Silas and Seth exchanged meaningful looks. "Will you excuse us for just a moment, Mr. Esh?"

"Nee," he shook his head. "Supper is on the table; whatever it is can wait until after we have eaten."

"Yes sir," they relented. Thirty minutes more couldn't hurt they supposed.

Leroy hid his smile until after they had shuffled inside. He had grown to care deeply for these two. They had become the sons der Herr had not seen fit to provide through birth. He wasn't sure how things stood between his eldest and Seth at the moment but one thing was unmistakable; the way they looked at one another was the same way he and Ruth used to moon at each other many years ago when they were still young and in the midst of courting. He would be happy to welcome either of them permanently into his home as his own sons; as long as his Amish brethren had no objection. The un-timely death of Deacon Yoder, sad as it was; had never-the-less lifted a great burden of worry from his heart. He had died before ever get-ting the opportunity to tell others what he had seen. The boys had proven their worth many times over, both on his farm as well as Isaac's. If no further 'incidents' occurred perhaps the suspicions of his people would be allayed enough to finally accept them.

He followed them up the porch steps and into the kitchen where Rebecca was waiting for them. After grace, they tucked into generous servings of chicken, green bean and potato salad and noodles with buttered crumbs. Rebecca seemed unusually quiet and introspective but her father shrugged it off as a passing mood.

As soon as supper was done, Silas grabbed his brother by the arm and hauled him out of the house. "We'll be back soon, Mr. Esh." He said, tipping his hat on his way out the door. The screen door bounced shut behind them as they hurried down the porch steps.

"Stop pulling me!" Seth growled, shaking his brother's arm off. He slowed to a stop, reluctant to finally confront reality.

"We can't put this off any longer, Seth; you know that." Silas' face was grim. "Let's get it over with."

Seth stared at his brother still unmoving as though his feet had been cast into quick drying cement. "Has anyone ever been granted an exception before?"

Silas shook his head slowly then put his arm around his brother. "C'mon...maybe you'll be the first?"

Seth nodded but still trudged like a condemned man into the field where they had seen the "star" fall. They each carried a flash-light and searched through the flattened vegetation for a good hour.

"It's not here, let's go." Seth sighed; feigning disappointment. Silas wasn't fooled. He shook his head.

"We search until we find it," he replied. After another hour they found the communication device; undamaged by its descent to Earth.

Seth picked it up and stared at it. For purposes of concealment it had been made to look like a cell phone.

Silas sat down on the ground Indian style. "Go ahead, Seth."

Seth emitted a long shuddering sigh then sat down across from him, inserting the ear bud and turning on the device. Silas waited patiently as a slender beam of light issued from the device and ascended into the night sky finally disappearing high into the stratosphere and beyond. Seth's eyes were closed and his lips barely moved while Silas looked on; hoping with all his heart his brother might receive the answer he desired. After several long moments' pause, a single tear slid down Seth's face. He removed the communication device and remained as still as stone.

Silas leaned forward; anxious to know the outcome. "Well?"

Seth slowly opened his eyes then shook his head; his face clearly indicating the response had not been what he hoped for.

"I'm sorry, Seth."

Seth held up his hand palm out to silence him, stood to his feet and shoved the device into his brother's hands.

Silas followed him silently, suddenly fearful of what his brother would do next. It would do no good to try and talk sense into him; the only one Seth might possibly listen to on this matter would be Rebecca…

Silas froze and shook his head. Why had he not thought of it before? He would have to find some way to speak to Rebecca privately without Seth's knowledge and it would have to be soon; before he violated their king's will and endangered their world forever.

Chapter Seventeen
"When Three Worlds Collide"

Jessica couldn't get back to the Inn fast enough. She carefully put her packages onto the table then turned on the laptop, kicking off her shoes and climbing onto the bed while she waited for the computer to boot up. She had 84 emails but the only one she was concerned about was Hal's. She opened it up and groaned. There were at least 75 hits on the name "Esh".

"Who'd have thunk?" she murmured to herself with a scowl. Here Hal had assumed there would be nothing; she had hoped there would be *something* and the ending result was basically "TMI" (TOO MUCH INFORMATION). She would just have to be methodical and look up each link one at a time by clicking on it and hope the gods of journalism were smiling down on her.

She had gone thoroughly researched 15 links by the time it grew dark outside and her stomach reminded her she had forgotten to eat dinner. She turned off the computer and stretched out full length on the bed, cracking her back, neck, arms and shoulders. She picked up her purse and headed downstairs where she waited patiently for the Innkeeper to get off the phone.

The woman ended the call and smiled up at her. "How can I help you?"

"Is there any place close by where I could get some dinner?"

"There's quite a lot; what do you feel like? Fine dining, fast food?"

"How about something in-between that has some atmosphere?"

"There's Annie Bailey's Irish Pub; it's located in downtown Lancaster."

"Sounds perfect! I sure could go for an ice-cold beer on tap after the day I've had."

The Innkeeper smiled and gave her a map of the area, yellow-highlighting the roads she would need to take as well as writing down the address so she could use her Smartphone to navigate the way. "I'll call in a reservation for you; it's quite a popular place so I can't make any promises..."

"No worries, thanks!" Jessica flapped the map at her in farewell as she went out the door. It was already dark and she felt sad that she had missed the twilight flight of the fireflies. She found the pub after a good fifteen minute drive and eased into the last available parking stall. "Luck of the Irish," she noted with a smirk. The front of the establishment was inviting with its rich wood trim painted red and stained glass windows. She could hear the sounds of laughter, talking and an Irish band blaring from within. She had to plug her ears to hear herself when the hostess greeted her.

"HI! THE ROCKY SPRINGS B&B CALLED IN A RESERVATION FOR ME ABOUT FIFTEEN MINUTES AGO? JESSICA LYNCH?"

The hostess scanned her computer screen then nodded; not even bothering to try and shout over the din. *Follow me*, she gestured.

Jessica followed her back into the public room where she was seated at a 2-top near the fireplace and handed drink and food menus. Adjacent to her table, the band hailed as the Dubliners was in full performance mode; making speech and hearing impossible. After a few minutes wait her waitress appeared with a smile; dressed all in black shirt, apron and jeans.

"JUST POINT!" she shouted; meaning the menus. She leaned forward and peered closely, writing down Jessica's selections, then gave her a 'thumbs up' to indicate she had gotten it. Moments later her pint of Guinness arrived soon followed by a dinner salad and her fish and chips. Jessica ate slowly while she studied the patrons around her. Most were business people; single, she assumed; who didn't want to bother fixing dinner after a ten-hour shift at work. There were quite a few men her age who gave her a nod and smile now and again to test the waters but did nothing more. Finally one of them got brave enough and sauntered over to her table.

"Is that seat taken?" He was tall, slender, clean-cut and had a nice face.

"Feel free," Jessica shouted, indicating the chair.

He put his beer down on the table, slipped in opposite her and held out his hand. "Jerry."

"Jessica."

"Oh-oh; we already sound like a sit-com!" he grinned at her. "You're not local, right? I haven't seen you in here before."

"Which must mean that you are," Jessica smiled; popping a sweet potato fry into her mouth. Perhaps she should mix a little business with pleasure and get some information while she was at it?

"Your powers of deduction are impressive," Jerry shouted with a smile; helping himself to one of her fries.

She slapped his hand playfully. "Hey! Get your own food!"

"I'm just waiting for it."

"What did you order?"

"Shepherd's Pie. So, Jessica...what do you do?" he yelled.

She had already prepared herself with a response; telling people she was a reporter usually shut them up tighter than a drum. "I'm here on vacation," she screamed over the sound of the band.

He was customarily incredulous. "Alone?"

"Not at the moment," she grinned, turning on the charm.

Jerry grinned back then waved frantically to get the waitresses' attention who was looking for him with his Shepherd Pie.

She set it down and pointed to his empty glass. "Another beer?" she shouted.

Jerry nodded.

"Fat Tire right?"

A big thumbs up.

The waitress left at the same time the band broke for a 30 minute break. The decibel level decreased exponentially.

"Much better!" Jerry said in a normal tone of voice. "I love it here; the food and atmosphere but your ears ring for the next two days. It's almost impossible to talk most of the time." He scooped out a steaming portion of Shepherd's pie and offered her the first bite. "Try it," he encouraged.

Jessica politely accepted the taste. "Then we better make the most of the break," she suggested. Being that her time was limited, she cut to the chase. "I read in the paper you've had a lot of weird stuff going on lately."

"You mean the UFO's?"

She nodded; glad he brought it up first.

"Yeah; it's had everyone pretty unnerved for the last few months but it's been mainly happening in the countryside where the Amish live. Still – I won't drive after midnight if I can help it."

"That's what the UPS driver at the Shady Maple was telling me."

"First a delivery man and now an auction broker; you're moving pretty fast there, missy!" he joked in his best John Wayne impression.

"It wasn't like that; I just overheard him talking to his buddies at the table next to me. Anyway, the paper said it all came to an abrupt halt?"

"Yeah; for months it's been like Star Wars here and then the day before yesterday [he snapped his fingers] it all came to a screeching halt; not that I'm complaining; I lost a lot a sleep with all the weird goings-on; I live out in the affected area." He shifted; obviously a little uncomfortable at discussing it. "So where are you from?"

They chatted amiably for the next twenty minutes; exchanged emails then Jessica and Jerry finished their meal in companionable silence except for the band which was again playing music loud enough to wake the dead.

When he walked her out to her car she pointed to her ears with a grimace. "Did you say it lasts two whole days?"

"If you're lucky," he grinned, giving her a peck goodbye on the cheek. "If you'd like I can show you around so you don't have to spend your entire vacation alone."

"I may take you up on it!" Jessica grinned, climbing into her car. She waved goodbye as she drove off. Normally she would have been grateful for the silence after enduring two consecutive hours of auditory assault on her eardrums but it just made the ringing more pronounced. She stopped off at a local minimart and got a half-split of wine so she would be able to sleep and returned to the Inn half an hour later.

It wasn't until after the effects of the wine and heavy dinner kicked in; when she was already snuggled under the duvet that it hit her like a ton of bricks. She rolled out of bed with a groan, snapped on the light and turned on her laptop. She opened Hal's email and scrolled down until she found the link she wanted: ESH QUILT FETCHES RECORD-BREAKING PRICE AT AUCTION. She was trembling as she rolled her mouse over it and clicked. As she read her eyes got wider and wider; there was a photo of the two Amish boys with the weird eyes in the piece despite their efforts to hide their faces. *"Ho-leeeee mackerel!"*

It was approximately 2:00 am when Rebecca felt the summons. It had awakened her up out of a troubled sleep filled with nightmares of darkness, anger, sorrow and unrelenting pain. She found herself bathed in sweat; her heart was racing when she sat straight up; glad to realize it had all just been a dream. She went to her bedroom window and saw his figure standing below; calling silently to her. He had never done it so late (or early) before but the pull was as irresistible as ever. She wrapped a cloak about herself and tip-toed downstairs and out into the yard, closing the door silently behind her.

Instead of opening his arms up to her, he beckoned with a finger for her to follow him and led her away until they stood in the middle of the flattened cornfield.

"Rebecca,"

"Silas!" She was absolutely flabbergasted. "What on earth are you doing here? I thought you were-"

"Seth." He finished for her.

She turned to go; suddenly fearful.

Silas caught her arm; firmly but gently. "Please don't; I must speak with you privately and this may be my only chance before it is too late."

"Too late for what?"

"For my world…"

Rebecca crept back into her room and sat in her rocking chair; struggling to hold back her tears. She had been worried enough when she had overheard them talking the night before but after he had fully explained everything she was absolutely terrified. It was all so incredibly familiar and at the same time alarmingly new. The elusive memory, which had tormented her since she overheard the brothers arguing earlier, suddenly and violently came into razor sharp focus.

She lit the bedside lantern and turned it up as much as she dared in order not to wake Hannah. Then she got her Bible off the nightstand and flipped to the third chapter of Genesis, reading it over and over again. She closed the holy book and squeezed her eyes shut; her entire body shaking with terrible fear.

"*Sei so gut, der Herr*...give me the strength to do what is right in your sight; I could not endure my life if I were the cause of such devastation! Please help me! Please help me!" She slid onto the floor and lay prostrate, face down; spreading her arms outward as she directed her pleas heavenward to God's throne. She lay thus, praying until the cock crowed and just before her sister woke up. Rebecca stood, took out a pencil and paper and began to write furiously. When she was done, she folded the letter in half, stuck it in an envelope then ripped the page she had been reading from out of her Bible and tucked it inside as well, sealing it shut and laying it on her night stand.

"What are you doing, Becca?" came Hannah's sleepy voice. "Is it time to wake up yet?"

"Nee," Rebecca said, sitting down on the bed to brush away the hair from her sister's face. "I love you, Hannah."

"I love you too, Becca." murmured Hannah sleepily, turning over in bed to catch a few more winks.

"Gil – I'm not crazy. Whatever they are, they're hiding in plain sight among the Amish! You've got to get a news crew down here and break this story wide open!" Jessica's hands were trembling with excitement. She had waited until 6:00 am to call her producer; whom she knew would already be on his treadmill working out before going into the station.

"I can't make you any promises, Jess, until I see what you got," he huffed, the whine of the treadmill going full bore in the background. "You got one shot at this so you better hit it out of the ballpark!"

"Got it! One shot...ballpark...I'm on it." Jessica hung up and began compiling the information she had collected in one long, news pitch backed up with hyperlinks, local news excerpts, YouTube videos of UFO's in Lancaster and the tape-recorded conversations she had secretly made of the UPS drivers and the bank executive, Robert Brown. She bcc'd Ted Booker, her cameraman, to include the Doppler images and section of video as well as the still photo that clearly showed the creepy silver eyes of the Amish boy that had shown up at the auction she had read about the night before. She paused a moment, shutting her eyes in a silent plea to the gods of journalism then hit the SEND button. Tomorrow she would drive through the heart of Amish farmland. Perhaps a little face time with some of the Amish would help her discover where the Esh family lived. She carried hard copy photos of the strange boys with her.

"Daed – I need you to do a favor for me," Rebecca said, catching her father before he went out the door to milk the cattle. It was still very dark outside and no one else was up yet.

"Jah? Was ist los?"

"I need to leave…immediately."

Her father stared at her; his bushy salt and pepper brows knitting together with anxiety. "Has Seth done something improper?"

"Nee…it is just very important that I leave right now," she replied, her eyes pleading for understanding.

Leroy stared hard at his daughter. She did not lower her eyes in shame but met his directly which told him immediately that nothing inappropriate had occurred between his eldest and Seth.

He nodded. "What do you want me to do?"

"Just keep Seth occupied and out in the fields long enough for me to go to Sarah Miller's house. If they agree I will stay with them beginning today and through the winter months while Seth and his brother work on their ship. None of you will see me until you send word that they have left. I won't be attending Meeting or any social functions until then; I have to remain out of sight."

Now Leroy was really becoming concerned. "Rebecca…was ist los?" he repeated.

"I can't explain, daed; but it is a matter of life and death."

A chill went down his spine at these words. "Whose life? Whose death?"

"The world they come from. As soon as you take them into the barn I am going over to her house; just keep them in there as long as you can."

Leroy nodded as he cupped her face in his hands. "Is there anything more?"

"Jah, please don't tell anyone where I've gone; not even mamm or my sisters."

"Rebecca Louise Esh, you are frightening your daed," he whispered. "Is this something I need to warn our people about?"

She shook her head. "No, this only concerns their world. Please don't ask me to explain anymore right now; I just need you to trust me."

Her father stared at her long and hard then finally nodded. "Jah, do you want me to give you a lift there in the buggy? It's a long walk in the dark."

Rebecca shook her head and held up a flashlight. "Nee, I don't want Seth to suspect anything or figure out where you've taken me. I'll just take the scooter as soon as you've all gone into the barn; the basket should hold all my things."

Leroy nodded and left the house, closing the door behind him. Seth and Silas were waiting for him outside. "I have much work to be done in the barn today," Rebecca heard her father tell them through the door. She watched from behind the window as the lantern bobbed up and down then disappeared into the blackness of the barn where the cows awaited them. As soon as the door shut, she was out the back door with her black cloak and bonnet on for concealment and riding the scooter in the dark for the Miller's farm. She knew the way almost by heart so did not need to use the flashlight until she got onto the main road.

"Rebecca! What are you doing here?" Sarah exclaimed, elbowing aside the front door so she could enter. Her hands were caked with flour from the morning's baking. "It's barely sun-up! Is something wrong?"

"I need to speak with you first before I talk to your parents," Rebecca replied, entering into the house. She had always liked the Miller's house immensely with its many windows that let in a lot of light.

Sarah looked down at Rebecca's arms which were filled with items of clothing. "Are you running away from home?" she grinned.

"Something like that. Is there someplace we can speak in private?"

"In the kitchen is gut; mom's in bed with a head cold and everyone else is already in the barn and chicken coop. Here, put your clothes down and have a seat. Do you want to help me finish the biscuits while we talk?"

Rebecca nodded with relief and embraced her for a moment. "I'm so glad to have you as my *freund*, Sarah."

Sarah handed her an apron. "Here put this on and go wash up then we can talk!" She returned to the kneading. Rebecca joined her at the kneading board. "Okay, Becca...spill the beans...what's going on?"

"I need to stay here for a while...several months...no one but your family must know and they can't tell anyone!"

"This sounds like one of my cloak and dagger books," Sarah remarked. "Are you in ...*trouble*?" She emphasized the word.

Rebecca immediately caught her implication and shook her head. "Nee, nothing like that. I need to stay away from Seth until he and his brother can fix...I mean, until they return home to their families."

Sarah paused from her kneading and stared at Rebecca's troubled face. "You're in love with him, aren't you?"

The pointed question immediately brought tears to Rebecca's eyes. She nodded.

"Is he in love with you?"

Again Rebecca nodded.

"Has your father refused to let you marry because they are so strange?"

Rebecca shook her head.

Sarah was thoroughly confused. "Then, *was ist falsch*?"

"This is not something I think I can explain, Sarah; it's just very important that we stay apart from one another until they leave."

Sarah nodded but her disappointment at Rebecca's refusal to confide in her was evident.

Rebecca decided to throw her a crumb to assuage her hurt feelings. "I also need to stay away from Jacob Zimmer."

Sarah's ears perked up. "Jah? Have you got some kind of love triangle going on here?"

Rebecca nodded.

"Tell me everything!" Sarah grinned, wiping her hands of flour. "Can you get these cut out and in the oven while I start the coffee?"

"Jah." Rebecca began rolling out the dough with a pin. "Jacob has begun courting me but I got scared and almost left for Indiana to visit my cousins. He still thinks I'm on my way there and I don't want him to know any different; I'm hiding from him too."

"*Was in der welt, Rebecca Esh*?" Sarah stood there gaping at her. "How are you going to avoid both of them when we all go to Meeting *and* Singing?"

This was the question Rebecca had been dreading. "I won't be able to go with you. I can't leave this house or be seen in public by anyone until Seth and his brother have left. If you host a Meeting then I will have to stay hidden in our room. If I am discovered to be here word will get back to them and he'll come looking for me. HE MUST NOT FIND ME, SARAH!"

"Seth or Jacob?"

"Seth!!"

Sarah just stared at her for a few moments, the coffee pot frozen in mid-air. Rebecca's face had gone pasty white with terror and her eyes looked wild. She needed to be calmed down.

Sarah turned back to the stove and put the pot on the burner. "Well I sure wouldn't mind having you around to help me with the kinner but it's up to daed and mamm. I don't think they would object either."

Rebecca relaxed somewhat and nodded, placing the biscuits on the baking sheet and sliding it into the hot oven; still trembling.

At that moment Bridget and Lilly entered the kitchen, their arms carrying baskets filled with multi-colored eggs in blue, brown and speckled white.

"Becca!" Lilly the youngest exclaimed; setting down the basket before hugging her. "Why are you here so early?"

"I'm helping with breakfast!" Rebecca smiled, hoping the answer would satisfy the curious seven years old.

"Did you bring Mary with you so we can play together?"

"I'm afraid not!"

"Put the eggs into the refrigerator, Lilly!" Sarah reminded, hoping to distract her little sister. "Leave about a dozen out for breakfast."

Next came John Miller, their father, and Sarah's two brothers, all who stopped abruptly to stare at Rebecca in surprise upon entering the kitchen.

"Rebecca Esh! *Was machst du hier*?" asked Mr. Miller.

This was the moment she had been dreading and rehearsing for during the entire ride over. "May I speak with you in private, Mr. Miller?"

The question caught him off guard but he nodded and beckoned her out to the service porch. "Jah – the rest of you get cleaned up for breakfast and stay inside."

Sarah watched from the kitchen window as Rebecca spoke quietly to her daed. She couldn't hear what was said but when it was over her father was nodding his head and then embracing Rebecca as he often did when Sarah was distressed about something. They re-entered the kitchen minutes later where Sarah noted that Rebecca's anxious expression had been replaced with relief.

Sarah slipped an arm about Rebecca's waist. "Come, let's get breakfast on the table and then I'll get you settled in my room, jah?"

"Jah," Rebecca nodded, tears of relief sliding down her cheeks.

"JESS, I'M NOT SENDING A NEWS CREW THERE UNTIL YOU CAN FIND OUT WHERE THIS FAMILY LIVES AND THAT'S ALL THERE IS TO IT!!" Jessica held the cell phone away from her head; eliciting glares from the other residents of the Inn who were trying to eat breakfast in peace. One of them pointed to a wall sign that read PLEASE REFRAIN FROM USING YOUR CELL PHONE IN THE DINING ROOM. She gave them an apologetic smile and then shrugged as if she couldn't read English.

Gil continued. "Just get me some actionable information like an address and I'll make sure we send everything we got over there."

"But that could take me weeks!" Jessica hissed, shouldering the phone so she could use her hands to eat. "I've only got 2 weeks of vacation time left."

"Then you know what your deadline is, bloodhound."

"Ugh – you're no help." She hung up the phone and stared down at her plate of country ham, cottage potatoes and fresh fruit. She had only been here fourteen days and had already put on two pounds; she was going to have to start running in the morning before it got too hot. She ate the ham and fruit and left the potatoes before heading to the Innkeeper's desk.

"Can you show me where the Amish farms are on this map?

The Innkeeper smiled at her as if she were an idiot. "Honey they are all over Pennsylvania. Do you just want to see what they look like or are you looking for anything specific?"

Jessica decided to level with her. "I'm actually looking for an Amish family by the name of Esh. I read about a quilt they had auctioned off for $10,000 and wanted to see if I could buy one from them. They must make some pretty incredible quilts!"

"I heard about that auction too!" The Innkeeper smiled. "But if you want to buy an Amish quilt you can go to Fisher's Hand Made Quilts on Old Philadelphia Road. It's not too far from here."

The Innkeeper wasn't making this easy. Jessica tried another tact. "I was also curious to meet the family who sold that quilt. I'm an...author and I'm doing a story on the Pennsylvania Dutch." It wasn't stretching the truth too much...she did write after all and she was doing a story...

"Oh you're an author? Well there are quite a few Esh's around here but I don't know them personally. I suppose the best thing to do would be to go to the shops they frequent and start asking around. They are a pretty close-knit community so I'm sure you'll find someone that knows the right family. If I know about that quilt auction you can be sure they do too!"

"What shops would those be?" Jess prodded sweetly.

The Innkeeper searched through the cubbyholes of her roll top desk until she found a colorful brochure. She handed it up to Jessica.

SHOP WHERE THE AMISH DO! screamed the banner advertisement. Inside was a list, complete with a detailed map and legend that showed all the stores and establishments where the Amish transacted their business.

"This is great!" Jessica said. "Thanks so much!"

"Just remember, no picture taking; it's against their religion," the Innkeeper warned. "Also, you may not want to mention that you're writing a book; they shy away from stuff like that. If you want to find the right family I would just mention that you are interested in buying a quilt from the Esh's and you may get further."

"I'll keep that in mind, thanks." Jessica smiled, before returning to her room. She could always use her Smartphone to take pictures and video. She was pretty sure the Amish wouldn't catch on to the fact that she was recording them using a phone instead of a camera until it was too late.

As soon as the morning chores were done, Seth made a beeline for the Esh kitchen. He had wrestled all night with the choice that lay before him. His mind and Silas telling him one thing and his heart another. He needed to speak with Rebecca…alone; needed to feel her in his arms again before he made the irrevocable decision that no one from his world had ever done before; to willfully disobey an order from their king.

He barely heard the screen door slam behind him as his eyes searched the front room and kitchen. He saw Ruth at the stove and Hannah, Mirriam, and Mary bustling about, but no Rebecca. "Where's Rebecca?" he asked.

All three women turned around, her faces etched with concern. "Ach! We don't know, Seth. She disappeared this morning before we all got up," replied Ruth; looking every bit as bewildered as he felt.

Silas put a hand upon his shoulder. "*Was ist falsch* (what is wrong)?"

Seth turned to accuse him but he could read his *bruder* well and saw no subterfuge in his eyes. He seemed truly at a loss as well.

"Where's Rebecca?" Silas asked.

"No one seems to know," Seth replied, fighting to maintain his composure. "Perhaps we should go look for her? She could be in trouble!"

"Nee," spoke Leroy's voice behind them as he entered the house. Seth watched him go to the kitchen sink and wash his hands. Leroy knew where she was!

"Please, Mr. Esh…I must speak with her! I know you know where she is."

Ruth looked at her husband; aghast that he would withhold such information from her. "*Ist das wahr?* Where is she?"

Leroy turned around and looked at each shocked face in turn; his expression somber and steadfast. "Rebecca is safe but she will not be returning home until after you both have left for your home." At this last his eyes homed in on Seth.

Seth felt the earth beneath him spin off its axis. Bile rose in his throat. "Please, I only need a moment with her," he whispered.

Leroy strode forward and for the very first time, gently laid his hands upon Seth's broad shoulders in an open display of affection. "I'm sorry Seth; but this you may not have. It is her wish to remain hidden until you and your bruder are able to fix the ship and leave."

Seth returned Leroy's stare; unable to believe that Rebecca would do this to him when he had been ready to sacrifice everything for her. Tears welled up in his silver eyes; stricken at heart. He turned away and went out the door to the *dawdi haus* where he could nurse his broken heart in solitude. Everyone just watched him leave; confused as to exactly what was going on.

Silas plunked down at the kitchen table and dropped his face into his hands with mixed relief and sympathy for his brother. Little Mary went up next to him and put her arm about his shoulder, patting him softly.

"Leroy – where is Rebecca?" Ruth still wanted to know.

Leroy sat down at the table and cleared his throat; obviously uncomfortable at having to withhold information from his wife. "I will tell you after the boys have left. For now you shall just have to be satisfied with that."

Chapter Eighteen
"The Bloodhound Picks up the Scent"

An entire week of fruitless searching had passed by with agonizing slowness. Jessica Lynch was growing increasingly anxious at the expenses she was racking up at the Inn and she only had a week and a half left to find the proverbial Esh needle in the Amish haystack or she would be returning to the station with her bloodhound's tail between her legs.

She would never hear the end of it from her colleagues in the news room. They had always taken perverse delight in playing elaborate practical jokes upon each other and would no doubt find some clever way to humiliate her. She ought to know, she had frequently been the ring leader. They would all be chafing at the bit to exact revenge on her! No doubt she would return to find her cubicle redecorated all in fluorescent green crepe paper and accessorized with every available "UFO" knickknack available for purchase off the internet.

"Off to visit the Amish shops again?" The Innkeeper smiled as she exited.

"Yup!" Jessica nodded glumly.

"Good luck!"

"Thanks!" She would need it. As the Innkeeper had warned; the Amish had been polite but tight-lipped about the doings of their brethren. She had visited more than half the shops already and made countless inquiries but had gotten nowhere. The FBI and CIA could learn a thing or two from the Amish about keeping confidences!

She got into her car when her phone beeped, signaling that she had received an email. When she checked she was pleasantly surprised to discover that it was from Jerry, the good-looking guy she had met at the Irish restaurant.

HI JESS – IF YOU'RE STILL IN TOWN AND NOT DOING ANY-THING I WAS WONDERING IF YOU WOULD LIKE TO SPEND A DAY OR TWO TOGETHER? I'VE GOT A FEW DAYS OFF. OUR OFFICES ARE BEING RENOVATED. CALL ME IF YOU'RE GAME.

She dialed the number immediately.

"Is this the beautiful blonde I met at Annie's?" answered Jerry's friendly voice.

"How'd you guess?" Jessica grinned.

"Caller ID," he chuckled. "So are you going to take me up on my offer?"

"That would be great; I'd love to. I'm rather tired of being alone on this vacation. Hey - since you're a local, perhaps you can help me figure out how to find a particular Amish family who sold a quilt recently for several grand?"

"The Esh's?" Jerry replied, sounding mildly surprised.

Jessica almost dropped the phone. "You know them?" *Stay calm! Stay calm! Stay calm!* She began to hyperventilate.

"Well yeah…my firm is the one that organizes all the auctions around here; I thought I told you that?"

Now Jess began to tremble violently with excitement. Her throat began to constrict. "Hang on!" she wheezed, clawing through her purse for her inhaler.

"Hanging…" returned Jerry's voice from the phone on the car seat.

She took several deep inhales and waited for her bronchial tubes to relax. "Sorry – I get attacks whenever I get too excited," she apologized. "Anyway you were saying?"

"No worries. I just looked up that auction while I waited and I've got their contact information right here. What did you need it for?"

Think fast. "Well first I'm doing research for a book on the Amish and, two: I might be interested in commissioning a quilt from them. Do you know them personally?"

"Only on a purely business basis," Jerry replied. "How about we meet for lunch at Annie's then we can leave your car there and I can take you out to meet them?"

"That would be wonderful!" Jessica nodded, trying to keep herself from squealing aloud with joy. "See you in 20 minutes?"

"It's a date!"

She hung up and immediately speed-dialed Gil Henderson. "I found them!" she crowed the instant he picked up.

"Found who?"

"The Esh's!!"

"The who-ses?"

Jessica could have thrown her phone out the window. She couldn't believe he had forgotten already. "THE ESH'S! THE AMISH FAMILY I'VE BEEN LOOKING FOR, FOR THE PAST THREE WEEKS!!!"

"Oh! Great sleuthing, Jess. Let me know what happens."

"Aren't you going to send a crew out here?"

"First verify these are the right people by asking them a few uncomfortable questions. If you're still convinced they have anything to do with all the weird UFO stuff that's been going on out there I'll not only send in a news crew; I'll call out the National Guard. Fair enough?"

"Yeah...." Jessica slumped in her seat. "You keep moving the bar, Gil! Just have them standing by ready to deploy because if the 'aliens' get wind of this they'll be sure to disappear." She hung up in a huff; feeling a bit weird at using the terms UFO and alien so frequently. Gil was his usual self; setting up one more hoop to jump through! She was going to make him pay big time if this story turned out to be as big as she thought it was. She started the car with a roar and backed out of the lot; arriving at Annie's fifteen minutes later where Jerry was already waiting for her.

A week had passed since Rebecca's disappearance and in all that time Seth had refused to eat and barely slept. He turned away every meal brought in to tempt him by the Esh's who were becoming increasingly worried about him. Silas often saw him standing outside at night like a statue, calling out to her with his heart but getting only silence in return. Dark circles were growing larger and larger under his eyes and he had grown so weak he could barely function anymore. During the day he lay on his bed in the *dawdi haus*, refusing to do even the most basic things to take care of himself and at night he pined for her. Silas could no longer bear watching his brother eat himself alive with torment and decided to take action.

It was eight days after Rebecca's disappearance when he finally confronted Seth in the privacy of the dawdi haus. He was surprised to find him sitting upright with the communication device in his hands.

Silas squatted next to him and put an arm about him. "Are you alright?"

Seth shook his head. "No." He lifted a face full of anguish to his brother's. "There's no point staying here any longer, Silas. I've contacted a nearby ship and they're going to teleport us out of here tonight when everyone is asleep. Then they'll destroy all evidence of ours."

All Silas could do was nod. It was the right thing to do both for his brother and for their world. He gave an almost audible sigh of relief. "Very well, should I go and extend our goodbyes to the family?"

"No, I'll just write them a letter and leave it on the table after they go to bed. I don't want them to know ahead of time."

Silas knelt beside his brother; wishing he could take away the heartache. "I'm sorry," he whispered. "I know you truly loved her."

"Love, not loved." Seth replied. A sob caught in his throat. "Silas; how am I to go on without her?"

Silas shook his head. "I don't know," he admitted. "But I'll always be here to help you."

They embraced for a brief moment then Silas left him alone to write the letter while he joined Leroy in the fields for their last day on Earth.

"Why is it that men will never stop and ask for directions?" Jessica moaned when she saw the same covered bridge they had passed twice before. "Your navigation system needs to be recalibrated!"

"I think it's getting confused on the difference between Pequea Lane and Pequea Street," Jerry grimaced, pausing to check a paper map. "Let's just drive a little further and I promise, the first farmhouse I come to I will get out and ask for directions, okay?"

"Okay," grumped Jessica. She had never felt this antsy in her life. She was so close to breaking a huge story only to be stymied by a malfunctioning navigation system. Ten minutes later they pulled up to an Amish farmhouse and got out. Two young women were out in the yard, cultivating the garden but they paused to see who had arrived.

"Excuse me," Jerry said, drawing close with a friendly smile. "I've gotten lost; I'm trying to find Leroy and Ruth Esh's farm?" Neither Jerry nor Jessica noticed when one of them went rigid.

Sarah Miller glanced at Rebecca nervously whose face had gone white as a sheet. She stalled for time. "Gut morgan, Mr. Fuller! What brings you out here?"

"Oh Sarah! I didn't recognize you for a moment. My offices are closed for the next couple of days so I was just showing my friend around. Jessica – this is Sarah Miller; Sarah – Jessica Lynch."

"Gut to meet you, Jessica." Sarah replied, extending her hand. Rebecca remained rooted to the spot; a terrible, unnamed fear growing upon her.

Jerry continued. "Jess heard about the auction on the Esh quilt a while back and wanted to meet Ruth. She's an author doing research and also wants to buy a quilt."

Sarah nodded and offered the blond woman a weak smile. "How nice."

There was a long awkward silence. "So can you help me?"

"Help you?" repeated Sarah; distracted by Rebecca's nails digging into her back.

"Yes, could you please give me directions to their farm?"

Rebecca's nails dug in harder.

"Ach! Uh…jah." She pointed reluctantly in the direction of the Esh farm. "If you go that way and turn left at the first lane it should take you there." She couldn't lie, not even for Rebecca's sake. She had already been baptized and lying was against the Ordnung.

"Thanks! Give my best to your family!" Jerry waved, getting back into the car.

Jessica got in on the other side, her door slamming shut as Jerry started the engine. "Did you happen to notice that other girl's face? I thought she was going to start crying or something."

"No, I didn't. Really?"

Jessica shook her head. "Men!"

The instant the car left the driveway Rebecca rounded on Sarah. "Why did you give them directions?"

"They asked me point blank, Becca, I'm sorry!" Sarah apologized. "Word is out all over town that some woman has been asking around for your family for weeks. I bet that was her!"

Rebecca clapped a hand over her mouth to stifle her sob then ran for the barn. She grabbed a bridle and slipped it over the head of Miller's horse. "Give me a hand up, quick, Sarah!"

"Becca, what are you doing?"

"I have to warn my family!"

"Warn them about what?"

"Please Sarah!!! I don't have time to explain!"

Sarah dropped her basket of vegetables and intertwined her fingers into a step for Rebecca. Rebecca put her left foot in and flung her right over the horse. She slapped the bridle reins hard on his rump. The horse took off at a gallop for her farm, taking a shortcut across the fields. In the distance she could see a cloud of dust as the car took the back roads to her home. She kicked the horse in the ribs, urging him faster but it was too late.

"Hey, could you slow down for a minute?" Jessica asked as she spotted two Amish men working in the field. She rolled down the window.

"Is this the Esh farm?" she hollered so they could hear her.

Leroy automatically looked around when the female voice addressed him; followed by Silas who didn't realize his error until it too late. The female's eyes locked upon his golden ones and in a split second he knew she had found what she had come looking for. Her mouth gaped open first in shock then in triumph; her hand holding her phone up as though it were a camera. Silas lowered his hat brim immediately and pretended to go back to work, but his heart was pounding. They had been discovered!

Leroy stepped forward and shook Jerry's hand as he approached the fence; unaware of what had just happened.

"Gut to see you again, Mr. Fuller," he said, tipping his hat as the blond woman got out of the car.

"This is my friend, Jessica Lynch. I've been showing her around but she wanted to meet your wife after reading about the quilt we auctioned off for you a couple of months ago."

"Ach? Well, I'm sorry but Ruth has been under the weather lately," Leroy apologized. "Perhaps another time?"

If the blond woman was disappointed she hid it well, Leroy observed.

"Well then I'm sorry to have bothered you, Mr. Esh. Please give my regards to your wife and your family?"

"Jah, I will." He nodded, waving goodbye.

Jerry and Jessica returned to the car. "Sorry I took you on a wild goose chase for nothing," he apologized. "But we could still see the sights. How about going to the Hershey Amusement Park with me tomorrow?"

Jessica nodded and smiled at him; trying to remain calm. "That sounds great. Perhaps I can just write Ruth a letter and ask her to make me a quilt since I will have to be returning to Philly soon? Could you give me the address?"

"Sure," he smiled, giving it to her.

"Perfect!" Jessica smiled at him as she wrote it down. He started the car and as he drove she played back the video she had taken of the Amish boy, praying under her breath that it would show his strange eyes.

"Thank Gaaaawwwd!" she suddenly bawled aloud unintentionally, her head falling back in relief.

"What are you so happy about?" Jerry grinned, resting his hand upon her shapely knee.

"Oh! Um…I just got an email from my mom that my sister just gave birth and that mother and baby are in good health!" she fibbed. She began typing furiously on her phone as she tried to upload the video in an email to Gil. It was a frustrating task because the car kept bouncing up and down upon the uneven payment. Eventually she got it through. It was only a matter of hours now before the media would descend in full force upon the peaceful farm of Leroy Esh who, she was now convinced, had been knowingly harboring an alien for months. She waited for a few moments; holding her breath for Gil's response. It was make or break time.

GOT IT! The subject line read. She opened the email. NEWS CREW ON ITS WAY IN CHOPPERS SO HOLD ON TO YOUR PANTYHOSE; ETA IS 20 MINUTES. YOU REALLY BLEW THE LID OFF IT THIS TIME, BLOODHOUND! Jessica crowed again, pumping her arms for joy.

"What now?" Jerry asked, wondering what the big hoopla was.

"It's a boy!" Jessica lied.

Rebecca sat on the horse watching from a distance as the car paused by her farm then drove off minutes later; completely torn as to what to do. She had no way of knowing what had just transpired between the passengers and her father so should she still go and warn her family or should she return to the Miller's and remain in hiding?

Suddenly without warning, strong arms pulled her down off the horse and onto the ground. A face appeared over her, blocking out the sun's glare.

"Rebecca!"

She panicked the instant she saw Seth's silver eyes glowing white hot above her. He had her pinned down by her wrists and was kneeling over her. Before she could find her voice, his lips were upon hers, his arms pulling her beneath him in the field. She wanted to fight; to struggle; to run away but she was no match against the power of his feelings. They washed over her like a tidal wave; pouring into her soul and filling her with a love so intense she became immobilized. As his mouth ravaged hers she felt his fingers go into her hair and pull it free of her kapp and bobby pins. He pulled at her tresses while kissing her face unabated until her hair was spread out around her like a golden fan. Rebecca's body was quaking with the internal struggle to resist him. She had to stop him; had to speak with him to warn him but her rational mind was swiftly becoming drowned out by the cries of her heart. She returned his kisses with equal ardor, her arms sliding across his broad back to pull him closer. Their tears mingled together.

"I thought I'd lost you forever," he whispered fiercely in her ear, raining kisses upon her cheeks, eyelids, brow and nose before nuzzling her neck. "I was going to leave and return to my world without you because I thought you no longer loved me." His hands cupped her face; a smile of joy breaking like the dawn over his features. "I was a fool."

He pulled her up to a sitting position, cradling her in his arms and stroking her face. "We'll never be parted again," he declared, pulling her mouth to his again.

"STOP IT!" she straight-armed him back, her eyes wild. "I won't let you do this!" Rebecca pushed away from him and struggled to her feet, running for the horse. It neighed loudly and danced about as she struggled to control it with the reins. Rebecca flung herself onto its back belly first then struggled to swing her leg over as Seth ran up and grabbed the bridle so she couldn't get away.

"Becca please!" he moaned, not understanding. "I thought you came back for me."

Sobs convulsed Rebecca's body as she struggled to remain on the horse. The look on his face was enough to rend her heart in two. She dashed the tears away which were blinding her eyes.

"I do love you, Seth...with all my heart and soul I love you!" watching his face transformed by momentary joy. *That is why I will not allow myself to become your world's Eve!*" Before she could change her mind she wheeled the horse about and galloped for home while he ran after her, calling her name over and over again.

"Thanks for taking me around today, Jerry." Jessica said as they arrived back at the pub where her car was parked. Adrenaline had been coursing through her veins from the moment she had received Gil's email. Now the trick was for her to remain calm and composed until she could get back into her own car and drive back to the Esh farm where she would meet up with news crew.

Jerry rolled down the window as she got into her own car. "Shall I pick you up around 10:00 a.m. tomorrow?"

"Sounds great; I'll text you the address of the Inn where I'm staying," she nodded, slamming the door shut and gunning the engine. Jerry watched in amazement as her tires spun, kicking up gravel until the rubber caught hold and the car roared out of the parking lot, leaving behind a cloud of dust.

"Excitable girl," Jerry muttered with a shake of his head.

They felt and heard the hum and throb of the helicopters long before they appeared over the horizon in the glare of the setting sun. Ruth, Hannah, Mirriam and Mary all left the house and ran outside to see what was going on. Out in the field Leroy and Silas were running towards the house. In the distance was a lone figure galloping towards them on horseback with blond hair flying behind. In the distance, on the usually empty road came a long caravan of cars and news vans.

"Was ist das? Was ist los?" Ruth cried, running out to meet Silas. Her eyes were wild with fear.

"The found us," he replied grimly, running past her into the dawdi haus.

Ruth twisted around, desperate for answers. "Who? Who found you?"

"The media," Leroy told her as he came into the yard; huffing and puffing with exertion. "Jerry Fuller had a newsperson with him although I'm sure he didn't know it."

"How do you know this?" Ruth asked, watching in horror as three helicopters began circling their fields and training high-powered telescopic lenses upon them. The news vans pulled up in front of their home; ejecting numerous people from within. Hannah, Mirriam and Mary all watched with mouths agape as a panel slid back on the top of several vans and long poles began to telescope upwards towards the sky with satellite dishes.

"There's been talk in town of a woman who's been snooping around and inquiring about us," Leroy said, putting his arms about his wife to calm her. "As far as I know none of our people said anything but she managed to find us anyway."

"Daed! Daed! Look! It's Rebecca!" Mary was jumping up and down and pointing to the figure on the galloping horse. Rebecca was hard to mistake with her golden hair blowing behind her in the wind as the horse cantered up to the house. The cameras trained upon her to capture every frame of the beautiful Amish girl with her hair flying free.

"Becca! Where is thy *kapp*?" Her mother cried, horrified.

Rebecca slid off the horse and ran up to them, her dirty face streaked with tears. "Where is Silas?"

"In the dawdi haus…where have you been all this time?"

Rebecca ran past her and burst into the dawdi haus where she found him standing in the middle of the room. He held a small device in his hands that pulsed with a blue light while his mouth silently formed words. She waited, trying to catch her breath until he was through.

He opened his eyes; stunned to find her standing before him. "They're on their way to pick us up," he said, looking past her. "Where's my bruder?"

"I left him standing in the field," Rebecca confessed. "He is probably on his way back here. What are you going to do? There are helicopters and news vans outside, they have us surrounded."

"My people will deal with that; the important thing is to get Seth here in time."

Rebecca swallowed hard. "What do you need me to do?"

Silas gripped her hands, his face grim. "Now that he's seen you Seth won't come with me and I can't force him into coming.

You will have to be the one to do it. You will have to bring him to the rendezvous point out by our ship."

"You want me to deceive him?" Rebecca gaped. She almost laughed at the irony of it all.

"Yes; is this not commonly done on your world often times for the good? So it must be now. I cannot do it. Say whatever you must, Rebecca, but at all cost you must get him there in less than ten minutes or he and our world will be in dire peril."

"I will need you to create a distraction so I can ride back out to him," she said, about to go out the back door.

"I will do what I can, now go!" Silas nodded.

Rebecca paused for a moment as she remembered something. She ran up to her room then flew down the stairs a moment later and pressed an envelope into his hand. "Give this to him after you've left," she said, planting a kiss upon his cheek. "Goodbye...I will miss you!"

With that she was out the back door and running for the barn to get Joe.

Silas withdrew the 'watch' device from his pocket and manipulated the buttons before walking outside the dawdi haus. There was now three times as many reporters and cameramen as there were before with more still arriving. Overhead several more helicopters had joined the others, buzzing in low circles round and round the farm to film the action. The moment the screen door on the dawdi haus slammed behind him all the cameras swung around to train their lenses upon him. The Esh's were huddled together trying to get into their home but the blond woman named Jessica who had been there earlier was now blocking their way; peppering them with questions.

"There he is!!" she screamed suddenly, pointing her finger directly at him. Silas made sure he kept his eyes downcast this time while his hands fiddled with the device in his pocket. It began to pulse.

"What planet do you come from?" Jessica asked, thrusting a microphone in his face. Silas kept his head down, refusing to answer when a big gust of wind almost knocked her against him. Undeterred, Jessica repeated the question but still he refused to answer her. The sky began to go dark and clouds began to form and boil overhead. Fat drops of rain began to fall.

"Look!" someone in the press crowd shouted. "The sky's turning green; this is twister weather!"

"Get the 'copters outta here!" someone yelled.

"No! It's a trick! He's doing this!" Jessica shrieked; not realizing how deranged she sounded.

The cameras left the Esh's and began pointing upwards.

"Don't be so gullible!" Jessica yelled at them, waving her arms heavenward. "He's doing this to distract you! Look! The clouds are only over this farm!"

Silas pushed another button turning her words into a lie in the very next moment. The sky from one horizon to the other turned dark and ominous. Rain mixed with ping-pong sized hail began to pelt down. The press corps ran for their vans to take shelter when the lightning began striking mere yards away as if it were being aimed at them. Silas disappeared around the side of the house in the ensuing melee and headed directly for the field. With their way now clear, the Esh's escaped into the shelter of their home and locked the door behind them as lightning and thunder continued to explode outside.

Rebecca galloped Joe out to the field and quickly found Seth who was on his hands and knees pitifully crawling towards her home.

"You came back!" he said, his face joyous.

"Yes, I've come back for you, Seth," Rebecca smiled, feeling like a cheat and traitor. "Can you climb up behind me?"

"Just watch me," he smiled weakly, struggling to his feet. With great effort and after numerous attempts he managed to get onto the horse belly first then swing his leg over. He collapsed against her. "Are we going home now?" he asked wearily as she wheeled Joe about and headed towards her farmhouse. She could hear the exhaustion in his voice and feel it in the loose grip of his arms about her waist.

"Yes," she nodded; glad he couldn't see her tears. "Hold on tight, Seth, don't let go."

Seth didn't seem to notice as they sky grew dark overhead or the rain began to sluice down. All he seemed to care about was that she was in his arms again and that she had come back for him. She gave Joe a good kick; urging him to go faster. She guided the horse away from the house and out into the field where his bruder stood waiting for them. The wind was now howling and lightning bolts were striking in a perimeter that surrounded the field like a protective barrier. Silas was looking up at the sky, a worried look on his face.

"Help me!" she called out to him, sliding down off of Joe. Silas ran forward to help her pull Seth safely off the horse. "What's wrong with him? Why is he so sickly looking, Silas?"

Silas gathered his brother into his arms and held him close.

"Becca?" murmured Seth, wearily reaching for her.

"He hasn't eaten or slept since you left," he informed her with a sad smile. "He's weak and heartsick."

The words sent pain knifing through her heart.

"Becca?"

She drew close and held Seth's face in her hands; her hot tears blending with his in the cold rain. "I'm here, Seth."

"Knew you'd come back," he murmured, struggling to focus his silver eyes upon hers. "I knew you never stopped loving me."

"How did you know that Seth?" she whispered.

"Because I never stopped feeling you in here," he said, pointing to his heart.

A sudden beam of blazing light shone down upon them.

"It's time; they're here." Silas said. "You need to step back beyond the beam of light or you will be taken with us."

Rebecca froze and stared at him. She didn't want to be parted from Seth. She shook her head at Silas, refusing to budge. "I want to come with you."

Silas had not seen this coming. "You can't." he stated flatly. "It is not possible."

"Why?"

"It cannot be, Rebecca."

"Please," Rebecca implored him, her eyes lingering upon Seth. He stared back at her, a ghost of a smile upon his lips.

"Stand back, Rebecca; I will not have your death upon my conscience!"

"No…" she began to protest then felt strong arms pull her backwards. NO! She was ready to scream but stopped when she saw it was her father.

"Come away, Rebecca," he said gently, his eyes filled with compassion. "Come with me now."

Rebecca allowed herself to be pulled away, oblivious to the rain soaking her hair and skin and the lightning exploding all around. She kept her eyes locked upon Seth's silver ones until the very last moment when the beam of light became too intense to look at anymore then suddenly disappeared, taking the brothers with it.

"Nooooooooooo!" she wailed, collapsing to her knees. "Please take me with you!" Her cries were swallowed up in the storm and they were no longer there to hear her.

Her father bent, lifted her into his arms and carried her into the house where her mother was waiting with a warm blanket. Rebecca collapsed into sobs as they wrapped it about her.

"Are they gone, Becca?" whimpered Mary, sitting down next to her upon the bench.

Rebecca nodded and drew her little sister close; still weeping. "Yes, Mary; they're gone…gone forever."

"Well that was a total waste of time and money, Lynch!" Ted Booker growled as he viewed the video playback from inside the van. The storm was still raging outside. "Gil isn't going to be very happy."

Jessica sat down next to him, her eyes blazing. "What are you talking about? Didn't you get the footage of his eyes or how he manipulated the weather?"

"Look for yourself," Ted said, pointing to the screen.

"All I see is static," Jess complained, punctuating her sentence with a loud sneeze.

"Precisely; that's all I got. That's all any of us got."

Jess stood up and hit her head on the roof of the van. "Ow! What are you talking about?"

"We got nothing, Jess. I even checked with the choppers and they got nothing but static too. It's like we had an electromagnetic pulse that wiped everything clean or something."

Jessica sat back down with a heavy plunk; her too short career flashing before her eyes. "Guess my name is mud from here on out instead of bloodhound," she surmised grimly.

EPILOGUE
"Sweet Sorrow"

"Silas?"

"Yes?" Silas knelt next to his brother's sleeping pod on the ship, gripping his hand as they made the jump to light speed.

"Where's Rebecca?" Seth asked wearily.

"She's home," Silas replied truthfully. "Are you doing all right? Can I get you something to eat?"

Tears leaked from his eyes. "She didn't love me enough, Silas. I would have given up everything for her."

"She loved you more than enough, my bruder," Silas corrected him, fishing in his pocket and laying a crumpled envelope upon his chest. "She loved you enough to give you up."

"What's this?" Seth struggled to sit up.

Silas got behind him and helped him up to a sitting position, using his body as a backrest. "Open it; she made me promise to give it to you after we left."

Seth ripped open the envelope and out fluttered two pieces of paper. The first was in her handwriting and the second was typeset with the words GENESIS 3 at the top.

My dearest Seth,
I'm sorry we cannot be together but I couldn't let your
world incur the same fate as mine when it was in my power
to prevent it. The Bible passages I have enclosed can ex-
plain better than me just what your world would have suf-
fered had I given in and let you disobey your king on ac-
count of me. You cannot imagine the endless suffering,
death, wars and heart-ache that would have resulted which
☙we here on earth have endured for centuries. A fate I
would not wish upon anyone.

In Plain Sight

*I will love you always and never forget you. No
matter the distance between us my heart will always belong
to you. Now when I look up into the night sky it will not be
the cold stars I see shining down upon me but your beautiful
silver eyes.
My life for eternity…Rebecca.*

℘ Q

Rebecca sat listlessly in the early spring sunshine, staring
blankly at the piece of notepaper that was her only remaining keep-
sake of Seth. They had been gone for months and the media attention
had disappeared almost the same day as the brothers had, the media
evidently having gotten nothing of substance to broadcast. Even the
brother's ship which had crash-landed in their field had somehow
mysteriously disintegrated during their departure.

Jacob Zimmer had come over to help her daed till the soil
and hopefully to pick up with her where they had left off. A week or
two more and it would soon be ready for planting. Her father's workshop had been cleared of all the boxes of parts the boys had ordered;
returned for a full refund to their places of origin by Craig their
friendly UPS man.

Life for all intents and purposes had gone back to normal;
now if only her heart could. A heavy rock of despair had taken the
place of a heart of flesh that had once beaten with fevered abandon
when Seth held her in his arms. Now she was left wondering if she
would ever be able to love again or if she would be doomed to live
out the rest of her days pining for what she could not have.

She was sitting with her family in the audience at the spring
auction, waiting for their quilt to come up for bid. This time they
were not worried about a bidding war that would result in hard feelings from their fellow Amish.

"Excuse me," said a male voice beside her. "But I couldn't
help noticing the text on that piece of paper you have there."

Rebecca looked up to find an older gentlemen smiling at
her. "May I?" he asked reaching for the paper.

She handed it over to him, a strange feeling growing upon
her. "Can you actually read this?"

"Of course," he smiled, his gray eyes twinkling. "I'm Jewish! I was raised in an orthodox Jewish home where I had to learn Hebrew!"

Rebecca's heart began to pound. All this time she had thought the letters to be in an alien language. She had never even seen Hebrew before.

She leaned close as he pushed his spectacles higher up upon his nose to look at it better.

אני שאני

"What does it say?" she asked.

The man handed her back the note. "If I were still orthodox I wouldn't be able to tell you," he teased.

"Why not?"

"Because it is forbidden to speak aloud the name of God." He pointed to the strange letters. "This is the name God gave Moses upon the holy mount when Moses asked how he would answer the Israelites about who had sent him."

Tears sprang into Rebecca's eyes as she recalled Seth's almost identical words to that effect about his king and began to slowly comprehend the awesome significance of this revelation.

"Can you tell me now?" she whispered, the stone encasing her heart beginning to fade away.

"Yes," nodded the man with a gentle smile. "The name God gave Moses is translated into English as: I AM THAT I AM."

"Danki!" Rebecca said, clutching the paper to her breast. "Danki!" She settled back in her seat and let the healing tears flow down her cheeks, neck and eventually onto her heart.

Seth wasn't lost to her forever. Maybe not in this lifetime but surely in the next they would be reunited where there would be no more fear of separation…of any kind.

In that blessed realm, the Savior himself had promised to wipe away all tears from their eyes and that was a blessed hope she could cling to.

THE END

RECIPES

Leroy's Favorite Oven Fried Chicken

1/3 cup canola oil
2/3 stick of butter

2 cups all-purpose flour
2 tsp salt
2 tsp black pepper
4 tsp paprika
2 tsp garlic salt
1 tsp oregano
2 tsp dried marjoram

8-9 chicken pieces (breast, legs, thighs)

Melt butter and oil in glass baking dish in 375°F oven. Set aside once melted. In large mixing bowl, blend together all the dry ingredients. Rinse chicken in cold water, pat dry then submerge thoroughly in large mixing bowl containing 2 beaten eggs mixed with 1 cup milk and ½ tsp hot sauce. Dredge coated chicken in flour mixture and place skin side down in glass baking dish with melted butter and oil. Bake for 45 minutes then with a spatula, flip chicken over and cook on the other side for additional 5-10 minutes or until top begins to bubble.

Rebecca's Baking Powder Biscuits

6 cups all purpose flour
½ cup instant nonfat dry milk powder
¼ cup baking powder
¼ cup sugar
1 tsp cinnamon
2 tsp salt
2 tsp cream of tartar
1 cup of cold lard, cut into chunks
1 cup cold butter, cut into chunks
1-3/4 cups buttermilk (approx.)

Preheat oven to 400°F. In extra large bowl, mix all ingredients except for the shortenings and buttermilk. With a pastry blender, cut in shortenings until mixture resembles coarse crumbs. Make a well in the center and pour in buttermilk. With a fork, quickly and lightly combine the ingredients (not all of the flower will be incorporated at this point).

Turn the dough out onto a well-floured pastry cloth or board and with floured-covered hands, knead 8-10 turns until smooth. Roll out dough to ¾" thickness. Use 1 2-½" biscuit cutter to cut the dough. Prick each biscuit 3 times with fork.

You can either bake the biscuits now or freeze for later baking. If baking immediately, place 2" apart on oiled cookie sheet and bake for 13-15 minutes (or golden brown). If you wish to freeze them, place unbaked biscuits on sheets in freezer. When hard transfer to plastic bags. To serve, remove biscuits as needed and bake frozen on an oiled cookie sheet in 400°F oven for 15-18 minutes.

Beef Stew

2 lbs beef stew meat, cut into ½" chunks
3-4 red potatoes
3-4 carrots
2 celery stalks
3 small yellow onions
1 28oz canned tomatoes (purée)
¼ cup water
5 Tbsp minute Tapioca
2 Tbsp Worcestershire sauce
1 Tbsp brown sugar
1 Tsp salt
½ tsp ground black pepper
½ tsp ground allspice
¼ tsp dried marjoram
¼ tsp dried oregano
¼ tsp dried thyme
1 bay leaf

Preheat oven to 300°F. Cut meat into bit-size chunks. Peel and cut potatoes into pieces a little larger than the meat. Clean carrots, celery and onions and cut all into 1" hunks. In large heavy roasting pan or crock pot, combine all the ingredients. Bake covered for 5 hours without stirring. (Don't freeze).

Ruth Esh's Beef & Noodles

3 lbs beef (chuck, trimmed)
1 large yellow onion in quarters
8 whole garlic cloves
1 shallot, minced
1 bell pepper in quarters (seeds & ribs removed)
2 large carrots, peeled, and cut in thirds
3 stalks of celery, cut in thirds
1 cup fresh parsley sprigs
2 bay leaves
¼ cup instant beef bouillon granules
½ tsp ground black pepper
1 8oz pkg medium quality noodles

Preheat oven to 325°F. Place mean in large Dutch oven or heavy roasting pan with all the ingredients except the noodles and parsley. Cover and bake for 3 hours. Remove pan from oven and transfer meat to a chopping board. Remove vegetables from broth with slotted spoon and discard bay leaves. Shred meat into bite-size pieces and chop vegetables finely. Return meat and vegetables to the broth and add in uncooked noodles. Cover pan and return to oven and bake for 1 hour and 15 minutes longer or until noodles are tender. Stir once being careful not to break up noodles. If broth evaporates, add additional broth as needed.

Zook's Famous Chocolate Coconut Candy

¾ cup butter
1 14oz can sweetened condensed milk
1 tsp pure vanilla extract
1 tsp almond extract
½ tsp salt
5-2/3 cups powdered sugar (1-1/2 boxes)
1 lb flaked coconut
1 lb pecans finely ground
3 oz paraffin
1-1/2 lbs semisweet chocolate morsels

In large saucepan, melt butter over low heat (do not allow to brown). Whisk in condensed milk, vanilla and salt. Add confectioners' sugar, coconut and pecans. Mix quickly using your hands. Coat a 9x13" baking pan with Pam. Transfer candy mixture to pan and pat in firmly in place using palm of hand to smooth and make it even. Cover and store in coldest part of refrigerator overnight.

In a double boiler set over hot (not boiling) water, melt the paraffin and chocolate morsels. Cut the cold candy into 1" squares and using a toothpick, dip candy into melted chocolate. Put on a cookie sheet lined with wax paper then put into refrigerator to harden. When candy has set, transfer to storage containers and keep cold until serving.

Ruth Esh's Blueberry Jam

1 quart blueberries sorted and washed.
½ cup cold water
4-1/2 cups of granulated sugar
Grated rind and juice of one lemon

Combine all ingredients into a large, heavy saucepan. Place over low heat and gradually bring mixture to a boil, stirring constantly for about 10 minutes. Cook at rapid boil for 2-3 minutes, skimming off the foam. If jam has not thickened enough, cook a bit longer. DO NOT HEAT THE JAM TO 220°F on a candy thermometer. Pour into 3 hot, half-pint sterilized canning jars. Let cool.

Ruth Esh's Ham Loaf

1 lb ground ham.
1 lb ground sausage (room temp)
2 cups Italian bread crumbs
2 eggs
1 cup sour cream
1/3 cup minced onions
2 Tbsp fresh lemon juice
1 tsp curry powder
1 tsp ground ginger

1 tsp dry mustard
1/8 tsp grated nutmeg
1/8 tsp paprika
¼ tsp ground pepper

Sauce
1 cup golden brown sugar
½ cup water
½ cup apple cider vinegar
¼ tsp black pepper

Preheat oven to 350°F. In large mixing bowl thoroughly combine the meats and crumbs (using your hands). In medium bowl, beat the eggs and add sour cream, onion, lemon juice and spices. Mix well, pour over the meat mixture and blend. Mold into a loaf and place on an oiled 9x13 inch baking dish. Bake uncovered for 1 hour.

While it is baking, prepare the sauce. In small saucepan, combine brown sugar with the remaining ingredients and bring to a boil. When the loaf has baked for 45 minutes, remove from oven then drain off excess fat. Pour the sauce over the loaf and continue baking for another fifteen minutes, basting now and then with the pan juices.

<u>Roast Duckling with Sauerkraut and Apple Stuffing</u>

2 Tbsp butter
1 large yellow onion, chopped
2 cups finely chopped apple (either Pippin or Granny Smith)
5 Tbsp chicken broth or white wine
1 cup very well drained sauerkraut, the juice reserved.
½ cup chopped fresh parsley
¾ tsp dried thyme

¼ tsp marjoram
¼ tsp black pepper
¼ tsp celery seed
6 cups soft ½" bread cubes
1 egg
1 7-lb. Duckling

<u>Basting sauce:</u>
½ cup molasses
1/8 tsp black pepper
1/8 tsp dried thyme
2 tsp melted butter

In large skillet brown 2 Tbsp's butter over medium heat until deep gold. Add onion and sauté until it begins to brown (about 2-3 minutes). Add the apple and 3 Tbsp's of broth or wine and cook covered on medium heat for 3 minutes or until apple is slightly cooked. Add sauerkraut, parsley, thyme, pepper and celery seed and stir to combine. Remove from heat. Put bread cubes in a large bowl and pour apple-sauerkraut mixture over it and toss lightly. In a small bowl, beat the egg and add the remaining 2 tbsp of broth or wine. Pour over dressing and toss lightly again just to combine and set aside.

Preheat oven to 375˚F. Remove neck and giblets from duck's cavity. Rinse duck under cold water and pat dry with paper towels. Fill duck cavity with the dressing, packing loosely. (Leftover dressing can be baked separately.) Secure opening with skewers and truss with kitchen cord. With fork, pierce duck all over to allow fat to drain off. Place duck, breast side up on rack in a shallow roasting pan.

In small bowl, combine the basting liquid ingredients along with ¼ cup of reserved sauerkraut juice Baste duck with a brush and roast, allowing 20 minutes per pound (approximately 2 hours for a 7 lb duck), basting every 20 minutes while roasting. If duck starts to get too dark, cover lightly with a piece of aluminum foil.

Home-Made Ice-Cream

10 egg yolks
2 cups sugar
¼ cup vanilla extract
Dash of salt
1 quart of half-and-half
2 quarts of heavy (whipping) cream
Rock salt

In large bowl, beat egg yolks until well blended. Add sugar and beat until fully incorporated. (This can be done the day before and stored in the refrigerator to make the texture even smoother and add volume.) Pour mixture into the freezer can of an ice-cream maker and pack freezer with 5 parts of crushed ice to 1 part rock salt. Freeze until mixture is thick and frozen. The ice-cream will be soft. You can tell when it's done by the grinding sound of the electric motor or aching arms in you are doing this with a hand crank. Drain off water and repack the freezer using 8 parts ice to 2 parts rock salt. Cover with a thick terry-cloth towel and allow to stand and rest for at least an hour.

Schnitzel with Noodles

4 slices veal scaloppini (thin veal cutlet)
Salt and freshly ground pepper
1/4 cup flour
1 lg. egg, beaten with
1 tbsp. water
1-1/2 cups cracker meal
4 tbsp. butter, plus more if needed
4 tbsp. butter
1/2 cup finely chopped parsley
12 oz. thin egg noodles, freshly cooked and drained

Sprinkle veal with salt and pepper. Place flour on a large plate and egg mixture in a shallow bowl. Place cracker meal on a large plate. Dredge each veal slice in flour. Dip in egg mixture and then dredge in cracker meal.

Heat butter in a large heavy skillet. Sauté the veal on one side. If the skillet is not large enough to hold the veal in one layer, this procedure will need to be repeated.

When the veal is browned on one side, turn and cook on the other side. Total cooking time for each slice is about five minutes, depending on the thickness of the meat. If necessary, add more butter to the skillet until all veal is cooked. Toss the freshly cooked and drained noodles with salt, pepper, butter and parsley. Immediately serve the schnitzel with the noodles on the side.

Marlayne Giron's Spaghetti Sauce w/Whole Grain Pasta

1 lb. Italian sausage (sweet or spicy) removed from casings.
1 lbs. ground meat
2 Tbsp Olive Oil
2 cloves garlic, minced
1 tsp white pepper
1 tsp salt
1 tsp Italian Seasoning
½ onion chopped well
2 jars of your favorite Spicy Marinara or Spaghetti Sauce
1 8oz can diced Italian tomatoes
1 4oz can tomato paste
1 Tbsp Worchester sauce
A generous splash of a full bodied red wine
½ 4oz can of diced mild green chilis

Remove Italian Sausage from their casings and brown in skillet. Add ground meat and brown. Remove meat, drain pan. Add 2 Tbsp olive oil to pan and sauté onions and garlic until translucent. Add back the browned meat and pork and mix well. Add in the rest of the ingredients and mix well. Allow to simmer for a good ten minutes at least until thoroughly heated. In a separate pot, boil water for your pasta and cook according to package directions then drain and add to the meat sauce.

Pennsylvania Dutch Sandwiches

8oz Gouda cheese, julienned
8oz boiled ham
1 cup mayonnaise
1 8oz can sauerkraut, well drained
½ tsp caraway seeds
Softened butter
12 slices of dark rye bread

In medium bowl combine everything except bread and softened butter. Chill overnight. Spread butter on one side of each bread slice. Top with cheese-ham mixture and another slice of buttered bread.

Apple Dumplings

6 Roma apples, peeled &
cored
Lemon juice
½ cup White sugar, approx
1tsp Cinnamon
Brown sugar
¼ cup chopped nuts
Butter
2 Pie pastries for 2 pies

Sugar sauce:
2 cups Water
¾ cup Sugar
2 tsp Vanilla extract
1 tsp Almond extract
2 tbsp Butter
¼ tsp Nutmeg
¼ tsp Mace

Roll out pastry and cut into squares enough to cover apples completely. Peel and core apples. Roll in lemon juice. Then roll in white sugar and cinnamon combined.

Place on pastry square. Stuff the apple core cavity with brown sugar, butter, brown sugar and chopped nuts in equal parts. (The amount depends on size of core cavity, just stuff full.) Fold pastry up around apple to completely enclose it. Place in pan.

Prepare sugar sauce by mixing water, sugar, vanilla, butter, nutmeg, and mace and boiling for 1 minute. Let cool slightly. Pour over Apples. Bake in 375° F oven for 1 hour. Serve warm with vanilla ice-cream.

Whoopie Pies

4 cups all-purpose flour
1 tsp baking soda
1 tsp baking powder
1 tsp salt
1 tbsp cream of tartar
1 cup unsweetened cocoa powder
½ cup softened butter
½ cup lard, softened
2 cups sugar
2 tsp vanilla extract
2 eggs

1-1/3 cup soured milk*

Filling:
1/3 cup + 3 tbsp all-purpose flour
1-1/2 cups milk
1-1/2 cups (or 3 sticks) of butter
¼ tsp salt
2 tsp vanilla extract
3-3/4 cup confectioner's (powdered) sugar

Preheat oven to 375°F. Sift together the flour, baking soda, baking powder, salt, cream of tartar, and cocoa. Set aside.

In large mixer, cream the butter, lard, sugar and vanilla together until well blended (about 3 minutes). Add the eggs one at a time, blending well after each addition. Add the flour mixture to the sugar-butter mixture, alternating with the milk and beginning and ending with the flour. Blend well but don't over mix. It should look like cake batter and might look curdled.

Line cookie sheets with aluminum foil. Use ¼ cup of batter for each cookie and drop onto cookie sheet, one in each corner then one in the middle, making as round as possible. Each cookie should be about 2-1/2" in diameter and 3-4" apart. Bake for 6 minutes and if necessary, reverse cookie sheets from front to back so they bake evenly then bake for 10 more minutes. They are done if you can touch with your fingertip and the cookie springs back quickly. Slide foil off sheet and allow them to cool for 2 minutes then remove from aluminum foil with spatula to wax paper-covered racks to cool. Use scissors to trim them into rounds while still warm. You can reuse the foil to bake the rest of the batches until the batter is used up.

Filling: Place flour in medium saucepan and add the milk gradually whisking smooth. Cook over moderate heat, whisking until mixture becomes thick and bubbles up in the center. Simmer over low heat for 2 minutes. Remove from heat and let cool.

Place butter into large mixing bowl and beat until it is slightly softened. Add the salt, vanilla and sugar gradually and beat for 2 minutes. Gradually add 1 large spoonful at a time of cooled milk mixture to butter then beat on high speed for 1 minute till filling is smooth, light and fluffy. If it is too soft; refrigerate until it firm up a bit.

Arrange cookies in pairs, flat sides up. Spoon ¼ cup of filling on half of the cookies and spread until it is 1/2" from the edge. Top with another cookie, flat side down. Press together so filling comes to the edges. Chill and wrap each cookie individually in plastic wrap and store in refrigerator. Serve at room temperature.

*If you don't have soured milk, add 1 tbsp + 1tsp cider vinegar to 1-1/3 cups regular milk and let stand for ½ hour.

Noodles With Buttered Crumbs

3 quarts water
½ tsp salt
1 Tbsp olive oil
8 oz thin or medium sized noodles
2/3 cups butter
2 cups bread crumbs
3 Tbsp minced fresh parsley or coriander
¾ tsp poppy seeds
¼ Tbsp black pepper
Paprika

Bring water to roiling boil in deep kettle with salt and oil. Pour in the noodles and return to boil. Cover tightly, remove from heat and allow noodles to stand for 25 minutes or until tender. Drain in a colander. Add 1/3 cup of the butter to the noodle kettle and melt it over low heat. Return the drained noodles to kettle and toss lightly.

In medium skillet melt the remaining 1/3 cup of butter over medium heat and add the cracker crumbs. Stir and toast until crumbs turn golden. Add parsley or coriander, poppy seeds and pepper then blend. Transfer buttered noodles to serving dish and sprinkle the buttered crumbs on top then sprinkle with paprika.

Made in the USA
Lexington, KY
31 March 2012